Breathless Part 3 – Love Without Limits

Chapter 1: A Chill In The Air

"I want this one," I said to the sales lady, pointing to a gorgeous, one carat diamond ring, with a white gold band. The stone was pear shaped, and matched a pendant that the intended recipient already owned.

I had a dinner date with my lovely Amy to look forward to that night. It had been weeks since I had seen her or even talked to her, and I could instantly tell during our conversation that she was upset I had gone so long without returning her calls or visiting. She initially sounded withdrawn and distant, but warmed up a bit when I explained how busy I had been with work, as well as the fact that I had just found my

cellphone and had literally hundreds of text messages and voicemails to sift through. I had felt guilty for failing to prioritize our relationship, but wanted to make it up to her.

After much deliberation, I made an important decision. I wanted to spend the rest of my life with my rag doll. I wanted to marry her. It was time.

The plan was to propose to her at dinner. I had called ahead at the restaurant, intent on making the event as romantic and memorable as possible. After the main course, I would get down on one knee to propose. Once Amy accepted, the waitstaff was going to come over with a bottle of champagne, a bouquet of roses, and a slice of cheesecake, which was one of Amy's favorite desserts.

After I had purchased the ring, I went home and got ready for the big date. I had purchased a new outfit just for the occasion, and had gotten a haircut as well as a manicure. The feeling of nervousness was rather intense, but I was excited as well. I had texted Jon and Daryl about it, along with a photo of the engagement ring, and they were so happy for me.

My two best mates were struggling in their own unique ways. Christmas was just weeks away, and Daryl's recovery from his car accident injuries was delayed by a bad case of the flu. As a result, he went from being able to walk unassisted to being bedridden for over a week. Tracy had fallen ill as well, most likely catching the virus from her boyfriend.

Jon had been drug free for over a month, but was still terribly depressed. He hadn't joined his parents when they had gone to Daryl's rehab facility for Thanksgiving dinner, electing to spend the entire day crying in bed. Additionally, he had opened up to me that he now had a fear of driving, which had manifested the day after Thanksgiving when he had attempted to drive himself to therapy in his Tesla. This was understandable, given the trauma of his motorcycle accident back in July. The driving phobia destroyed his self confidence, but he was determined to get over this fear so he could go on a long-awaited coffee date with Candy.

With all that was going on, I decided to splurge on a casino trip for New Year's Eve. We all needed to get away for a while and have a little fun. It could double as an engagement party for Amy and me, assuming she accepted my proposal. Daryl was due to leave the rehab facility by mid-December, so this would also be a great way to celebrate his recovery. Jon was reluctant to go, since he hadn't traveled farther than five miles in months, but I told him that he desperately needed something to look forward to.

"I will let you know, mate," he had said with a sigh. "These days, I'm a bloody cripple."

Although I hadn't said it out loud, I knew one reason Jon hesitated to go to the casino for New Years is because he wanted to avoid bumping into Lisa and Nick, who, according to a social media post, announced a plan to visit the northeast for the holidays. Lisa enjoyed gambling and also loved going out for New Year's Eve, so chances were high that she would visit Pequot Moon with her new husband. Jon was still friends with his ex as well as Nick, but felt like he needed more time before seeing the two newlyweds in person.

For the hundredth time that evening, I checked my hair and my outfit, insisting on looking perfect for my Amy. I splashed some aftershave on my face, placed the tiny jewelry box in my pocket, and put on my jacket before going to Amy's house to pick her up.

She was already waiting outside by the time I pulled into her driveway. Her royal blue jacket contrasted nicely with her porcelain skin, which glowed with pink blush. Her hair was curled in soft waves. My heart raced when I laid eyes on her and I smiled broadly.

"Hello, my lovely girl," I said, as she approached the car with a shy smile. "You look stunning tonight. I've missed you so much. Allow me to get the door for you."

I got out of the car and opened up the passenger door like a proper gentleman, making sure to give her a huge hug and passionate kiss beforehand. Perhaps it was simple paranoia due to nervousness about proposing, but I thought I felt her body tense up when I embraced her. I wrote it off as a fluke and let her get in the car. Then, we were on our way.

We made small talk on our way to the restaurant. She was very busy with school, trying to catch up after falling behind from being sick for so long. As we chatted, I realized how much I had missed her, and felt like a jerk for letting so much time pass without talking to her or seeing her.

The restaurant was a beautiful place, very fancy and completely decked out for the holiday season. It was the perfect venue for a marriage proposal. Per my request, we got a table next to the stunning fireplace. Amy loved fireplaces, and the fire casted a lovely glow on her beautiful face. I took off her jacket, marveling at the lovely blue dress that she wore. I removed my coat, pushed her chair in, and then I sat down. I moved my chair closer to hers and placed my hand on her thigh. She tensed up visibly.

"What's wrong, doll?" I asked with a sweet smile. "Perhaps you need some wine?"

Just then, the waitress came over and took our drink order. I splurged on an expensive bottle of red wine, which arrived within minutes.

I poured Amy a glass, then poured one for myself.

"To us," I said with a sexy smile, before clinking my glass to hers.

As the alcohol flowed, so did our conversation. I asked her what her goals were for the future, and she told me that she wanted to work in the pediatric ward of a hospital once she finished with nursing school.

"Hmm," I said with a gentle smile. "I love children." I pictured Amy and me walking through a park, pushing a baby stroller occupied by a little boy or girl of our own. The thought warmed my heart. I placed my hand

on her leg again, moving up until I was inches from her crotch. She winced and backed away.

"Kenny, not here," she said coyly as she blushed.

The waitress reappeared and took our food order. We both got filet mignon with asparagus and rosemary potatoes. I began to feel more nervous, knowing full well that I was perhaps twenty minutes away from popping the big question. We sat in comfortable silence for a few moments as we took in the sights and smells of the restaurant, and sipping wine. I decided to ask her something else.

"What else do you plan for the future, aside from the career goals you just mentioned?" I smiled at her sexily.

Amy took a sip of wine as she thought of an answer. "Well, I definitely want to stay local so I can be near my family and friends. And I do want a family of my own some day. How about you?" She asked shyly, fidgeting slightly.

I had a sense that she was holding something back from me, but decided to put that nagging feeling aside and share my goals with her. "I want to continue working at the gym, because I love what I do. But I want to settle down and have a family myself. I feel like that's the one thing missing from my life, settling down with someone special, and starting a family." I placed my hand on hers, gently.

Before Amy was able to react, the food arrived. Despite my increasing anxiety, I was ready to eat.

The steak was the best I had ever eaten, and I reveled in its juicy flavor. I was such a lucky bastard, sitting in one of my favorite restaurants with one of the most beautiful girls I had ever known. Amy and I ate in near silence, the only words being "yum," "wow," or "delicious" over the next ten or so minutes. I was down to my last morsel of steak, when Amy cleared her throat and looked at me. Her facial expression was a combination of "serious" and "frightened."

"Kenny?" she began sheepishly. "There's something I have to tell you." Her voice shook slightly.

I placed my hand on hers and smiled reassuringly. "Of course. What is it, sweetheart?"

Amy sighed and took another sip of her wine before continuing. "I'm not sure how to say this but..."

My heart rate sped up as I tried to imagine what she had to say. "You can tell me anything," I said softly.

Her eyes filled with tears of what must have been guilt or shame. "When you were...busy with work and not reachable by phone, it was hard for me, and I didn't know what to think. I felt abandoned. So I had started spending more time with Eugene. He and I have been friends

our whole lives. I know that you and I have been a thing, so when he asked me out I was hesitant. But then one day I said yes. And, well, we have been on about eight dates, and have spent a lot of time talking and hanging out when not on those dates. He wants to make it official and be my boyfriend. I want to give it a try with him because, as much as I hate to admit it, I'm falling for him." She blushed and bit her lip, ready to cry but managing to hold it together.

I sat there frozen, barely able to talk. I encouraged her to continue.

"Kenny, I'm so sorry to drop this on you right now, when we are just starting to see each other again. But I think that once you check your phone messages, you will understand a little better why I pulled away from you and looked to Eugene for comfort.

"There were some things that happened to me, things that I tried to share with you that are too painful to talk about here. And when you were absent for so long, it hurt so much. I still want to be friends and hang out, but Eugene and I have a certain...pull. There's a chemistry I can't explain. I'm so sorry again, Kenny. Last thing I want to do is break your heart. I wanted to tell you later but I decided there's no 'good' time to say all this. I still love and care about you and I'm grateful for the time we were together. And I'm glad we at least tried to give it another shot. Please know that. Ok?" She smiled gently.

I felt like I had been hit by a bus. I downed the last of my red wine and nodded, trying to resist the urge to take the jewelry box out of my pocket and throw it into the fireplace.

"I must be honest, Amy," I began in a soft voice, determined to stay calm and rational. "I'm very sad about this. Heartbroken, in fact. But, I do see chemistry between you and Eugene. He's a kind man, and I think that he would be a good match for you. I love you so much, Amy. And I want you to be happy. And if your happiness means having to give you up, I will do it. You're special, sweetheart. I will always be here for you."

Amy smiled with relief. "I'm so relieved. I thought you would take it so much worse. Thank you for understanding. And I'm so glad we have this time together tonight. If you don't mind, I have to use the ladies room."

I nodded. "Of course, dear. And I can order us some dessert."

Her face lit up. "Sounds great!"

Then she got up and headed to the loo. The waitress came over with a smile on her face.

"So are you proposing to her when she comes back from the restroom?" She asked enthusiastically.

I shook my head as I fought back tears. "Sadly, no. She just told me she's leaving me for another man. So there's no need for flowers or champagne, I'm afraid."

The waitress's expression turned to one of shock and sadness. "Oh, no. I'm so sorry to hear that. Heartbreak is so tough, but you will get through it. I have been there myself. Can I get you anything?" She asked with a sympathetic smile.

"Yes, a slice of cheesecake for her and an Irish coffee for me," I said, as I poured myself another glass of wine and chugged it down. "And a shot of tequila, too. Top shelf."

"Coming right up," She said with a smile before walking away.

Tears began to spill down my face, which I hastily wiped away as I checked my phone. I had a text from Jon.

"Did you ask her yet?" The message read, with a smiley face and diamond ring emoji next to the question.

I began to type a reply but couldn't bring myself to share the tragic news, much less via text. Somehow, by keeping the information to myself, it felt less "real."

Amy returned from the ladies room with a sweet smile on her face and sat down, taking a sip of her wine. It broke my heart to think that, if not for her news, I would have been getting down on one knee around that time. I had to get up and clear my head for a few moments.

"Excuse me, darling," I said as I got up and went to the men's room.

I promptly found a stall and sat down on the toilet for a few moments, letting the tears fall freely. After a few moments of sobbing, I took the jewelry box out of my pocket, and took out the ring, studying it. Amy would have loved the ring so much. But, as long as she didn't love ME, or at least wasn't IN LOVE with me, I had to forget about what might have been and had to focus on what might be with someone else. Despite my temptation to throw the fucking thing down the toilet or return it to the jeweler, I placed it back in it's pretty little box, holding out hope that one day I would find someone else to give the ring to.

I bawled for a few more minutes before exiting the stall and splashing water on my face before returning to the table.

The drinks and dessert had arrived, and Amy was eating her cheesecake. I sat next to her and downed the shot of tequila, winking at her.

"Are you ok?" She asked sweetly. "Your eyes are red."

I nodded as I drank my Irish coffee. "Yes, doll," I lied. "The spicy potatoes always get to me."

Amy nodded and smiled, eating the rest of her cheesecake with enthusiasm. The waitress brought the check and smiled sympathetically at me, knowing I must have been in agony and couldn't wait to get out of there. She was right.

I promptly paid the bill and then we headed out of the restaurant. Amy turned to me once we were in the parking lot, gently placing her hand on my shoulder.

"Since my mom is working the night shift, would you like to hang out at my house for a little while, to relax and watch a movie? And maybe have a drink?" She asked with a gentle smile.

Despite my heartbreak, and despite the fact that I wanted to drop her off and rush home to curl into a ball, I didn't want the night to end. I still loved her, and wanted to savor what time we had left before she was "officially" Eugene's.

I hesitated for a few moments before agreeing. "Sure, why not? What's the harm in a few drinks?"

Three hours later...

We lay naked and sweaty on Amy's bed, panting from our marathon sex session. I hadn't intended for us to wind up in bed, but the moment we had reached the front door of her house, our eyes had locked. Within seconds, we were kissing passionately and ripping off each other's clothes.

Her body had felt so warm and her skin and hair so touchably soft, I felt so happy to hold her and make love to her one last time. My emotions had run high as my hands traveled all over her beautiful body, my maleness buried in her womanhood. I wasn't sure how the hell I was supposed to let her go. I couldn't think of that just yet. So I had simply enjoyed the pleasure of the moment, savoring every kiss, every thrust, and every caress. The orgasms had been intense and plentiful, and the tears had fallen like rain. I loved my sweet Amy.

I ran my fingers through her hair as we lay next to each other. She turned to me and smiled sleepily, running her hand over my stubble. I smiled back, studying every inch of her body. I wanted the moment to last forever.

We held each other gently, as we gazed into each other's eyes. Sleep was so tempting but I forced myself to stay awake, partly to savor the moment, but also because I had no intention of spending the night at her place. I wanted to go home so I could cry, call my best mate, and get really drunk before passing out in my own bed.

"Despite our conversation tonight, I still love you," I whispered to my rag doll, whose eyes were closed. "And I'm still here for you."

She smiled gently, without opening her eyes. "I still love you too, Kenny," she whispered softly.

My eyes began to fill with tears once again as I lay there, holding her. The night could have ended so differently. We could have been

engaged. Amy could have been wearing the lovely ring. Her mum would have been overjoyed at the news, and would have loved the ring as well. I stifled a sob.

Just then, Amy began to snore quietly, so I knew she was fast asleep. I slowly let go of her and carefully rose from the bed, getting dressed. I had to get out of there. Once I had finished dressing and had put on my shoes, I leaned over to whisper in her ear.

"Goodnight, Amy," I said, before kissing her on the cheek. She didn't stir. I slowly backed away from her, watching her sleep peacefully. More tears fell from my eyes.

Munchkin, perhaps sensing my emotional state, greeted me on my way out the door, so I gave the beloved cat a kiss and a scratch behind her ear before heading home, where multiple bottles of strong alcohol awaited me.

I cried so hard on the short drive home that I had to pull over to the side of the road at one point to collect myself. My heart was so completely broken, and I didn't know how I was supposed to function. Just when I was ready to be in a relationship again, it ended. There's only so much loss a person can take, and, between losing my parents and sister, losing my wife, and losing my would-be fiancée, I wanted to just give up.

I made it the rest of the way home without incident. Then, once I had collapsed on the couch in a fit of fresh tears, I got out my cellphone. I had a voicemail from Jon.

"Hey mate," the message began. "Let me know how tonight went. In my experience, no news isn't necessarily good news, but then again you could also be shagging her to celebrate. Either way, call me. I love you."

I lit myself a cigarette then opened the bottle of vodka sitting atop the coffee table and took a swig from it. Then I reluctantly called him, taking some deep breaths to try and calm myself.

"Well? What's the verdict?" Jon asked excitedly.

I sniffled a few times, unable to talk right away. He must have known what happened without my having to say anything.

"Oh dear," Jon began. "Did she say no?"

"Worse," I sobbed. "I didn't even get a chance to propose. Right after we had finished our dinners, she got a serious look on her face and said she had something to tell me. Long story short, she dumped me for Eugene." I began to cry harder.

Jon sighed. "I am so sorry, Ken. That's awful. Did she explain why?"

I repeated what Amy had said to me, going into detail about how I had been unreachable for many weeks and she had felt abandoned, and

that there were things that had happened to her during this time that were hard for her to deal with alone. So she had turned to Eugene for comfort and support, and that she was falling for him after going on a bunch of dates with him, and...per his proposal, wanted to be his girlfriend.

"Bloody hell," Jon muttered. "Sounds like what happened with Lisa and me, when she had fallen for Nick. I'm really sorry, mate. It hurts so much right now, and it feels like you will never heal from it. But you have healed from worse. And you're strong."

I bawled some more. "I don't feel strong," I sobbed. "When I dropped her off at her house, I had made love to her one more time. I didn't want to do it, but I couldn't let her go just yet. I wasn't ready to say goodbye." I took another swig from the vodka bottle and a drag off my cigarette.

"You needed closure," Jon said soothingly. "It's only natural. Aw, man. I wish I were there to give you a big hug, and cuddle with you. Maybe even get shitfaced with you." He chuckled, as did I. "THAT'S what you need to do, mate. Get totally shitfaced in the comfort of your home, and take a nice bubble bath. Eat some chocolate, cry as much as you need to, and call me whenever you need to talk. I will leave my phone on all night just for you."

I sniffled. "Thank you, Jon."

"Any time, mate. Oh, and here's some good news that might cheer you up: I've decided to join you at the casino on New Year's Eve."

My eyes lit up and I smiled. "Really? Oh, that's great. We will have so much fun."

"Well, first I have to survive my coffee date with Candy, which is in three days. I'm so nervous, mate. You would think I was preparing for a bloody space shuttle launch." Jon chuckled.

"You will be ok," I assured. "Maybe you can bring her along to the casino?"

"Hmm, we will see. I'm not the same person she knew so many years ago. I'm even a stranger to myself. I mean, shit, in a few short months, I went from leaping out of airplanes, bungee jumping, and riding motorcycles, to being afraid to drive a car. Instead of a beach front home in Malibu, I'm residing in my parents' in-law apartment. Instead of traveling the world, I'm traveling to and from my therapy appointments, with my mum as my chauffeur. My hands shake like an old man's, I still can't get an erection to save my life, AND I haven't worked in months. It's bloody embarrassing."

Listening to Jon's plight helped me put my own life in perspective. All things considered, I was in a fortunate place. My heart ached, but I knew it was temporary. In any case, I had to let Jon know how proud I was of him.

"Jon, don't be so hard on yourself. You have overcome so much in a short time - healing from a breakup, then recovering from an assault, then surviving a motorcycle accident, and getting a handle on a decades-long eating disorder and drug problem. You might see yourself as broken and unrecognizable, but to me, you're a hero. I'm so proud of you."

Jon giggled shyly. "Go on, mate," he teased. "Thank you for the kind words. Now go on and take a nice bath, maybe watch some porno, masturbate, and do whatever else you have to do to heal through this. And call me anytime. I don't care if it's five o'clock in the fucking morning and you're straining on the loo. I'm here."

I laughed heartily for the first time in days. Jon always knew what to say to help me feel better. We exchanged pleasantries for a few more moments before hanging up, then I got up to start my bath.

The vodka bottle was empty by the time the tub was full, and I was in full-on "crybaby mode" once again. I turned on some music as I lay in the hot, sudsy water, occasionally closing my eyes and pretending Amy was with me. After wallowing in the water and bawling my eyes out for god knows how long, I drained the tub, toweled off, and set out to complete the dreaded task of going through all the messages on my phone.

The majority of the messages were run-of-the-mill, and many of them were business related. There were a few from Daryl and Jon, and a few

from Lawrence. Some of the messages were ones of concern. I saved Amy's for last.

Amy's texts were pretty ordinary, asking if I was alright and expressing a desire to talk. There were a few that sounded a touch more urgent, and suggested that she had something important to tell me. I moved on to her voicemails. She had left four in total. The first two were short and sweet, expressing a need to talk. The third one was different, and she was crying. I forced myself to listen as my own tears spilled down my face. I so hated hearing Amy upset.

"Hi, Kenny," Amy had begun in a tearful voice. "I, uh, don't know where you are or when I will hear from you again. I wish I could tell you this in person but it can't wait. I took a pregnancy test. It came back positive. I'm going to see my doctor to confirm that it's not a false alarm. I wish you would talk to me. I... I need you. I really need you. Please call me..." She had sobbed into the phone before hanging up.

My entire body began to shake as I realized what I had done. My poor Amy had needed me so badly and I was completely unreachable. I imagined how frightened she must have been, a fourth year nursing student, dealing with a positive pregnancy test, and the baby's father being absent for weeks on end. I cried tears of shock before knocking back a shot of whiskey and lighting a cigarette, then made myself listen to her final voicemail.

"Hello, Kenny. I just got back from the doctor, and it turns out that it was a false positive and I'm not pregnant after all. I'm relieved, but I do hope you get back to me soon so we can talk. It's been a very stressful

couple of weeks for me. I hope to reach you before Thanksgiving. Call me, okay? Bye."

Fuck. I needed to call Jon. My fingers shook as I struggled to use my phone to dial my best mate.

"Hey, mate," he whispered. "You ok?"

I stammered. "N-no. Sh-she... she'd had a pregnancy scare weeks ago and had tried to tell me, but I wasn't there..." My tears fell nonstop as I curled up on my couch, phone in hand. "I just listened to the voicemails I had missed. I'm an awful person!" I began to hyperventilate because I was crying so hard.

"Ken, it's ok," he soothed in his soft, hypnotic voice. "Just breathe. You had no way of knowing, hmm? This isn't your fault. I know it hurts, mate. You would have been there for her if you had known what was happening. You're a great person, and you were a great boyfriend to her. You must forgive yourself. Read that last book I gave you, the one on the power of forgiveness. Apply it to yourself."

"I can't..." I began as I sobbed.

"You CAN," Jon insisted. "You must. Don't torture yourself. I did that when Lisa ended things, and the guilt consumed me. All those drugs, the countless sexual encounters, the bingeing and purging were all acts of self-punishment. Granted, I wanted to escape my pain, but I also felt

like I needed to abuse my body to make up for the mistakes I had made with her. I soon realized that wasn't working for me. So I started being kinder to myself. I still have a long way to go before I no longer feel guilty about all the shit I'd done wrong during our twenty years together, but I'm on my way to feeling worthy again, to feeling whole. I have faith in you, Ken. I have faith you can make it through this in one piece. Forgive yourself."

Jon's words had resonated with me after we had ended the phone conversation. I lay in bed, replaying his advice. He was right. In order to move on from Amy's and my breakup, I had to forgive myself. I was going to enjoy my Christmas, and book an epic trip to the casino for New Year's Eve.

Three weeks later...

The casino was completely decked out for the holidays, and the place was bustling with activity. Nearly everyone was dressed up, and music swirled through the air. The reservation had cost a pretty penny, but Jon had insisted on treating to a row of suites on the top floor.

"Check in is over HERE, Deedee," I said to my date, who was busy staring at a huge Christmas tree in the main lobby. I smiled and winked at her. "You work here," I teased. "You're not supposed to be impressed by the decorations!"

Deedee stuck out her tongue and laughed. "I have a thing for Christmas trees," she said with a wink. I was glad I had chosen her to be my date,

and had made sure to pack my restraints, a bull whip, and the sharpest knife I owned. It would be a night she would never forget.

We got in line with the other people checking in. After a short wait, we got our room keys and went to our suites. She and I were the first ones to arrive at the casino. Jon, Daryl, Tracy, Amy, and Eugene were due to arrive shortly, and we were going to attend a new year's dance party in the ballroom. It was a formal affair, and I had rented a tuxedo for the occasion.

The suite was gigantic, with a view of the river that ran through the property. The bed had a sumptuous velvet cover. My cock hardened and I dropped my bags. It was time for a quickie.

I grabbed Deedee's arm, making her jump.

"I wanna fuck the shit out of you," I growled.

Before she could react, I picked her up and threw her on the bed, ripping her clothes off as well as my own. I kissed her hard on the mouth as I did this, muffling her protests.

"Shut up, cunt!" I spat in between kisses. By this point, we were naked. I rapidly lined up my rock hard cock with her wet, stubbled pussy and slammed into her.

SMACK!

I slapped Deedee in the face so hard her nose bled. Then I held down her arms as I pounded her mercilessly. She began to cry and fight me, but gave up after a few moments and wound up having such an intense orgasm that her body shook like a leaf. My thrusts were relentless as I restrained her with my strong arms, and I made her climax over and over. Then, just as soon as the ambush had begun, it came to an explosive end. As much as I wanted to continue fucking, I couldn't hold back any longer.

I pulled out and climaxed all over her ample breasts, licking off the cum like a thirsty dog.

"Ready to party?" I asked breathlessly as I helped her up from the bed.

She stared at me in disbelief before nodding and wiping her nose. "Yeah," she panted.

We spent the next half hour getting dressed for the night. She looked radiant in her dark blue dress and matching heels. Her dark brown hair was done up in a classy updo, and her lips were a kissable shade of burgundy. I wore my black tuxedo, and a new designer wristwatch that Jon had given me for Christmas. The package had arrived on my doorstep on Christmas Eve. The watch, like most gifts Jon got me, was very expensive, but he had wanted me to have what he referred to as "one of the most exquisite fucking timepieces on the planet." I hadn't seen Jon since October, back when Daryl had been in an accident.

I complimented Deedee on her looks and we walked hand in hand down to the elevator, which reached the lobby in a matter of moments. We still had time to spare before the others were scheduled to arrive, so we decided to gamble for a while and have some drinks.

Deedee and I were sipping martinis and sinking a ton of money into our respective slot machine games, when I felt a tap on my shoulder. I turned around abruptly.

"Hey, buddy!"

Nick stood above me, looking very handsome in a black tuxedo and his dark hair slicked back into a ponytail. I immediately stood up and gave him a huge hug.

"It's so great to see you!" I said as I embraced my old friend. "Is Lisa with you?"

Nick nodded. "She's getting a drink. Did you or your friend want one?" He asked as he looked at Deedee with a smile.

I shook my head. "No, thank you, we are still working on our martinis." I turned to Deedee, who stood up and shook Nick's hand with a sexy grin. I couldn't wait to tie her up later and run a knife over her flesh!

Just then, Lisa showed up with two highball glasses. She was wearing a lovely light blue dress and her curly blonde hair was done up in sparkling barrettes. Her eyes widened and she smiled broadly as she saw me. She set down her drinks to give me a hug and kiss.

"Oh my GOD!" She gushed. "Kenny, I'm so happy to see you!"

After Lisa and I finished hugging and making small talk, she and Deedee exchanged pleasantries and introductions. Then the four of us headed down to the ballroom for the long-awaited New Year's Eve dance party.

About an hour later...

After the four of us had danced and enjoyed a few drinks at the party, Daryl arrived with Tracy. I was amazed by how good my best mate looked after being in the rehab place for so long. He walked with a slight limp, but looked perfect otherwise in his tuxedo and fresh haircut. Tracy looked like a movie star, wearing a dark pink gown and matching jewelry. Eugene and Amy arrived shortly after, and I felt that familiar twinge of jealousy. My lovely rag doll looked more beautiful than ever, wearing a navy blue gown with sequined flowers adorning the bodice, as well as the pendant with the pear-shaped diamond. Her boyfriend looked dapper in his tux, which sported ruffles. We all exchanged hugs and made small talk as we waited for the last of our group to arrive. Instinctively, I checked my phone to see if Jon had texted me. He had.

"Running a few minutes late," the message read. "Candy drove, and she had to pull over a few times so I could throw up. My meds gave me motion sickness."

I texted a quick reply letting him know it was ok and would see him soon. Then I swallowed and blinked back tears as I thought of my best mate reduced to a shell of his former self - going from motorcycle riding daredevil to frightened young man with a driving phobia, and on psych meds that made him sick. Still, I was happy to learn that Candy was coming with him. He had yet to tell me how their coffee date went. When I had asked him about it several weeks prior, he had told me he would fill me in the next time he saw me. In any case, I had a feeling that Candy was a keeper, and just the person Jon needed in his life to feel cared for and nurtured.

The ballroom was beautifully decorated, and I felt like I was on a movie set. Shades of red and gold dominated the sumptuous landscape. A live band played popular tunes, and the alcohol flowed freely. We all danced to our hearts' content, laughing and talking as we did so. Despite my recent heartbreak, I felt like I was in heaven.

"Hi, Ken!" A familiar female voice called out from behind as I danced with Deedee. I turned around.

Candy stood in front of me, wearing a dark red ball gown and matching lipstick. Her platinum hair was curled to perfection and her bronze skin shone like a goddess's. I smiled and gave her a huge hug before introducing her to Deedee and letting her exchange greetings with everyone else.

"Where's Jon?" I asked Candy with a smile, scanning the ballroom for my best mate.

"He's ordering a shot at the bar," Candy explained. "The poor guy has been a nervous wreck all day. His hand tremors have worsened on his new meds, so I helped him shave and dress, and I also did his hair and makeup."

My eyes widened. "Oh, dear me," I said with a sigh. "I had no idea it was that bad. You're so kind to do all of that for him." I patted her on the arm.

Candy shrugged. "My father had Parkinson's, and I took care of him up until the last year of his life, before he was admitted to a facility. So this is no big deal for me. Besides, Jon and I are old friends." She smiled warmly.

Before I could react, Jon appeared behind her. He looked absolutely incredible, just like he had six months ago. His freshly cut and styled hair sported new blond highlights, and his tuxedo fit perfectly. His newly tanned skin was flawless, as was his beard. He grinned ear to ear when he saw me, revealing teeth that were even whiter than usual.

"Hey, mate," he said in a quiet voice as he held out his arms for a hug. I eagerly embraced him, feeling his body tremble as I did so.

"I've missed you so much. You look amazing," I said as I held him.

"Candy did a great job," Jon said as he backed away from me. "But I still shake like a son of a bitch," he added with a chuckle. Just then, he noticed Lisa standing in front of him and smiling. His posture changed slightly and he appeared a bit more nervous than before, but after a few moments of hesitation, he returned her smile and exchanged hugs with his old flame.

"I've missed my little lioness," Jon said as he held Lisa. Despite the still-recent breakup and the drama that ensued, it was clear they still loved each other very much. They exchanged a brief kiss before Nick approached Jon shyly.

"Hey, buddy," Nick said with a gentle smile, holding out his hand.

Jon shook his head. "No, mate, you're getting a hug." He wrapped his arms around Nick, who broke down in relieved laughter as he embraced his old friend.

After hugging Nick, he moved on to Daryl, Tracy, Eugene, and Amy. Then I introduced Deedee to my best mate and his date. Lastly, Jon introduced Candy to Lisa and Nick.

"I had the pleasure of meeting this lovely young lady over twenty years ago," Jon said with a huge grin. "She's the daughter of David Klein, the acting coach who helped me master an American accent. We lost touch

for a very long time, but we reconnected when I was in the hospital recovering from my accident. This girl has saved my life." He smiled lovingly at Candy and placed his arm around her. She blushed and giggled.

Lisa smiled. "That is such a sweet story," she said warmly to Candy. "Jon had mentioned you years ago, talking about how much fun you two had during the first summer that he moved to the states. He said you were his first real crush!" She chuckled.

Candy tilted her head back and laughed heartily. "He was also MY first crush," she admitted. "When my family and I moved away, I was so upset. Then I had gotten really depressed and lost touch with all my friends, including Jon. I wound up gaining a ton of weight and dropped out of high school for a while, but finally got myself together around my senior year and graduated. Then I went to college for exercise science, lost weight, and got my personal training certificate. I actually met Daryl and Ken when I was a member at their CrossFit gym, before moving several towns over and deciding to work at a gym in my new town. It's funny because I didn't even know that Daryl was Jon's brother until after I had ended my membership and moved away. Then back in July, Ken told me Jon was living on the east coast again, and recuperating from an accident at county hospital, where I volunteer. So I decided to pay him a visit. And the rest is history." She winked at Jon, who, in that moment, looked absolutely smitten with her.

Lisa and Nick looked so happy for Jon just then, as did the others. "Candy is a keeper," Nick said to Jon with a wink and a smile. Everyone laughed.

Just then, the band started playing a great song from the 80's, so we all decided to dance.

It felt great to let loose in that grand ballroom, laughing and singing along to the music as our bodies moved to the intoxicating rhythm. The fact that it had become an impromptu reunion made it all the more special. I was so happy to see Jon looking healthy, with a lovely lady at his side. The more I found out about Candy, the more I liked her. After dancing with Deedee for a while, I decided to switch partners. So I gently broke away from Deedee and touched Candy's arm.

"May I have this dance?" I asked.

"Hey, what if I don't want to give her up?" Jon interjected jokingly.

Candy laughed as she backed away from Jon and took my hand. We began dancing passionately to the music, spinning around and giggling.

"You are SO good for Jon," I said with a smile. "I haven't seen him look this happy or this healthy in a very long time."

Candy smiled broadly. "He's as good for me as I am for him," she confessed. "He makes me so happy. And I have no intention of letting him go. In fact, tonight I'm going to tell him how I feel. I'm going to tell him I'm in love with him."

My eyes widened and I grinned ear to ear. "Oh, wow. I'm sure Jon will be so happy to hear that. And I bet he feels the same way about you. I can see how he looks at you. Besides, you two go way back and I know that by the time you moved away so many years ago, he was head over heels for you but couldn't do anything about it. And now, so many years later, you get to make up for lost time."

"We haven't made love yet," she said shyly. "I wanted to wait for the right moment. Maybe tonight, but I won't push it."

I nodded. "It will happen when it's meant to happen. And when it does, I'm sure it will be an amazing experience."

Candy and I danced for a while longer, and I got an erection as I pictured Jon making sweet love to her. I envisioned their toned, naked bodies gently entangled as they held each other, gazing lovingly into one another's eyes and kissing, wrapped in the satiny white sheets that adorned the hotel's king size bed, soft music and candles helping to set the mood. I got lost in my fantasy until I felt a tap on my shoulder. It was Jon.

"Hey, mate, let's step out into the lobby for a smoke," he said with a wink.

I nodded, and gave Candy a kiss on the cheek before Jon and I headed out of the ballroom and into the main lobby, where smoking was allowed. Jon and I found a bench next to an ashtray and sat down, promptly lighting up.

Jon's hand trembled as he held his cigarette, but he looked rather normal otherwise. He took a drag then smiled at me.

"I wanted to tell you about my coffee date with Candy," he said, smoke pouring out of his mouth and nose.

I nodded and grinned before taking a drag. "Yes, please fill me in."

He sighed and continued, a blissful smile spreading across his face. "It was just...magical."

I raised my eyebrows and smiled broadly. "No kidding?"

"Well, the night had started out on a rather awful note because I wound up having a panic attack in my driveway. I couldn't get myself to drive. Our plan was to meet up at the coffee house and I was going to go in my Tesla. But I sat there frozen with the engine idling, unable to get myself to put the car in gear. So I called her up crying, telling her I had to cancel because I was too scared to drive. Wouldn't you know, she insisted on picking me up and driving us there? I reluctantly agreed, and chainsmoked so many cigarettes before she showed up.

"By the time we arrived, I was a nervous wreck and my hands were shaking so badly from the meds. But I pressed on and did my best to hide my hands as we sat down in the cafe and made small talk. I

ordered a coffee as well as my favorite soup. Little did I know how badly my hand would shake when trying to eat that shit. After a few failed attempts at feeding myself, I threw down my spoon and started to cry. She was so sweet and asked me what was wrong, and I was just so embarrassed. I told her this was a bad idea, that we had to leave. I told her I wasn't the same person she met years ago, that I was damaged goods and couldn't even drive a car or fucking feed myself. I told her I thought she was a very nice girl, but that she deserved better." He paused and took a drag.

I patted him on the arm. "Oh, Jon," I said softly.

He shrugged. "Next thing I knew, she placed her hand on mine and looked at me so kindly, and said, 'Let's get this soup to go, and head over to my apartment.' Then I blushed and had to tell her I couldn't have sex because it was impossible for me to get an erection. She laughed and said she didn't care about sex and just wanted to spend time with me, said she had special utensils at home that would make it easier for me to eat my soup. I finally agreed but asked her, 'What could you possibly see in me?' And she said, 'The way you handle yourself at your worst makes me curious about how you are at your best.'" His eyes filled with happy tears as he uttered that last sentence.

"Oh my god," I said with a grin. "That's so sweet. And I'm guessing you rode with her to her place?"

Jon nodded. "I wound up spending the night. But nothing happened. We just talked and held each other until we fell asleep fully clothed on her couch. And I got to eat the soup using a weighted spoon meant for

Parkinson's patients. It vibrates slightly, which helps to cancel out the tremors. Her father apparently used to eat with them. It was so cool, eating with the same utensils my late acting coach had used towards the end of his life. It was like I was connecting with him somehow. Strange, I know. But anyway, this was the first time I had spent the night at a girl's house without having sex. It felt nice to just talk and cuddle. We also kissed that night, and I gotta tell you, mate, there were fireworks!" He winked, and I laughed. "Best of all, though, I woke up with a semi-erection. My first one in months. Can you believe that?"

I chuckled. "It's a start!"

Jon nodded and laughed. "Indeed it is. We have been inseparable since that night, talking on the phone every day and visiting that same coffee house, sometimes chatting for hours without knowing how much time has passed. We have been out to dinner a few times as well, and to the movies. We even drove to downtown Providence to look at Christmas lights. She makes me feel so...taken care of. I've never felt this way before, mostly because I've never really allowed anyone to take care of me. Now I realize that, after so many years, always being 'in charge' gets old. Anyway, I'm going to tell Candy how I feel tonight. She deserves to know that I'm... head over heels in love with her." His eyes once again filled with tears.

I put my arm around Jon. "I'm so happy for you. She's special. And she takes great care of you, too. You deserve to be happy."

Jon smiled and kissed me on the cheek. "So do you, mate," he said gently. "What's the deal with Deedee? You're just friends?"

I nodded. "Yes. I'm still recovering from the Amy incident, so I don't want anything serious right now."

"Understood. Hey, um, slightly off subject, but... How in the hell did you AND Daryl manage to have sex with Candy before I have?" He raised his eyebrows and smirked.

My eyes widened and I felt my face turned red. "Oh, shit! I'm sorry, Jon. These incidents happened before either of us knew who she was."

Jon put his hand on my shoulder and smiled assuringly. "Ken, it's totally fine! I'm not upset about it at all. In fact, I'm very impressed that my younger brother of all people managed to bang her. Candy and I have talked a lot about our sexual history - things we have done, people we have been with, et cetera. She wasn't fazed at all by the fact that I've fucked over a thousand people, or even that I raped you. She simply said, 'Nobody's perfect. I'm no saint myself.'" Jon shook his head and chuckled before continuing. "But, I must tell you, she told me EVERYTHING about her experiences with you and Daryl, mate. She talked to me about the time you took her home from a bar and fisted her, and the champagne bottle adventure at Tracy's birthday party, then the four-way with Daryl and her friend Adrian. And how you fucked her with the barrel of a gun?" He raised his eyebrows, impressed.

I blushed and nodded. "Candy's idea. I was so fucking nervous!"

Jon laughed. "Even I haven't done that! The most I have done with a firearm was hold a .38 caliber pistol to a girl's head while she blew me. She had asked me to, and I had to get stupid drunk before I agreed to it. You know of my experience with handguns, mate. What happened when I was ten? It traumatized me. I mean, I've visited shooting ranges and have gone hunting, so I'm comfortable using rifles and pistols. But this was completely different. So it took a lot for me to avoid panicking when I saw her take that thing out of her purse."

I thought of my experience with Candy, remembering how scared I was handling that gun. Just then, I saw a red haired girl that looked so much like Anna that I could have sworn it was her. I stared as she came closer, only to realize it wasn't her after all. I was at once relieved and disappointed.

"You miss her, don't you?" Jon said softly, having somehow read my thoughts. "You miss Anna."

I smiled sheepishly and nodded. "Guilty as charged."

"I think you should call her. Or at least text her. If only to say hello and happy New Year. I have a hunch that she's here." He winked.

"Have you seen her?" I asked, my eyes wide.

Jon shook his head. "No. But I have keen intuition. I think she misses you as much as you miss her."

Daryl and Tracy emerged from the double doors of the ballroom, followed by Nick and Lisa. Everyone but Daryl took out their packs of cigarettes and lit up, then sat around Jon and me, making small talk. I barely paid attention to the conversation as I lit another cigarette, thinking of Anna. If anyone could help me get over Amy, it was her. My mind wandered to the first time Anna and I had sex, so many months ago. What I wouldn't do to tie her up and sodomize her right in the middle of the fucking casino...

"Earth to Ken!" Daryl said with a laugh as he waved his hand in front of my face. He was pretty tipsy, but it was nice to see him enjoying himself. "I said, do you wanna go back inside and dance some more? And have another round of drinks?"

"Yes," I said, as I rose to my feet. "Sorry, I was lost in thought!" I said with a chuckle.

"Were they DIRTY thoughts?" Daryl teased, making everyone laugh.

I smiled mischievously. "The best kind to have!"

We all headed back into the ballroom for more partying.

An indeterminate amount of time later...

I got so fucking drunk that it was hard to dance, but I managed to remain upright, dry humping and fondling everyone from Deedee to Amy, to Lisa, to Tracy, to Candy, and anyone else who was up for the verticalized, non-penetrative coitus that passed for "dancing."

Daryl was nearly as sloshed as I was, and even planted a drunken kiss on my lips at one point. Jon remained comparatively sober, and had cheered and clapped as his younger brother acted wild and crazy. As the night wore on, more and more people arrived at the ballroom. Similar to Times Square, the closer it got to midnight, the more crowded it got. I could tell that Jon was getting increasingly agitated, and had to step out of the ballroom with ever-increasing frequency for cigarette breaks. After perhaps the sixth or seventh time he stepped out, I decided to join him.

"You alright, Jon?" I asked, as I approached him outside the ballroom, sitting next to him on the bench. I lit a cigarette.

Jon trembled as he smoked, appearing close to tears. "I'm just overwhelmed," he confessed. "This is the farthest I've been from home in months, and it's so crowded I can't breathe. And I know that Candy is going to want sex tonight. But I don't know if I can get it up for her. I feel like a failure, mate." He wiped a tear from his eye.

I put my arm around him. "Don't put pressure on yourself," I said softly. "Candy really cares for you and she won't care if you can't perform sexually."

Jon sniffled. "But I care," he said as his lip trembled. "I just want to be normal again. Todd, Andre, and Noelle FaceTimed me from Times Square before, and I was happy to hear from them but I was also embarrassed to talk to them, because I'm so different now. I'm not the man I was. I'm a shell."

I held him tighter. "Jon, you're a force," I insisted. "Recovering from all the shit life threw at you takes time. I'm amazed at all you have overcome. You're my hero, remember?"

Jon blushed and smiled. "Stop it," he said with a chuckle.

I smiled broadly. "I mean it! Now, let's go back inside and party, hmm?"

Jon took a few more drags off his ciggy and nodded slowly. "Ok."

I took Jon by the hand and led him to the bar, ordering us both Long Island iced teas. We chugged the strong drinks, getting good and buzzed before returning to the dance floor.

Tracy, Amy, Lisa, and Deedee had all removed their panties, and took turns dancing with each of us blokes. Candy was already commando, and had teased the other girls for removing their knickers so late in the evening.

"Such amateurs," she had said with good natured laugh, as she pointed to the pile of undies sitting atop the round table we shared. Then she walked up to Jon, who was sitting down to take a breather. She held out her hand.

"Would you dance with me once more?" Candy asked with a sweet smile.

Jon looked at her with stars in his eyes and nodded as he rose to his feet. The chemistry between them was beautiful. They floated along the dance floor, completely enamored with each other. Similarly, Amy and Eugene appeared completely smitten as they sat at the table, talking and laughing. Nick and Lisa were having a smoke outside the ballroom, and they hadn't left each other's sides all night. Last but not least, there was Daryl with his darling Tracy, who were hanging out at the bar, holding hands and having a grand old time.

I felt that familiar feeling of jealousy form in the pit of my stomach, and decided in that moment that I would channel my frustration into my treatment of Deedee that night. That's right, once the ball dropped at midnight, I was going to drag that bitch up to my room, tie her to the bed, whip her, and run a knife all over her naked body before fucking the shit out of her. Perhaps I would even urinate on her, if the mood struck me. She wasn't getting a "safe word," either. I would only stop when I felt like it.

The busty brunette bitch emerged from the ladies' room, and I roughly grabbed her hand, leading her in an aggressive dance that was closer to an assault. I hadn't even given her time to process what I was doing as I

dragged her around the dance floor, groping her periodically. She laughed and squealed playfully, occasionally gasping when I handled her roughly. The clock on the wall read, "11:15," and I had a hunch that the party was about to get even wilder. My hunch was spot-on.

More and more people piled onto the ballroom floor, in anticipation of the balloon drop that was to happen at midnight, along with a showing of the ball drop in Times Square on a giant screen that covered one of the walls of the ballroom. The air thickened with the number of people crammed inside, and I was glad I had a decent buzz to help me feel less claustrophobic.

Deedee provided a welcome distraction from the pandemonium, kissing and groping me as we danced to the music. Daryl and Tracy were completely inebriated, laughing and half-dancing as they leaned on each other. Eugene and Amy slow danced as they gazed into each other's eyes, seemingly unaffected by the activity around them. My eyes filled with tears of longing as I looked over at my rag doll, thinking how I could have been with her instead of Eugene.

I spotted Nick and Lisa, who were talking with Jon and Candy in what appeared to be an intense conversation. I noticed how Jon's face got red as he spoke, and how he was occasionally shaking his head, appearing embarrassed or ashamed of something. Lisa and Nick had their backs to me, so I couldn't tell how they were reacting to what Jon was saying. I decided to be nosy.

"Excuse me, dear," I said to Deedee with a peck on her cheek as I made my way through several dancing couples to talk to Jon. By the time I had

made my way over to him, Nick and Lisa had hugged Jon and Candy before heading to the bar, calling out reassurances to Jon and telling him not to worry. I placed my arm around my best mate, who was shaking and looked ready to cry. Candy stood next to him with a concerned expression.

"What's going on?" I asked Jon.

Jon hesitated before answering. "Lisa and Nick proposed a four-way with Candy and me, and I had to tell them about my little 'performance problem.' As someone who has spent his entire adult life being a sex-crazed dominant with no history of erectile dysfunction, it was fucking humiliating to explain to my ex and her husband what has happened to my body in just a few short months."

I swallowed and wrapped my arms around his waist, enveloping him in a warm hug. "I'm sure they understand," I said softly. "They are old friends of yours and they love you no matter what. You will get through this."

Candy chimed in, embracing Jon from behind. "Yes, you will," she assured sweetly.

Jon sighed as he hugged me back, then returned Candy's embrace. "You're both so good to me," he said through tears.

Just then, I felt someone sock me on the shoulder. I broke my embrace with Jon and turned around abruptly.

"Heeeey!" Daryl slurred in my ear with a goofy smile, before turning his attention to an amused Jon and Candy. "We all gonna start fucking soon or what?! Let's all dip into the 'Candy' jar! I have dibs on her pussy and you blokes can fight over her two other holes. What ya say?"

Candy, Jon, and I stared at Daryl for a few brief moments before bursting into raucous laughter. I so loved when my more strait-laced best mate let loose and acted crazy, and this time was no exception.

"What would Tracy think of this plan?" Jon asked after he had finished laughing. Candy nodded through her chuckles.

"Oh, Tracy can video the whole thing!" Daryl assured with a hiccup.

We once again broke into crazy laughter. Then Daryl suddenly wrapped his arms around Jon and gave him a big bear hug, which his amused elder brother returned.

"I fucking love you, big brother!" Daryl proclaimed as he covered Jon's laughing face in kisses.

"I love you too, you little shit!" Jon replied in a good natured way as he embraced his younger brother. "Now go fondle Tracy. I'm sure she's horny and can't wait for the ball to drop so she can drop her knickers!"

We all laughed at Jon's comment. Then Daryl broke the hug and gave us a thumbs up and a wink before staggered through the ever-thickening crowd. He quickly located his girlfriend, and wasted no time planting a sloppy kiss on her pretty face. I made my way back over to Deedee, who was touching up her lipstick.

"I can't wait to tie you up and fuck the hell out of you when the ball drops," I growled into her ear as I spanked her in the ass, making her squeal.

Just then, another herd of people crammed their way into the ballroom and, before long, there was very little room in that place. We were practically elbow to elbow with everyone. The live feed from Times Square appeared on the large screen, and the band began playing exciting music to get the partygoers pumped. Deedee and I danced as best we could, making the best of the crowded conditions.

The time was 11:30. The temperature in that place must have increased by ten degrees within a matter of minutes, with all the people crammed inside. I looked around me once more, having a hard time locating my friends in the crowd. Just then, I saw Nick and Lisa waving me over and noticed the others were with them. They couldn't have been more than thirty feet away. They were all bobbing to the music, except for Jon, who stood motionless and stared at the big screen with an anxious

expression on his face. I took Deedee's hand and slowly made my way through the herd to join my friends.

Lisa wrapped her arms around me and kissed me on the lips. "Glad you decided to join us," she said flirtatiously. "Remember, our bed is open in case you and Deedee want to double your pleasure." She winked.

I laughed, very tempted to take her up on the offer but deciding not to, out of respect for Jon. "I'm afraid Deedee is going to be rather... tied up later!" I quipped, to which Lisa giggled. "Besides, I want to break her in slowly before introducing third parties. But rain check for sure."

Lisa nodded. "I totally get it! Just wanted to offer."

Deedee leaned over and kissed me on the cheek as she moved her hips to the music, and I held her more closely. I was so ready to fuck the shit out of her. Midnight couldn't come fast enough.

Just when I thought it wasn't possible for any more people to pile into the ballroom, they did. It became even harder to dance, much less move. I did my best to ignore the ever-thickening crowd and keep my eyes trained on the big screen.

The clock now read 11:50. I looked around me, noticing the crowd and then my friends. Amy and Eugene were already kissing, as were Nick and Lisa. Daryl and Tracy were barely able to stand, and were drunkenly

giggling as they leaned on each other. Lastly, there was Candy and Jon. What I saw made my heart speed up.

Jon was trembling and had his head in his hands, appearing to be in complete distress. Candy had her arm around him, and was talking to him soothingly. She must have sensed that I was looking at them, because she made eye contact with me, then smiled sympathetically.

"Is he ok?" I mouthed to her, pointing to Jon.

Candy shook her head. "He wants to go back to the hotel room!" She called out. "He's having a panic attack."

I nodded and managed to inch my way over to my best mate, who was still covering his face with his hands.

"Jon?" I said, making him abruptly uncover his face and look at me with a red, tear streaked complexion. "You gonna call it an early night?" I winked, trying to keep the mood light.

Jon wiped his tears and nodded. "Yeah," he gasped, struggling to keep it together.

"Need me to help you to your room?" I looked at him then at Candy, who shook her head.

"It's ok, Ken," Candy assured with a sweet smile. "We can manage. But thank you so much. It was a wonderful party. We will touch base later. Happy New Year!" She leaned over and kissed me on the cheek.

I hugged her, then hugged Jon, who began crying and shaking badly.

"I'm sorry, mate," Jon said in a trembling voice as I held him. "This is just too much for me."

I backed away from him and smiled gently. "It's alright, Jon," I assured. "I'm proud of you for even showing up. I love you so much. Take care of yourself and have a happy New Year. I will call you later."

Jon nodded and took Candy's hand, letting her walk him through the hoards of people, off to the safety and quiet of their hotel suite.

My heart broke so badly for Jon, who normally would be dancing on table tops and having a blast. But at least he had Candy to take care of him. I took some deep breaths and re-joined Deedee, who smiled and was completely immersed in the happy energy of the party. Similarly, the others were hypnotized by the music along with the live feed of Times Square on the big screen.

Before long, the countdown to midnight began, and the ball started to drop. Everyone in that ballroom participated in the countdown,

including myself. Once there were five seconds remaining, I turned to Deedee and smiled as I grabbed a fistful of her hair and pulled.

"HAPPY NEW YEAR!" The crowd bellowed.

Confetti and balloons fell on us from the ceiling as everyone turned and kissed their plus-one. The live band began playing an upbeat rendition of "Auld Lang Syne." I wasted no time jamming my tongue down Deedee's throat, violently tugging at her hair as I did so.

"Ow!" She yelped. "That hurts!"

I tilted my head back and laughed sadistically, then noticed my friends all locking lips with their romantic partners. Everyone was with the love of their life except for me. Instead of being with Amy or Anna, I was stuck with a silly tart who was blessed with a double helping of chest and half a helping of brain. Jealous rage began to radiate through me.

"Let's go back to the hotel room," I growled in Deedee's ear.

"But I still want to party," she whined. "There's a champagne toast going on!"

"I don't give a fuck what you want!" I shouted, then began to drag her through the crowd.

About an hour later...

"Kenny, can we stop?" Deedee gasped through tears as she lay restrained on the bed with clamps on her nipples and a giant dildo up her bum. Red welts covered her stomach, thighs, and back from when I had whipped her. "This hurts so much. I need a break. Please?"

I tilted my head back and laughed evilly. "We stop when I say we stop, you little bitch."

"But, Kenny-"

"Shut your fucking mouth or I will put tape over it!" I warned as I slapped her in the face, making her scream in surprise. "I'm leaving the goddamn room. I'm tired of looking at you!"

Deedee's eyes grew wide. "You're not just gonna leave me here tied to the bed, are you?" Her voice shook.

I smirked. "You bet I am. If you keep quiet, I MIGHT let you go."

With those words, I turned around and opened the door to the bedroom and stepped out into the suite's living room. I slammed the door behind me and abruptly turned on the tv, intent on drowning out Deedee's protests.

I turned up the volume, mildly guilty that I had abandoned her while she was in "subspace" and needed aftercare. I pushed those guilty feelings to the back of my mind as I lit a cigarette. I was fucking done being nice to anyone. I wanted to be a mean bastard and look after myself. To hell with what anyone else wanted. It was time to focus on Ken Smith. I cranked up the volume on the telly.

Knock, knock.

I abruptly looked over towards the door and got up to answer it. Who the hell could be knocking at my door at such an ungodly hour? I quickly put on my robe and opened the door to my hotel room.

"Hi, Kenny," Amy said in a soft voice, smiling shyly. She was still wearing her lovely blue dress. I felt my heart rate speed up.

"Hello, Amy," I said with a gentle smile. "What brings you here?"

Amy blushed. "Well, you left the party so quickly that I didn't have time to wish you a happy New Year, so I wanted to do that."

I nodded and smiled, placing my hand on her shoulder. "That's awfully nice of you. Happy New Year, sweetheart."

Amy smiled sweetly. "There's something else," she said timidly. "I feel bad about breaking your heart, and I just wanted to thank you for being such a good boyfriend. I'm sorry that things happened the way they did." Her eyes filled with tears.

I placed my arms around her tiny waist. "Oh, honey, it's ok," I assured in a soft voice. "I'm so glad you and Eugene wound up together."

Her eyes lit up. "Really?" She asked.

I nodded, then gave her a big hug, which she returned. We held each other for several minutes, and I began silently crying for what might have existed between us. I inhaled her scent and savored the feel of her petite body, picturing her and me as a couple, then trying my best to replace my face and body with Eugene's. The imagery made my heart break all the more. I slowly broke the embrace and looked at her with wet eyes and a trembling lower lip. I tucked a lock of her hair behind her ear and leaned in close to her face.

"Go to him," I whispered in a trembling voice. "He's waiting for you."

Amy's eyes filled with fresh tears. "Yeah," she gasped, as she wiped her eyes. "I guess I should. Goodnight, Kenny."

I swallowed. "Goodnight, my rag doll. I love you." More tears rolled down my face. "Bye."

I slowly closed the hotel room door as she tearfully waved goodbye and started down the hall to her suite. It was official: Amy now belonged to Eugene.

Devastated and grief stricken, i hobbled to the couch. I felt as if I had lost Amy all over again. I sat down, rapidly downed a shot of vodka, and began to bawl my eyes out.

"Kenny, are you ok?" Deedee asked through the door. I guess my sobs were louder than I thought. I cleared my throat.

"Yes," I said shakily. "I will be right in to undo the restraints."

I wiped my eyes with a tissue and blew my nose before opening the door to the suite's bedroom. I wasted no time releasing Deedee from the restraints, then removed the nipple clamps and dildo. She abruptly sat up from the bed with a sigh of relief. I sat next to her on the bed and held out my arms.

"Let me hold you," I said gently, to which she nodded. In truth, I probably needed a hug more than she did.

Deedee eagerly wrapped her arms around me, resting her head on my shoulder. We both cried as we embraced, providing much needed comfort to each other.

Some time in the early morning...

I lay on the king size bed asleep, when suddenly the screen to my phone lit up. I took a look at it, and discovered it was a text from Jon.

"Candy and I made love," the message read. "It was beautiful. Turns out my equipment is working after all. I think I will extend our stay another couple nights. We have a lot of 'catching up' to do, if you know what I mean. Haha."

I smiled broadly as I pictured Jon making passionate love to his darling Candy. It was about time my best mate caught a break. I was about to put my phone down and go back to sleep when my phone lit up once more with a new text. My heart raced when I saw who sent it.

"Happy New Year, stranger! I'm at Pequot Moon. What better place to celebrate New Years than at the casino, right? Maybe we can grab a bite to eat soon? Miss you!"

I wasted no time replying to Anna, overjoyed that she was at the casino. It was time to meet up with my favorite redhead.

Chapter 2: "Lions, a Tigress, and Bears, Oh My!"

She sat at one of the benches in the main lobby of the casino, her long red hair contrasting nicely with her black sweater. It had been so long since I had seen her, and my heart beat faster and faster as I got closer to her. God, how I had missed my Anna.

Deedee had awakened early, and we had chatted over coffee in the hotel room before getting ready to check out. I had thanked her for being my date and wished her the best, telling her to keep in touch. We had exchanged a passionate kiss in the empty elevator before parting ways.

Meanwhile, I was only a few feet away from Anna. She was looking down at her phone and must have sensed my presence, because she suddenly looked up and saw me coming towards her. She smiled broadly and stood up, holding out her arms for a big hug. I wasted no time embracing her.

"It's so great to see you," I said as I held her. "I have missed you so much."

"Same here," she said in a soft voice as she backed away from me, planting a soft kiss on my lips. My knees nearly buckled.

We walked through the casino for a while, making small talk and eventually finding a restaurant for breakfast. It was so surreal, talking with Anna after months of silence.

After chatting for a while over coffee and eggs, she revealed to me that her boyfriend had broken up with her a few weeks before Christmas, leaving her for his ex. I smiled inwardly, knowing I once again had her all to myself.

"I had a similar experience myself," I said, as I took a sip of my coffee. "Amy and I had been dating for a while and she broke up with me the night I planned on proposing to her."

Anna's eyes grew wide and she placed her hand on mine. Her touch made tingles go down my spine, and my heart sped up. "I am so sorry that happened to you. That's awful."

I shrugged. "Heartbreak sucks."

She tilted her head back and laughed. "Indeed it does!"

I took a few bites of my eggs before deciding to ask an important question. "You know, we can be a comfort to each other, if you like? It doesn't have to be anything serious, but I wouldn't mind hanging out with you, maybe catching a movie? Perhaps dinner as well?" I felt a bit out of my comfort zone asking Anna to go out with me, since fucking was more my strong suit than dating.

Anna blushed and smiled. "Kenny, are you actually asking me out on a date?"

I cleared my throat as I felt my face grow hot, with a shyness that wasn't characteristic of me. "Well, um, in a manner of speaking, I suppose one might call it a 'date.' But, um, we don't have to really call it anything. We can just say we are hanging out. I-I mean.... Um, unless you WANT to call it a... a date?" I squinted and bit my lip.

Who the hell was I? Mr. Confident, reduced to a stuttering mess when confronted with the idea of being interested in more than sex. Needless

to say, Anna's facial expression was more than a little amused, and she wasn't used to seeing me so inarticulate.

"I say we go out on a limb and call it a date," she said with a wink.

I blushed again and nodded hastily. "Well, then, I, uh... suppose it's a date. Good." I cleared my throat. "Great, even."

I wanted to bang my head against a wall for being so clumsy and awkward. Before I had a chance to do so, however, my phone vibrated. Daryl had texted me. "Excuse me, sweetheart," I said, as I took out my phone and read the text.

"Good morning and happy new year, mate," the message read. "You ran off so fast last night that I didn't have a chance to talk to you, but wanted you to know I had a great time, and so did Tracy. And I finally told her I loved her. She and I are ordering room service before checking out. Sometimes breakfast tastes better in bed! Talk soon."

I replied quickly, telling him I had a great time, then let him know I was at a restaurant in the casino with Anna and had just asked her out on a real date.

"About bloody time!" Daryl replied.

I laughed and put my phone away so I could give my redheaded friend my undivided attention.

"So," I began as I placed my hand on hers, "Where should we go for our...date?" I raised my eyebrows.

Anna smiled broadly.

Three days later...

"Oh, my fucking god, yes!" I panted as I ejaculated inside Anna, whose face was beet red as she lay strapped to the inversion table.

I had initially purchased the table as a way of relieving tension in my spine, but ultimately decided that, with its straps and copious amounts of padding, it would make a nice piece of sex furniture. It did take a fair amount of balance and strength to keep myself from falling off the inverted surface as I fucked the shit out of Anna, but adrenaline and blue balls fueled me. And before I knew it, I was riding my favorite redhead like it was nothing.

We hadn't even made it to the movie theater, like we had originally planned. After all, what was the point of devouring popcorn and staring at a big screen when we could devour and stare at each other's bodies instead?

I undid the straps and released Anna from the confines of the inversion table. Semen dripped down her inner thighs as she stood on wobbly legs, breathing heavily with a tired smile on her face. I wrapped my arms around her.

"Shall we do dinner?" I asked with a sexy smile.

Anna took some deep breaths before answering. "Sure."

We both cleaned up and got dressed, and were about to head to my car when I got what I needed from under my bed.

"Turn around and bend over," I said to Anna.

She hesitated, at which point I slapped her in the face. Then she quickly turned around and bent forward at the waist. I yanked down her skirt and underwear and inserted the object deep into her pussy, making her squeal.

"You can stand back up now."

Anna slowly stood up straight then pulled up her underwear and skirt.

"How does the egg feel?" I asked.

She shrugged. "It feels ok right now, but I don't know how it comfortable it will be when I'm sitting in the restaurant," she said timidly.

"Just imagine how challenging it will be to eat comfortably when it starts to vibrate at random," I said with a sinister grin, taking the remote control out of my pocket.

Anna's eyes grew wide. It was going to be a long dinner!

About an hour later...

The little red-headed slut did an impressive job talking and eating with the vibrating egg going off at random in her pussy. Her ability to multitask was beyond sexy, and it took every bit of willpower for me to avoid fucking the shit out of her in the restaurant parking lot.

Round three of the evening consisted of me fisting her up the arse while forcing her to remain bent over a bar stool in my kitchen, her arms restrained with zip ties, and the egg on the highest vibration setting. I so loved seeing her squirm and whimper in pain and I pumped my fist in and out of her tight bum. I used my other hand to pleasure myself as she struggled.

"Just try to escape," I growled as my fist raped her tight hole. "I dare you. I would LOVE to see how far you get with that egg up your cunny and your arms tied behind your back. And let's not forget all the alcohol you consumed at the restaurant. You're my captive, my SLAVE. This is what you get for being away for so many months. Take it like a big girl, Anna. Take it! TAKE IT!"

Anna began to tremble as I violated her back door, doing her best to stay calm. She was so sexy. I had missed her so much. I had missed kissing her, touching her, and fucking her. Mostly, I missed talking to her and simply being in her presence. Lustful thoughts aside, I valued her as a person. Perhaps one day, I could even love her.

"Ohhh, god!" Anna moaned as she began to cum. It seemed that the combination of the vibrating egg with the anal fisting was conducive to orgasm! A broad smile spread across my face as she succumbed to rapture.

Once she was covered in a fine film of sweat and her moaning quieted, I gradually removed my fist from her bum and the egg from her cunny. I washed my hands at the kitchen sink before wrapping my arms around her still-trembling body. I breathed in her sweet scent.

"I bet you have missed this?" I crooned in her ear as I held her.

"You have no idea," she gasped as she wrapped her arms around me.

We exchanged a passionate kiss for several minutes before deciding to take a bubble bath together. Spooning in the water with my lovely Anna was exactly what I needed.

As I filled the tub with water and Anna's favorite bubble bath, I checked my phone. Jon had called me and left me a voicemail.

"Hey mate!" The message began. "Guess who just got behind the wheel of a car for the first time in months? That's right. Candy let me drive her Jeep for the last few miles of the trip back from the casino. I can't tell you how good she is for me, Ken. We spent the better part of three days in bed, and it was like being in heaven. I'm talking nonstop orgasms, room service, spa treatments right in our suite, and amazing conversation. I really love her, mate. Anyway, I wanted to invite you to dinner at my parents' house tomorrow night. Candy, Daryl, Tracy, Nick, and Lisa will be there as well. Amy and Eugene can't make it because they are taking a day trip to Newport to celebrate Eugene's birthday. Anyway, maybe you would want to bring someone along, perhaps Deedee or Anna? It would be fun for all of us to hang out and catch up. Call me later and let me know if you can make it. Ciao!"

I smiled broadly and turned to Anna, rubbing her shoulder. "Jon just invited us both to dinner at his parents' house tomorrow night. Daryl and Tracy will be there, and a few other people who I would love for you to meet. Want to come?" I raised my eyebrows in anticipation of her answer.

Anna nodded and grinned. "I would love to!"

"Great! I will let Jon know."

I decided against a phone call since I was eager to jump into the tub with Anna, so I texted him a quick reply to let him know I would be there, with my favorite redhead as my date.

His reply was hilarious in its crudeness. "Excellent! Be sure to lick her auburn-tinted landing strip for me, and give her a good bum-fucking."

"I already bum-fisted her and shoved a vibrating egg up her cunny," I wrote back. "But sure, I can lick her for you!"

"You sex crazed monster, you!" Jon quipped. "See you tomorrow!"

I chuckled and shook my head in amusement, then put my phone on the counter. I wrapped my arms around Anna's dainty waist. "Let's get in the tub," I said in a soft voice.

Anna and I stepped into the sudsy water, which was piled high with luxurious, rose-scented bubbles. We spooned in the tub, lying in relaxed silence for several moments. My thoughts traveled back to several years prior, when Jon had showed me a list of questions that he had asked Lisa. These questions involved edgeplay, specifically what the submissive would be willing to do, or not do. I had a copy of the list and had every intention of sharing it with Anna once we were done with bath time.

In the interim, I busied myself with her perky breasts, squeezing and running my hands over them as I nuzzled her neck. My fingers traveled farther south until I was touching her clit, making her moan.

"Would you go down on me underwater?" Anna gasped. "I love when you do that."

I smiled broadly. "Of course, sweetheart."

Then I repositioned myself in the tub so I was kneeling between her legs. I took a few moments to take some deep breaths then filled my lungs with as much air as possible before submerging myself.

I buried my face in her tender womanhood, my tongue gliding over her outer lips and clit. I gently nibbled at her inner labia for a few moments and caressed her stubbled mound with my fingers, then jammed my long tongue deep into her hole. She moaned softly as I devoured her from beneath the surface of the water.

Thoughts of my wife traveled through my mind as I ate Anna's pussy, and I recalled how turned on she would get whenever I went down on her underwater. Jon's ex was similar, and loved a good session of cunnilingus in the pool or tub at the end of a long day, or any time for that matter. Jon, true to his daring personality, took things to an extra level, going so far as letting go of all his breath, blowing countless bubbles into Lisa's hole, and holding a vacuum for minutes at a time.

Because of his drowning fetish, he admitted to occasionally swallowing and inhaling tiny amounts of water to get what he called "the taste of death" as a tense finale to oral sex underwater. It was never enough for him to "just" hold his breath; he had to go for broke. And if Lisa took too long to climax? Jon would punish her by holding her under.

After about seven minutes, I suddenly felt emboldened and began to blow bubbles into Anna's cunny. I wanted to experience the thrill of near drowning, if only to better understand my best mate's mentality. Before long, I had no air left in my lungs. My diaphragm spasmed slightly as I resisted the urge to inhale or swallow water, busying myself with Anna's pussy lips as I prayed for her to climax soon. My tongue flicked her clit repeatedly and I stuck two fingers in her hole, pumping in and out as I struggled to remain conscious. How in the hell did Jon manage to stay underwater for so long, with no air in his lungs? I pressed on, tempted to come up for air if she didn't have an orgasm soon.

My body shook as I forced myself to stay underwater, deciding in that moment that I would punish Anna for taking so long to cum. Yes, surely that's what she deserved. That little bitch needed to pay the consequences for disappearing for so many months. I felt my diaphragm contract once more as darkness overtook me. Was there a power outage? Or was I simply losing consciousness? My heart sped up and I got nervous, having no clue what was happening. Before I was able to determine what was going on, everything went completely black.

A short time later...

"Ken?" An unfamiliar male voice called out. "Come on, buddy."

A bright light was shining in my face and I opened my eyes slightly as I coughed and sputtered. My lungs felt heavy, the way they did when I had a bad chest cold. I coughed some more, then took some deep breaths.

I took inventory of my surroundings and realized I was lying on the bathroom floor, paramedics surrounding me. Anna stood to the side with a relieved expression as I came to.

"What happened?" I asked the paramedic who knelt next to me.

"You almost drowned," he said to me. "It seems you lost consciousness when you were underwater, according to this young lady." He motioned to Anna with a nod. "Do you want to go to the hospital?"

I sat up slowly and gave myself a few moments to breathe and orient myself, then shook my head. "No, that's quite alright."

The paramedic nodded, and checked my vitals once more to make sure they were normal. Satisfied with the readings, he got up off the floor and two of the men helped me to my feet. Thankfully, I was wearing a towel.

Anna came up to me and hugged me tightly. "I'm so glad you're ok," she said.

"Me, too," I replied as I held and kissed her.

After a few more moments, the paramedics left, telling me to take care. It was strange but, despite the fact that I had almost died, I felt high. I understood Jon's mentality a wee bit better. Emboldened by the fact that I had cheated death, I was more than ready to share with Anna "the list of questions to ask a submissive." I was curious to see what she was willing to do to please her master.

The following evening...

The ten of us sat around the dining table at Jon's parents house, talking and laughing over pizza. It was so nice to have a wholesome evening with some of my closest friends. Anna got to meet Nick and Lisa for the first time, as well as Jon and Daryl's parents. Needless to say, they all loved her.

After dinner, we all retreated to the living room to watch a movie. About midway through the film, I received a text from Jon, who was sitting merely a few feet away on the couch and cuddling under a blanket with Candy.

"Hey Houdini," Jon's message began, in reference my bathtub incident. I stifled a laugh. "I'm texting you for privacy reasons. Did you share THE list with Anna yet?"

"Yes, indeed," I wrote back. "She replied 'yes' to everything except for the question where I asked if it was ok to pierce her clit."

"Haha! Not surprising. I hadn't even asked Lisa when I had done it to her. I actually added that question to the list because she had been so traumatized by the event, and I didn't want to risk getting the same reaction with another girl."

"Have you shared the list with Candy?" I asked.

"Not yet," he wrote after a pause. "She's been asking to do edgeplay with me, but I'm hesitant. Truth is, I've never been in a monogamous, 'vanilla' relationship in my entire life, so I wanted to stay away from the hardcore stuff for at least the first couple months. The other day when we were making love in the suite, she took my hands and moved them from her breasts to her throat, and all I could do was rest them there. I just couldn't bring myself to choke her. I still think of her as that sweet, angelic girl with pigtails who I met so many years ago, and I don't want to 'corrupt' her. Silly, I know, but it's how I feel. She was, and still is, my little angel."

I smiled, impressed that my kinky, sadistic best mate was turning over a new leaf by giving monogamy and "vanilla" sex a try.

"Not at all," I wrote. "Maybe you should show her some of the edgeplay videos of you and Lisa, so she can see what it's all about and make her final decision."

"Good idea," Jon replied. "Best case scenario, she will find the videos edgy and kinky, and will be ready to try BDSM. Worst case, she will think I'm a sadistic monster and will want nothing to do with me. Praying it's the former!"

I chuckled softly and replied with a laughing emoji before directing my attention back to the movie, and to Anna. I held her a little more tightly.

After the movie was done, Lisa suggested we go outside and make snowmen. There was about six inches of snow on the ground from a recent storm, just the right amount for making snowmen...and for snowball fights. I smiled as I pictured Anna's expression - squealing and laughing with a mound of snow covering her lovely head of hair.

"I'm game!" I said with a grin. Everyone else agreed. We all put on our coats, gloves, and boots, then headed outside.

Most of us lit cigarettes, with the exception of Jon's father, Candy, and Daryl. We made small talk for a few moments as we smoked, then paired up and began gathering piles of snow for the snowmen. Halfway through the "building" process, I felt something hit my back. I turned around.

Daryl was standing about eight feet away from me, a smirk on his face. He quickly grabbed a handful of snow and made another snowball to throw at me. I smiled broadly.

"Wanna fight?" I asked with raised eyebrows as I picked up a wad of snow and packed it into a ball, throwing it at his chest. He immediately did the same. We repeated the process several times, forgetting about our respective snowmen. Anna watched in amusement, as did the others, who started to join in, and before long, it was an all-out brawl and everyone was throwing snowballs at each other.

I became incredibly horny as I saw Anna laugh and squeal with delight, her long auburn tresses getting streaked with snow. In fact, I was determined to fuck the shit out of her once I left Jon's parents house. I had only had sex in the snow once before, and it had been an exhilarating experience. There was a secluded area not far from my home, and it was very scenic with lots of trees. I would shag her there.

Two hours later...

"That's it, take every inch of me!" I panted as I pounded the hell out of Anna in the snow, my hot breath escaping my mouth in plumes as it met the crisp January air.

It was about a half hour before sunset. Snow-covered evergreens surrounded us, as did a small lake that was frozen over. The view was

nothing short of majestic. I pile-drove even harder into Anna while she lay in the snow, the cold weather doing little to lessen my erection OR her wetness.

Anna's eyes suddenly widened and she appeared startled.

"Ken, did you hear that?" She asked.

I stopped thrusting momentarily to listen. There was a faint rustling in the background, which got louder in volume. I withdrew from Anna and pulled up my pants, deciding to investigate the sound of the noise. Most likely, it was someone being nosy and enjoying the free show.

"Is someone there?" I asked, as I walked slowly towards the source of the noise. That was when I saw it. I ran back to Anna as fast as I could, grabbing her arm.

"Quick, pull your pants up!" I gasped as I began to half carry her down the snow covered path to my car. "We gotta leave!"

"Why? What's wrong?" Anna asked as she struggled to get dressed, trying to keep up with me as I pulled her along.

"There's a bear!" I panted.

Anna began to scream and broke into a sprint. I did likewise. Thankfully, the car was parked fairly close to where we had been fucking. As for the bear? He could have been harmless, but I refused to take chances. Just when I thought we were in the clear, I saw two people running through the woods towards us, and it looked like they were struggling to put their clothes back on as well. In the semi-darkness, it was hard to make out their features, but I could tell who they were once they got closer.

"Oh my god," I gasped, an amused smile crossing my face as I stood near my Mercedes. "What are you two doing out here?"

Nick and Lisa panted as they broke into giggles. "We decided to have some fun in the woods before we encountered a bear!" Lisa said breathlessly. Nick started laughing as he put his arm around her.

We all broke into laughter. "So did we," I said. "Good thing we parked close. I was afraid Mr. Grizzly was going to follow us to the parking lot. But it looks like he prefers to stay in the woods! Where did you guys park?" I asked, scanning the parking lot for their car but seeing nothing.

"We parked on the street," Nick said. "We thought it would be good to get some exercise, but I didn't think that would include running from a big bear!" He said with a chuckle. "What are the chances of two Leos being pursued by a bear? Aren't bears usually afraid of lions, and not the other way around?" Nick asked with a wry smile.

"I guess we're the 'cowardly' type!" Lisa quipped with a smirk. We all chuckled at her comment.

"Would you like us to drive you guys to your car?" I offered. "Just in case the bear makes an encore appearance?"

Lisa and Nick laughed heartily. "Sure," they said in unison.

An idea popped into my horny head. "Did you two want to come by my house for a bit, to hang out with Anna and me? Maybe have some... hot chocolate?" I licked my lips and smiled suggestively.

Lisa smiled sexily at me, then at Anna, knowing that I wasn't just referring to the beverage.

Later that evening...

"Hello, everyone," Jon said, his face appearing on my laptop's screen. Candy snuggled next to him, so she would appear on the screen as well. The headboard and several pillows served as their backdrop, and they had a black satin blanket draped over them. It was clear that they were naked under those covers, and their faces appeared slightly flushed from what must have been a recent lovemaking session. They looked like the ultimate "cozy couple," and my heart melted at the scene. I smiled and waved, as did Anna, Lisa, and Nick.

"Hey, Jon!" Lisa said with a sexy smile, as she positioned the laptop closer to the edge of the dresser. "Glad you're able to 'join' us, even if

it's virtual. It's been a while since you've had a chance to be a voyeur. And now Candy gets to see some of the action, too. Hi, Candy!"

Candy smiled and waved. "Hi!"

Jon cleared his throat. "I wish we could be there in the flesh but I feel a bit under the weather, like I'm getting a cold. Candy here just made me a cup of tea, and made me some soup earlier. Sweetheart that she is." He turned to look at her and gave her a sweet kiss on the lips.

"Aww!" Lisa gushed. "That's so nice! You're in good hands with this one, Jon." She winked.

Jon smiled back. "Indeed I am. And we can't wait to see all of you get down to business," he said with a sexy smirk.

Lisa smiled sexily, and began taking off her sweater. The rest of us began undressing as well.

The vodka-infused hot chocolate provided a nice buzz, and I couldn't wait to watch Lisa and Nick have their way with Anna, who was more than a little inebriated as she pulled down her pants and knickers. My favorite redhead was about to get a nice little treat from her new friends. This would be Anna's first four-way, and I was very excited for her.

Once I was completely nude, I leaned across my king sized bed and landed an aggressive kiss on Anna's lips, pulling her red hair as I did so. Lisa looked on, licking her pretty pink lips as she pulled down her tiger-print undies. Her vagina was predictably bald, with a diamond earring adorning her clit. Nick, who was still in his black boxers, unhooked Lisa's bra, which matched her knickers. Her luscious D-cup titties stood full attention, and Nick wasted no time grabbing and sucking them as he pulled down his boxers. His thick cock was fully erect.

"Looks like my little lioness has turned into a little tigress for the evening," Jon crooned as he lit a cigarette. "Love the lingerie, honey."

Lisa giggled as she fingered herself and ran her hands through Nicks hair. He was still busying himself with her breasts, not that I blamed him. "Thank you," she said. "It was a Christmas gift from Nick."

Jon nodded as he took a drag off his ciggy, holding onto Candy a little more tightly. "Good job, Nick. Although I prefer her naked!"

Everyone laughed. I pulled down Anna's underwear as I licked her bare breasts, reveling in the feel of her flesh. I gently pushed her backwards onto the bed and kissed her bare crotch, then gently slid my finger inside her dripping wet hole. She moaned sexily. Just then, Lisa got off the bed and took what appeared to be lingerie out of her overnight bag. When she put it on, it was clearly not lingerie. It was something much more exciting. My eyes lit up, as did Jon's.

"Holy shit," Jon gasped. "You brought the strap-on. The big one, no less."

Lisa nodded as she got closer to the laptop, showing it off to Candy and Jon. "It's ten inches," she bragged, then turned her attention to Nick. "Get on your knees," she said in a low voice, as she spat on her hand and ran it over the impressively sized silicone shaft.

Nick nodded. "Yes, Mistress," he said softly as he got into position. Lisa lit herself a cigarette then knelt behind him, lining the head of her strap-on penis with her husband's bum. Very gently, she entered him, and he moaned sensually.

I got so incredibly horny as I watched Lisa bum-fuck Nick, and wanted very badly to do the same to Anna. As if on cue, my lovely red haired friend got on her knees and lifted up her lovely arse, turning to look at me with eyes full of lust.

"Fuck me, Master," Anna breathed in a sexy voice, as she stared at me with those bedroom eyes. She didn't have to ask twice.

"With pleasure," I growled, as I spat on my cock and wasted no time pounding her tight bum from behind, grabbing her breasts as I did so.

Lisa began to pull Nick's hair and slap his arse cheeks, making Jon even more excited. He smiled broadly before taking a long drag off his ciggy.

It was clear my best mate was in his glory, and Candy looked on with wonder at the sordidly sexy scene.

"Ken," Jon began as smoke trailed out of his mouth and nose. "Why don't you have Anna eat Lisa's bum while she fucks Nick? To make it an official foursome?" He raised his eyebrows.

I smiled and nodded, and Lisa squealed with delight at the prospect of having her salad tossed by Anna, who crawled closer to Lisa's arse while my cock remained buried inside her. Anna then crouched down and began eating Lisa's bum. I pounded Anna harder, doing my best to avoid ejaculating as my dick slid in and out of her tight hole.

Lisa took another drag off her cigarette as she moaned with pleasure. "Anna, your tongue feels so good," she purred, smoke escaping her mouth in thick bursts.

I looked over at the laptop screen, and surely enough, Jon was lighting another cigarette with the lit end of the old one. He so loved chainsmoking during sex, even as a voyeur.

"This is so fucking hot," Jon breathed as he smoked, running his hand through Candy's blonde locks. "This is my first time watching Lisa fuck someone with a strap-on. I've always been on the receiving end up until now. This whole scene is making my dick hard as a rock. You're all so sexy." He turned to look at Candy. "Almost as sexy as this little gal I have lying next to me." He winked at Candy, who giggled and smiled.

After a while, we switched positions and Nick went down on Anna while Lisa continued to bum-fuck him with the strap on. I stood above Lisa so she could suck me off. She soon lit another cigarette and gave me one of the best smoking blow jobs I had ever experienced, blowing tons of menthol smoke all over my balls as well as up and down my shaft. Once I was on the brink of climax, I pulled out at the last minute and ejaculated all over Lisa's pretty face. She squealed with delight as her flawless complexion became covered in my semen.

"Have Anna lick Lisa's face clean," Jon suggested, before lighting another cigarette.

I nodded and smiled sexily as I leaned over to talk to Anna, who was in her glory as Nick buried his face in her auburn-stubbled pussy. A sexy grin spread across her flushed face.

"Anna, darling," I said as I ran my hand through her luscious red locks. "Would you be a sport and lick the jizz off Lisa's face?"

Anna chuckled then nodded, slowly getting up as Nick backed away from her vagina. She then knelt next to Lisa and stuck out her pretty little tongue, tentatively licking her cheeks in shy sweeps.

"More tongue!" Jon said gleefully with a broad smile, as smoke trailed out of his nose and mouth. Candy laughed at his comment.

Anna complied with Jon's request, sticking her tongue farther out and flicking it over Lisa's face as if she were licking a penis. Lisa moaned sexily.

"Mmmm," Lisa began. "I can't wait for you to go down on me. After knowing how your tongue feels on my backside and my face, I'm sure it will feel even better on my lady parts."

Jon laughed heartily. "Ahh, Lisa," he began good-naturedly. "Always so polite when referring to anatomy. I want you to say the 'C' word. Would you do that for me?" He raised his eyebrows and took a drag off his ciggy.

Lisa smirked sexily. Then she slowly withdrew from Nick, lit a fresh cigarette, removed the strap-on, and crawled over to the edge of the bed so she was closer to the laptop's camera. She took a long drag and French inhaled, holding the smoke in her lungs for a good thirty seconds before speaking. "Cunt."

As if it wasn't sexy enough to see a big cloud of smoke billow out of her mouth and nose as she spoke the word, the tone of her voice was low and sultry, and her enunciation precise. Jon was clearly pleased.

"Good girl," he crooned.

My cock hardened once more, and I felt an overwhelming need to fuck the shit out of Jon's "little lioness."

"Hey, Lisa," I growled as I ran my fingers through her blonde mane, "Why don't you let Anna lick your cunny while you give me a hand job, and Nick can face fuck you?" I turned to Nick, who nodded in agreement. "Then after Anna makes you cum, I want to fuck the shit out of that delicious, pierced pussy of yours."

The three of them giggled at my words before getting into position. Jon and Candy looked on with eager, horny eyes, caressing and kissing each other.

Lisa's strong hand gripped my cock as Nick stood at the foot of the bed, his manhood positioned above her pretty mouth. She tilted her head back and took an impressive amount of his shaft into her mouth and down her throat. Then Anna crouched down between Lisa's legs and began nibbling at her labia, occasionally fondling her clit piercing. After a few moments of gentle play, Anna went for broke and shoved her face into Lisa's womanhood. While this was happening, Lisa tightened her grip around my member, and moved her hand faster and faster. It didn't take long for me OR Lisa to achieve orgasm, and I was ejaculating onto Lisa's hand at the same time she squirted over Anna's face. As a kinky surprise, Nick withdrew from Lisa's mouth, bent down and licked my semen off Lisa's hand, then licked Anna's face clean.

"Open wide, little tigress," Nick said to Lisa with a sexy smirk, then gave her an aggressive open mouth kiss so she could swallow Anna's and my cum. Lisa moaned as she hungrily devoured Nick's mouth, digging her nails into his back as she did so. Nick grunted as he tolerated his wife's long talons breaking his tender flesh, eventually drawing blood.

Jon was so aroused that he was panting, and his face was covered in a film of sweat. Candy smirked with amusement, and I had a feeling that she was pleasuring Jon under the blankets. Determined to maintain his composure, Jon wiped his brow then cleared his throat.

"Lisa, darling," he panted, "Be a good girl and lick the blood from Nick's wounds."

Lisa slowly backed away from Nick's lips, which sported a minor cut from her aggressive kissing. Then she got behind Nick and stuck out her long tongue, running it up and down his back, lapping away at the bleeding wounds. It was so sexy in its depravity, and despite the fact I had just orgasmed, I found myself getting hard again.

I looked at Lisa with lust, pushing her down on the bed. "Open those legs nice and wide, sweetheart," I growled.

Lisa nodded and obliged, and I forced her legs open even wider before impaling her diamond-adorned womanhood with my rock hard shaft. Nick sucked at Lisa's breasts for a few moments before turning his attention to Anna, who began fondling and sucking Nick's erect cock. This was glorious!

Lisa began to moan and pant, squirting all over my dick within perhaps five minutes. I withdrew from her, then licked her pussy clean before looking up at Nick, who was still sucking and biting Lisa's tits.

"Hey, old friend," I said in a low voice, eyeballing him like he was a filet mignon as I ran my fingers through his long, wavy black hair. He backed away from his wife's breasts to look up at me with a sexy smile. "It's been a while since we've...connected. I've missed your tight bum. Now that Lisa's broken you in with the strap on, how would you like MY ten inch member?"

Nick grinned from ear to ear, appearing giddy at my proposal. Anna, as if on cue, gently let go of Nick's penis and began to finger herself, appearing more than a little aroused at the idea of Nick and me having sex.

"You don't have to ask twice, buddy," he panted, before getting on all fours.

I spat on my dick then lined myself up with Nick's arsehole, penetrating him roughly as I held onto his hips. I glanced up at the laptop and saw a smirk form across Jon's face.

"Make sure you're nice and rough with Nick," Jon growled as he lit another cigarette. "I love seeing him in pain."

Lisa lit up once more, grabbing a leather paddle from her bag then handing it to me with a sadistic smile. "Would you do the honors?"

I nodded then took the paddle from her, whacking Nick in the arse several times. He gasped in pain and surprise, as red welts formed on his buttocks. Meanwhile, Lisa turned her attention to Anna.

"Lie down and spread your legs for me," Lisa purred as she took a drag off her ciggy, then took a giant two-way dildo out of her bag. Anna obliged, her eyes opening wide at the sight of the toy. Lisa straddled her. Then she spat on her end of the dildo and eased it into her pussy, then spat on the opposite end and slid it gently into Anna's. Lisa got a good rhythm going, rocking her hips as she grinded against the little redheaded whore. I got so turned on seeing the two of them fuck, and my cock became even harder.

WHACK! WHACK!

I slammed the paddle against Nick's raw arse cheeks once more, making him jump. Jon smiled sexily, pleased that I was getting rough with his ex's husband. Lisa decided to join in on the rough play, slapping Nick in the face, then twisting Anna's nipples until she squealed in pain. Nick began to fondle himself as I fucked him, panting with arousal within seconds. This charade continued for a while, until all four of us approached orgasm.

I moaned sexily as I ejaculated inside Nick's bum. Then Anna and Lisa climaxed a few seconds later, covering the double dildo in their pussy juice. The second I withdrew from Nick, Lisa backed away from Anna and removed her end of the dildo, then crouched down to Nick's bum. She spread apart his arse cheeks, sucked the cum out of his hole, and

crawled over to the laptop to show Jon and Candy the contents of her mouth.

"Open wider," Jon crooned as he smoked another cigarette. "Show daddy what you've got in your pretty mouth."

Lisa obliged, revealing a mouth full of the semen that she had sucked out of Nick's violated bum. Then she abruptly turned to Nick and kissed him hard on his wounded mouth, forcing him to swallow the contents. As per usual, he gagged but managed to force down the questionable substance. Jon gave a satisfied smirk as he saw his ex's husband do his best to choke down the load of cum.

Before Nick had a chance to recover, Lisa grabbed the leather paddle off the bed, then lit another cigarette. The expression on her face made it clear she was up to no good. She took a drag them stood at the foot of the bed.

"Be a good boy and turn your back to me, and get on all fours," she ordered as smoke poured out of her mouth.

Nick hesitated but did as she asked. "Yes, Mistress."

"Now, you have been a bad boy for taking so long to swallow the load I gave you. So, as punishment, I am going to paddle you five times per cheek. After each strike, I want you to say, 'I am mommy's good little boy.' Understand?" She raised her eyebrows as she took another drag.

Nick swallowed, knowing he was about to endure some pain. "Yes, Mistress, I understand."

Lisa took a long drag off her cigarette, drew her arm back and whaled Nick on the arse with the paddle.

WHACK!

"I am mommy's good little boy!" Nick cried out.

"Nick....Nick....Nick," Jon said in a resigned tone as he rolled his eyes and shook his head. "Still a big baby. Say it like you have a pair. Project your voice. C'mon. You're a Leo. A lion. King of the bloody jungle. Act like it." Jon smirked as he took a drag off his ciggy. It was obvious he enjoyed being the "director" of this voyeur session.

Nick cleared his throat. "I am mommy's good little boy!" He shouted, using a louder voice than before.

Jon nodded. "Better. Now Lisa, I want you to paddle him harder. And don't stop until you finish your cigarette. You're the lioness, the QUEEN of the jungle. Don't hold back. Be fierce. Rawr!" He winked.

Lisa giggled and nodded, taking a drag and drawing her arm back once more.

WHACK!

This time, Anna and I winced at the sound of the paddle slamming hard against Nick's bum, which turned a darker shade of pink.

"I am mommy's good little boy!" Nick shouted once more.

This charade continued for several minutes, by which time Nick was shaking and choking back tears. His arse cheeks were bright red, with streaks of blood. Lisa was panting slightly with a slight smirk on her face, satisfied with the job she had done. She took a final drag off her cigarette before putting it out, then directed her attention to Jon, who was sipping tea from a mug.

"How did I do, Daddy?" Lisa asked in a sexy voice, running her hand up and down the length of the paddle.

"Outstanding, darling," Jon crooned between sips of his tea. "Just outstanding. And you, too, Nick. Great job, old pal." He winked.

Nick wiped tears from his eyes and cleared his throat. It was clear he was in some pain. "Thank you," he mumbled as he grabbed a tissue from the dresser and blew his nose.

Lisa's expression softened, then she gently placed her hand on Nick's shoulder. "May I hold you?" She asked in a sweet voice.

Nick sniffled then nodded. The two "lions" embraced each other. There was so much love between them. It was beautiful to watch.

I turned to Anna and ran my fingers through her long red hair. She smiled sweetly at me, then leaned in for a kiss. We locked lips passionately. Out of the corner of my eye, I saw the laptop screen. Surely enough, Jon and Candy were gazing into each other's eyes and caressing each other, before exchanging a prolonged kiss.

Lisa and Nick noticed the two love birds as well, smiling at the scene.

Candy and Jon backed away from each other's faces and exchanged an amorous glance, while suddenly Candy got out from under the sheets, uncovering Jon as she did so. Then she took the laptop and placed it farther away, revealing her beautiful naked body in its entirety, as well as Jon's. Then she lay next to Jon once more, wrapping her leg around his hip and stroking his penis. In response to this, Jon began kissing her passionately while squeezing her lovely breasts and cupping her shapely bum. His hand eventually made it to her shaved vagina, and he wasted no time shoving most of that hand inside her. Their moans were audible, as was the occasional "I love you," whispered between kisses.

The two lovers embraced even more tightly as they devoured each other's mouths. It was clear that they couldn't get enough of each other. Their bond was so strong, in the literal and figurative sense. Scratch marks appeared on their skin as they took turns digging their nails into each other's flesh, their lips remaining locked. Their breathing quickened, as did their movements. It was one of the sexiest things I had seen in ages, and I wasn't the only one who thought so because everyone else's eyes remained riveted to the laptop screen, sexy smiles on their faces.

Jon slowly backed away from Candy's mouth and he looked at her with an expression of love intermingled with lust. Then he reached behind Candy's pillow, and pulled out a black blindfold. Candy's eyes widened and a smile spread across her face.

"Let's play," Jon crooned, as he held up the blindfold.

Candy nodded excitedly, and Jon fastened the blindfold over her baby blue eyes, tying the long satin straps in a secure bow behind her head. He kissed her tenderly on the forehead, then crawled towards the laptop with a mischievous look on his face.

"See you guys at lunch tomorrow!" Jon said cheerfully with a wink.

We all began to protest. "Noooo! Don't turn off the camera!" Lisa said earnestly. "We want to see some fireworks!"

"I will record a video for you. Bye, all." Then Jon blew a kiss and waved before closing the lid on the laptop.

The rest of us booed and jeered, as we had been looking forward to watching Jon and Candy have sex. But I knew my best mate would spare me few details of their encounter, and the video he would send me the following morning would be testament to that.

In the interim, the four of us took a shower together then relaxed in front of the tv, talking about plans for the following day. Lisa and Nick were flying back to California that afternoon, but we were going to meet up with them for lunch beforehand.

After Lisa and Nick had fallen asleep on my couch and Anna had gone to bed in my room, I opened my junk drawer and took out the infamous document, then retreated onto the deck for a quick smoke as I read it over.

A Short List of Questions to Ask a Submissive

Answer yes or no to each question

1. Would you let your master blindfold you?

2. Would you allow your master to run a knife over your body, and possibly cut you?

3. Would you be willing to be held underwater by your master?

4. Would you be willing to be burned with the lit end of a cigarette?

5. Would you get a tattoo of your master's choosing to prove your devotion?

6. Would you sleep in a cage overnight to please your master?

7. Would you allow your master to give you a body piercing, including the genital/clitoral area?

8. Would you allow your master to either force-feed you, or deny you food as punishment?

9. Would you allow your master to give you electric shocks?

10. Would you be willing to have sex with another person while your master watches?

11. Would you wear a gag or similar device that restricts speech in order to please your master?

12. Would you let your master tie you to a bed for hours at a time, and as long as overnight?

Mind you, I had already done several of these things to Anna already, but the point of the document was to get an idea of what she would allow me to do in the future. Also, people can change their minds, and just because she allowed something to happen before, didn't mean she would allow it again.

I was impressed that Anna had answered "yes" to everything except for question number 7. However, I also wasn't entirely convinced that she would do some of these things more than once.

My wife, for example, had been claustrophobic and didn't like sleeping in a cage. In fact, she would be up almost all night until sheer exhaustion took over. Lisa was similar, and would actually start begging Jon to let her out after several hours. As I have mentioned, Jon engaged in very intense BDSM sessions with his ex, usually without a "safe word" or any option to end things until he said so. As such, he rarely caved when it came to edge play, usually waiting for a medical emergency to happen before letting up. But hearing Lisa cry and beg was sometimes enough for him to stop playing the "master" and go back to being her kind partner.

I finished my ciggy and went back inside to go to bed with my sweet Anna at my side. Sleep came quickly, as did a vivid dream of being attacked by vicious bears. I had awakened in a cold sweat, holding Anna a bit more tightly before drifting back off to sleep. Sometimes our minds create bigger monsters than what exists in reality.

Chapter 3: The Master Is Back

"Get on your knees and beg for forgiveness," his deep voice demanded. He was fully clothed, unlike his submissive, who stood before him completely nude and vulnerable.

She bit her lip and did as he asked. When she opened her mouth to speak, however, she broke down into peals of laughter, covering her mouth in shame.

"I'm sorry!" She said through giggles as she nervously ran her hands through her light blond hair. "I don't mean to laugh."

He stood above her, hands on his hips and an exasperated expression on his handsome face.

"You think this is a joke? Hmm?" He crouched down so his face was closer to hers.

She appeared panicked, trying her best to stop laughing and look serious. "N-no, I don't think it's a joke. I'm just not used to this."

He sighed, then got even closer to her. "Then get used to my hand."

With those words, he got behind her and smacked her rear end very hard, landing a strong blow to each cheek. She gasped in pain. That was when the video ended.

I put down Jon's phone and looked at him with sympathy.

"I see what you mean," I said to him and we sat outside on my deck, smoking. It was a beautiful day in early March, and spring was already in full bloom.

"Yeah," Jon sighed as he took a drag. "Candy is proving to be a tough nut to crack. I mean, I love how things are going with us, and with life in general. My gym is doing great after being open for only two short months, the house hunting is going well, and I'm finally driving on the highway again. I even have an acting gig coming up next week, my first one in almost a year. But I'm so used to being taken seriously as 'master' by my subs. I'm not used to laughing. It's so FRUSTRATING, mate!" He said through clenched teeth with a chuckle.

I laughed appreciatively. "It will come," I assured. "Maybe you need to be more stern with her? Possibly try some new form of punishment besides spanking?"

Jon's brow furrowed. "I know, mate. Problem is, I'm nervous. Imagine me of all people, king of all things 'edge play,' hesitant to whip out the heavy artillery. But I'm used to things being more vanilla with her and me, so this is still very new. I mean, you saw that 'blindfold' video of us back in January. It was good old-fashioned lovemaking, with sensory play in the form of ice cubes and my tongue."

I nodded as I thought of that video, which had been erotic but so romantic and sweet, with gentle-yet-passionate lovemaking that made it clear how much Candy and Jon loved each other. Jon had initially handled her so tenderly, like a delicate flower, only getting rougher after she had gotten rough first.

"I love what you did for her on Valentine's Day," I said with a smile as I took a drag. "You completely spoiled her. The diamond bracelet, a fancy

dinner, a trip to a five star spa in Newport, a huge box of chocolates, and that enormous bouquet of roses? She was clearly in heaven."

Jon smiled broadly. "I love pampering my little angel," he said softly. "It's like, we have a connection that goes beyond the physical and the emotional. It's a sort of...spiritual connection that we have. She's such a great person. So kind. So pure. So nurturing. So..." His voice trailed off as he looked for another word.

"Giggly?" I offered with a smirk.

Jon laughed heartily. "Well, yes."

A thought popped into my head. "I know you have mentioned putting it off, but I think it's time for you to show Candy some videos of you and Lisa. It would allow you both to ease into edge play since you won't have to really DO anything to her. And, she can take her time deciding what she wants to do."

Jon thought about what I said for a moment, and swallowed. "I think you're right, mate. I HAVE been putting that off for a while. Speaking of edge play, how are things going with Anna?"

I flashed Jon a mischievous smirk. "Let's just say, enemas aren't her cup of tea."

Jon raised his eyebrows and laughed. "Wow! You finally did it! Bravo, mate." He patted me on the back, then looked at me intensely. "I want to hear all about it. All the dirty, depraved, sordid details. You know how much I LOVE a filthy story." He lit a fresh cigarette with the end of the old one, inhaling deeply as a sexy smirk formed on his face.

I spared him few details as I recounted what had happened over the weekend with my little redheaded sub.

Two days earlier...

Anna met me at my house after work, showing up at my doorstep in the outfit I had instructed her to wear - pretty black dress, high heels, and no panties. She also wore red lipstick and a pretty pearl necklace. Her hair was done up in a sexy style. I looked her up and down, then nodded.

"You look adequate," I said coldly. "Come in."

"Yes, Master," She said timidly.

I wore a black button down shirt with dark jeans, and my hair was styled in a sexy, tousled way. I stood before her with my hands on my hips, fully in charge and ready to give her a lesson in humility.

"Tonight, we will be testing your endurance," I said in a low voice.

Anna looked at me with a look of fear in her eyes. "What does that entail?"

I glared at her for a few moments, then decided to get right down to business. "Turn around and bend over. Then lift up your dress so your bum is exposed."

She swallowed. "Yes, Master."

My cock hardened as I saw her firm, luscious bum. I grabbed the enema bulb off the kitchen counter, then roughly spread her arse cheeks. She squealed with surprise. Without warning, I shoved the tip of the bulb inside her arsehole, and squeezed the liquid contents of the bulb into her bowels. The water was warmer than it needed to be, and she moaned in discomfort. Once the bulb was empty, I roughly removed the tip from her arse and slapped her cheeks several times, making her gasp.

"Stand upright and pull down your dress. Then turn around and face me." I put down the enema bulb and picked up the broom and dustpan.

She sniffled then did as I said, wiping tears from her eyes as she did so. That was when I handed her the broom.

I put out my cigarette and walked up to the bathroom door, trying the knob. It was locked.

"Anna?" I called out, knocking lightly on the door. "You alright in there, sweetheart?"

Anna sniffled. "No, I'm not," she sobbed. "Leave me alone, please. I'm so humiliated!"

I swallowed, suddenly feeling guilty about what I had done. "Ok, honey. Take all the time you need."

Anna continued to cry as I walked away from the bathroom door and went to the kitchen to pour myself a stiff drink, which I downed rapidly. Then I got out the cleaning supplies, intent on scrubbing the floor.

Similar to Jon, I had a cast iron stomach. Body fluids have never made us squeamish. Perhaps our experiences helping Daryl with potty training had something to do with it, as did cleaning up after his chemo-related sickness. Jon and I had helped Martha tidy up after Daryl many times, cleaning everything from vomit, to urine, to poop off the floor and toilet. We had even helped change his nappies when he was a baby. The sight of blood never bothered us either, so we were happy to help disinfect and dress Daryl's wounds whenever he injured himself. That's right, Jon and I were natural caretakers from a very early age. It seemed we were both born to take charge.

Dominants often make good "helpers," due to their ability to take control of situations and people. It is rare to find a dominant who is a pure "sadist." While it is true that dominants can become aroused by watching scenes involving others' discomfort, many are highly empathic, and inflict pain primarily as a means of giving pleasure to the submissive.

Once I was satisfied with the cleanliness of the floor and put away the supplies, I knocked on the bathroom door once more. Her crying, despite being softer, continued.

"Anna, sweetheart?" I said in a gentle voice. "May I come in, please?"

Anna sniffled before answering. "Promise you won't whip me?" She called out in a shaky voice.

I smiled and shook her head, amused that she thought I still wanted to hurt her. "I promise I won't whip you. I don't want to hurt you. I know that you're already upset and I want to comfort you. Would you let me do that?"

More sniffles. Then she unlocked the bathroom door and opened it. Her eyes were swollen and bloodshot, and her face was streaked with tears. She shook slightly.

I smiled gently as I walked inside the bathroom. She had taken the time to clean herself, as evidenced by the film of water on the shower curtain and bathtub, and the scent of body wash. She backed away from me as I walked in, still hesitant to let me touch her. I sat at the edge of the tub.

"Come sit next to me," I said in a soft voice.

Anna swallowed then nodded shakily, taking shy steps towards the edge of the tub then slowly sitting down. She looked at me shyly.

I placed my arm around her and leaned in for a kiss. Our lips locked for a few moments, and she was the first to back away.

"What are you thinking?" I asked, rubbing her back with my hand.

She began to cry again. "I don't want to do that again," she said through sobs. "Please don't make me. It was so uncomfortable and embarrassing."

I held her tighter. "Oh, honey," I cooed, as I ran my fingers through her long, auburn hair. "You don't have to do anything you don't want to. We don't have to do an enema again. I promise. I'm proud of you for letting me do that to you just this one time. Not everyone would. But you did. You're brave and you're strong. And you did a great job cleaning my floor." I winked.

Anna turned to look at me, her eyes red from crying. "Would you draw me a bath?" She asked timidly.

I laughed and kissed her on the forehead. "Of course I can, sweetheart."

I spent the rest of the evening pampering Anna, taking a bath with her, cooking her a lovely dinner, and rubbing her feet on the couch as we watched one of her favorite movies. By night's end, she was so happy and relaxed, and I lay awake watching her as she slept in my bed. I studied every curve of her body, thinking of what a future with her would be like. I started to feel something in the pit of my stomach, something akin to nerves. It was a familiar feeling. I felt like I was beginning to fall in love.

Present day...

Once I was done with my enema story, Jon raised his eyebrows and smiled broadly, looking at me for a few moments.

"What?" I asked as a smile spread across my face.

"You're falling for her, aren't you?"

I blushed, having kept that part of the story to myself. Somehow Jon's intuition was spot on. "What makes you say that?" I asked nervously.

"The look you get in your eyes when you talk about her, it speaks volumes. I could see stars in them. And you get a little smile on your face. Even the way you say her name, it's like you're elongating it, savoring it. 'Annaaaa....,'" he exaggerated in a breathless tone.

I chuckled and shook my head. "You're crazy!"

Jon nodded. "Yes, this is true. But I'm right, mate. Admit it." He smiled warmly.

I sighed. "You ARE right," I admitted. "I'm just not sure how to tell her, or when."

"You will know when," Jon assured. "It will just FEEL right. That's how it was with me and Candy on New Years. She and I had arrived at our suite shortly before midnight, and she had begun to loosen my tie and unbutton my shirt as she looked intensely into my eyes with a gentle smile on her face. My tremors were still pretty bad then, but my hands were unusually steady as I unzipped the back of her dress and ran my fingers through her hair.

"Before long, the clock struck midnight and the fireworks show started, and we had an amazing view of it from the top floor. So there we stood, in a partial state of undress, window shades wide open, watching the fireworks. She turned to look at me with that lovely smile, and I could see the reflection of the fireworks in her baby blues. I cupped her chin,

leaned in close, and said in a voice barely above a whisper, 'Candy, I have a confession: I'm in love with you.'

"Her eyes filled with tears of joy, as did mine, and she replied, 'I'm in love with you too, and I'm glad you said it first because I was too nervous.' Then we locked lips, finished ripping each others' clothes off, and spent the next 72 hours fucking like bunnies!" Jon laughed at the memory, as did I. "So just remember, if you're nervous about telling Anna how you feel, chances are that she's nervous, too. I see how she looks at you, Ken. She feels the same way you do. Keep that in mind when you feel too scared to open up to her."

I digested what he had just told me and slowly nodded. "Thanks for the advice, Jon."

He smiled. "Any time. Oh and by the way, you were WAY too easy on Anna," he said with a smirk. "You totally should have whipped her for getting shite all over your beautiful floor."

I tilted my head back and laughed heartily. "I guess I'm becoming soft!"

"No," Jon began in a quiet voice. "You're not becoming soft. You're simply a man who is falling in love." He patted me on the back.

I felt myself blush as I considered what he said. Love was a powerful force, and had a way of changing a person. I had experienced what falling in love had done for my outlook many years ago with my wife,

then more recently with Amy. Now I was seeing what love had done for Jon since he and Candy had reunited. It becomes easier to express vulnerabilities, and to share the most intimate parts of yourself with someone else. You begin to care for another person more than yourself. The world seems kinder. YOU become kinder.

In less than a year, Jon went from being an emotionally closed-off narcissist with an occasional soft side to a sensitive, gentle soul who was finally healing from a life of trauma and addiction. He had even made me and Daryl equal partners in the gym business, insisting that we each get 33 percent of the profits. Daryl and I had been shocked at Jon's proposal, which he had pitched over beers at Daryl's favorite bar, the same one with the "sticky table" Jon had complained about the previous year. The meeting had ended in tears of joy on Daryl's end, and hugs all around. I believe that Candy's love had changed Jon, had healed him some. And I was so happy for him.

As for the consequences of what love had done for MY life so far? It had made me fall so hard for another woman, to the point I had lost myself in her. So much of my identity was caught up in the beautiful soul that I had called my wife, and I had no idea what to do with myself once she was gone. Then, several years later, when I was ready to love again and dared to be vulnerable, I got my heart stepped on once more by sweet little Amy. Love could be a positive thing, of this I was certain, but it had also ruined my life. So for the moment, I decided to hold off on telling Anna how I felt. I couldn't risk having my heart broken again. Unlike Jon, I simply wasn't ready.

Several weeks later...

"Where are you taking me?" I asked with a chuckle as Jon led me blindfolded down the beach.

"You'll see," Jon said as he held onto my arm and guided me through the sand.

I figured he was probably showing off a new boat of his, but this would prove to be a bit larger than a boat.

After a few minutes of walking, we stopped and he took off my blindfold. We stood before a large, white, 2-story, contemporary house with floor to ceiling windows and balconies galore. It looked very much like his old home in Malibu, except a bit larger, and was merely five houses away from mine. I smirked in disbelief.

"Don't tell me this mansion is yours?" I asked.

Jon nodded. "It is, indeed, mate!" He said with a huge smile. "I bought it with cash! Move-in day is next week. It has an indoor pool with a high diving board, a sauna, five bedrooms, five and a half baths, a wet bar, a two car garage, and a jacuzzi in the master bedroom. There's even a pool table left over from the previous owners. And? It was half the price of my place in Malibu, despite having more square footage. Isn't it great? We're gonna be neighbors, mate!" He put his arm around me.

I was overjoyed with the news. "Congratulations!" I said with an ecstatic smile. "That's wonderful. I want to see inside. Can you give me a tour?"

Jon nodded. "Absolutely," He said as he walked with me to the front door, and unlocked it. "The place is mostly empty but you can at least see the general layout."

We entered through the spacious foyer. Similar to his old home, there were high ceilings and luxury touches throughout - granite floors, stainless steel appliances, and an impressive view of the ocean.

The formal dining area had an impressive chandelier and room for a large table. The wet bar near the kitchen was impressively sized, and the former owners had left a vast array of liquor.

There was a fireplace, which his old home lacked, as well as ceiling fans. The downstairs bathroom had a claw foot tub and was very old-school, and the adjoining bedroom similarly had a vintage charm. There was another bedroom that was smaller in size, which would do well as an office or guest room. Jon intended on converting the larger of the two bedrooms into a home gym, complete with treadmills, a rowing machine, a stationary bike, and an assortment of strength equipment.

The winding staircase led to three more bedrooms, one of which was enormous and had the aforementioned wet bar and jacuzzi tub. Each upstairs bedroom had its own balcony and an incredible view of the beach. Even the master bath had a stunning view of the water, with a large window next to the oversized tub.

As for the swimming pool? It was Olympic sized. The pool room itself had glass walls and a glass ceiling, so you practically felt like you were outdoors. An infrared sauna was tucked away in the corner of the pool room. Across from the sauna was a mini bar. The pool room had a door that led to a nice outdoor patio area, which sported a fire pit and a jacuzzi, as well as a mini gazebo. It was direct waterfront, of course. The house was like a mini hotel, and I was so happy for Jon.

"This place is amazing," I said. "I'm so thrilled. You've got to have a housewarming party once you're settled."

"Of course," Jon said with a grin. "This place has everything I wanted. The only thing that's missing is a girl to share it with." Jon's expression turned wistful, then apprehensive. "I need to think of a way to ask Candy if she would move in with me. I know that she and I haven't been together that long, but we have an amazing bond. Plus, it's not like we've just met. But still, I don't want to scare her off by asking her too soon."

I thought of what he had said. "I know what you mean. Well, maybe bring it up casually? When she first comes over, ask her if she could see herself living in a place like this and see how she reacts."

Jon's brow furrowed. "Hmm, not a bad idea. She lives pretty simply, so I'm sure that moving into a place like this would be an adjustment for her. Maybe she would need time to think about it, who knows? It's just... I can see us living a beautiful life in a home like this. Waking up to the sound of the ocean, going for morning swims in the heated pool,

making love in the sauna and the jacuzzi, candlelit dinners on the patio..."

Jon's gaze appeared faraway as he spoke, and I couldn't help but feel spellbound by what he was saying. It really did sound like a beautiful life. I couldn't imagine Candy refusing, or even "needing time to think about it."

BEEP! BEEP!

My phone's alarm broke me out of my daze. I looked at my device and silenced it.

"Well, looks like I must return home to let the girl out of her cage," I said with a sigh. "She's been in there since last night. I reckon she needs me to take her for a walk and feed her."

Jon gave a wry smile. "Of course, mate. Do what you gotta do. A dog needs his master... or should I say, HER master."

He and I walked back to my place, then we exchanged hugs and pleasantries before agreeing to talk later.

"Don't hold back on discipline if she misbehaves," Jon said with a smirk as he walked to his car.

I chuckled and waved, then went inside the house. I could hear the sniffles and whimpers right away. I wasted no time marching up to the cage and opening the metal door.

"It's time for a walk and a feeding," I said as I pulled her forward by her collar. She reluctantly crawled out of the cage, her body trembling slightly. I set down the dog bowls on the floor, one of which contained water. The food consisted of oatmeal. She looked up at me quizzically.

"Eat!" I demanded with my hands on my hips.

Anna reluctantly picked up the bowl full of oatmeal and tilted the ceramic container towards her lips. She did her best to control her shakiness but her hands still trembled despite her efforts. My manhood hardened and a smirk spread across my face as I watched my little pet slave eat from a dog bowl.

"Be sure and finish it all like a good girl," I said in a low voice as I stood above her with my arms folded across my chest.

She finished the oatmeal within a few more moments and took a few sips of water from the other bowl. Then she looked up at me, awaiting my next command.

"Stand up," I ordered, and she complied. I grabbed one of her dresses from the couch and handed it to her. "Put this on. I am taking you for a walk on the beach. I will be keeping you on a leash so everyone will know you're my pet." I smirked.

Her eyes grew wide but she did as I said, quickly pulling the floral print dress over her head. Then I grabbed the leash and hooked it to her collar, and we headed out of the house and onto the beach.

"You're lucky I'm not making you walk on all fours," I said coldly as I pulled on her lead, forcing her to walk faster through the sand. "Thank me for letting you remain upright." I glared at her.

Anna sighed. "Thank you for letting me remain upright," she recited robotically as she walked behind me.

I pulled the leash roughly, startling her. "And what else?" I raised my eyebrows.

Anna's eyes filled with defiant tears. "Thank you for letting me be your slave." Her voice shook.

I smiled gently. "You're welcome. Now let's continue."

I pulled her along the beach for about five minutes before we encountered another person walking. It was an older woman I hadn't

seen before. Upon seeing Anna on a leash, she covered her mouth in surprise and did her best to avoid eye contact, then walked around us. I had to bite my tongue to keep from laughing out loud. I knew Anna was mortified, so I mercifully turned around and walked her back to the house.

Once inside, I unfastened the leash from her collar, and kissed her on the cheek. Her eyes were bloodshot from tears of embarrassment.

"Great job, Anna," I said in a soft voice as I wrapped my arms around her waist. "I'm so proud of you."

She cried into my shoulder as we embraced. Several minutes passed before she spoke.

"Do you really think I have what it takes to be your slave for a whole week? I feel like I crumble so easily," she said with a sob.

I backed away from her tear-streaked face, and kissed her forehead. "Yes," I assured. "You handle yourself with tremendous grace, Anna. This is a process. We must start slowly. First, one night and then two, and so on. Go easy on yourself, dear. I mean, you were confined to a cage overnight and forced to eat from dog bowls, and then I walked you on a leash in public. It's a lot to go through." I ran my hands through her hair and kissed her on the lips. "You did great," I whispered in her ear. "Now, lets do something fun. You deserve a reward. Anything you like."

She ultimately decided on a trip to the spa. This would be our first spa visit as a couple. I excitedly called her favorite place and booked an appointment for her to get a pedicure and massage, as well as a haircut for myself. I so loved treating her, and taking care of her after intense play. This "slave training" session was the first of what would prove to be a grueling experience for Anna, one that would push her loyalty - and our relationship - to the limit. But in the meantime, pampering was in order.

One week later...

The commercial begins with a black and white scene of a handsome, shirtless, 30-something male with a chiseled physique. He is standing in a dark bedroom and is nude, holding a white sheet that covers his groin but only partially conceals his bum. He is smoking a cigarette in a sexy way, taking long drags and letting the smoke trail out of his nose and mouth in a seductive stream. He looks at his designer watch before glancing out the window at a busy city, his gaze intense.

The next scene is shot in full color, and shows the same handsome man dressed in a suit and holding a briefcase while walking towards a train. He looks at the same watch once more, before stepping through the train's doors.

Scene number three is shot entirely underwater. The man is wearing a white button down shirt and black slacks, diving into a pool with his clothes still on. His watch has fallen to the bottom of the pool, so he swims down to the bottom, grabs the watch, and puts in on. While down there, he encounters a woman with short blonde hair, who turns

out to be a mermaid. They swim closer to each other, smiling. The man looks at his watch once more, and the camera zooms in on the watch face. The watch still works despite being in deep water, and continues to tick away the seconds. When the camera zooms back out, it is revealed that the man is no longer wearing his shirt or pants, because he is now a mermaid as well. He holds hands with the mermaid woman, who is wearing her own wristwatch. It is the same brand as his, but with a slimmer wristband. They kiss.

The final scene shows the man once again in a suit, waking up on the train from what appeared to be a dream about the mermaid. However, as he gets off the train, he notices the same woman he saw in his dream, now wearing a blue dress. She looks at her watch (the same one as in his dream) then looks up to see the man watching her. She smiles at him, and he smiles back. The screen then fades to black and a closeup picture of the watch fills the screen, and a man's deep, soft voice begins talking.

"Crafted from sleek titanium, waterproof for up to 200 meters, and a lifetime warranty, this is Nautilus. It isn't just a time piece. It's quality time. Available at fine retailers everywhere."

I clapped and cheered. "Bravo, Jon!" I said with a smile as I handed my best mate's phone back to him. We were sitting outside on the patio of Jon's new place, enjoying a smoke and a cocktail before the other guests arrived to the housewarming party. Candy was in the downstairs loo, getting ready. "That's a great commercial," I said.

"Thanks, mate," Jon said with a grateful smile. "The black and white scene was a bitch to film because it took forever to get the lighting right, and there was a draft that kept messing up the motion of the smoke through the air. I wound up going through almost an entire pack of cigarettes. As for the underwater scene? Noelle and I did it in one take. The mermaid fins were CGI so all we had to do was undress. We were down there for more than three minutes. The cameraman was impressed, said we were real-life mermaids. I told him I was an experienced freediver, and demonstrated how long I could stay submerged. Wound up hitting a new record for holding my breath: thirteen minutes and four seconds. Must be from cutting back on smoking. I'm down to two packs a day, and I haven't smoked weed in months."

"That's great," I said as I took a swig of beer. "You did a terrific job with the voiceover at the end, too. I loved your American accent."

"An American accent is ok, but an Italian one is better," a familiar male voice said.

Jon and I spun around and our jaws dropped. "Holy shit," Jon gasped as he stood up. "Mario! You made it!"

The three of us exchanged hugs and pleasantries, offering our old high school buddy a seat as well as a beer, both of which he took.

"Nobody answered the door so I just walked around the back," Mario said as he took a swig of beer.

Jon nodded. "That's fine. The girlfriend is inside getting dolled up. Otherwise she would have answered. I can't wait for you to meet her."

Mario lit a cigarette and nodded. "Girlfriend, huh?" He asked with a smirk. "I haven't had one of those in years. Not since my heart got stepped on. Fucktoys, yes. But girlfriends? No."

Jon and I laughed at Mario's comment. Mario, whose nickname was "Momo," was full-blooded Italian with dark brown hair, a short beard, and honey brown eyes. He was about 6'2 and had a muscular build. He spoke with a sexy Italian accent and had a confident personality that made him irresistible to most. He was the closest thing Jon ever had to an idol of sorts.

I had felt neglected by Jon for half of my freshman year of high school, especially after Mario had beaten the crap out of Nick in a wrestling match. This had happened right after Nick had beaten Jon in a previous match, humiliating my best mate. Jon then began to see Mario as his new hero, inviting him into our little clique, where he rapidly assimilated. After all, Jon was a self-proclaimed "alpha male," and Mario was the only bloke who Jon considered worthy of the same title.

Around this time in my life, Jon started calling me his "bitch," introducing me as such to Mario at a party, and saying I did whatever I was told to do. I had laughed off Jon's nasty comment, explaining to Mario that Jon and I had been best mates since we were little. Jon had scoffed, mumbling, "whatever" under his breath, and proceeded to order me around for the rest of the night. He had expected me to fetch

him drinks, help him up from his seat, bring him food, and even light his cigarettes for him. When I tried to talk to Jon, he would ignore me, and when I tried to talk to others, he would interrupt me. After hours of this, I had snapped at Jon and stormed off, telling him I wasn't his slave, and that he needed to get his own fucking beer and stop acting like a dick. His facial expression had been one of total shock; he was completely unaccustomed to me blowing up at him.

Following that party incident, I had gone weeks without speaking to Jon, by which point he was trying so hard to patch things up with me. He had eventually invited me out to dinner at my favorite restaurant and wanted to treat. "Just us two blokes," he had said. In those days, we rarely hung out one-on-one anymore, so this was a big deal.

During the dinner, he had apologized and promised to be nicer. He had explained that he got aggressive and sometimes blacked out when drunk and high, and said things he didn't mean. Also, he had assured me that calling me his "bitch" was a term of endearment, that I was a great friend to him, and that he loved me so much. After that, he had shown me a video of him playing a beautiful song on the guitar, one that he had written just for me. I had loved hearing him sing in his soulful, baritone voice. After the video, tears had filled his expressive green eyes and he placed his manicured hand on mine, asking for my forgiveness. At that point in my life, it had been one of maybe three times I had seen Jon get emotional. I had caved, on account of his charm and persistence, and we exchanged hugs. I had even agreed to his offer to give me a handjob in the car, a form of make-up sex for his behavior.

Over time, he would revert back to his old tricks, bossing me around and even engaging in sexual foreplay with me at gatherings with friends. He would rationalize it with the explanation, "They're our close mates

and they're drunk; they don't care if we fool around." If I resisted, he would either sulk or use force to get me to go along with it, insisting we had a "special bond." These public advances left me feeling humiliated, but I did my best to convince myself that I was choosing to go along with what he wanted. On one occasion, I resorted to closing my eyes while he held me down and sucked me off on his couch during a party, crying silent tears that I hoped nobody noticed. This would be our pattern for a very long time, and it would be almost two decades before I would get up the courage to admit to myself that these public acts were not consensual.

Mario later confessed to me that he didn't really like Jon that much in the beginning because of the way he treated me and Nick. Aside from making me his "bitch," Jon had blatantly made fun of Nick at one point when we were all hanging out together, laughing at him and calling him "pathetic." Then he had encouraged Mario to join in on the bullying. Mario, to his credit, had sat there stone-faced, refusing to be influenced by Jon. At the time I had defended my best mate's behavior to Mario, saying he was just "a bit rough around the edges." Of course, in hindsight, Jon was straight up abusive at times, and it would take years for the dynamic to shift between us.

Mario was the strong, independent sort, and took no shit from anyone. Because of this, he was the only one of our mutual friends who Jon had consistently treated with respect. Mario was known to disappear for months or even years at a time and resurface at random, needing to retreat periodically. And here he was again, connecting with us blokes like no time had passed. It felt good to see him again.

It was uncanny how much Mario and Jon had in common from day one, and the joke in high school was that Mario was the Italian version of

Jon. Mario's last name was Morrone, and Jon's last name was Moore, so our mutual friends referred to them collectively as "Momo" and "Jomo."

They were both born on the 20th of the month, bisexual, born in Europe to wealthy families, multilingual, very athletic, and dominant in bed. They both acted and modeled for a living, and had musical ability. In fact, Jon and Mario played in a band for a number of years in high school, and they had slept together by the end of sophomore year. They were both talented singers. Mario had continued to hone his craft while attending college in Connecticut, taking voice lessons. Eventually, he moved to New York City and landed a gig on Broadway, scoring lead roles in several musicals. These days, he was a professional singer, and had just signed a contract with a major music label. According to his post on social media, his debut album was scheduled to come out very soon.

Jon showed the Nautilus watch commercial to Mario, who absolutely loved it.

"I like how the ad features three things you're good at: being naked, smoking, and holding your breath." Jon and I both laughed. "I just wish I had known you were filming in New York a few weeks back," Mario added. "We could have met up."

Jon nodded as he smoked. "I know. It's just that I was only in the city for one day, and I was crazy busy. That gal who starred in the commercial with me? Old friend of mine. Her name is Noelle. She and I went out for an early dinner after we had finished shooting, and our photographer

friend Jeannie joined us. Well, poor Noelle wound up having way too much to drink, so I agreed to drive her to her apartment in Brooklyn. She had come onto me a number of times, and I had to explain to her I was in a monogamous relationship. She got a little upset but eventually settled down, and I put her to bed. We have a history of fooling around, and she's used to me being polyamorous, but she was very understanding once she had sobered up. She and Jeannie were impressed with how much I have changed since last year. Guess I was a bit of a man-whore before!"

Mario chuckled. "Yeah, look at you," he said. "All monogamous and shit. You have definitely been to hell and back over the past year, all the shit you told me over the phone. Between the breakup with Lisa, the drug issues, the motorcycle accident, and the stint in rehab? It's a lot. But you landed yourself a quality girl AND you got a sweet new crib. You gotta give me a tour!"

Jon grinned ear to ear. "Oh, definitely. Once I finish my ciggy I will give you the grand tour of my castle."

Mario nodded then turned his attention to me. We made small talk for a few minutes. I told him about the business expansion with Daryl and Jon, as well as my relationship with Anna. Per his request, I showed him a photo of her.

"Tasty!" Mario said with a wink, making me laugh. "Will this fiery redhead be joining us tonight?" Mario asked.

I nodded with a smile. "Indeed she will be. She should be coming over in about ten minutes, according to her text."

Mario's brow furrowed. "Looks like I'm the odd man out," he said wistfully. "Seems everyone else is taken except me."

I patted Mario's shoulder. "That's not true," I said. "Our neighbor Brittany is coming over, and she's very single. I think you two would hit it off."

Jon nodded with a wolfish grin. "I totally agree. Brittany is a lovely girl. Ken and I got to, um, 'sample' her last July."

Mario laughed heartily, as did I. "You filthy dogs, you! Some things never change."

"Indeed they don't," Jon agreed as he stood up from his chair and put out his cigarette. "I'm just going to use the loo and then I will give you a tour. Be right back."

Mario nodded as Jon went into the house, then he leaned in closer to me. "Hey, does Jon still act all rude to you, and call you his 'bitch?'"

I shook my head and smiled. "Nope. We had a heart to heart in July and things changed after that. He was dealing with a lot of personal issues

for years and it wore on him, made him act mean. But he's addressed those issues and now he's like a new man."

"It's about damn time," Mario said with a smirk. "He seems nicer, and more mature. He was a total dick back in the day."

Before I could respond, Jon came back, this time with Candy in tow. They were talking and laughing, the epitome of a blissful couple. She truly looked like an angel, and was dressed in a beautiful, flowy white dress and matching cardigan.

"Mario, I would like you to meet my lovely girlfriend, Candy." Jon beamed as he showed off his "little angel."

Sparks immediately flew between Mario and Candy, and it was immediately clear that they already knew each other. Mario stood up from his seat, a lovesick expression on his face. Candy smiled at him, her eyes misting over with an expression of longing. They just looked at each other for several moments. Mario was the first to speak.

"My god," Mario gasped as he took Candy's hands in his and squeezed them. "Candy. Wow..." He drank in the sight of her, barely able to speak as his jaw dropped.

"Hi, Mario," Candy replied shyly as she bit her lower lip.

Jon stared at them both, somewhat dumbstruck. "You two....um, you two know each other?" He stammered, already knowing the answer.

They both slowly nodded, in a trance as they gazed at each other lovingly. "We go way back," Mario said in a soft voice.

Many hours later...

Mario, Jon, and I held each other on the living room couch as we cried, having spent the last hour pouring our hearts out over our respective heartbreaks. I had shared the story of my wife, and Jon had gone into detail about Lisa's miscarriage and the tragic breakup that ensued. Last but not least, Mario had talked about his ill-fated relationship with Candy. That's right: Mario was Candy's ex-boyfriend. They had dated seven years prior, and had been together for a year. Candy had been the one to end things, not long after both her parents had died.

During the hour, we had managed to polish off an entire bottle of vodka, but it felt good to get properly shitfaced and let out all the emotions we had kept bottled up. The party guests had left by that point. The only exceptions were Candy and Anna, who were sleeping in the guest bedroom. Like us, they had both had a lot to drink and needed to sleep it off.

It had been a great party overall. We got to catch up with friends we hadn't seen in a while. Daryl, Tracy, Amy, Eugene, Martha, Jon Sr., Noelle, Andre, Todd, Jeannie and Brittany had made it, along with a few other neighbors of ours. Tracy had hugged Andre and Todd when she

had met them, thanking them through tears for helping her the night of her rape. As for Brittany and Mario? Jon's prediction had been spot-on. They had hit it off, and had exchanged numbers and drunken kisses by night's end. Even my brother Lawrence and his wife Diana had stopped by for a while for a nibble. It was still rather strange seeing my brother being friendly with Jon after so many years of being enemies, but I was happy to see them get along.

Many of the guests had brought swimsuits, and were able to enjoy the indoor pool. After the alcohol had been flowing and most of the guests had left, Jon, Mario, Candy, Anna, and I had gone skinny dipping. I had seen the way Jon had glared at Mario when he had flirted with Candy in the pool, at which time my best mate had swum up to her and began making out with her aggressively. I couldn't help but feel bad for Jon, who was once again dealing with jealousy, and having to compete with another man for a girl's attention.

Now? Jon and I were comforting Mario, who was beside himself as he shared the details of his breakup, which had completely turned his life upside down for years.

"We had met in my freshman year of college and quickly became friends," Mario said as he wiped his tears away. "I was living off campus at my uncle's house, while working part time at the Italian restaurant he owned. She had come into the restaurant one day for pizza. We got to talking and I learned that we went to the same college. I told her I was a fine arts major and was pursuing an acting career. Then she told me her father taught theater at Yale but he was also an acting coach who gave private lessons. So I started taking lessons to help me master an American accent."

Jon's eyebrows raised. "No shit. I went to her father for the same thing when I was ten, right after I had moved to the states. Small world, huh?"

Mario nodded. "Yeah, what are the chances? Anyway, we were friends for years until I finally decided it was time to ask her out. She said yes, and we had a great time. Wound up having sex on the first date, and it was fucking amazing. You know that hot, heavy, wild sex that happens after years of pent up sexual tension? The kind of sex that lasts for hours and leaves you completely covered in sweat and totally spent? THAT kind!"

Jon and I laughed, as we were both familiar with the kind of lovemaking he was talking about.

Mario took a swig of beer before he continued. "Things progressed pretty quickly after that, and after about six months of being together, I knew I was in love with her. I had never been in love before, had never even had a serious girlfriend. But she was different. Anyway, her mother suddenly passed away in her sleep, and she was devastated. I helped her get through it as much as I could. Unfortunately, she didn't even have time to mourn, because her dad started failing around the same time. He had been battling Parkinson's for a few years but after the death of his wife, things got worse for him, and fast. I helped her take care of him until he got sick enough to move to a facility. Three months after moving there, he died." A tear fell from his eye, which he hastily wiped away.

Jon and I put our hand on Mario's back, knowing how hard it was for him to talk about this.

"I did my best to comfort her but she was inconsolable. I wanted so badly to lift her spirits and I felt like I could picture myself spending the rest of my life with her, taking care of her. So I bought a beautiful engagement ring and, after taking her out for a nice dinner, I drove her home and we had some wine, listened to some music, talked. Then I lit some candles and dimmed the lights, to make the mood more romantic. Then I got down on one knee, and popped the big question. She..."

Mario put his head in his hands and started to cry once more. Jon and I simply patted and rubbed his back, patiently waiting for him to continue.

"She told me she had to think about it. I was disappointed but still hopeful. So I waited a few days and brought it up again. That's when she broke up with me. We had been together for a year. I was so heartbroken, I just broke down sobbing. She began to cry too, saying she felt awful and that it wasn't anything I did, but that she just didn't have it in her to be in a relationship with anyone. She felt broken after losing both her parents in such a short time and needed to be alone. I tried to tell her I would help her, that I would be there for her and she said she still wanted to be friends but couldn't marry me, or even be my girlfriend.

"We spent one more night together, for closure. That night, we had made love for hours, had cried in each other's arms until we both fell asleep holding each other. When I woke up, she was gone. She had left

me a note on the bed, saying she would always love me and not to blame myself. I fell into a horrible depression that lasted months, and it took years before I felt 'normal' again. I moved to New York not long after that, to start fresh. I couldn't be around anyone or anything that reminded me of her. Since that breakup, I haven't risked putting myself out there again. No relationships, just one night stands. But I'm glad I got to see her tonight. And I'm happy for you, Jon. You're perfect for her. So, congratulations, old pal."

Mario and Jon exchanged warm hugs, then I joined in. The three of us cried as we embraced.

Jon sniffled and backed away after a few moments. "Candy had told me about this, but I had no idea that you were the one she was talking about. She said that she did feel terrible about ending her relationship with you, and that this was why she had moved back to Rhode Island from Connecticut, and was single for so long. I'm glad you were able to connect again and talk about things, after so many years."

Mario nodded. "She needed to heal from her losses. I get that now. But you two belong together, I can see it. Tonight, she told me all about your history together, meeting when you were kids and that you were her father's student. Then she filled me in on how she had lost contact with you for a very long time, and confessed to me that she felt this longing for you over the years that never went away."

Jon's eyes filled with tears of joy. "I felt the same for her. She's my little angel."

I smiled at the two blokes, thinking of Anna. The three of us headed outside for a smoke and chatted some more, then got ready for bed. Mario went to sleep in one of the upstairs bedrooms, Anna and I took a downstairs one, and Jon and Candy headed to the master bedroom.

Anna fell into a deep sleep right away, but I lay awake as I listened to the sound of Jon making love to Candy. Their soft moaning punctuated the sound of the bed creaking, and there was an occasional slapping sound followed by a muffled squeal. I smirked as I imagined what Jon was doing to her up there, and I developed a massive erection. At that moment, I slid my hand down the front of Anna's panties and slipped a finger into her pussy as she slept. I kept my other hand on my manhood and masturbated myself to sleep.

Sometime in the middle of the night my phone buzzed. Jon had texted me.

"I showed Candy the edgeplay videos of Lisa and me. She's convinced they were staged. I'm going to show her how very real those acts were. The girl needs to start taking me seriously and stop laughing, or I will slap that little smile off that angel face of hers."

I rubbed my stubble, then decided on a reply to my frustrated best mate. "Yes. It sounds like she needs to know who's 'master.' Did she fill out that 'list of questions to ask a submissive' yet?"

"Indeed she did, answering 'yes' to everything. Apparently she's ok with me piercing her clit, 'as long as it's the hood and not the glans.' She

literally wrote that next to the question. I guess she's done her research on clit piercings, haha. Then I added a question specifically for her since she carries a pistol. I asked if it was ok to use her gun during play, and she wrote, 'as long as it isn't loaded.' With a smiley face after it. It's like she thinks this whole thing is funny."

"Take her by surprise," I wrote. "I say invite her over one day and just tie her up. Don't even tell her what you will be doing to her. Take charge. Mess with her head. Make her feel powerless. Stop treating her like your little angel. Corrupt her. Whip her. Bite her. Spit on her. Ejaculate on her. Piss on her. Cut her with a razor. Shove the barrel of her gun in that pretty mouth of hers after it's been inside her tight bum. And as she's lying there, tied up and helpless, covered in blood, spit, semen, and piss, shoot blanks at her for fun. Better yet, invite me over so I can watch."

Jon replied with a string of laughing face emojis, then wrote, "Wow! Listen to you, mate. You're one hardcore sadist. Fucking brilliant."

I smiled. "I learned from the best of them," I replied. "You should have her come over on the weekend of your birthday. What better way to celebrate your 34th than by breaking in your little angel?"

"Good idea," he wrote. "It's only a few short weeks from now. And I will definitely let you watch. Oh man, I'm gonna have some sweet dreams tonight!"

We wrapped up our text conversation then I turned off my phone, directing my attention to the lovely redhead next to me. I watched Anna's chest rise and fall with her breathing and before long, my eyes got heavy and I fell asleep. I dreamed about Anna and Candy being tied up while Jon and I took turns shooting blanks at them with Candy's gun.

4/19, the night before Jon's 34th birthday...

The three of us sat in a circle in Jon's living room, holding hands with our eyes closed. Soft music played from the stereo, and candles adorned the tables.

Jon, Candy, and I had just finished dinner and a round of cocktails. Now, we were getting into the zone with a meditation session, preparing ourselves for what Jon called, "Candy's awakening."

Jon had gone out and purchased special costumes for the role play that would take place, and when I had asked what the costumes looked like, he had smirked at me, telling me it would be a surprise.

After we were suitably relaxed, Jon got up and blew out the candles then turned off the music. Then he helped Candy from the floor, and picked her up. He gazed lovingly at her.

"Let's go upstairs," he crooned, then looked over at me with a gentle smile. "Follow us, mate."

I smiled and nodded, excited for what would follow. Jon carried Candy up the stairs and I followed behind them. He had her go into the walk-in closet to put on her costume, while Jon went into the loo to put on his. Meanwhile, I chilled out on the chaise lounge in the palatial master bedroom, which sported a wet bar, mini-fridge, and an oversized jacuzzi tub that I couldn't wait to take a dip in. I fondled myself as I tried to picture what would happen next.

Candy emerged from the closet several minutes later, and I was able to hear her giggles before I saw what she was wearing.

She took tentative steps towards me, doing a little twirl for me. I smiled sexily as I took in the sight of her.

"Nice wings," I said with a grin.

"Thank you!" She said with a chuckle.

She wore a sleeveless white dress with lace flowers adorning the bodice, as well as matching angel wings made of feathers. Her dress sported slits that went up to mid-thigh. The costume was the perfect combination of innocent and sexy.

We made small talk for a bit, and then her expression turned serious.

"I'm nervous," Candy admitted to me, looking down in shame as she sat down on the king size bed.

I smiled sympathetically. "You're in good hands," I assured her. "Jon wouldn't do anything to seriously hurt you. He loves you very much. And I'm here for moral support."

Candy smiled shyly. "Aren't you also here to 'watch?'" She asked with raised eyebrows.

I chuckled. "Well, yes, but I also keep Jon in line. If he gets carried away, I intervene. We have an agreement."

Candy nodded. "I trust you guys."

Suddenly, the lights in the room dimmed, sensual music came on the stereo, and a shadow appeared in the doorway.

The faint glow of his cigarette was visible, as was the silhouette of his body. When he stepped into the room, it became clearer what he was wearing, and my eyes widened.

The first thing that grabbed my attention was the set of red horns, which looked very realistic and appeared to grow out of his head, as if they always belonged there. Next was the sensual, floor-length, black velvet cape, which emphasized the broadness of his shoulders. Lastly,

there were his eyes. Normally a sultry green, they now had a demonic red hue, thanks to special effects contact lenses. The inner rims of his eyes were lined in black. The new eye color, combined with the makeup, made his gaze even more intense than usual. That's right: Jon Moore was the devil.

He came in closer to Candy, staring at her with his red eyes as he took a drag off his cigarette. She stood up from the edge of the bed and struggled to keep a straight face as he glared at her, smoke streaming out of his nostrils. Candy was the first to speak.

"You're one hot devil!" She said with a giggle, as she ran her hands up and down his front. His cape opened slightly, revealing his bare torso and a pair of black boxer briefs. Jon smirked and put his cigarette in his mouth, opening his cape wider. His erection was visible through his knickers, and his nipple jewelry was updated with new black hoops. His pecs and abdominal muscles popped even more than usual.

Candy continued to touch him, running her hands over his nipples, and taking the time to play with the new jewelry. Then her hand traveled farther down, until she had reached his underwear. She smiled sexily at him and began teasing his package through the silky material, making him moan.

He took a long drag off his cigarette and French inhaled. Then he put it out in the nearby ashtray, leaned in close to Candy, and blew a thick stream of smoke in her face. Then he grabbed the back of her neck and began kissing her. His kisses became more aggressive as the minutes passed, and he began pulling her hair and grabbing her crotch and bum,

making her squeal and moan with desire. Suddenly, he picked her up and threw her onto the bed.

Jon wasted no time placing her dainty wrists in the leather restraints, followed by her ankles. A nervous smile spread across her face as she lay atop the black satin bedspread, and she did her best to stifle her giggling. I could tell my best mate was getting annoyed.

Once the restraints were in place, he straddled her and glared at her.

"Wipe that little smirk off your face, bitch," he growled.

Candy bit her lower lip and took some deep breaths, trying her best to be serious. Predictably, she broke out into full-on laughter.

Jon abruptly got up from the bed and removed his cape, followed by his boxer briefs. He was now fully nude, except for the devil horns atop his head. His enormous manhood was fully erect, and he had a new cock piercing. He stood at the foot of the bed with his hands on his hips, staring at Candy as she tried in vain to control her laughter.

"I warned you."

With those words, Jon climbed back onto the bed and positioned himself so his cock was in line with Candy's mouth. She gazed at his

pierced member, fascinated by the jewelry that dangled from the front of his shaft. She then looked up at him, hesitant.

"Don't just stare at it, EAT it!" Jon barked, making Candy AND me jump.

She opened her mouth and began sucking Jon's dick, and he began face-fucking her hard. He practically fell atop her face as he squatted up and down with increasing speed. It was clear that she was struggling not to choke on his penis, and she began to make gagging sounds as he raped her mouth. Saliva dripped down the sides of her face as she struggled.

Jon smirked down at his slave, enjoying every moment. "That's it," he panted as he thrusted. "Choke on the devil's cock, like the good little angel you are."

I once again began to fondle myself as I lay on the chaise and watched the fuckfest. It was so incredibly sexy, watching my best mate defile his "innocent" little girlfriend. I couldn't wait to see her reach a breaking point. Jon, perhaps sensing that I was smiling at him, looked up at me and winked.

"Mmmm..." Candy began to groan as more spit formed around her mouth and down her face as she did her best to suck Jon's cock. He grabbed the back of her head, forcing himself even deeper into her mouth. Tears formed in her eyes and she made more gagging sounds. It was clear she was trying not to throw up.

"Shut up or I will punish you," Jon growled as he continued to violate her. He intensified his grip on her head.

Candy's face began to turn red as she choked on his penis, her teary eyes pleading with him to let up. He continued to mercilessly fuck her mouth, until it was clear she had thrown up.

Luckily it was only a wee bit of bile, but it was enough for Jon to let go of her head and back away from her mouth to let her breathe and assess the amount of vomit. Candy looked up at him with shame in her eyes, a combination of spit, tears, and bile streaking her angelic face.

Jon examined his vomit-covered penis and wiped it dry. Then he glared at Candy, and got in close to her face.

"Look at the mess you made," he growled. "You're about as pure as yellow snow. You don't deserve angel wings, OR a white dress."

Jon leaped off the bed and grabbed something from underneath it. What I saw made my heart speed up something terrible. Candy gasped and her eyes grew wide. It was a machete!

"Jon, what are you going to do?" I asked in a shaky voice.

He looked at me with those devilish red eyes, looking almost inhuman as his face morphed into a frightening mask of rage. A vein popped out

of his forehead and his nostrils flared. His arm muscles popped as he tightened his grip on the shiny weapon.

"Watch me," he said with a smirk, then diverted his attention to his slave, who appeared horrified.

"I'm going to do some surgery," he explained to Candy as he climbed back onto the bed. "You're about to become a mere mortal."

With those words, he began sawing away at Candy's angel wings, until they were mere stumps. Feathers piled up on either side of her on the bed as she tried to breathe deeply and stay calm. Once he was done with the wings, he moved onto her dress, cutting it off of her. Candy began to tremble and whimper, but Jon continued on, his expression cold. Next was her bra, and then her panties, all ruined beyond repair by the sharp and deadly object. Before long, Candy was nude, and Jon held the machete in front of her scared face before slowly lowering it until it was level with her vagina.

"I could kill you so easily," Jon said with a sadistic grin as he held the machete inches from her labia.

Candy began to shake even harder. "If you kill me, you can't make love to me anymore," she said timidly, trying to reason with him.

Jon's lips curled into an amused grin and then he broke into an evil laugh. "What the fuck makes you think I want to make love to a little

cum slut like you? Hmm? You're delusional. You're just a toy to me. A play thing. Nothing more."

He began to slowly move the machete up and down her torso, watching her struggle to keep her cool. The cold blade grazed her breasts, her inner thighs, and even her pussy lips. She struggled against the restraints and shuddered something terrible as the machete made its way across the most delicate parts of her anatomy. I became increasingly worried that she would get cut. But Jon's movements were smooth as could be, and just when I thought she would either lose her cool or wind up injured, he let up and tossed the machete to the floor. I breathed a sigh of relief, as did Candy.

Jon glared at Candy as he straddled her, his erect penis merely inches away from her vagina. He began running his fingernails down her abdomen, going hard enough to leave scratch marks. Once there were marks on her stomach, he moved to her breasts, squeezing and digging at the same time. Candy winced at the sensation, squirming under his touch.

"You're lucky this is all I'm doing to you right now," he growled as he dug his nails deeper into the flesh of her breasts. "I'm about ready to get a lot rougher."

"Jonny Boy...," Candy muttered in a sing-song tone.

This got Jon's attention and he stopped scratching, his expression appearing surprised and rather wistful. "Jonny Boy" has been his mum's

nickname for Jon when he was a baby, and at age 11, he had shared this piece of information with Candy, who had insisted on calling him the same thing. As a sort of inside joke, he had invented a nickname for Candy as well.

"Remember when we were younger, and you used to call me your 'Candy Girl?' It was right after you told me about your mom's nickname for you. We were at the beach when you told me about that nickname, and I thought it was so sweet and kept calling out to you from the water. I would call out, 'Jonny Boy!' And you would call back, 'Candy Girl!' It became our version of 'Marco Polo.' It was such a nice memory." Her eyes filled with tears as she smiled sweetly at him.

Jon swallowed. Then he looked at her with such love and admiration, and his heart seemed to melt. In all the years of role play, I had yet to see him break character. But in that moment, that's what seemed to be happening. His hands began to massage her breasts gently, and he leaned down towards her face, as if he were ready to kiss her.

"You know what I think of that memory?" He said in a soft voice, a gentle smile on his face.

Candy smiled at him. "What?"

"I think... that 'Jonny Boy' is dead, and so is 'Candy Girl.'" He spat, as his expression turned sour and his red devil eyes glowed with rage. "It was a million fucking years ago. These days, I go by 'Master,' or 'Sir.' And you?" He raises his eyebrows and pointed to her chest. "You don't even

HAVE a name right now. You're a fucking hole to be filled. So you better wipe that amused smile off your face, and stop 'topping from the bottom.' Stop trying to make me crack. Stop trying to distract me. Stop trying to 'dominate' me. And stop trying to make me get emotional. You hear me?!" His face was inches from hers by this point, and he looked furious.

Candy's face was flecked with the spit that had flown from Jon's mouth when he had shouted at her. With frightened eyes, she nodded and she trembled slightly, biting her lip. "Yes, Master," she mumbled.

It was obvious that she was crushed, despite the fact that she had successfully penetrated through Jon's armor, and had found a way to make him "feel." I could read my best mate like a book, and I could tell from his body language that Candy had really thrown him a curve ball. For the briefest of moments, Jon Moore, the king of being in control, had lost control.

"You're gonna pay for this," Jon growled as he spat on his hand and rubbed the saliva on his dick, before bending down, spreading her cheeks, and spitting onto her arsehole. "Get ready to be bum-fucked by my pierced cock!"

He barely gave Candy time to prepare for his huge penis before lining it up with her back door and slamming into her. She screamed in pain and surprise.

Per an earlier conversation with Jon and me, Candy had an aversion to anal sex, partly due to Mario's obsession with bum-fucking but also due to her experience with my anal fisting. Similar to Jon, Mario was very well endowed as well as dominant, and had a clear preference for anal. In fact, she had credited Mario for popping her back-door cherry, having remained a self-proclaimed "anal virgin" until she was 24 years of age. She had merely tolerated the anal sex, neither hating it nor enjoying it, but Mario had been such a passionate and skilled lover that she had decided it was worth it to let him fuck her anally, as a sort of reward. By the end of their relationship, Mario had managed to get her to orgasm while sodomizing her, but it had been a "one and done" experience. And now, years later? She had no choice but to tolerate Jon's cock in her arse while restrained.

Her facial expression gave away her discomfort, which encouraged Jon to treat her more roughly.

SLAP!

Jon actually smacked Candy in the face, making her squeal in surprise. A red mark appeared on her cheek. He pounded her harder, and her wrists strained against the leather straps.

"Does it hurt?" Jon asked in a mocking tone as he fucked the hell out of her back door.

Candy nodded. "It feels like a stabbing pain," she whimpered as she did her best to deal with the sodomy.

Jon hesitated and he slowed down the tempo of his thrusts. For the briefest of moments, his face showed a look of concern, before morphing back into a look of contempt. Despite the intensity of the role play, it was obvious he loved her and didn't want to hurt her. He swallowed and did his best to stay in character.

"Well, I don't hear the safe word," he said with a sneer as he violated her bum. "So until you say it, I'm not stopping. In fact, since you just whined at me, you must now endure a new level of pain. Understood?"

Candy bit her lip as she winced, continuing to tolerate the rough sex. "Yes, Master," she gasped.

Jon looked over at me with raised eyebrows. His red eyes glowed and it was clear he was up to no good. "Would you grab my black belt from the closet?" He asked with a smirk.

I swallowed and nodded, waking up to the closet and grabbing Jon's black leather belt. Then I walked up to the bed, ready to hand him the belt.

Jon shook his head. "No. Help me take the restraints off this little whore. I want to bum-fuck her doggie style while whipping the shite out of her."

Candy's eyes grew wide upon hearing Jon's words. But I did as he asked, abruptly undoing the straps on her wrists as well as her ankles. Once the restraints were off, Jon quickly withdrew from her. His cock was covered in blood but he didn't care. He glared at Candy, who was rubbing her sore wrists.

"Turn over and get on your knees, you little whore," he growled, as he wiped blood from his manhood and licked his hand, before smearing some of the blood on her breasts.

Candy looked ready to throw up when she saw Jon taste her blood, and when he wiped some of it on her tits, she covered her mouth with her hand in shock.

SMACK!

Jon slapped her in the face again, this time with a hand covered in blood. She squealed and whimpered as she looked at him pleadingly, blood smeared on her cheek.

"I SAID, turn around on your KNEES, bitch!" Jon bellowed.

Candy obliged, her limbs shaky as she positioned herself on all fours. I got in closer to her and Jon, belt in hand.

Jon climbed up behind her and once again spat on his cock, then lined himself up with her traumatized bum. Then he grabbed her hip and slammed into her. She gasped in pain as she was forced to endure further torture. He pounded the hell out of her, roughly grabbing her hips as he fucked her from behind. Slapping sounds filled the air, as did the smell of blood. After a few moments of hard thrusting, Jon turned to me with an ominous gaze.

"Now hand me the belt."

I reluctantly handed Jon the heavy leather strap. He took it from me with a smirk, then took some deep breaths, preparing to whip the shit out of his little slave.

He continued to thrust as he drew his arm back. "Get ready for some REAL pain," he warned Candy.

I looked on with wide eyes, watching Jon get ready to whip Candy with the belt. But there was something wrong and his cocky expression morphed into one of fear. He swallowed as he continued to thrust, and closed his eyes for a few moments. Then, just when I was convinced he would change his mind about the belt, the sound of the heavy leather colliding with flesh filled the air.

CRACK!

Candy's screams echoed off the walls as she endured a succession of painful blows to her back and bum as Jon continued to plow into her from behind. About midway through the whipping, Jon encouraged me to disrobe and join me on the bed. Once I had climbed onto the king size bed, he looked at me with those intense red eyes.

"Choke her," he said in a low voice.

I smirked and nodded, getting into position at the head of the bed until my manhood was merely inches away from Candy's tear streaked face. She looked at me with fear in her baby blues, her eye makeup smudged.

"Get ready to fight for air, sweetheart," I growled as I placed my hands around her throat.

Candy choked and gagged as Jon continued to rape her anally, punctuating his hard thrusts with an occasional strike from the belt. Red welts covered her back and her arse cheeks, and some of the welts began to bleed. This went on for some time, and I became more and more impressed with Candy's ability to remain calm. Her stamina rivaled Lisa's, and she was incredibly poised for a first time "edge player."

Suddenly, Jon pulled out and began to masturbate, his hand moving faster and faster over his shaft. I decided to do similar with my own member, and choked Candy's throat with my left hand as I choked my manhood with my right. After a few moments, Jon ejaculated all over Candy's back, then spread some of the semen over her cuts. She

I was thinking. He winked at me knowingly then turned to Candy. By that point he had stopped urinating and had let go of her wet head.

"You have done a respectable job maintaining your composure during this intense scene," he said in a kind voice, removing the devil horns from his head. "Because of this, I will allow you a ten minute break, during which you are permitted to clean up and grab a drink and a nibble."

Candy nodded and wiped her eyes, and began to get up from the bed. Jon and I gave her a helping hand, making sure she was steady on her feet, which she luckily was. She began to walk out of the room and down the hallway towards the loo to clean herself up.

Jon walked to the doorway and popped his head out. "Remember, ten minutes!" He called out.

"Ok," she called back with a giggle.

Jon scowled at the sound of her laughter. Then he took the soiled bedspread off the bed and placed it in the nearby hamper, replacing the bedspread with a fresh one. Once he had finished making the bed, he turned to me and smiled, grabbing his pack of cigarettes from the top of the dresser. He offered me one and I accepted. We both lit up.

"So," I began, as I took a drag and sat down on the chaise, "What's next on the menu for your little angel?"

Jon smirked and sat down on the edge of the bed and he took a long drag. He held in the smoke for a few moments before answering. "Gun play."

Smoke trailed out of his nose and mouth in thick bursts as he breathed those words, and his red eyes glowed ominously.

I raised my eyebrows. "You think she's ready for that?"

Jon shrugged. "I have yet to see her lose her cool. I think she's more than ready. But mostly, I want to see how much she can handle before she breaks down. She's tough, mate. Possibly the toughest I've ever seen."

I nodded. "I can't believe she giggled when you told her she could only have ten minutes."

Jon rolled his eyes. "That's the other thing. The laughter is getting on my nerves something awful. It seems that no matter what I do or say, it's just a joke to her. Which is why I'm adding a little secret twist to the gun play, one I think is bound to scare her serious."

He got up and whispered in my ear. My eyes widened at what he told me. "Seriously? She will surely piss herself. I mean, shooting blanks is nerve wracking enough, but the possibility of the gun-"

"Shhh!" Jon said, as he placed his finger on my lips. "I can't risk her overhearing. These walls are thin, and the floor doesn't creak; she could sneak down the hallway and suddenly pop into the room, and we wouldn't hear her coming."

"Ok, sorry," I said, taking a few drags off my ciggy.

With those words, Jon got up from the bed and walked over to Candy's purse. He took our her .38 caliber pistol and studied it for a few moments.

"It always amazes me how heavy these little things are," he said, as he turned over the weapon in his hand, looking at it from different angles with a look of awe. "Such a small tool...with such potentially large and devastating consequences."

I nodded. "Guns scare me something awful," I admitted as I looked at the pistol in Jon's hand.

Jon looked up at me. "Me too, mate."

Down the hall, Candy was humming to herself, oblivious to the fact that she was about to be tortured at gunpoint, with her own gun. The sound of her humming grew in volume and it was clear she wasn't far away.

"She's coming," I whispered.

Jon nodded, then took a hasty drag off his cigarette before putting it out and sitting down at the foot of the bed, deadly tool in hand.

Candy emerged through the bedroom door, her hair wet from a recent shower. She wore a towel around her torso and held a martini glass in her hand. Her facial expression was so blissful and carefree, you would think she was on vacation. As soon as she saw the gun in Jon's hand, however, she froze. Her blue eyes widened.

"I found your gun," Jon growled as he pointed it at his sub.

Candy swallowed as she did her best to stay calm. She put down her martini glass and readjusted the towel covering her body. "I-I see that," she stammered.

"I also found your bullets," he said with an evil grin.

That did it. Tears filled her eyes and she covered her mouth in shock. Her towel fell to the floor, revealing her naked body, which sported some scratches and bruises from the rough play.

Jon stood up from the bed and got closer to her, aiming the gun at her face. "I am...SO...FUCKING...SICK and TIRED of you laughing at me! It's

about time you learned how to take me seriously! Lie down on the bed."

Candy nodded as she wiped her eyes, practically running to the bed then lying down. "Please don't do anything crazy," she pleaded in a shaky voice.

Jon tilted his head back and laughed as he continued to point the gun at her. "Depends on how you define 'crazy.' But we ARE going to play a game. The first round will consist of you being gun-fucked up the arse while I fist your tight little pussy. And then? We get to play a little Russian Roulette."

Candy shook her head in horror. "There's no way you would do that," she began shakily. "You wouldn't load it. No way. You love me too much to risk killing me."

Jon glared at her. "How do you know it's not loaded? You have no fucking idea who you're dealing with!"

Just then, he spun the barrel of the gun, aimed it perhaps a foot to the right of Candy, and pulled the trigger.

BANG!

The sound of the gun going off was deafeningly loud and I couldn't help but jump. Candy predictably screamed, backing away from Jon as he crawled up onto the bed.

"Open your legs," Jon growled as he aimed the gun at her pussy. His manhood was once again standing attention, and his face formed a sneer.

Candy obliged, scared of what he would do to her if she refused.

Jon spat on the barrel before lowering it to her vagina, then slid it inside. She flinched as the cold material entered her womanhood. He pushed harder, and began moving it in and out of her pussy at a faster and faster pace. She closed her eyes tightly and bit her lip, doing her damndest to tolerate being violated with the barrel of her own (possibly loaded) gun. Unlike the time I had gun-fucked her, Jon was aggressive with the deadly tool, jamming it repeatedly into her ladybits as a sinister smirk formed across his face.

"I thought you had a gun fetish," Jon growled as he pounded her with the barrel of the pistol, occasionally pinching her nipples.

Candy winced and moaned before replying. "I do, but you're being very rough," she panted.

Jon laughed evilly. "This is just the warmup, darling. After this, the gun is going up your arsehole and my fist in your cunt. So shut up and take it, bitch."

"Yes, Master," Candy whimpered.

As much as I loved a good edge play session, this particular scene was hard for me to watch. Guns made me incredibly nervous, and I felt a craving for some liquid courage. I got up from the chaise lounge and helped myself to a nip of top shelf vodka from the mini-fridge that Jon kept in the room, next to the wet bar.

Jon looked over at me. "Hand me one of the vodkas, will you?" He asked. "Actually, make that three. Two for me and, uh...one for the bitch." He glared at Candy. "Maybe some 80 proof goodness will make you less uptight."

Candy opened her mouth to speak but thought better of it, electing to keep quiet. She eagerly took the small bottle of vodka out of my hand when I presented her with it, downing the contents rapidly. As for Jon, he looked at me with lust in his eyes.

"Would you feed them to me?" He asked with a smirk.

I nodded, opening both bottles. I held the first one to his lips and he tilted his head back, guzzling the strong booze. Then I gave him the

second bottle, which he finished just as quickly. Then he winked and smiled.

"Much better," he crooned, before slowly taking the barrel of the gun out of Candy's pussy. He examined the juices covering it, and licked it clean. "Mmmm, delicious...just the perfect amount of blood," he said as he licked his lips.

Candy lifted her head up from the pillow and looked at him with alarm, then down at her crotch. "Am I bleeding?" She asked with concern.

"Just a wee bit," Jon said as he continued to clean the gun with his tongue. "There might be more blood after I fist you."

Her eyes filled with frightened tears and, once again, Jon's facial expression was kind and reassuring. He placed the gun on the bed.

"You know the safe word," he said softly, caressing her face with both his hands. "Just say it if things get too intense."

Candy swallowed and nodded. "Any chance I can have another vodka?" She asked sheepishly.

Jon chuckled softly. "Of course, darling. I will have another one myself."

He got up from the bed and went over to the mini fridge, taking out 2 nips of vodka. He turned to me and offered me one but I declined, intent on remaining clear headed for the intense scene to come.

Once Candy and Jon had downed the booze, Jon began spitting on his hand and fondling her, intent on getting her wet with a combination of his saliva and her secretions. She moaned as he touched her womanhood, and began bucking her hips. As she did this, Jon grabbed the gun from the edge of the bed, and spat on the barrel.

"Ouch!" Candy gasped.

Jon had shoved the barrel of the pistol up Candy's bum, taking her by surprise. He continued to fondle her pussy with his other hand, grooming her for the fisting he planned on doing to her.

"Close your eyes," Jon breathed. "It will help. Trust me."

Candy nodded and clenched her baby blues closed. I watched wide-eyed as Jon slowly inched his hand deeper and deeper into her vagina, starting with the fingertips, then the fingers, then the knuckles. She whimpered as her limits were tested, one agonizing inch at a time.

"Deep breath," Jon whispered, as his hand disappeared inside her all the way to his wrist. He was about to form a fist with his hand and the sensation would indeed be very intense. Although I had successfully fisted her the year before, this time would definitely be more

challenging, as she now had the barrel of a gun up her bum, and she wasn't nearly as drunk as she had been that night. This would hurt.

With her eyes still shut tightly, Candy took a deep, jagged breath, filling her belly with air. Then it happened.

"AAAHHHH!!!"

Her scream was loud and piercing, and her breathing turned to panting. Jon's fist was now stretching her walls, and challenging her tolerance for pain.

"You're doing great, Candy," Jon assured with a smile as he held his fist inside her, the gun still securely embedded in her backside. "Just breathe. Tell me if you want to stop."

Candy shook her head as tears fell from her closed eyes. "No, don't stop, I'm coming," she panted. "You're on my g-spot! Just keep the gun and fist still and let me move my hips."

Jon raises his eyebrows in incredulous surprise and looked up at me. "Can you believe this one?"

I shook my head and smiled in amusement. "She's a legend. Hardcore all the way." I put my hand on my cock and began to diddle myself, loving the way Candy bucked her hips while being dual penetrated.

"Like candy," Jon and I blurted out at the same time. The three of us laughed. It felt good to experience a moment of comic relief after so much tension. Little did we know that this light hearted moment would lead to the most intense part of the evening.

One hour later...

"Woohoo!!!" Jon exclaimed after he spun the chamber of the gun and shot what was luckily a blank at an empty bottle of booze, making me and Candy jump.

After licking Candy's juices from his hand and arm, Jon had taken the time to disinfect her abrasions, and we all took a much needed break from the hardcore play. Now, the three of us were more than a little buzzed on shots of vodka, and were therefore emboldened to handle Candy's gun with less apprehension. Candy was the most sober of us, and looked on with horror as Jon continually used various objects in the room for "target practice."

"Here, mate," Jon said to me as he held out the gun. "Have some fun with it."

I swallowed and hesitantly took it from him. Even with liquid courage coursing through my veins, the gun frightened me something awful. I spun the chamber, cocked it, then aimed it at a lamp situated in the

corner of the room. This would be my first time firing a gun. My hand shook slightly, but I took some deep breaths and closed my eyes.

BANG!

My body shook like a leaf as I stood shaking with the gun in my hand, and Jon looked at me with a broad smile on his face. He began clapping.

"Bravo, mate," he said with a big grin. "Now aim it at me."

I swallowed and hesitated before taking aim at my best mate's chest. The gun shook something terrible as I once again spun the chamber and put my finger on the trigger. I closed my eyes.

BANG!

"Yesss!" Jon exclaimed, as he stood unharmed, coming in for a hug.

I let him wrap his arms around me as I stood numb, completely shocked at what I had just done.

"You alright?" He asked as he backed away from me, his expression concerned. "You're shaking so badly."

I nodded. "I'm fine," I lied, deciding to sit down and recover. I placed the gun on the table next to me and rubbed my temples.

Jon patted me on the back. "It's ok, just take some breaths." Then he picked up the gun and backed away from me, turning his attention to Candy. She sat in shock, her hand over her mouth. He spun the chamber then took aim at her.

"Jon, please don't shoot it at me," she said in a trembling voice. "Hand me the gun."

Jon raised his eyebrows, and lowered the gun respectfully. "I will hand you the gun, under one condition."

Candy swallowed. "What's that?"

He walked up to her until he was only a foot away. "Shoot me."

Candy shook her head. "No."

Jon smirked. "Have it your way." He then suddenly turned to me and aimed the gun in my direction.

BANG!

I screamed and jumped a foot in the air, not having had any time to prepare mentally. "Dammit, Jon!" I barked as I began to shake and cry. "Just give her the gun!"

Jon put his hands up and nodded, instantly remorseful for what he had done. "Ok, ok." He handed Candy the firearm, and she eagerly took it. "But I still want you to shoot me." He backed up several feet.

Candy sighed. Then she stood up and hesitantly spun the chamber, then aimed at Jon. She closed her eyes, her finger primed on the trigger as her hands shook.

"Come on, baby," Jon said in a soft voice. "Be a good girl and pull the trigger. I'm not afraid to die." He held out his arms and closed his eyes, a little smile on his face.

Candy's hands shook badly as she stood there and she was doing her best not to cry. The standoff continued for a few moments, until, suddenly, she dropped the gun and began to cry. Before long, she was sobbing uncontrollably.

Jon opened his eyes and looked at her with concern. "Hey, it's ok, honey," he assured, as he got closer to her. She recoiled and backed away.

"Don't touch me!" She sobbed, then picked up her gun, grabbed her purse and her set of clothes, and ran out of the room.

Jon took after her. "Candy, please don't leave," he pleaded, rapidly putting on his robe and following her down the hallway.

But she ran down the stairs so quickly, bawling her eyes out as she did so. A few moments after that, the front door opened and slammed shut, followed by the sound of Candy's car peeling out of the driveway.

By this point, Jon was downstairs, frantically grabbing his car keys and putting on his slippers, intent on catching up with her. I went after him before he reached the front door, placing my arm on his.

"Let her go," I said softly. "She needs to process this alone."

Jon looked at me with his eyes full of tears and a trembling lip. "I don't know if she's coming back," he said in a shaky voice. "I pushed her too hard, mate." He broke down crying.

I wrapped my arms around him, letting him cry into my shoulder. "She will come back," I assured.

I spent the rest of the night comforting Jon, even going so far as to cuddle with him in bed. It was his birthday and, since Candy had run out on him, he needed company. After all he had done for me, I was glad to

be there for my best mate. We fell asleep in each other's arms. Before drifting off, I couldn't help but wonder how differently the night might have ended if Jon had filled her in on one little secret, the one that he had whispered to me earlier: the gun hadn't been loaded.

The following morning...

Jon's was soaking in the jacuzzi and sipping an espresso that he had made with the new espresso machine I had gotten him for his birthday, when suddenly his phone buzzed. He answered it after only one ring.

"Hello, Candy," he said in a tentative voice, looking over at me with fear in his eyes.

I sat up in bed, suddenly more alert and feeling nosy. A few minutes went by before Jon spoke again.

"Yes, of course, darling," he said in a gentle voice. "Come on over."

Candy arrived within minutes, having stopped at a nearby store. I decided to remain upstairs while she spoke with Jon, wanting to give them some privacy. Still, my curiosity got the best of me, and I eavesdropped on them from the top of the stairs. The dialogue was somewhat muffled but I was able to make out most of the words.

"I just felt completely overwhelmed," Candy said in a shaky voice. "I'm not used to being out of control. And I didn't realize you hadn't loaded the gun until I had gotten home and checked the chamber. It was just so hard to believe, that you would risk killing me, or risk me killing YOU." She sniffled.

"Oh, honey, I'm so sorry," Jon soothed. "I pushed you so hard. But I do love you very much. You did a great job. You're so incredibly strong, and poised. I'm glad you came back today."

"I got you something for your birthday," Candy said shyly. "Well, two things. One I bought from the liquor store and the other I made. I recall you telling me about your boa constrictor named Samantha, and showing me pictures of her, so I did a painting of her for you."

There was some crinkling of paper, followed by the sound of Jon breaking down in tears.

"Oh, my god," Jon gasped through sniffles. "It's a beautiful painting. You're an incredible artist, Candy. I'm going to put this up in my bedroom, right above my bed. AND you remembered my favorite beer! Oh man, this is turning out to be a great birthday already! Thank you so much, honey!"

I smiled as I leaned over the staircase, watching my best mate embrace his little angel. They held each other for several minutes, with Jon being the first to back away.

"I have an important question," Jon began. "I know that you and I haven't been together that long, but we have known each other for a long time and we have an amazing connection. The thing is, this house is too large for just me. And I know you mentioned that your lease is up in July. So what I want to know is, would you like to move in with me when your lease is up?"

Candy's answer was quick and enthusiastic. "Yes! Absolutely!" She squealed. "I was waiting for you to ask me. I've dreamed of living in a place like this with someone I love. I would be honored."

By that point, I could no longer contain my enthusiasm and let out a cheer. Jon and Candy laughed and invited me to join them downstairs for celebratory breakfast on the patio.

Late that night...

I was lying in my bed, my darling Anna fast asleep next to me. I took out my phone and began watching the video that Jon had sent me.

Jon's birthday had been a lovely day, full of sunshine, amazing food, and wonderful company. After spending the better part of the day walking on the beach and swimming in Jon's pool, his parents had come over for dinner, along with Daryl, Tracy and Anna. And now Candy was moving in with him. I had gone home around 11pm, intent on letting Jon have

some "alone time" with his little angel, and take care of unfinished business of the "edge play" variety.

In the video, Candy stood naked before Jon, who was fully clothed.

"You have been a bad girl," Jon began in a stern voice, "walking out on me like that. Get on your knees and beg for forgiveness."

She slowly got down on her knees, then looked up at Jon with pleading eyes. "Please forgive me, Master," she said timidly.

Jon knelt down, running his hand through her hair. "I forgive you." They exchanged hugs.

Then he looked at the camera and winked, satisfied.

I wasted no time texting him. "Wow, she actually kept a straight face. AND you convinced her to move in with you. Talk about a nice birthday!"

"Yes indeed," Jon replied. "I feel like I did several years prior, before things in my life started going to shit. I feel like I'm back, mate. The MASTER is back."

I smiled broadly, agreeing wholeheartedly.

Chapter 4: Love Is Not Enough

Early morning. Anna sat naked in the cage, a dazed expression on her face. She had spent the better part of two nights in that confined space, with nothing but a pillow, blanket, and water bottle for company. After much resistance, I had agreed to let her have her cellphone, under the condition that she agreed to use it only to play games, listen to music, or watch videos.

I crouched down to speak to my little slave. "Good morning, my pet," I said softly. "How was your second night in the cage?"

Anna shrugged, her eyes vacant. She looked simply exhausted.

"Did you sleep?"

She shook her head. "N-no," She stammered.

My facial expression softened, feeling rather heartbroken over the thought of my lovely red haired girl being awake all night in a cage. I opened the door to the metal enclosure, holding out my hand. "You can come out, sweetheart."

Anna looked at me like a frightened animal as I helped her get to her feet. Then she collapsed against me, letting my arms envelop her in a comforting embrace as she cried softy.

"Great job," I soothed as I held her. "After a bit more practice, you will be more than ready for 'slave week.' Why don't you lie down in bed for a while? Get some rest. Then when you wake up, we can grab a nibble before we head out to Providence for the show."

Anna backed away from me and smiled wearily, then I walked her to the bedroom. "I can't wait to hear Jon and Mario sing," she said.

That's right: my best mate was performing at Capitol Brewing Company with our high school buddy, THE Mario Morrone. Not long after our little reunion at Jon's housewarming party, Mario had invited Jon to perform alongside him at Rhode Island's largest brewing company, which also sported a huge stage and impressive sound system. The venue was known for hosting a number of famous bands and singers over the years. I joined Anna in bed and we slept for several hours, and I dreamed about Jon and Mario having a foursome with Anna and Candy on a stage, a huge audience cheering them on as they fucked.

Later that evening...

The venue was full, with hundreds of people cheering and clapping, anxiously awaiting the main event. There were about four dozen tables that seated up to ten people, all filled to capacity. On the outer perimeter there was booth seating, for up to four. There was a dance floor in front of the stage, which lit up in different colors. The place felt more like a high-end discotheque than a brewery, and I was more than a little impressed. As for the food and beer? Amazing selection. Anna and I had both ordered fish and chips for dinner, and a local IPA on tap. The opening act had been a local punk band, and the performance had been terrific. However, everyone was there to see the main event, which happened to be Rhode Island's own Mario Morrone and Jonathan Moore.

Lisa and Nick had flown in for the show, along with their firebreather friend Chris, who had visited Jon back in July when he was in a coma. Then there were some friends from New York, including Noelle, Todd, Andre, and Jeannie (who had agreed to take professional photos of the

event), and several of Mario's friends from the city as well. Martha and Jon Sr. were there, as well as Daryl, Tracy, Amy, Eugene, Lawrence, Diana, and, of course, Candy. My lovely neighbor Brittany was dating Mario by this point, so she was also in attendance. Even a few gym members came, eager to see "Coach Jon" perform.

I placed my hand on Anna's leg as I sipped beer and waited for two of my best mates to appear on stage, when suddenly the venue went completely dark.

Just when we all thought there had been some sort of power outage, the sound of electric guitars filled the air, the curtains re-opened, and the stage lit up, revealing a full band with Jon and Mario at the front. The crowd began applauding loudly, and I joined in, along with everyone else at our table. They were both dressed in leather pants and unbuttoned white shirts, and their hair was styled sexily in tousled waves as they played their shiny guitars with impressive skill. They truly looked like "rock stars." After hearing just a few introductory notes from the guitars, I already knew the concert would be incredible.

Jon's bass-baritone voice mixed well with Mario's baritone-tenor voice, and they sang in harmony for the majority of the first song. Many people got up to dance, feeling a desire to move their bodies to the infectious beat. I stood up and looked at Anna, then held out my hand.

"Would you dance with me?" I asked with a sexy grin.

Anna smiled and nodded, taking my hand. And so began a wonderful evening full of dancing, incredible music, and random electric shocks to the pussy. That's right: there was a shock collar tucked inside the panties of my red-haired submissive, and I held the remote control.

Normally used as a tool intended to train willful dogs, the shock collar had value as a torture device in the BDSM world, and was a popular accessory among doms to keep their subs on high alert. I delighted in watching her grimace and jerk as she felt the jolts travel through her groin. Jon smirked in my direction several times, knowing full well what was happening to my redhead.

The highlight of the concert was when Jon and Mario began a duet with acoustic guitars, singing a brand new song that they had co-written. It was inspired by Candy, and the name of the tune was "Bambolina." When translated from Italian, the word meant "little doll," and Mario had given Candy that nickname when they were dating. As for Candy, she was completely starstruck as her current boyfriend and ex-boyfriend serenaded her, inviting her onto the stage towards the end of the song. Once the song had ended, Jon and Mario kissed her on the cheek and introduced her to the crowd as the inspiration for the song. She had blushed adorably before stepping back down onto the dance floor.

After the concert, Jon and Mario posed for pictures with fans and gave autographs as well. By this point, we were all good and tired. Daryl, Tracy, Eugene, Amy, Noelle, Lawrence, Diana, Jeannie, Martha and Jon Sr. decided to call it a night, as did the members from the gym. The rest of us, however, were excited for the second part of the evening that would take place in a luxury suite on the top floor of Providence's fanciest hotel: the afterparty.

Three hours and multiple drinks later...

"Oh yeah! Shock me again, Daddy!" Lisa panted as the shock collar around her neck went off for what must have been the tenth time. She continued to ride Nick, who was in heaven as he moved his hips in time to her undulations.

Jon held the remote control and was having a jolly good time zapping his ex girlfriend as he pounded the shit out of Candy, who lay panting with her legs against Jon's front.

While this was going on, Brittany and Mario looked on with amused smiles as they fucked doggie style on the floor. Chris, Andre, and Todd enjoyed a threesome on the nearby couch, occasionally breaking out into laughter. I was with Anna, of course, and we shagged on one of the king sized beds, switching from one acrobatic position to the next. It was glorious.

We hadn't originally intended for there to be an orgy, but after so many shots of booze and occasional hits from a bong, the sexual tension ran high. So before long, we were all fucking.

Partner swapping was rampant, and before long I had fucked nearly everyone in that room except for Candy and Jon, who remained with each other. I was impressed by how faithful my best mate was to his girlfriend, only allowing an occasional kiss from the others. I could see

Jon's jaw tighten when, mid-fuck, Mario suddenly separated from Brittany and approached Candy.

"How about a kiss for your old flame?" Mario asked drunkenly. Candy lay on her back running her hands up and down Jon's chest as they made love. Jon's thrusts slowed down and he bit his lip, doing his best not to appear jealous.

Candy nodded and smiled, turning her head as Mario bent down to kiss her lips. It was quick and sweet, and I could see Jon's face relax when their lips separated. Mario then turned to Jon for a kiss, who grabbed the back of his neck and devoured his mouth. When they separated, they exchanged smiles. I couldn't help but get turned on seeing my two rock star friends kiss each other. My manhood hardened as I continued thrusting into Anna.

Before long, Lisa got up from Nick and walked over to Candy and Jon. The two blonde girlies kissed for a few moments, playfully tugging at each other's hair. Then she leaned over to Jon, who began kissing her rather aggressively, going so far as to push the button on the remote of the shock collar, which she still wore around her neck. She yelped as the device went off, backing away from Jon with a startled expression. Her lower lip had a wee bit of blood on it.

"You bit me," Lisa whimpered as she wiped her lip.

Jon nodded and grabbed a handful of her hair, pulling her alarmed face closer to his. She gasped as he pulled at her tresses, their faces inches apart.

"I still own you, baby doll," Jon growled with a smirk. "Understand?"

Lisa nodded hastily as she swallowed, knowing full well he was still her master and there was nothing she could do to change that. "Yes, Daddy," she whispered.

Jon let go of her hair. "Good girl. Now go disinfect that lip. There's peroxide in the loo."

Lisa scurried off to the bathroom to clean her lip, and Nick followed behind her to help. Then Jon turned back to his darling Candy, whose eyebrow was raised.

"That wasn't very nice," Candy said as she shook her head. "You should apologize to Lisa and clean her wound."

Jon stared at Candy, his mouth hanging open in shock and disbelief. He wasn't used to subs questioning his judgment. EVER. Anna and I looked on in fear, as did the others in the room. Things got so quiet in that hotel suite, you could hear a pin drop. Candy was going to get a rude awakening of some kind - perhaps a hard slap in the face, a bite on the nipple hard enough to draw blood, or worse.

Surprisingly, Jon's expression softened and he nodded slowly. "Ok," he said softly before kissing Candy on the forehead. "You're right. I was too harsh." Then he withdrew from her and got up from the bed and began walking to the loo to check on Lisa and apologize.

"Thank you, Jon. And also, can you fix me a drink afterwards? Please?" Candy asked sweetly.

Jon turned around and smiled gently. "Of course, love." Then he disappeared into the bathroom.

We were all very surprised at what we had just witnessed. Jon never tolerated that sort of "backtalk" from anyone, and detested taking orders. I looked at Candy, who had a calm, self-assured smile on her face. That was the moment it occurred to me: Jon had found a woman who matched his dominance.

I looked at Anna, who had her arms wrapped around me and was smiling sweetly. Suddenly, I realized how thirsty I was.

"Would you like a drink, sweetheart?" I asked as I ran my fingers through her long red hair.

She nodded. "I would love one."

I got up and headed to the suite's kitchen. Out of the corner of my eye, I couldn't notice Mario staring at Candy like she was a medium-well ribeye. The look on his face was nothing short of predatory. I decided at that point to keep an eye on the bloke.

Jon soon joined me in the kitchen, intent on making a drink for himself as well as Candy.

"How's Lisa?" I asked, as I began mixing juice with vodka.

"She's alright, aside from being completely spent," Jon said with a sigh. "Nick and Chris said they were rather exhausted too, probably from the plane ride. I know they took a red eye flight out of LAX. Looks like they will be headed to their room in a bit. Then I heard Andre, Todd, Mario, and Brittany talking about going to bed as well. It might just wind up being you, me, Candy, and Anna tonight, mate."

I nodded. "I'm all for an intimate gathering."

Jon raised his eyebrows and tentatively placed his hand on the small of my back. His green eyes twinkled as he looked at me. Then he leaned over and kissed me gently on the lips. It had been a long time since we had kissed, and, unlike many times in the past, it felt natural and unforced. "I love you, Ken." His voice was barely above a whisper.

I smiled and put my arm around him. "I love you too, Jon. It was a great show tonight. You're an incredible performer."

Jon chuckled as he blushed. "Oh, go on!" He chided as he began to place ice and a variety of liquors in a blender. I took a spoon and began to stir the two screwdrivers I had made for Anna and me, when suddenly Andre, Todd, Chris, Lisa, Nick, and Brittany came into the kitchen. They were all wearing either robes or pajamas.

"We are all headed to bed," Lisa said tiredly with a weary smile. "Wish we could stay up longer but it's been such a long day!"

Jon and I were still naked as we fixed drinks and began making fun of them good-naturedly about the night being young as we said our goodbyes and exchanged hugs.

"More fun to be had tomorrow at my house," Jon reassured with a wink, as he handed Lisa a cocktail glass, which she accepted with a smile and a kiss on Jon's cheek before heading out of the suite with the others.

They left, and we resumed making drinks and chatting in the kitchen. Jon began running the blender, intent on making daiquiris for himself and Candy. At that moment, I had a vague feeling that something was wrong.

I grabbed the drinks, stepped out of the kitchen, and began to eavesdrop on Candy and Mario, who were in the second bedroom. The

door was closed but I could make out the dialogue. What I heard made my stomach turn.

"Mario, please," Candy gasped. "I don't want to! Get off me!"

"Shut up, you stupid bitch!" Mario growled. "You need some Italian sausage in your life!"

"Noooo!" Candy cried out.

My blood ran cold. Anna was fast asleep on the couch in the living room, a blanket over her lithe body. I quietly set down the drinks on the coffee table next to the couch, and was ready to barrel through the door when, suddenly, I saw Candy's purse sitting on the end table. I unzipped the top and immediately saw her gun. I grabbed it and opened the door.

Mario and Candy both froze when they saw the pistol in my hand, which I aimed at Mario's head. He was lying atop a naked Candy. He was naked himself and was holding down her arms, clearly ready to rape her. He began to slowly get off of her, holding up his hands.

"Easy there," Mario said nervously. "Nothing happened."

"Yeah, thanks to my coming in here at the perfect time!" I barked.

Candy lay there, shaking and crying, in complete shock. She covered herself in a blanket and curled into a ball as she did her best to collect herself. Just then, the door opened and Jon was there, drinks in hand. He gasped and nearly dropped the drinks when he saw I was holding a gun and aiming it at Mario.

"What the hell just happened?!" Jon bellowed, looking at Mario, then Candy, and then me. He placed the drinks on the table next to the bed. "And why are you holding Candy's gun, Ken?" He raised his eyebrows.

"Mario was trying to force himself on Candy," I explained. "And now he's going to take a little walk with me to the bathroom." I got in closer to Mario, making him walk backwards as he held his hands up.

Jon's eyes grew wide and he glared at Mario, looking ready to charge at him until Candy began to sob. Seeing that I had the situation under control with the gun and appearing heartbroken at the sight of his little angel in distress, he went to comfort her. She began to tremble as she cried into his shoulder. "What are you going to do?" Jon asked me in a shaky voice as he held his girlfriend.

"I'm going to make him pay," I said coldly. Then I turned to Mario, who was looking more and more frightened with every passing moment. "Come on! Let's take a little trip to the toilet!" I held the gun closer to his head.

Mario staggered to the loo, looking ready to piss himself. He was clearly inebriated but I didn't give a shit. I had zero tolerance for rape, and had I not been there at that precise time, he would have violated Candy. And I would have fucking shot him. But since he had only attempted to rape her, I would give him a chance to redeem himself. First, though? I would make him suffer.

Once we were in the bathroom, I closed the door behind us. "Fill the tub with hot water," I ordered.

Mario did as I said, his hands shaking as he did so. "Please, Ken, I didn't do anything. I got carried away but nothing happened." He looked ready to cry.

KNOCK, KNOCK, KNOCK!

"Ken, what are you doing in there?" Jon asked. "Can you open up?"

"No, Jon," I shouted through the door. "This is between me and Momo! He doesn't get to lay a hand on his ex girlfriend and use drunkenness as an excuse! I'm tired of his cocky ways, so he needs to learn a lesson!"

I heard mumbling coming from the outside of the door, followed by Candy's voice.

"Ken, please don't kill him," she implored. "Promise me?"

I swallowed, suddenly realizing how crazy they must have thought I was for reacting to what turned out to be nothing more than a drunken sexual advance. But my experiences with Jon had traumatized me, and I knew firsthand how quickly behavior could escalate if left unchecked.

After Jon had tried to rape Amy on the Fourth of July, I had been too slow to respond and had also foolishly tried to reason with him afterwards. I had never stopped feeling guilty for not coming to Amy's rescue that night. I often wondered if she would have gone for me instead of Eugene, had I been the one to save her. I also wondered if I could have prevented Jon from raping ME that same night, had I been more assertive with him. As for Tracy? I hadn't even been there when she was raped. So I felt like this was the perfect time to redeem myself, to come through for someone I cared about, to be the hero.

"I promise I won't kill him," I said. Then I checked the water temperature, which was suitably very hot. I turned off the faucet then smirked at Mario, who was shaking and beginning to cry.

"I'm sorry," Mario began.

"Sorry won't cut it," I growled. "Get in the tub."

He shakily lifted his leg and placed it into the tub. He flinched. "It's boiling hot," he whimpered.

I placed what I knew was an unloaded gun against his head, making him whimper and cry. "I don't care! Sit down in the water or I will shoot you!"

Mario shakily lowered himself down into the scalding water. I then placed my foot on his stomach to keep him from getting up. Within seconds, he began to cry and scream in pain as his skin turned red.

"Please! It burns! Please let me out of the water!" He begged as he thrashed around. After a few more seconds, I lifted my foot, allowing him to rise from the water.

BOOM! BOOM! BANG!

Just then, the door flew open. Jon had broken it down, and stood there with Candy, who looked upset.

Mario wasted no time jumping out of the tub, grabbing a towel, and sitting on the toilet to cry. It was clear he was in distress, and his skin was a bright shade of red. He would undoubtedly have first and second degree burns to deal with. But I felt his discomfort was a small price to pay for what he had done.

"Give me the gun," Candy said firmly. Jon had his hand on her shoulder.

I handed it over to her. "I'm sorry for taking your gun but he was hurting you, and I couldn't have that. Plus I was just using it to scare him. He didn't know it's not loaded."

Candy swallowed. "Um, actually, it IS loaded."

"WHAT?!" Jon and I both blurted.

Candy nodded. "That's why I insisted that Jon break down the door. I was convinced you were going to shoot and kill him. As annoyed as I am at his advances, I don't want him dead, or even hurt. He's drunk, and probably won't even remember this in the morning. He's prone to blackouts."

Jon nodded. "Candy's right. He tends to not recall things the next day after a heavy night of drinking. And I'm sure he will feel very badly about this incident when we tell him. So I say we all just go to bed and we can talk to him about it once he's sobered up." Jon turned to Mario, who was crying. "Come on, old pal, lets get to bed, hmm?"

Mario nodded as he wrapped the towel more tightly around his shoulders and let Jon help him to his bedroom, where Brittany lay in a dead sleep.

I turned to Candy. "I'm sorry I got so carried away but I care about you so much. You're Jon's soul mate, his little angel. and I couldn't let Mario hurt you."

Candy nodded and gave me a big hug. "I know, and thank you for coming to my rescue. But next time, use your fists instead of my gun," she said with a chuckle.

"Fair enough," I said with a faint laugh.

That night, I slept with Anna on the fold-out couch while Candy and Jon slept in the first bedroom, and Mario and Brittany in the second one. It had been one hell of a crazy night but I had no regrets about threatening Mario with Candy's gun, or forcing him into a tub of hot water. Before we all went to bed, Jon admitted that the only reason he wasn't more pissed at Mario for what he had done is because he knew firsthand how easy it was to behave poorly after drinking heavily. He also said that, had Mario actually raped Candy, he would have been much less forgiving.

The following morning, Anna and I woke up super hungry and went into Jon and Candy's bedroom to wake them up for breakfast. That was when I noticed the barrel of Candy's gun peeking out from under Jon's pillow. The incident must have made him feel compelled to keep himself - and his girlfriend - protected, in case Mario decided to attack again. I elected to keep my mouth shut, as I had a feeling that Candy might not approve of Jon keeping her loaded gun on his person.

"Hey, guys," I whispered.

Candy and Jon both opened their eyes a crack and smiled when they saw Anna and me.

An hour later...

The six of us ate breakfast in the dining area of the suite, electing to get room service. Despite the drama the night before, everything felt normal, almost as if nothing happened. Brittany was very affectionate with Mario, and kept feeding him little bites of French toast. It was clear they made a great couple. At one point, Mario examined his skin and made a comment about how he must have fallen asleep in the bathtub.

"You know how I love my hot baths!" Mario commented as he rubbed his pink arm. "This wouldn't have been the first time I've dozed off in the tub." Jon and I exchanged knowing looks, deciding to tell Mario the truth after we had finished eating. Anna and Brittany decided to take a soak in the suite's hot tub that was situated in the living room, and we agreed to join them once we had finished speaking with Mario.

As to be expected, Mario was horrified to learn what he had done and the reason for his reddened skin, and apologized to Candy through tears. Needless to say, she was forgiving. After the conversation, Mario excused himself to the bathroom to wash his face. After a few moments, Jon cleared his throat.

"Would you excuse me?" Jon asked as he stood up from the dining table. "I must speak with Mario alone."

Jon went to the bathroom and knocked on the door. Mario let him in. Curious, Candy and I got up and decided to eavesdrop. We pressed our ears to the door.

"Mario, you and I go way back," Jon began. "And you know I love you. But my Candy is precious to me. What you did to her last night was unacceptable. Candy filled me in on some extra details before we went to bed. Not only did you try to rape her, but she said you called her a stupid bitch and told her she 'needed Italian sausage in her life.' She also has bruises on her wrists from where you restrained her, and she said your penis actually grazed her vagina at one point. My little angel is NOT stupid, and she's NOT a bitch. As for your 'Italian sausage?' She has long since upgraded to 'British bangers and mash.' She doesn't want to have sex with you. And she's in love with ME now, mate. Get over it."

"Jon, I'm sorry-"

"I KNOW you're sorry. And I accept your apology. But make no mistake. If you EVER make unwanted advances towards Candy again, I will hurt you. And I will hurt you badly. I won't need a gun to do it, either. Just my bare hands. You stay AWAY from her, mate. Or it won't just be a couple of painful seconds in a tub of hot water. I will DESTROY you. Understood?"

"Yes, Jon. I get it. I won't touch her again." Mario's voice shook something awful.

"Good. Glad we had this talk, mate. Let's shake hands, hmm?"

There was a pause, and I could make out the sound of Mario grunting in pain, presumably from having his hand crushed from the handshake. Candy and I winced at the notion.

"See you outside, yes?" Jon said in a cheerful voice. "Very well, then. And put some ice on that hand. I've been told I have a...strong grip."

At that moment, Jon unlocked the door and we quickly backed away and sat back down at the dining table. He opened it and walked out with a confident smirk on his face, giving a Candy a huge hug. She initially appeared shocked from the exchange between the two blokes, but her expression turned to one of gratitude as they embraced.

"I love you, Candy," Jon said as he held her, planting gentle kisses on her lips. "I will always make sure you are safe."

"Thank you," Candy said as she held him. "But please don't hurt him anymore, ok? I think he gets the picture."

Jon backed away from her and ran her fingers through her blonde locks. "Ok, doll. You have my word."

Mario came out several minutes later, looking disheveled with bloodshot eyes and a frightened expression on his face. He made a

beeline for the kitchen. I got up and decided to pop my head inside the kitchen, where I saw him grab the ice pack from the freezer and wrap it around his right hand.

I walked back to the dining table and looked at Jon quizzically. "How hard did you squeeze his hand?"

"Hard enough to know that if he crosses the line with Candy again, he's dealing with something much more severe," Jon whispered ominously. "You know of my grip strength, mate. I have crushed hands hard enough to break bones. Years of rock climbing and gymnastics have made my hands incredibly strong. But hopefully I won't ever have to unleash my wrath on our dear friend. In fact, we have plans to perform together again, and to record a few songs together in his studio." He smiled.

Candy and I looked at him with happy surprise. "Wow," Candy began. "That would be great. You and Mario recording songs together? Aww, my baby's a rock star!" She gave Jon a hug as he chuckled.

"I think Mario has learned his lesson," I said as I took a sip of coffee. "He's not the type of guy who doesn't learn from his mistakes."

"Agreed," Candy said with a nod. "Can we join Anna and Brittany in the hot tub now?" She asked excitedly.

Jon smiled broadly as he took off his robe and revealed his chiseled body. "You don't have to ask twice!"

Candy and I followed suit and stripped before joining the girls in the hot tub. Mario stayed in the kitchen, nursing his injured hand and what I imagined was his dignity.

About an hour or so later, we checked out of the hotel and made our way back to Jon's house for a second wave of partying. It was a beautiful spring day, and everyone had a wonderful time enjoying the beach as well as Jon's pool, sauna, and jacuzzi. There was no shortage of food or alcohol, and I was able to convince Anna to shag in the sauna.

It was the sweatiest sex I'd had in a long time, and the orgasms were plentiful. I loved the way her womanhood smelled and tasted in that hot and sultry environment, and she loved the cunnilingus I gave her. For the grand finale, I bent her over so her face was uncomfortably close to the hot coals and sodomized her, then forced her to go down on me after I climaxed inside her tight bum. I delighted in the sight of her choking and gagging on my sweaty cock and balls, doing her absolute best to clean me with her tongue.

Not long after the sauna sex, Mario and Jon wound up having a heart to heart, while Anna cooled off in the pool. They invited me to join in on the conversation, since we were all good friends. It was during this talk that Jon disclosed the sordid details of his past to Mario, discussing everything from his molestation, to the sex acts he pressured me into from puberty onward, to the physical abuse he endured during Lisa's drunken rages, to my rape. Mario had initially been shocked at the story but finally understood why Jon had been so hard on him earlier in the day, because if anyone knew how much destructive behavior could spiral out of control without early intervention, it was Jon. My best

mate had been a sexual predator for the better part of two decades, with drugs playing a huge factor in the way he had behaved.

"Hey, boys!" Jeannie said cheerfully. "I hate to interrupt, but I wanted to show you some of the pictures I took from the concert!"

Jon got excited as Jeannie handed over her phone. Mario and I got in close to look at the photos. They all looked incredible, and I was able to see several of them that looked suitable for an album cover, or even the front page of a magazine. Jon and Mario both looked like rock gods, with their shiny guitars, handsome faces, and muscular bodies clad in designer clothing. Mario looked more than a little impressed, and complimented Jeannie on a job well done. I chimed in. Jon, however, appeared less than thrilled and his face contorted into a grimace as he looked over several pictures of himself playing guitar and singing.

"What's wrong?" Jeannie asked Jon as she placed her hand on his back.

Jon swallowed and shook his head. "N-nothing," He stammered. "I, uh, I just think I look a little... big in some of these photos, that's all. Not your fault. You're a wonderful photographer."

Jeannie's eyes widened. "Oh, honey, I think you look amazing! And you're as lean as always! You're definitely not 'big,' especially not for your height. You're slim and muscular. And incredibly handsome. A rock god!"

Mario and I agreed, reassuring Jon that he had very little in the way of fat on him and could even afford to put some meat on his bones. Jon smiled shyly, blushing at our compliments. I knew that Jon still had body image issues, and did my best to reassure him every chance I got that he looked fit and trim.

Eventually, the four of us bonded over more drinks and began to mingle with the others, but I noticed that Jon didn't eat anything the rest of the evening and insisted on wearing a t shirt when he swam in the pool.

That night, Anna and I fell asleep on Jon's living room couch, holding each other. I dreamt about her being my live-in slave, sleeping in a cage and waiting on me hand and foot. I intended on challenging her more and more over the next few weeks, training her to be my maid, my servant, my whore.

One month later...

"May I please have some water?" She begged in a shaky voice from the confines of her cage.

I sighed and got up from the couch, deciding it was time to be humane towards my slave. She had been living with me for about two weeks, agreeing it was time to take our relationship a step further. I had proposed the idea to her over a romantic dinner and had been delighted when hearing the word out of her beautiful mouth. "Yes," she had breathed with a lovely smile. I had so cherished that first night together, making passionate love for hours on end, shagging

everywhere from the kitchen, to the bathtub, to my king sized bed. And now? She was little more than a slut to me. I was in full on "Master" mode and wasn't in the mood for her shit.

I filled her water bowl, opened the door to her cage, and slammed it down on the floor in front of her haggard face. "Here!" I spat.

"Thank you, Master," she muttered with a timid expression. Then she picked up the bowl and began slurping greedily at the contents. My heart silently broke for her, as I knew how grueling this experience was. She was now able to endure three nights of being confined in a cage, with minimal food and water.

Jon had given me some pointers on how to make her more comfortable in the tiny space, suggesting I line the bottom of the cage with a velour bedspread and provide memory foam pillows. I had initially balked at the idea, insisting it wasn't meant to be a bloody hotel room.

"Well, do you want her to have the energy to clean the whole house in the wee hours of the morning, and top it off with a quality blow job and a shag?" Jon had asked with raised eyebrows and a smirk.

"Well, yes," I had replied with a laugh.

"Then make her as comfortable as possible. Your dick will be happier, trust me." Then he had winked and lit a cigarette.

I laughed internally as I thought of what Jon had told me, and, to his credit, his advice had worked. With a more comfortable environment in the cage, Anna was able to sleep through the night and fellate me to the point of orgasm at a moment's notice, after being awakened to do the dishes at 5am.

Not long after the concert in Providence (and the incident with Mario), Jon had gone on to record some songs at the studio. Everything seemed to be just fine between the two blokes, but I knew things were strained in Jon's personal life. Seeing those pictures of himself looking "big" had really impacted his self esteem, and even Candy had begun to express concern for his eating habits.

"I'm worried that Jon might be relapsing with his eating disorder," Candy had confided to me in a whisper, after I had joined her and Jon for dinner at a nearby pizza place that had outdoor dining. Jon had barely eaten, preferring to chainsmoke cigarettes instead.

"I don't need all that pizza," Jon had explained to Candy with a gentle smile as he held a cigarette in his hand, kissing her sweetly on the lips. "Your love sustains me."

Candy had giggled and shook her head. "Love is not enough," she had said in a motherly tone, placing her arm around him. "You need to eat, too."

After that, Jon had made more of an effort to eat, taking some small bites of his pizza in between drags of his cigarettes. He had been wearing a baggy sweater despite the warm temperature, and his beard appeared fuller, perhaps in an effort to camouflage his weight loss. My heart sank for him as I thought back on that night, hoping what Candy had said wasn't true.

Several days after going out for pizza, I had called Jon from work to check in with him. He had been reassuring, telling me he was very busy with the gym as well as the music project with Mario and wasn't as good about eating regularly. He WAS running the gym himself, which meant doing a ton of exercise in addition to the activity he already did in his spare time, but said he planned on hiring another person to help out so he could get a break. It had seemed like a valid explanation to me and I was satisfied.

But several weeks had passed since that conversation, and I was no longer getting replies from Jon via phone or text, and when I had tried popping by his house a few times, he wasn't home. He had even missed a barbecue I had invited him to for the 4th of July.

I eventually talked with Candy, who told me even she had barely seen Jon over the past few weeks, and that when she did see him, he appeared exhausted and increasingly gaunt. In fact, she revealed to me that he didn't even want to appear naked in front of her lately, insisting on having sex doggie style or in a pitch black room. He was even wearing baggy pajamas to bed when he usually slept in the nude or in boxer briefs. Worse yet, she hadn't seen him eat since we had gone out for pizza the month before.

By the second week in July, Candy's concern grew all the more. Jon had taken her to her favorite amusement park in Connecticut for her birthday, as well as a five star restaurant for dinner and drinks. Not only had he avoided eating anything at the park, but he hadn't touched his meal during dinner, insisting he wasn't hungry. As for cigarettes? He now smoked constantly, going through at least a carton every two days. I expressed my alarm, and told her to keep me in the loop. She shared my concern for him and promised to update me.

Meanwhile, Anna and I were getting on just great as a couple, and she was a very compliant little slave. As time went by, I felt increasingly confident that she would be ready for "slave week." I continued to throw little challenges her way - restricting food and water intake, limiting her sleep, forcing her to spend the night on the floor of my bedroom, and holding her underwater when taking a bath with her. For part of her breathplay training, Jon agreed to let me use his pool and his jacuzzi whenever I wanted, and even gave me ankle weights to place on her so she would remain submerged. When I wasn't forcing her to hold her breath for painfully long periods of time, I was locking her in Jon's sauna with the temperature on the highest setting, then fucking the shit out of her sweat covered body for an hour straight.

After so many days of torture, Anna's outer veneer of toughness began to crack. We were having dinner at my house when she suddenly broke into tears.

I placed my hand on hers and looked on with concern. "Anna, sweetheart, what's the matter? Talk to me."

My sweet little redhead began to shake as she sniffled. I handed her a tissue, which she graciously took. "I'm just so overwhelmed," she said through tears. "I don't know what to do with my life right now. I love being a teacher but I feel like I need more. A new certification of some kind. Or maybe a new hobby. And I'm also trying to be a good girlfriend to you, and a good sub but I don't feel like I'm cut out for that either. Ugh..." She put her head in her hands and cried quietly.

I placed my chair closer to hers and put my arm around her. "Oh, honey," I soothed. "I'm very proud of you. I think you're doing a tremendous job, both at home and with your career. Perhaps a new hobby would do you some good, though. I know that Candy enjoys painting. Maybe you two girls can take some classes together? Jon mentioned that she goes to a nearby art studio and takes lessons once a week. You might like it."

Anna wiped her eyes dry and nodded, leaning her head against my shoulder. "Yeah, I might actually like that," she said in a quiet voice. "I need an outlet of some kind. I love my students but they require a lot of energy, and the things I do with you are even more challenging."

I ran my fingers through her hair. "I can only imagine. This is a big adjustment for you, moving in and being subjected to all this torture. You deserve a little fun. Let's give Candy a call after dinner and see about setting up a date for you two gals to do some painting? It would also give me a good excuse to have a night out with the boys."

Anna smiled sweetly at me and nodded. "Let's do it."

Three days later...

Daryl and I sat at our favorite bar watching sports on the telly while sipping beer and devouring a delicious plate of buffalo wings. Jon was supposed to meet up with us, but neither Daryl nor I could get a hold of him. We shrugged it off, deciding to go have fun without him and pop by his house later to check in. Jon wasn't the flaky sort, so we were both a bit concerned but felt like enjoying ourselves anyway.

As I was having some "bro time," Candy and Anna were doing a paint night at a restaurant several towns over. They had become fast friends, getting on very well the moment they had met the previous year. I was very happy that my lovely red haired girl was discovering a new hobby and having fun with a new gal pal. My manhood grew in size as I pictured Candy and Anna swapping spit atop a restaurant table, covering each other in watercolor paint as patrons looked on in awe.

"Hey, earth to Ken!" Daryl said with a chuckle as he waved his hand in front of my face. "How are you and Anna doing? Things still good, yes?"

I nodded. "Sorry, I was just, uh, lost in thought for a moment," I said with a wink, to which Daryl smirked. "Yes, things are quite good. She's decided to take up painting with Candy."

Daryl nodded as he took a sip of his beer and helped himself to another chicken wing. "Speaking of girls," Daryl said with a sly grin, "Tracy and I are having our own little adventures in the sack."

I raised my eyebrows. "Really? No shit! Tell me more, mate."

Daryl blushed and cleared his throat. "A few nights ago, I handcuffed her to the bed post." He bit his lip and turned an even darker shade of red.

I smiled broadly. "Way to go, Mr. Vanilla!" I teased good-naturedly. "Glad to see you branching out a wee bit. What else happened?"

Daryl took another sip of beer. "I, uh... I fisted her."

My eyes widened and I nearly dropped the chicken wing I had been holding. "No bloody way!"

Daryl chuckled and nodded. "I know it's hard to believe, but it happened. I went slow and it only lasted a few seconds but I did it. She was in pain for sure but she was a trooper. It wasn't my idea. She had asked me to do it."

I laughed. "I would have been surprised if it WAS your idea. You're such a proper gentleman."

Daryl's expression turned serious. "I'm worried about Jon." He looked at me with sad eyes.

I felt a lump in my throat and nodded. "Me, too. Let's pop by his house afterwards and check on him."

Daryl and I sat at the bar and watched the telly for a while longer, making sure to finish our delicious plate full of wings. It felt so nice hanging out with him; he was always so stable and easy going. I never had to worry about Daryl, because he was so level headed. His elder brother, on the other hand, was always one to keep me, and others, on their toes.

We drove in Daryl's car to my house, electing to walk the several hundred meters down the beach to Jon's place. The light was on in his kitchen as well as his bedroom, and his car was parked in the driveway. Daryl knocked on his front door.

"Hello? Jon? It's me, Daryl. Ken is with me too. Can we come in?"

No reply. I tried the door knob and it was locked. We walked around the back and tried the sliding glass door that led to his living room. It was locked as well. Daryl looked at me and shrugged.

"He's probably sleeping," Daryl suggested. It is after 11pm after all, and I know he goes in early to open the gym. Let's give him another day to get back to us."

I swallowed and nodded, doing my best to keep calm and not jump to conclusions. We walked back to my house and ate some ice cream before Daryl headed back home to be with his lovely Tracy.

My gut told me that Jon was in some kind of trouble. I fell into a fitful sleep that night, where I had a nightmare about him drowning and I was unable to save him.

Nearly two days later...

The paramedics had found Jon lying in a heap on his kitchen floor, a small pool of blood collecting near his head, where he had a huge gash from having collapsed. The refrigerator door was wide open, and broken dishes surrounded him. His phone was in his hand. He must have tried to call for help after he had fallen. After I had placed his device in the charger, it was confirmed: he had tried to text Daryl and me to say he couldn't make it because he felt dizzy and had to lie down, but he had never hit "send." He had also tried dialing 911 but only made it to the first two digits, at which time he must have lost consciousness.

Several of the members of Jon's gym had shown up at Daryl's and my gym the morning after we had gone out for beer and wings, noting that the door was locked and the lights were off at Jon's, so they had come to our gym to work out instead. This was unusual, because Jon was due to open the gym that morning at 8am. After driving to Jon's gym and seeing that it was indeed closed, I had contacted Candy, who had a spare key to Jon's home, but she was away for the next few days visiting her aunt in New York. She asked me to keep her updated, because if it was an emergency she would return home. I agreed then called Jon's

mum, who also had a key and agreed to stop by his house as soon as she could. That was when she found him and called the paramedics.

When Martha had arrived at his house, Jon's lifeless body had appeared completely emaciated, his bathrobe open to reveal a prominent ribcage and hollow stomach. Like many of us, she hadn't seen her son in over a month and was shocked by his appearance. His breathing had been very shallow and his heart was barely beating, and she knew he was in horrible shape.

The doctors at the hospital estimated that Jon had been lying in his kitchen for at least 36 hours, if not longer. He was severely dehydrated and malnourished, and barely alive. He needed to be given fluids via IV and required supplemental oxygen. Candy returned home from her aunt's as soon as she had gotten the news, heading straight to the hospital along with me, Daryl, Martha, and Jon, Sr.

"What are the total damages?" Candy asked shyly when she had met us in the visitor lounge.

Martha wiped tears from her eyes then cleared her throat. "He has a concussion from falling and needed staples in his head to close the gash on the back of his head. On top of that, he's severely dehydrated and malnourished, and needs intravenous fluids and nutrition to get his weight back up and his hydration levels adequate. His heart is in poor condition from starving himself and his oxygen levels are low, so he's on supplemental oxygen. That's all we know for now."

Candy's eyes filled with tears. "I feel so bad," she said in a trembling voice. "He's been so distant lately, I've hardly seen him but when I have seen him, he's appeared so gaunt and so weak. I should have tried harder to help him."

Martha placed her hand on Candy's shoulder. "This isn't your fault," she assured. "You're a wonderful girlfriend. I haven't seen him this happy in a long time. But he still has an eating disorder, and the severity worsens at times, especially when he's under pressure. I know performing the concert with Mario and recording songs in the studio has added to his stress levels."

I nodded. "That's true," I said. "I think the trigger for him was seeing pictures from his concert, where he thought he looked 'big,' but it was simply the angle of some of these photos that was the culprit."

Martha began to cry again, and Jon Sr. comforted her. We all knew how fragile Jon was when it came to his body image, and were familiar with his triggers. As soon as we got the ok, we went up to visit Jon.

As we sat there sitting in his hospital room and watching him sleep, I felt a sense of deja vu. It had been almost exactly a year since he had gotten into his motorcycle accident. It was tragic to see him develop problems again, but I reminded myself that he was in better shape this time around than he was the year before. He no longer battled a drug addiction and wasn't recovering from an injured tailbone. He also wasn't dealing with the acute grief of his breakup with Lisa, or the trauma of his sexual assault at the hands of Andre and Todd. I felt

optimistic that he would bounce back from this. The only question was, how long would it take him?

Two weeks later...

"No."

Jon lay in his king size bed, dressed in his oversized designer robe, arms folded across his chest, his expression defiant. His satin blanket was draped over him. He had gained five pounds in the past few weeks due to being fed through a tube in the hospital, but was still considered very underweight for his height. He had been home for three days, having left against medical advice. So he was still very weak, and consuming only liquids. During his hospitalization, he had revealed that he hadn't eaten in over a month, surviving solely on water. He had lost over 30 pounds in that time period. Frightened for his life, his mum had decided an intervention was in order.

"But Jon, it would be good for you to go away to a treatment center," Martha begged, as she placed her hand on his shoulder. "It worked so well for you last time."

Candy and I nodded in agreement at Martha's advice.

Jon glared at his mum. "I need to do this alone," he insisted. "Last year I needed more help because I was recovering from more stuff. I promise I will eat and go to therapy. In fact, I'm eating already. I ate the breakfast

you made me this morning." He averted his eyes. It was clear he was lying.

Martha shook her head. "You're NOT eating, honey. I know this. I saw the uneaten breakfast in the garbage." Her expression looked so sad.

Jon raised his eyebrows. "You went rummaging through my trash?"

"No, but I was throwing away something else and saw the untouched food when I opened the lid. Anyway, your doctor said that if you don't start eating, then you will go back into the hospital again. You're very fragile, and you're the thinnest you've ever been. You will die, Jon." She began to cry.

Jon reached out and held Martha's hand, squeezing it. "Don't cry, mum," he said softly. "I will be ok. But I need to help myself through this. You can't do it for me. Nobody can."

I cleared my throat and placed three brochures on the nightstand next to his bed. "There are three treatment places your doctor recommends for your eating disorder," I began. "One of them is the place you went to last year in the Berkshires, and the other two are located out west."

Jon's nostrils flared as he stared me down with his intense green eyes. "Stop hounding me."

My eyes filled with tears. "Jon, I'm not-"

"Yes you are!" He barked, making the three of us jump. He took the brochures off the nightstand and looked at the cover of each one briefly, shaking his head and scoffing. "Unbelievable," he grumbled.

Candy placed her hand on his shoulder. "Honey, do you want some time to think about this? We can meet up later on and talk about it? How does that sound?"

Jon's expression softened as he looked at his little angel. He slowly nodded. "Yes, I think that's wise. I need some time to make my decision. Let's all meet up the day after tomorrow, same time."

We all nodded. Martha got up and gave Jon a bear hug that lasted a good twenty seconds. "I love you so much," she whispered. "We all do."

Candy and I took turns hugging Jon then made our way out of his house. We felt emotionally drained, but hopeful. In bed that night, I held Anna close to me, savoring the feel of her body and the scent of her hair. I was so grateful for her presence in my life, especially with all the drama going on. Unfortunately, the drama would only get worse.

Two days later...

Per Jon's request, both his parents showed up at his place, as did Daryl, Candy, and myself. We walked through the front door and found Jon sitting on the living room couch fully dressed, his hair and beard freshly trimmed. Despite the hot temperature, he wore his leather motorcycle jacket, which hung on his skeletal frame. He had multiple pieces of luggage on the floor next to him.

We all exchanged hugs with him and complimented him on his looks, then sat down to talk.

"I've made my decision," Jon announced. "I'm going away to a treatment center for ninety days. I picked the one in Scottsdale, Arizona. I already booked a flight and I'm leaving tonight."

Martha applauded, as did the rest of us. "That's wonderful, honey! I'm proud of you!" She got up and hugged Jon. "And you will be home just in time for the holidays! Of course, I would want you to call me every week while you're away, so I know how you're doing." Jon broke their embrace and began shaking his head.

"No, you don't understand, mum. Let me finish. See, there's a catch."

"Oh?" Martha inquired.

Jon's eyes filled with tears. "I don't want to be contacted during my time away. I need some time and space to find myself. But also?" Jon faltered.

"What is it?" I asked with a lump on my throat.

Jon took a deep breath. "I'm not sure if I'm ever coming back."

Everyone's jaws dropped, including mine. "What do you mean?" Jon Sr. asked in his deep, resonant voice.

He sighed. "My entire life, I have been in the spotlight. I never have privacy. Between acting, modeling, sports, dancing, and singing, I have constantly had to worry about how I look, how I behave, how I perform, and it's SO much pressure. It's killing me, and I can't handle it anymore. It's making me want to start fresh, begin a new life as an anonymous man, where nobody knows me. I need this time to heal. But I also know this could be a one way ticket, so I wanted to take the time to say goodbye to those I'm closest to."

Candy began to cry, as did the rest of us. Jon's expression softened as he saw us get upset. Daryl was the first to speak.

"I don't want you to go away forever," he said through sniffles. "I want you to come back after ninety days. We run a business together. And you would be leaving behind so many who love you."

Candy nodded, wiping her eyes. "I don't want to lose you," she said softly. "We just found each other again after so many years."

Jon bit his lip then got up from the couch to kneel before Candy. "Don't be sad, my little angel," he said softly as he ran his fingers through her hair. "I never said I wouldn't return home. I just said I MIGHT not. Nothing is written in stone. I'm just not sure right now."

Candy nodded. "I understand."

Jon smiled gently. "I knew you would."

We all talked some more before parting ways with Jon, each of us trying to hold out hope that he would come home after ninety days. Daryl and I discussed the logistics of hiring new people to help with the gym, and what to do if he decided not to come back home. Martha and Jon Sr talked with him for a while as well. Jon's plan was to hold off on selling his vehicles and house until he had a clearer idea of what he wanted to do, but was turning off the utilities and forwarding his mail to the treatment center for the time being. He had drained the pool and jacuzzi as well. Before long, everyone but me and Candy had left, having exchanged sentiments and tearful hugs.

Jon turned to me with a sad smile on his tear streaked face. "My best mate," he began. "I love you so much. I hate to do this to you and others I cherish, but I think it's the only way I can get better, and stay better."

Tongue tied, I gave Jon a prolonged hug, not wanting to let go. "I hope you return home," I whispered as I held him. "Or at least keep in touch."

He backed away from me with a sad expression. "I can't promise anything."

Candy began to sob, and Jon turned his attention to her, placing his hand on her shoulder. Tears spilled from his eyes. "I would like to speak with you alone, honey," he said softly. Then they retreated to the patio.

Feeling nosy, I stood inside with my ear next to the sliding door, which was partially open.

"My darling," Jon began. "This is so painful, but it's something I have to do. I'm...breaking up with you. And it's not because you did anything bad, and it's not because I don't love you. It's just...I'm SO damaged, and I need to find myself. And I have to do it alone. I know you were scheduled to move in with me by the end of the month, but I recall you mentioned your landlady is willing to rent to you on a month to month basis and hasn't found a new tenant, correct? I'm so sorry but I need to do this. I need to let you and everyone else go. I need you to spread your wings, my little angel."

Candy sniffled. "I don't want things to end," she said through tears. "I love you."

"I know. I'm sorry. And I love you, too, Candy. But you were right when you said that love is not enough. I need more than love to get through this mess. Please know that this isn't your fault. And I don't want you to wait for me, either. Don't put things on hold. Live your life."

Then silence. I poked my head out from behind the corner to see them embracing tearfully for several minutes. Jon was the first to back away. He wiped tears from Candy's eye with his thumb, looking at her with eyes full of emotion.

"Please leave."

Candy nodded then began walking off Jon's property, completely devastated, her head in her hands.

"I love you!" He called out to her, then broke down in sobs as he made it back inside. I quickly backed away from the sliding door.

Jon looked at me with a red face, hastily wiping away his tears. "Looks like you're the last one."

I nodded and pulled him in close to me, giving him a bear hug to end all bear hugs. I didn't want him to leave. The idea of never seeing him again was too much to handle.

"I love you, mate," Jon said into my shoulder as he cried. "I will always be with you."

I backed away. "I hope you come back."

Jon nodded sadly, then grabbed his luggage and began heading out into the front foyer. "My cab is almost here," he said in a forlorn voice.

I waited with him on his front porch until his cab showed up, then began to cry once again. "Good luck, Jon," I said tearfully.

Jon smiled as he wiped away his tears. "Thank you, mate. You're the best friend anyone could ever hope for. I mean that."

We walked to his cab, and I helped him load the bags into the car. Then we exchanged one more hug before he got into the back seat.

"Goodbye, mate," he said with his trademark smirk.

"Goodbye," I croaked, as fresh tears filled my eyes.

He closed the door, then the cab slowly began to drive down the street. I watched the car get smaller and smaller as it drove down the road,

until it had disappeared altogether. Suddenly, that's when it hit me: Jon was gone.

Later that night...

"Mmmm," Anna moaned. "You taste even better than you look!"

My lovely redhead ran her tongue down Candy's belly, which sported edible body paint. It hadn't been our intention to have a threesome, but grief and alcohol have a way of bringing out the sexpot in almost anyone.

Candy had been so devastated and heartbroken after Jon had broken up with her. After I had walked home from Jon's, I had seen her crying in her car, which was parked in my driveway. She had met me there prior to us walking to Jon's house, for what had turned out to be one of the most gut wrenching moments in recent history for me and several others.

I had wasted no time comforting her, letting her cry into my shoulder for as long as she needed to. After a while, we retreated inside, where Anna fixed us drinks and listened to us both bawl our eyes out over Jon. Multiple cocktails later, we all wound up swapping spit on the couch and stripping naked. Before we knew it, we were having full on three-way sex in my kitchen, complete with whipped topping, edible paint, and chocolate sauce. Suddenly, "paint night" had taken on a whole new meaning, and I realized how good a canvas a woman's body makes!

I took the paint brush out of the pot of chocolate sauce and drew a flower about an inch above Candy's shaved pussy. Anna smiled and wasted no time licking the flower off, then let her tongue trail down to Candy's tender pussy lips.

I fondled myself as I watched Anna go down on Candy, eventually positioning myself above Candy's mouth. Soon my cock was merely inches away from her pretty lips. She took hold of my dick and began sucking it. I facefucked her, delighting in the sound of her moans and the sight of Anna eating her womanhood.

Anna and I switched places after a few moments, and I decided to lick Candy's pussy as Anna sat on her face. I grabbed the edible paint and drew a red heart on her mound, rapidly licking it clean before burying my face in her cunny. My dick was hard as a rock and I so wanted to pound the shit out of Candy's bum, so I tossed her salad for several minutes then got my member nice and wet with my spit.

DING! DING!

My phone went off, as did Candy's. It was almost 1am. Nobody ever texted me at this hour. I felt myself go limp as I got up from the kitchen floor to see who the hell might be bugging me so late at night. My first instinct was that something tragic had happened, and that it involved Jon. Anna got up as well, so Candy could check her device.

I breathed a sigh of relief when I saw that it wasn't an emergency, but that it was a video Jon had sent of himself from his seat aboard the plane. I pressed "play."

"Hello," Jon said with a smile. "I just wanted to record a little something for you in case you got lonely and needed to hear my voice, and see my face. I know my departure was so sudden and I feel bad about doing it the way I did it, but I feel like it was the only way I could save myself. I want to be healthy for those I care about. I know it's easier said than done, but please try not to be sad. Please know I'm in a safe place, and a rather beautiful place, where I can heal, and live a healthy and happy life. I do hope to return home one day to be with my loved ones. Until then, remember that I love you and that I will always cherish the memories we have together. You are very special to me. Be well." He winked and flashed his self assured smile, then the video ended. I felt a lump in my throat and swallowed, already missing my best mate.

Candy's lip began to tremble and her eyes filled with tears as she watched the video of her now ex-boyfriend, which happened to be the same video he sent me. Anna and I wasted no time comforting her, assuring her that Jon would never stop loving her but that for her own mental health, it would be best to move on and let him go for the time being.

The three of us decided to go to bed, feeling exhausted from the events of the day as well as the impromptu sex party. Part of me felt very guilty for having sex with Candy, as I believed things weren't truly over with her and Jon but simply put on hold. Then I decided that, just as Jon was putting his needs first, it would be healthy for me to do likewise. I lay on my back, blonde to my left and redhead to my right, waiting for sleep to overcome me.

Anna was sleeping within minutes, her breathing deep and regular. I studied her as she slept, memorizing every curve and every feature of her lovely face. I caressed her red hair, gently, so she wouldn't stir. I opened my mouth to speak, deciding I would say to her what I didn't have the nerve to utter while she was awake. I got close to her delicate ear.

"I love you." My voice was a quiet whisper. She hadn't stirred, and continued to sleep peacefully.

I sighed in relief as I lay back onto my side, feeling both triumphant and slightly disappointed at the same time. I had finally told Anna that I loved her, but I also wondered if the words counted since she hadn't been awake to hear them. Just before falling into a deep sleep, I decided that, while love wasn't always enough for some, it gave me a reason to wake up in the morning and be the best possible version of myself, and put another person's happiness before my own. Perhaps my best mate could get to that point one day, but he needed to heal some. Until then? Love was NOT enough.

Chapter 5: "What's In the Box?"

"I do hope to return home one day to be with my loved ones. Until then, remember that I love you and that I will always cherish the memories we have together. You are very special to me. Be well."

I watched Jon's "farewell" video from July for what must have been the fiftieth time since he had left nearly four months prior. His ninety days at the treatment center had passed several weeks ago, and I waited patiently to see if he would contact me or anyone else. Aside from the occasional post card or care package, none of us had heard from him at all since he had flown out west to get help for his eating disorder.

Candy got occasional flowers or chocolate in the mail from him, with sweet little notes included, like, "You will always be my little angel," or, "Something to brighten up your day." For my birthday, I received a beautiful gift basket with various bottles of wine and snacks, with the note, "I'm with you in spirit. Happy 35th, mate!" His parents and Daryl got several gifts as well, complete with little sentiments assuring them he was safe.

These little tokens of love, however thoughtful, were no substitute for his presence in my life or the lives of others who cared about him. In fact, the gifts sometimes served as cruel reminders of his absence, physical evidence of the fact that he was still alive yet no longer reachable, by phone or otherwise. I had known him almost all of my 35 years and had never gone more than a few weeks without speaking to him. Even when he traveled overseas, we touched base consistently.

This total silence was an anomaly, and I found it increasingly unbearable.

Before long, the week of Thanksgiving arrived, and Anna and I had plans to celebrate with Daryl and his parents, along with Tracy, Amy, Eugene, and Candy. Jon's "little angel" would ordinarily be going to her aunt and uncle's house, but they had gotten the flu and didn't want to risk getting her sick. Despite Jon's absence, it was nice to have a holiday celebration to look forward to with some of my closest friends and my lovely Anna.

The night before the big feast at Martha's and Jon Sr's house, I drove with Anna to Boston to see Mario in concert. His performance had been phenomenal, and we were able to meet up with him and his lovely Brittany for drinks afterwards, in the bar at the hotel where he was staying. We even got to meet the other members of his band, who hung out with us for a while. Mario had also received some postcards from Jon, who had thanked his old friend for encouraging him to sing again and promised to keep in touch. Like the rest of us, Mario was sad Jon had to leave so suddenly but was relieved to know that he was getting treatment for his issues.

Anna and I had eaten dinner at a lovely bistro prior to the show, taking turns feeding each other little morsels of food as we gazed lovingly into each other's eyes. To spice things up, I had convinced her to wear a shock collar around her ankle, and within several weeks, she had become accustomed to receiving electric shocks of various intensity while doing everything from shopping, to cooking, to showering, to fucking. "Slave week" was coming up during Christmas break, and it was ideal timing since she had ten days off from her teaching job, and I had the same amount of time off from the gym.

Back in August, Daryl and I had hired extra people to help with the gyms, and business was going very well. Legally, Jon was still a business partner with us, but had actually sent checks to Daryl and me to cover what would have been his cut of the profits for three months. With the check, he had included a kind note: "You boys deserve my cut since you're doing all the work. I'm proud of you. Keep it up!" Daryl and I had been elated but not terribly surprised, since Jon wasn't the same miserly bloke that he had been up until the previous year, when he had insisted on getting ten percent of the gym's profits despite living across the country.

We had both decided to close the gyms for a period of ten days during the holidays, as it had been years since either of us had taken more than a few days off. Business was doing so well that, in addition to being able to afford vacations and time off from our jobs, we were able to give holiday bonuses to our employees and planned on giving them the checks the week before Christmas. Daryl planned on flying to Florida for a five day trip with Tracy and had encouraged me to accompany him, but I had told him with a wink that I already had "staycation" plans with my lovely redhead.

Anna and I had a wee bit too much to drink at the bar and didn't think it was safe to drive home. So we decided to crash in Mario's suite, which luckily had a spare couch. She and I showered together then put on the soft robes provided by the hotel and cuddled beneath the blanket. I turned on the Telly to help myself fall asleep.

Unfortunately, sleep wouldn't come for some time, because there was some "breaking news." It involved a hit and run accident, resulting in an

unidentified body found on a main road in Scottsdale, Arizona. The only specifics they offered was that the body belonged to a tall white male who appeared to be in his thirties, and they didn't show a picture. Scottsdale is the same city where Jon happened to have gone for treatment.

My brain went a mile a minute as I tried to talk myself down from a panic and think rationally. Perhaps he wasn't even IN Scottsdale anymore? Perhaps he was on his way back home? Also, he was far too smart to travel on foot without any form of identification. As for tall white males in their thirties? Millions would fit that description, including myself, right? I said a silent prayer that it was someone else's body.

As I prayed, I did my absolute best to keep my thoughts from going to "worst case scenario." Despite my efforts, I had a vision of Jon relapsing on drugs and wandering through the streets of Scottsdale after dark, no wallet, intoxicated out of his mind, crossing the street without looking and getting hit by a careless driver that decided to keep going, leaving my best mate to die on the side of the road.

Anna, sensing my feelings of dread, did her best to soothe me and be reassuring. I treated myself to a few hits of weed from the pipe I had brought, then changed the station to something more conducive to sleep: the home shopping channel.

My phone's alarm awakened me from a dream in which Jon was starring in an infomercial, selling a convection oven. The dream had ended with

him stripping naked and winking at the camera, urging viewers to "call now, before supplies run out!"

I saw a number of text messages on my phone as well - one from Daryl, one from Candy, and another from Martha - all concerning the "breaking news" about the missing body and resulting anxiety. I sent quick replies, reassuring them despite my own doubts regarding Jon's safety. It seemed I wasn't the only one worried, and asking the same question: "Was Jon alive?" My Thanksgiving was merely minutes old, and was already getting off to a rough start.

My nerves were shot, so I indulged in a "wake and bake," rationalizing that I still had at least two hours before I planned on heading home. After that, I would still have time to relax and change clothes before driving to Jon and Daryl's parents' house for dinner.

"Yo."

I jumped as Mario barged into the living area, greeting me with a smile as he offered me a cup of coffee, which I graciously accepted. My hand shook as I took the cup.

"You ok, Ken?" Mario asked with concern.

I nodded and took a sip of the coffee. Anna began to stir next to me on the couch and smiled sleepily at me as well as Mario. I ran my hand

through her hair and kissed her on the forehead. "Yes, I'm ok," I lied. "I just saw something on the news that worried me."

Mario nodded. "Oh, yeah. That body in Arizona," he said casually. "I saw the news myself last night. I know what you're thinking. It's not Jon. No way. He wouldn't go down like that. I know Jomo. He's resilient as hell. Trust me." He smiled confidently and placed his hand on my shoulder.

"Thanks, Mario, I'm sure you're right. I just wish I could call or text him but his phone is off, and has been since July. He's been completely unreachable for the past four months. Nobody knows where he is, not even his parents."

Mario raised his eyebrows. "No shit. Well, he's always been pretty rebellious. But I don't think he's gone away forever. In fact, I think he will be back before Christmas."

I nodded and took another sip of coffee. "I hope so."

"I have a keen intuition," Mario said with a smirk. "Sometimes I just KNOW things."

I thought of what Mario said, and cuddled with Anna for a few minutes before ordering breakfast via room service. Mario and Brittany joined us in the living room for breakfast, and the four of us tuned in to the thanksgiving parade on TV for about an hour. My anxiety level got a wee bit lower, to the point I could actually think about other things besides

the identity of the body in Arizona, and after exchanging pleasantries with Mario and Brittany, Anna and I began the trip back home.

As I drove, I couldn't help but look over at the passenger seat. My lovely redhead looked so beautiful in her wool coat, her long auburn hair cascading down her front. She turned to me and smiled, placing her hand on my thigh. I smiled back, doing my best to concentrate on the road as an erection grew in my knickers. By the time I drove past Providence, I couldn't take it anymore. I pulled over on the shoulder of the highway.

"Get in the back seat," I ordered as I pulled down my pants and freed my enormous cock from the confines of my boxer briefs.

Anna smirked as she climbed into the back seat of my Mercedes. I wasted no time doing likewise, tugging down her pants and underwear within seconds before lining myself up with her auburn-stubbled cunny. She was already wet so I teased her opening for a few seconds before plunging balls-deep into her. She howled with delight, her body grinding against the leather as I violated her. This was our first time having full on intercourse in a car. It was a tight squeeze with the two of us being back there but it still felt good, and the fact that it was taking place on the shoulder of a highway in broad daylight made it all the more exciting!

I held her arms down as I pounded her, my breathing quickening by the second. The windows fogged up as we panted in unison, our movements making the car shake ever so slightly. My thoughts traveled to other drivers, and I wondered how many would take notice of a

Mercedes parked on the shoulder, hazard lights blinking, windows fogged up, car rocking back and forth. I stifled a laugh and did my best to focus on the sensations going through my body, and the warmth of Anna's womanhood enveloping my member.

"Oh my fucking God!" Anna panted as she climaxed, her warm juices covering my dick, which exploded merely seconds later. We held each other tightly as we orgasmed, our bodies shuddering with rapture.

I slowly backed away from her flushed face, smiling broadly. "That was brilliant," I said breathlessly.

Anna nodded. "Agreed."

I withdrew from her and used a napkin to clean myself, handing her one as well. The windows were significantly fogged up, so I pulled up my knickers and pants then climbed back into the driver seat, and hit the defogger button. Anna got dressed and joined me, making sure to kiss me on the cheek before buckling up. I slowly merged back onto the highway, feeling a sense of relief and joy that was part post-coital euphoria and part love for Anna. One day I would need to get up the courage to tell her I loved her during waking hours, and not just whisper those words to her when she was in a dead sleep.

Several miles ahead, I noticed another vehicle parked on the shoulder, hazard lights on, foggy windows, and rocking slightly. Anna and I let out a hearty laugh, as it was highly likely that our activities had inspired at least one other couple to shag on the side of the highway!

The rest of the trek home flew by, and we arrived at my house by early afternoon. Anna and I showered together then got dressed for dinner at Martha and Jon Sr.'s. I made sure to grab the bottles of wine I had bought for the occasion then looked at my darling Anna, who was wearing a beautiful dark green sweater that made her red hair appear even more vibrant than usual. Seeing that we had time to spare, I decided it was a good idea for a quickie in the kitchen. I put down the bottles of wine.

I looked at her with longing, running my fingers through her hair. Then I wasted no time bending her over one of the bar stools. She yelped in surprise as I pulled down her satin knickers, freeing my own manhood from my trousers as I did so.

"How about a little appetizer before the feast?" I quipped, before entering her abruptly. Her moans echoed off the walls.

Nothing like some extra "stuffing!"

One hour later...

Nine of us sat around the dining table, laughing and sharing stories over deviled eggs and glasses of wine. We were all doing our best to be merry, despite the craziness earlier in the day with the "breaking news." The smell from the kitchen was nothing short of heavenly, and my mouth watered at the thought of the feast to come.

Amy and Eugene sat directly across from me and Anna. They looked radiant, both individually and as a couple, and whatever jealousy I had felt the year prior had long since dissipated. Amy's cheeks had a rosy hue, and she wore a beautiful blue sweater that flattered her porcelain skin tone. Eugene had grown out his red hair a bit, and looked rather handsome. He had grown up so much since I had met him several years before, when he was still dating Tracy.

As for Daryl's lovely girlfriend, Tracy was looking adorable in a fuzzy pink cardigan and pretty waves in her highlighted blond hair. She and Amy were scheduled to graduate nursing school the following year, and were excited to start work at a nearby hospital. I couldn't believe how quickly time was flying by, and it seemed only yesterday they were babies playing in a sandbox.

Candy sat on the opposite side of me, an empty chair next to her that would have been occupied by her boyfriend. She looked beautiful as always, her light blond hair curled in sexy waves that framed her face. She wore a white sweater that accentuated her "angelic" look, along with a diamond necklace Jon had given her. She laughed and joked along with the rest of us, yet there was a sadness to her face that I noticed, especially during the rare quiet moments in the dining room. I knew she was missing Jon something terrible. At one point, she caught me glancing at her during one of those "pensive" moments, doing her best to cover up the seriousness with a bright smile.

"You miss him, don't you?" I whispered sympathetically.

Candy's smile faded and her eyes filled with tears that she quickly blinked away. "Yes," she said with a nod.

I placed my hand on her shoulder. "Me, too."

Martha suddenly came up to the table with a platter full of cheese and crackers, a huge smile on her face.

"Dinner is almost ready, loves!" She announced, as she placed the platter on the table, grabbing a piece of cheese from the platter and popping it into her mouth as she scurried back into the kitchen.

We all cheered, helping ourselves to the new appetizers. The sound of holiday music started over the stereo system in the living room. Flurries of snow were visible outside the window. It began to feel like the holidays, and I felt myself getting into more of a festive mood.

I poured myself another glass of wine, doing the same for Anna and Candy. Jon Sr. launched into an amusing story about the neighbor's dog coming onto the property during a barbecue they had over the summer, and begging for ribs. In fact, the dog enjoyed visiting whenever there was a party involving food, and Jon Sr. figured it would only be a matter of time before the animal materialized, begging for scraps from the thanksgiving feast.

Knock, knock!

Someone was at the door. Not missing a beat, Daryl piped up.

"Maybe that's the neighbor's dog right now!" He quipped.

Everyone laughed. Martha removed her apron and walked over to the front door, wondering aloud who it could be since she wasn't expecting anyone else. I leaned back in my chair so I could see what was happening from the dining room.

"Special delivery," a man announced, and he was dressed in a delivery driver uniform along with another identically dressed gentleman. They were rolling a very large cardboard box on a dolly cart through the front foyer, then gently lowering the box to the floor. Martha signed a form that one of the men handed her.

"What could it be?" Martha asked. "I haven't ordered anything, at least nothing that would fit into a box this big."

One of the men shrugged. "Maybe it's an early Christmas present?" He suggested with a smile. "Have a happy thanksgiving, ma'am!" The men called out before leaving.

Martha smiled. "You as well, loves!" She closed the front door then grabbed a pair of scissors from a nearby drawer to open the box.

Jon Sr. got up from his chair and helped his wife open the box. "What's in the box?" He asked aloud, and did his best to try and lift the box but it was too heavy. I got up, as did Daryl, offering to help. Just then, Martha got the top open.

The box was filled to the brim with styrofoam packing peanuts, which Martha and Jon Sr. began removing from the box in small handfuls. Then the box began to shake. Martha let out a startled yelp, as did I, and everyone got up from their seats to join us in the foyer. What happened next was nothing short of incredible.

"Ho! Ho! Ho!"

A red form suddenly rose from the box. It was Santa Claus himself, holding a red velvet bag full of what I assumed were presents. He stood about my height and stepped out of the box with a flourish. His white beard had pieces of styrofoam in it, as did his red suit and hat. We all began to laugh and cheer, wondering why the hell someone dressed as Santa Claus would have himself shipped in a box to someone's house on Thanksgiving night!

Santa's true identity became apparent, however, when he removed his hat and beard in one swift motion. His hair was a lighter shade than usual, with flattering platinum blonde highlights contrasting nicely with his natural dirty blonde. His usual short beard was reduced to more of a pristine stubble, revealing sunkissed skin and cheeks that dimpled when he flashed his megawatt smile. His green eyes shone with a light that had been missing from them for some time. That's right: Jon Moore was back home!

"Jonathan!" Martha exclaimed with an ecstatic smile, eagerly wrapping her arms around her son. "You're back!"

We all began excitedly talking at once, praising Jon on how healthy he looked and how great it was that he was back from Arizona.

Jon put down the bag of presents, lifted his mum, and twirled her around, laughing joyfully as he did so. "Indeed, I am home," he said. "And I'm here to stay."

Jon Sr. was next to give Jon a bear hug, complimenting him on his looks. "You're blond like me, again," he said with a smile as he pointed to Jon's new highlights.

Jon nodded. "I got tired of darkening my hair after so many years and decided to go back to my 'roots,' so to speak," he said with a chuckle. "The Arizona sun definitely helped things along!" Everyone laughed at his comment, agreeing his natural blond suited him.

Daryl and I were next, and couldn't help but break down in tears as we held him. Amy and Tracy followed, and Jon picked them both up at once and twirled them around, as he had done with his mum.

"So good to see you again, Jonny," Tracy said with a broad smile as he set her and Amy back down on the ground. "You look great!"

"I FEEL great," Jon said with a grin. "I've gained thirty pounds."

We congratulated him on his improved appearance and health. Then he hugged and greeted Anna, and shook Eugene's hand, complimenting him on his longer hair.

Last, there was Candy, who was standing towards the back of the herd. She smiled shyly, taking tiny steps towards Jon, whose expression turned rather wistful.

"Hello, my little angel," he said softly, taking her hands into his. "You look so beautiful. I've missed you so much."

Candy's eyes filled with tears. "I've missed you, too," she said, before melting into his shoulder. She cried softly as he held her.

The rest of us smiled and got teary eyed as we saw the two lovebirds reunite, deciding to retreat back to the dining room to give them some privacy.

"Dinner will be ready in about ten minutes! I can't wait to hear about your trip!" Martha called out from the kitchen.

"Ok, mum," Jon called back. "Candy and I are going to talk alone for a few moments but we will be back." He put his arm around her and walked with her to the den. I was feeling curious so I excused myself from the table and discreetly followed behind them, pretending to go into the loo as Jon closed the door of the den behind him. I positioned myself close to the door so I could listen in.

"Jon, there's something I need to tell you. Well, two things."

"Of course, doll. You can tell me anything. What is it?"

There was a pause, and I felt my heart rate speed up. I had a feeling that Candy was going to confess to sleeping with me and Anna, and I was sure that my best mate wouldn't be happy about it.

"About two weeks after you had left for Arizona, I had a pregnancy scare."

Silence. I put my hand over my mouth in shock, imagining how scared and alone Candy must have felt.

"Oh, my God," Jon gasped. "I am so sorry you had to deal with that alone, and that I wasn't there for you. I can't imagine what that must have been like."

"Yes, well, luckily the test came back negative," she replied softly. "I've been on the pill for years, so my period is almost never late. My doctor figured it was stress related."

"You poor thing, honey. Learning about that just breaks my heart. But I'm here for you now. Let me hold you for a while."

I heard sniffling, and wasn't sure if it was Candy or Jon crying, or both. But I smiled as I imagined them holding each other.

Jon cleared his throat. "You, um, said there was something else you wanted to tell me?" His voice was kind and gentle.

Candy sniffled. "Yes. I'm really sorry to tell you this but... the night you left for Arizona I was devastated, so I got very drunk with Kenny and Anna. We started out just talking but one thing led to another and the three of us wound up... having sex. I'm sorry. I understand if this is a dealbreaker..."

Her voice trailed off and she began crying. Jon made some soothing sounds and let her cry for a few moments before speaking.

"Listen to me, darling, ok?" Jon began in a soothing tone. "You are one of the kindest souls I have ever met in my entire life. I'm not angry or upset by what you did. I understand that you did what you had to do to get through the terrible pain that I put you through by leaving so suddenly. I'm so sorry for hurting you like that, and I will do whatever I

can to avoid causing you any more pain, I promise. I am still head over heels in love with you, Candy. And I want to be with you. I'm back for good, and I want us to pick up where we left off. Would you move in with me? Please?"

Candy was quiet for a few seconds. "What's this?" She asked. "Is it a key to your house? It's beautiful! I know I left my original copy under the welcome mat the night you left."

"Yes, it is indeed a key to my house, but a custom version with your birthstone on it, as well as real diamonds, and there's an engraved message on the back. Turn it over and you will see."

Candy cleared her throat and read the message. "'Candy Girl: You have the key to my home & the key to my heart. Love, Jonny Boy'. That's SO sweet! Thank you!"

Jon chuckled. "Of course, Love. And you can wear it as a pendant. See? It comes with a clip."

"I do see that. I'm definitely going to wear it as a pendant, it's gorgeous. I love it, Jon, and I love YOU. And the answer is yes. I will move in with you. I want to give Gladys 30 days notice as a courtesy, but yes. Today is the... 21st? This means I can move in right before Christmas."

I heard more sniffling, which was most likely Jon crying tears of joy. I felt ecstatic for my best mate, who was once again healthy and happy. After all he had been through over the years, he deserved a bloody break.

"Oh, Candy," he whispered, "I'm so happy. You have no idea. I have my little angel back."

"You just have to promise me you won't take off again," Candy said in a joking tone.

"You have my word. I love you."

A thump emanated from the den, which I imagined was the sound of the two of them collapsing onto the leather sofa. This was followed by giggling, and the sound of clothing being unzipped.

"Dinner will be ready soon," Candy said through muffled giggles.

"First, I need to stuff the turkey," Jon quipped, making Candy laugh to the point that she snorted. "I want you so badly. I miss the feel of your body, and I can't wait until later. Just a quickie. Mmmm..."

I could hear them moaning and exchanging feverish kisses, and at that point I decided to give them privacy, so I walked back to the dining room. Anna smiled at me and I smiled back.

"Where's my brother? What's he doing?" Daryl asked drunkenly. "Stuffing Candy's turkey?"

I burst out laughing, as did everyone at at the table, including Jon Sr. Just then, Martha came up to the table with a huge platter of food, with a lovely turkey in the middle that was just begging to be eaten. My mouth watered.

"Dinner is ready!" Martha crowed with a huge smile. "You all help yourselves!"

One by one, we filled our plates with heaps of goodness. I was elated, knowing my best mate was back home. I piled several helpings of mashed potatoes on my plate along with copious amounts of stuffing, and helped myself to some more wine. Music continued to play from the speakers and I caught myself humming along. Anna smiled at me as she filled her plate, and gave me a quick peck on the cheek. Whatever apprehension had filled my mind earlier in the day had long dissipated. Life was good!

Martha sat at the table and filled her plate, questioning aloud where Jon and Candy were. Seconds later, they emerged from the foyer and made their way into the dining room with huge smiles on their flushed faces.

"The guest of honor has returned, along with his lovely girlfriend!" Martha announced proudly. Everyone else mumbled their approval, delighted to see him join us for dinner.

Candy's lipstick was gone, and her sweater was inside out. She wore the house key pendant on her necklace, which shone beautifully. I hid a smirk as she sat to the left of Jon, who sat to the left of me. He had taken off his Santa suit and was wearing a holiday sweater with a llama on the front, which had been a gift from Daryl. He smelled faintly of smoke from his post-coital cigarette as well as vaginal secretions, presumably from going down on Candy. He smiled and winked at me as he poured a glass of wine for Candy and then for himself.

Daryl, looking rather inebriated, addressed Jon with a wolfish grin. "Hey there, Santa llama," he slurred. "Did you slide down Candy's chimney?"

The entire table burst out laughing. Daryl was always entertaining when he was tipsy, and this time was no exception.

"Santa might have made a pit stop," Jon quipped, which led to more laughter. He piled more food on his plate then took some bites of mashed potatoes.

"It's so great to see you eating again!" Martha said cheerfully. "You have to tell me about your time in Arizona. I've never been there and have always wanted to."

The rest of us agreed, encouraging Jon to tell us about his travels.

"Oh you would have loved it," Jon said to his mum. "It's a beautiful state."

For the next twenty minutes or so, Jon bewitched us with stories about his time in Arizona, talking about his experiences in the treatment center, his hiking trip to the Grand Canyon, sight seeing in Sedona, his new meditation ritual, and the solo cross country road trip he had taken after the 90 days, using his red Tesla. That was when Daryl piped in, telling him about the news regarding the hit-and-run car accident with the unidentified body in Scottsdale, and how we could all assume it wasn't his body. Jon laughed heartily, as did the rest of us.

"That reminds me, I had actually paid one of the members at the gym to tow MY car all the way to Scottsdale," he said. "I so love my 'little cherry' and didn't want to wait until I was back home to drive it. In fact, he was one of the UPS drivers who 'shipped' me here tonight. I paid him and his coworker friend to do it. You know me, I had to make a grand entrance!"

I laughed, as did the others. "What was your favorite part of the trip?" I asked as I took a sip of wine.

Jon thought for a moment before answering. "I think my favorite part was the completion of my program. Forget all the sights and attractions, and the adventures. Learning how to develop a better relationship with food and to practice taking care of myself was really invaluable. In fact, I

didn't return home right away because I wanted to practice some of the skills I learned when I was in treatment. Travel has always been a trigger for my eating issues, so it felt like the perfect time to test myself, to make sure I was ready to return home. I wasn't coming back until I knew I was better."

Candy placed her hand on his shoulder and looked at him with tears in her innocent blue eyes. "I'm very proud of you," she said softly. "And I'm so glad you're home."

The rest of us agreed, congratulating Jon on his progress. Daryl smiled and raised his wine glass, leading a toast to his elder brother.

"I just want to say I'm so happy for you, and I congratulate you on your improved health. You are an inspiration. Cheers, Jon!" His younger brother grinned with pride, and we all took turns clinking glasses.

Jon took a sip of his wine and smiled gratefully at his brother, placing one arm around Candy and the other around mine. "The worst part of my trip? Being away from those I care about. The nights were the worst. I hated going to bed alone."

Candy kissed him on the cheek. "Now you don't have to worry about that anymore," she assured. "Because I'm moving in with you."

Martha's eyes widened and she smiled broadly. "Oh my goodness! That's wonderful!"

Jon nodded and kissed Candy gently on the lips. "That's right. My little angel takes such good care of me, and now I know I can take good care of HER. I can't wait for us to begin our life together."

My manhood stiffened as I imagined Jon fucking the shit out of Candy, taking the time to baptize each room in his palatial home, forcing her to tolerate every inch of his throbbing, pierced cock in all of her holes, making her lick semen off the floor and punishing her severely if she refused. As I finished my cranberry sauce, I placed my hand on Anna's thigh, and leaned over to whisper in her ear.

"I'm shaving your pussy when we get home then I'm eating pumpkin pie off of it," I murmured into her ear. I loved the way she blushed at my words, struggling to keep her cool. I drank some more wine and got a massive erection as I thought of what her womanhood would look like with pumpkin pie and whipped topping slathered all over it. Just then, Jon leaned in to whisper in MY ear.

"Two words," he whispered. "Dracula dick."

I swallowed and looked at him with raised eyebrows. "You going to make Candy give you that?" I asked in a hushed tone.

He smirked and nodded. Jon had invented the term a number of years prior, when he had asked Lisa to bite his penis hard enough to break the skin while going down on him, then licking the blood. He had loved the

sensation, the feeling of pleasure mixed with intense pain, and enjoyed doing it to whatever brave blokes would let him. He had tried to do it to me once and I had yelled out the safe word past a certain point, getting away with a mild laceration that healed within days. Knowing my best mate and his lack of inhibitions, he probably would have bitten halfway through my cock had I said nothing.

After dinner and dessert, we all retreated to the living room to watch movies, and Jon gave each of us a gift from the velvet bag he had brought with him. Candy already wore her gift around her neck. As for me, I got a bottle of my favorite scotch, Anna got a bottle of her favorite wine, Martha and Jon Sr. got a beautiful set of vases, Eugene and Amy got gift cards to their favorite video game store since they were avid gamers, Tracy got an expensive lip gloss set, and Daryl got new resistance bands for his home gym. My best mate had always been generous and a skilled gift giver. Some things never change.

Three hours and half a bottle of scotch later...

"Oh, my fucking god..." I panted as Anna went down on me, using her teeth a fair amount. I had forgotten how good it felt to get sucked off while drunk off my arse, and the fact that I had an audience made it all the more exciting.

That's right: Jon and Candy had front row seats to the fuckfest. They lay across from Anna and me, cuddling on my king sized bed, and naked as the day they were born. They occasionally fondled and kissed each other as they looked on with eyes full of lust. The new velvet bedspread and new satin sheets felt so good against my naked body, enhancing my

pleasure that much more. Jon had offered for Anna and me to crash at his place, but I felt like being in my own home and my own bed.

After dinner at Jon's parents' house, the four of us decided on strong drinks for an encore to the evening. Things started off civilized, with the four of us drinking glasses of wine in front of the television, and they ended with Jon and me licking shots of tequila and single malt scotch off Anna's and Candy's tits. With all the alcohol we had consumed, it was only a matter of time before the clothes started coming off.

"Shall I grab the razor and the pie?" Jon asked in between kisses from Candy, lighting himself a cigarette.

"Oh, yes," I panted, recalling my previous plan to shave Anna's pussy then eat pie off her mound. "And the whipped cream."

Jon smirked and nodded, taking Candy by the hand as they got up from the bed. "Coming right up."

I closed my eyes and moaned with pleasure as Anna took every inch of me in her mouth, occasionally grabbing my ballsack with her soft hand. Within seconds, Jon and Candy returned to the bedroom. He had TWO razors and TWO slices of pumpkin pie, along with a can of whipped cream. He and his little angel sat back down on the bed with smiles on their faces.

"We had an idea," Candy said.

I raised my eyebrows. "What's that?" I asked as I placed my hands atop Anna's head, her motions quickening.

"We want to turn it into a pie eating contest," Jon said with a sexy grin before he took a long drag off his ciggy then put it out. "Whoever finishes eating first wins. There's a fun little twist: The loser's girlfriend has to give the winner a blow job."

I chuckled and nodded. "I won't say no to getting a second one!"

Jon laughed. "We shall see who wins. Don't be so... cocky."

Everyone laughed, including Anna, who began sucking me off with ever increasing speed. I climaxed within a minute.

"Great job, Anna," I cooed breathlessly, caressing her flushed face as she swallowed my load. I handed her a bottle of water, which she eagerly accepted.

Jon cleared his throat and grabbed the shaving cream off the nightstand. "Now, both you ladies lie on your backs and spread your legs."

Candy and Anna smiled, lying on their backs with their legs open. Jon squirted some shaving cream into his hand and gently covered Candy's mound and outer lips with a thin layer, then handed me the can. I did similarly to Anna's private area, making sure the application was nice and even. After this, Jon and I grabbed the razors and began gently shaving, starting at the mound then working our way down gradually.

"Don't you worry, Candy," Jon said soothingly as she tensed up slightly. "I'm an old pro at this. I used to shave and wax Lisa all the time. Sometimes we would make a game of it, where she would blindfold me or turn out the lights in the room, just to see how I would do. In fact, we can do that right now." Jon turned to me with a sexy smirk. "What do you say, mate? Want to test your 'blind' shaving skills?"

I swallowed, knowing this was uncharted territory for me, but slowly nodded. "As long as the girls are ok with it," I said.

Anna and Candy nodded. "Just go slow," Anna advised, a bit of fear in her eyes.

"We will," Jon assured, turning off the lamp next to the bed.

The room was dark, but just light enough to make out the silhouette of the girls' bodies as well as Jon's. I would have to go by feel. I was less concerned about missing spots of hair and more concerned about making sure I didn't cut Anna by mistake. I placed the blade against Anna's skin and made slow, short movements. I saw Jon do likewise, and knew that Candy was trying to remain calm by taking deep breaths.

"That's it," Jon said in his velvety voice. "Just breathe. You're doing great. I'm almost done, love."

Several more minutes went by before I determined that I had done a rather thorough job, and Anna's mound and lips felt as smooth as a baby's bum. I leaned down and kissed Anna's freshly shaved mound, letting her know I was finished. My mouth watered and my cock swelled. I was ready for pie, in more ways than one.

"Smooth as can be," Jon whispered, before turning on the light. He smiled at Candy, who smiled back. "That wasn't so bad, was it?"

Candy shook her head. "Not at all. You have a gentle touch."

Jon winked then grabbed one of the pie plates and the can of whipped cream. I did likewise, excited for what was to come.

"Alright," Jon began. "Main rule: we must only use our mouths to eat. No hands allowed."

I nodded. "No problem."

With those words, Jon and I took the spoons and began piling the pumpkin pie onto our girlfriends' respective mounds. They both giggled

at the sensation of cool pie meeting their delicate flesh. Then we each squirted a generous amount of whipped cream on top of the contents.

"On my count," Jon said. "Five, four, three, two, one, and GO!"

I leaned down and began devouring as much of the pie off Anna's crotch as I could. Some whipped cream got up my nose as I did so, but I didn't care. I wanted so badly to win, to feel Candy's mouth on my manhood. But it wasn't meant to be. Because as soon as I finished the last mouthful of pie, I sat back up and saw Jon smirking at me. The bastard had won yet again.

"It was a close race. I finished TWO seconds before you!" He boasted with a satisfied grin, his arms folded across his chest.

Candy smiled up at him. "Great job, honey!"

Anna looked at me with a lovely grin. "You did amazing," she said as she sat up and gave me a gentle kiss on the lips.

Candy cleared her throat. "Hey, I have an idea."

The three of us raised our eyebrows, interested.

Candy looked at Jon. "I've always wanted to see you two boys together," she said shyly. "You have been friends your entire lives, and I get turned on by seeing men pleasuring each other. I would really love to see Ken go down on you, Jon."

My best mate smiled broadly at Candy. "The hell you say!" He said in a tone that was impressed as well as surprised. Then he looked at me with a gentle grin on his face. "I'm down for it but I will leave it up to you, Ken. What do you say? You ok with giving me a blow job? I know it's been a while."

I thought about it for a moment, and realized that it HAD been ages since I last did anything sexual with Jon. In fact, the last time we'd had any real sexual contact was the time he had raped me almost a year and a half prior. The threesome with Tracy the following day didn't count since, aside from a kiss, we hadn't touched each other. I looked at Anna.

"As long as my lovely redhead is alright with it?"

Anna smiled and nodded. "Of course! Candy and I BOTH want to see you guys get hot and heavy."

Jon and I began crawling towards each other on the bed. Lust was in his emerald green eyes and I could feel my heartbeat quicken. He gently ran his hand through my hair.

"I've missed this," he whispered. Then he grabbed the back of my neck and began kissing me. His lips were gentle at first, but then he opened his mouth wider until he was devouring me. He slipped his tongue into my mouth, and I did likewise. I grabbed the back of his neck, pushing his head even harder against mine as we kissed. He moaned with pleasure, then lay down on his back, pulling me with him so I wound up on top of his toned body.

I caressed his chest as I locked lips with him, playing with his pierced nipples from time to time as I did so. In turn, he ran his fingertips down my back and grabbed my bum. His touch felt so good, and I loved the way he bucked his hips from time to time, his manhood hardening steadily. Ever so slowly, I began crawling backwards towards his penis, leaving a trail of kisses down his front. His pecs and abs were rock-hard, and his pubic area clean-shaven. He ran his hands through my hair and began to moan with pleasure as I made my way down to his throbbing, pierced maleness.

"Oh..." Jon moaned as my hand caressed his hairless balls and my lips grazed the tip of his engorged manhood. "Ken.... Don't stop. Mmmm...."

I smiled and began kissing his penis, starting from the tip and ending all the way down to his ballsack. I even licked and sucked at his cock piercing, which he loved. After a few more seconds of kissing and sucking, he reached out for Candy's hand and held it, perhaps to let her know that, despite the intimacy going on between him and me, he was still "connected" to her somehow. I followed this gesture, grabbing and holding Anna's hand as I pleasured Jon.

"This is beautiful," Jon crooned as I took a fair amount of his shaft into my mouth. He then turned his head to look at Candy, a sexy smile on his face, then leaned in for a kiss.

Candy and Jon locked lips passionately as I sucked him off. That was when Anna took a hold of my penis and began pleasuring me with her soft hand. I moaned as I continued to deep throat my best mate. That was when a depraved idea came into my head.

I began using my teeth when sucking Jon's dick, to see how he would react. Predictably, a huge smile formed on his face, and he backed away from Candy's lips to speak to me. His green eyes sported that all too familiar sinister "glow" that I hadn't witnessed in a long time.

"That's it, Bitch," he growled as he began bucking his hips and placed one of his hands on top of my head, pushing me to take more of him inside my mouth. "Bite me."

I felt my face get hot with anger. It had been so long since Jon had referred to me as "Bitch," and I felt like I was instantly transported back in time. Whether he was deliberately trying to get a rise out of me so I would give him the aforementioned "Dracula Dick," or was simply getting carried away by the combination of alcohol and sexual arousal, I couldn't be certain. However, I DID know that I was pissed, and suddenly wanted nothing more than to bite his penis hard enough to break the skin.

My jaws clamped down more aggressively on his member, and I dared myself to bite harder. Jon's smile morphed into something closer to a grimace, and his moans turned into grunts as I bit down with more and more pressure.

"Mmmm," Jon groaned, backing away instinctively as my front teeth threatened to break the tender flesh of his maleness. "Wait.... time out, mate."

I backed away momentarily as I squeezed and twisted his balls, in full on "sadist" mode. Candy looked at Jon with concern and held his hand more tightly, worried that I would become unhinged. At this time, Anna let go of my penis and placed her hand on my shoulder, perhaps in an effort to calm me down.

"What's the matter, Jonny Boy?" I asked mockingly as I glared at him. "Chickening out because you no longer have any cocaine or pills to numb the sensation, hmm? Not like in years past? Too bloody bad, mate. You asked for 'teeth,' and that's what you're going to get!"

I didn't even bother looking at Jon's reaction to my words. Instead, I roughly grabbed his dick and began biting harder than ever.

"Ughhh!!" Jon cried through clenched teeth as he did his best to endure the pain of being bitten. Several agonizing seconds later, it happened.

I heard, as well as felt, a sickening "crunch," which was the unmistakable sound of teeth breaking skin, followed by Jon's loud scream. I rapidly backed away from his penis, the taste of blood taking over my mouth.

"You alright?!" I asked Jon, instinctively applying pressure to the wound. "What do you need?"

He was panting and his face began to lose color as he broke out in a sweat. "I need ice!" He gasped as he grimaced in pain, his eyes clamped shut. "And a towel and bandages! Holy shit, it hurts..."

Anna immediately rose from the bed. "I will take care of it," she said, then ran off to get the first aid supplies. Candy held Jon, who did his best to remain calm as his girlfriend spoke loving words and caressed his face, telling him he would be alright.

I examined the area where I had bitten, and realized my teeth had gone deeper than I had expected them to and felt a new surge of adrenaline. It appeared I had really hurt him.

SMACK!

Candy had slapped me in the face for what I had done. Her lip was trembling and she was clearly upset. As for Jon, he was now pale as a sheet and began to shake, appearing to be in shock. Candy held his

hand and ran her fingers through his hair, whispering assuring words to him as he tried to stay conscious.

I wiped the blood from my lips and held Jon's clammy hand, feeling like I was in a movie. Clearly, I had gotten carried away and felt awful.

"I'm so sorry," I began shakily, addressing Jon and his girlfriend at the same time. Just then, Anna reappeared with an ice pack and towel, as well as disinfectant and bandages.

The three of us got to work as Jon lay there panting with his eyes closed, wincing when I used disinfectant on his wounds. The bleeding had luckily slowed down, and I was more confident he wouldn't need to go to the emergency room or require stitches. When he was a bit more alert, I had him lift his head and look at the damage, and he agreed it didn't look too severe and that he would most likely heal up within a few days.

"I've suffered worse," he assured me with a wink as Candy applied antibiotic ointment and bandages, then handed him a bottle of water, which he eagerly drank from. "Remember the piercing incident in New York City?"

I shuddered and nodded as I recalled that harrowing ordeal with Todd ripping out Jon's genital piercing, and Jon having used his sewing kit to stitch himself up, and cocaine as a numbing agent.

"I just wasn't expecting it to bleed so badly," I said. "But then again, I've never bitten a penis hard enough to draw blood!"

Jon chuckled weakly, sitting up for the first time since the ordeal had begun. He took my hand. "This is ok," he said in a reassuring whisper. "I know you feel bad. Don't. You did nothing wrong, mate. I asked for this. When I had said I needed a time out, you had given it to me. All I needed was a few seconds before continuing. I could have stopped you, but I didn't."

I smiled gently. "Alright. I just didn't want to hurt you this badly. It was scary seeing all that blood and hearing you scream like that."

Candy nodded in agreement. "You turned so pale, too," she added.

Anna chimed in. "This could have been so much worse," she noted. "I heard on the Internet about someone who had half his penis bitten OFF and needed it surgically reattached."

The four of us winced as we pictured that, thanking god that this wasn't worse. Jon assured us that he wasn't in a ton of pain and would simply need to lay off blow jobs and regular sex for at least a week, but that his other two holes were "still open for business." We all howled with laughter at that one, then Candy piped up.

"Maybe you would let me use the strap on?" She asked as she placed her arm around him. "We haven't done that yet, and I know you expressed interest many months prior, but we never got around to it."

Jon grinned from ear to ear. "That would be a great 'welcome home' gift. Perhaps tomorrow night?"

Candy nodded and smiled. "It's a date!" A few seconds later, her expression changed, then she turned to me and placed her hand on my shoulder. "Sorry for slapping you," she said in a soft voice. "I was just scared."

I smiled and squeezed her hand. "It's quite alright, sweetheart."

The four of us made small talk for a few moments then exchanged hugs and kisses, relieved that Jon was alright and not seriously injured. Then we all got dressed and walked down the beach to Jon's house for a night cap as well as a dip in the pool. We hadn't packed bathing suits, so we all swam in the nude. Jon didn't want to get his bandages wet so he simply sat and watched the three of us from the edge of the pool, splashing at us periodically and laughing.

Despite the scare with Jon's penis, it was a great night overall, and I was so glad he was back home. By night's end, he had given me some pointers to help prepare myself mentally for Anna's "slave week," which was coming up in less than a month. He insisted that I needed to "be prepared for anything," including the possibility of Anna getting permanently injured or seriously ill if I didn't take proper precautions.

I could also expect her to develop some PTSD from the experience. Apparently, Jon had seen it happen to Lisa, as well as Noelle. For a long time, Lisa needed to sleep with a night light, due to Jon's repeated ambushes in a room he had made completely dark, to add to her feelings of panic and lack of control. She also liked to have a water bottle on her at all times - in her purse, in her car, and next to her bed at night - after she had become severely dehydrated due to Jon denying her anything to drink as punishment. As for Noelle, she had developed a strong aversion to anal sex for about a year, after Jon had forced a large butt plug inside her when she was sleeping.

Late that night, when I was spooning with Anna in bed, I thought about my own trauma and how it had changed me. Ever since Jon had raped me the year prior, I was unable to fall asleep on my stomach, perhaps out of a subconscious fear of being attacked from behind. Some things just sort of "stay" with us, whether we realize it or not.

That night I dreamed I was buried alive, in a box full of styrofoam packing peanuts. After screaming for what seemed like an eternity, someone rescued me from my grave and helped me out of the box. The person in question? My wife.

Chapter 6: The Longest Week of Our Lives

Christmas Eve

Anna and I were sitting on the comfy couch in my brother Lawrence's living room, watching Christmas movies and sipping red wine. His wife Diana was there, and the four of us had just finished a lovely dinner that my brother had cooked. One of the benefits of having a family member who's a professional chef is having amazing meals at holiday time. Diana, despite not being a chef, could hold her own in the kitchen, and had made an incredible pecan pie. I had consumed two slices, inevitability falling into a sugar coma in front of the telly.

Diana had complimented Anna on her choker necklace, unaware that it was the "slave collar" she wore in public. The one she wore in the house was an actual dog collar, made out of leather with silver spikes surrounding it.

"Slave week" was to begin at midnight, and, as a sort of Christmas present, I would allow her 2 free hours, just long enough to eat a meal with me and possibly watch a short movie. Jon had rolled his eyes when I let him know about my plan to give her two free hours, insisting one hour was enough. The conversation had taken place at the gym the day before Christmas Eve, when we were both getting in one last workout before closing up shop for ten days.

"But it's Christmas, Jon," I had said exasperatedly, in between sets of lifting weights.

"I don't give a fuck if it's the second coming of Christ or the bloody rapture," he had said in a deadpan voice as he did dumbbell curls. "You call yourself a dominant, but you're acting like a pussy. Either make her your slave, or don't. She needs to EARN the right to get 'free hours.' What happened to standards, mate? You've grown soft. I can see it."

My nostrils had flared. "What happened to the explanation you had earlier this year? When you had insisted I wasn't 'growing soft,' but simply falling in love? Hmm? Don't you see I really care about Anna, and I don't want to hurt her. I... I LOVE her."

Jon had studied me for a moment and smiled sympathetically. "I know. But she doesn't know that for sure, because you haven't TOLD her you love her. Keeping this information to yourself therefore gives you an excuse to be extra tough on her, at least just this once. Trust me, women need that verbal affirmation, of being told they are loved. Otherwise, they have no idea. Actions are only part of the equation. Anyway, my advice to get through the week is to pretend she's a stranger, or at least someone you don't have a strong connection with. You might even want to make her wear a mask, to create a sense of detachment. That little trick helped me when I did it to Lisa years ago. I felt like less of a monster."

I had digested what Jon had just said, and it made sense. In order to get through this, I would have to pretend Anna was someone else, someone I didn't care for.

"I know this is hard, Ken," Jon had said in a gentle voice as he put down the weight and placed his hand on my arm. "As you know, I called it

quits by day five of 'slave week' with Lisa, and I won't judge you if you do the same with Anna. Let's also not forget that I don't have the balls to make my OWN girlfriend my slave any time soon, and have no idea when I will. In fact, just the thought of locking Candy in a cage gives me the jitters. But anyway, you will know if it's time to end things during the week. Just remember one thing: You're in control. Ok? And I'm here if you need me."

"Thanks, mate." We had exchanged hugs then began closing down the gym, excited for the long vacation ahead. He and I had wound up getting together at our favorite bar later that night, to exchange gifts and have a quick beer, just us two boys. Anna and Candy were both visiting with family that night. As for Daryl, he had left with Tracy for Florida earlier in the day, and I couldn't help but express envy for the bloke for traveling somewhere warm, since it was a mere fifteen degrees in Rhode Island that evening.

"Since Candy moved in three days ago, I have HER to keep me warm whenever I like," Jon said with a huge grin.

"That's so wonderful," I said, as I took a sip of beer. "I'm so happy for the two of you!"

Jon beamed. "Me, too."

I smiled as I thought back on that moment in the bar with my best mate, who was finally getting a damn break after so much suffering. I wrapped

my arm more tightly around Anna, and helped myself to more wine when Diana offered to refill my glass.

Anna turned to look at me then gave me a sweet kiss on the lips. Then she whispered in my ear.

"I can't wait for midnight." Her voice was so sexy.

My cock nearly exploded right then and there. I then noticed the time. 11:30pm. I finished my wine as quickly as I could then said goodbye to Lawrence and Diana, thanking them for the dinner and the little gift basket they had given us. I let Anna drive, since she was more sober.

Despite the fact that it was barely a 20 minute drive home, I had her pull over halfway through the ride, insisting on a quickie in the back seat. She had climaxed, while I elected to hold my load, rationalizing that doing so would help me act more aggressively towards her, more dominant. My theory would prove to be right.

Shortly after midnight...

My slave knelt naked before me, her spiked collar adorning her neck and a satin blindfold over her eyes. I stood above her, hands on my hips as I took in the sight of her. I cleared my throat and had her recite her vows.

"Repeat after me," I began in an authoritative tone. "'I agree to be your slave...'"

Her voice was timid. "I agree to be your slave."

"'For a period of seven days.'"

She sniffled. "F-for a period of-"

SMACK!

I slapped her in the face, making her squeal. "Speak up!"

She whimpered then continued. "For a period of seven days," she said in a louder voice.

"'I agree to follow orders.'"

More sniffling. "I agree to follow orders."

"'I will avoid eye contact and will only speak when spoken to.'"

She fidgeted some. "I will avoid eye contact and will only speak when... when spoken to."

"'I will consent to any and all sexual favors.'"

"I will consent to any and all sexual favors." She coughed this time.

I leaned forward so I was an inch away from her face. "Stop with the sound effects," I warned. Then I continued.

"'I will wait on my master night and day.'"

Her lip trembled. I already could tell this would be a tough experience. "I will wait on my master night and day."

"'Failure to perform tasks properly will result in discipline from the master.'"

She cleared her throat. "F-failure to perform tasks properly will result in discipline from the master."

I smiled, satisfied. "Good girl."

I took the blindfold off her and had her read and sign a contract, highlighting in detail what she could expect over the course of the week as well as her rights as a slave. It was similar to the document I had given Amy to read and sign when she was my slave, so very long ago.

Once the vows taken and the paperwork signed, I placed the blindfold back on her then bent her over. I spat on my dick then lined myself up with her tight bum.

"Get ready, bitch," I growled before going balls deep into her arse. She squealed as I pounded the shite out of her. My thrusts quickened as I fucked her, and I thought of all the twisted shit I would do to her over the next seven days. I climaxed within minutes, then dragged her to the bathroom to clean her up, using more pressure with the washcloth than necessary. She grimaced as I rubbed her bum raw, then dried her off with a scratchy towel. After this, I took off her blindfold and had her go into her cage for the night. After I closed the door to the cage, I leaned in to talk to her.

"Have a good sleep," I said softly. "See you in the morning. Merry Christmas." I smiled gently.

She smiled back timidly. "Merry Christmas, master."

I grinned broadly, pleased that she had remembered to call me "master."

I retreated to the kitchen and poured myself a drink, pleased with the way things had started. I watched some TV then went to bed.

As I got under my satin covers, I developed an erection once again and began to fondle myself. After a few moments, my phone lit up with a text notification. I picked it up and read the message.

"How did it go?" Jon had texted.

"It went well," I wrote back. "She stammered a few times when repeating the vows but then she remembered to call me 'master' when I put her in the cage for the night."

"Very good," he replied. "Seems everyone stutters when reciting the vows. Something about the setting, about being forced to do things under pressure, that brings out the timid little lamb in everyone."

I chuckled, agreeing wholeheartedly. "Good point." Then I added a "sheep" emoji, to which Jon replied with a laughing face.

"I have a challenge for you, MASTER," Jon then wrote. "One you should reserve for the end of slave week."

"What's that?" I imagined Jon would suggest I pierce her nipples or some other grotesque thing I hadn't had a chance to do to her yet.

"Tell her you love her."

My heart raced as I sat there reading the words of that text. Somehow everything else seemed fine by comparison - keeping her in a cage, withholding food as punishment, and random ambushes felt like a walk in the park. But to tell her I LOVED her? To express those feelings for her? The notion still scared the crap out of me. My hands shook as I forced myself to reply back.

"Let me sleep on it," I responded with trembling fingers.

"Hahaha," Jon wrote. "That's what I thought. But a wise idea, I reckon. Goodnight and Merry Christmas, mate. I love you."

I smiled warmly at Jon's text. "I love you too, Jon. And Merry Christmas to you as well. Gnite."

I turned off my phone and fell into a deep sleep.

Some time in the wee hours of the morning...

As was often the case after having a strong drink before bedtime, the dream was vivid.

It took place four years prior, not long after Jon got engaged, and not long after Daryl and I had both lost our wives - his to divorce, and mine to an unspeakable event.

Daryl and I were riding in a taxi to Jon's house in Malibu. He and Lisa were hosting a Christmas party, and, to quote Jon, "Everybody who's anybody is invited, plus a few...extras." The conversation had taken place in November via video chat, and Jon had smirked at his brother when saying the word, "extras." Invariably, this had led to a blowout between the two blokes, with Daryl shouting and criticizing his elder brother for his "elitism," and Jon calmly berating his younger brother for being "white trash." Daryl had gotten so upset by the comment he had slammed the laptop shut, thus ending the video chat, and didn't speak to Jon for over a month.

When we had arrived at Jon's beautiful home, which was tastefully decorated for the holidays, Daryl knocked on the side door, which led directly to one of the dining rooms. There was no answer but he heard some strange noises from inside the house. I decided to turn the knob and the door opened. We were expecting Jon or Lisa to answer the door; instead, we were greeted with the sight of two naked bodies shagging on furniture typically designed for eating, with an expensive chandelier and grandfather clock for an audience. The air was thick with pot smoke.

Jon was standing at the side of the granite dining table, fucking the hell out of Lisa, who lay atop the table with her arse at the edge, and her legs resting against Jon's front. Her D cup tits bounced up and down and her moans were the result of pleasure mixed with pain. He was

pounding the shit out of her, not breaking rhythm even when he saw us standing in the doorway. Lisa, the more coy of the two, quickly covered her breasts and gasped in surprise, apologizing as she began to get off the table. Jon held her legs in place and shook his head.

"You stay right there, love," he panted as he fucked her, then turned to us. "Be right with you boys. Make yourselves at home in the pool area. My staff put out some nibbles and drinks."

I laughed and nodded, closing the door and making my way around the other side of the house to the pool area and back yard, which overlooked the ocean. Daryl, far from amused, scowled and walked away with a look of disgust, dragging our luggage through the gravel path that led to the pool area. He mumbled something about a long flight and respecting other people's time. I put my hand on his shoulder, knowing how annoyed he was with his brother at that moment.

The other guests wouldn't be arriving for a while, so it was just me and Daryl. Holiday lights adorned the palm trees and bushes that surrounded the Olympic size pool, and there were about a half dozen round tables with white tablecloths, and white poinsettia plants in the middle of each table. Christmas music played softly from speakers. At the far end of the yard, there was a long table with an impressive display: there was a huge assortment of hors d'oeuvres and various bottles of wine in buckets of ice. Several staff were busy arranging the food, plates, and silverware, making sure everything was "just so" for their boss, Mr. Moore.

Working for THE Jon Moore was a pleasure for anyone lucky enough to make the cut. The prospect would be very well paid, but he or she would have to be willing to work weekends, holidays and late nights, have no less than four references, pass a rigorous background check, and submit to a drug test (Jon needed to make sure anyone he hired wouldn't dip into his stash of coke, benzos, weed, ecstasy, or any number of other goodies he had in his 'bag o' yummies,' the nickname he had given the Louis Vuitton satchel that he had purchased for the sole purpose of storing his drugs). Twenty hours a week was considered "full time." Benefits included paid vacation, a health savings account with regular contributions, holiday pay, regular bonuses, free membership to an exclusive gym and spa that Jon frequented, free meals, free room and board in Jon's luxurious "guest wing" when they stayed overnight, and "quality time" with the boss man after hours. That's right: Jon would sometimes party with his staff when they were done with their work day, frequenting night clubs, getting drunk and high with them, and even taking them on vacations with him. Mr. Moore was generous with his body as well, so sex was a given, of course.

For day to day living, Jon had a personal assistant, landscaper, personal chef, and two housekeepers under his employ. For his parties, he also had several bartenders and waitstaff, as well as a DJ. Occasionally, he would hire one of several musicians to play live music. Jon spared no expense when it came to living well.

Daryl and I put our luggage next to one of the tables, then he turned to me, a scowl on his face.

"How about we chill out for a bit while waiting for his majesty to stop shagging?" He suggested bitterly while motioning to the refreshment table. I laughed and nodded.

We made our way over to the long table and saw an assortment of bottles of beer, wine, and nips of hard liquor on display, and guests were encouraged to help themselves. There was also a full service bar set up next to the table, for guests who preferred to have someone make their drinks. The bartender, whose name was Dale, was a stunning young bloke who worked as a model, and had met Jon at a gig. According to Jon, Dale had mentioned wanting a side hustle to bring in extra money, so Jon hired him as a part time bartender and waiter. Jon quickly learned that Dale was bisexual, and wasted no time making the moves on him. In fact, my best mate seduced him after his first day on the job.

"Hey, boys!" Dale said cheerfully as we approached the bar. "Great to see you again. What will it be?"

"A martini," Daryl and I said in unison, to which Dale laughed. He made us our drinks and we sat at the bar for a bit, sipping and making small talk.

After perhaps a half hour, Jon appeared through the sliding glass door, cigarette in his mouth, and still very much naked. He cockily walked up to Daryl and me, delighting in his younger brother's horrified facial expression.

"Sorry it took so long," Jon said as he took a drag off his cigarette. "Lisa took a while to climax, then she wanted to suck my dick after. Anyway, welcome to mi casa and Happy Christmas."

Daryl's face turned red as he looked away. He was furious. "Can you please cover yourself?" He asked.

Jon raised his eyebrows and stood there, smirking at Dale and the other two staff who were standing at the other side of the pool area taking a smoke break. They all looked more than a little aroused at the sight of their naked employer, smiling and blushing at him. Jon turned and winked at me, then his green eyes settled on his younger brother and his expression hardened.

"Fine," he said to Daryl in a low voice. "I will cover myself."

With those words, he reached over to grab one of the white tablecloths off a nearby round table, and violently yanked it off, causing the poinsettia plant to crash to the ground. Then he wrapped the tablecloth around his waist. One of the staff members scurried over to the table to clean up the mess.

"Better?!" He snapped at Daryl, who looked ready to beat the shit out of his brother.

Daryl suddenly got up from his seat. "I can't fucking handle this," he muttered as he grabbed the luggage and headed toward the house. "I

need to take a piss and I need to get away from my ridiculous brother." I got up and followed him.

"Hey, Daryl, just ignore him," I said softly as we headed inside the house to use the loo. "He's just trying to get a rise out of you."

Once we were inside the house, Lisa came up to us, looking beautiful in a red halter dress. She smiled broadly.

"Hi, guys!" She said as she gave us each hugs and kisses. "Merry Christmas! So glad you could make it. Sorry about before. Jon gets a little... carried away!" She said with a giggle.

Daryl blushed and smiled. He had always had a bit of a crush on Jon's long time girlfriend-turned-fiancée, not that I could blame him. "It's quite alright," he assured. "Merry Christmas to you as well. It's so great to see you. You look...amazing."

"Well, thank you!" She purred before excitedly grabbing our hands. "We are gonna have SO much fun tonight. We scored some of the 'good stuff.'" She winked at us, then grabbed a cigarette from a nearby table and lit it with her designer lighter. Whether ciggies or marijuana, that girl loved to smoke.

The "good stuff" referred to the high potency weed that Jon reserved for special occasions. It was laced with only who-knew-what, and had a penchant for turning most anyone into a greened out, sex crazed

monster. In fact, the first time I had tried it, I had wound up with an erection that lasted for six hours and had lost most feeling in my legs. Aside from initial paranoia about the government recording my bedroom activities and what I feared was imminent paralysis in my lower extremities, the sex had been glorious, and I had wound up fucking no less than eight people that night.

Lisa helped us with our luggage and got us settled in our respective guest rooms upstairs, then she went downstairs to the kitchen to help the chef with the food. Along with being an actress and model, Lisa was a chef herself and loved to bake and cook. The chef, along with the other "help," had their own designated rooms downstairs, each of which had the amenities of a mini hotel room. Whenever Jon had a party, the staff, along with the other guests, were encouraged to stay the night to sleep off whatever debauchery would take place.

Once we had gotten settled we made our way back downstairs to relax in front of the tv before getting ready for the party, which wasn't starting for another hour or so. Jon joined us in the living room within a few minutes, and was wearing a robe. This time, he was smoking a joint instead of a cigarette.

"Care to do a little pre-gaming?" He asked Daryl and me with a smirk. "It's the good stuff."

Daryl and I nodded, figuring we could use a little relaxation after the previous drama. We each took several somewhat wimpy tokes, deciding it was best to wait for the other guests to come before getting totally plastered.

Feeling pleasantly stoned, Daryl, Jon and I went upstairs to get ready for the party. I had packed my usual "casual party" uniform, which consisted of a basic black button down shirt made of silk, fitted blue jeans in a dark rinse that hugged my bum, and black leather boots. I also wore a silver necklace that my wife had gotten me years ago, a designer watch Jon had given me for Christmas the year prior, and a few rings I had bought myself. I still wore my wedding ring, simply because I wasn't ready to let it go. I trimmed my beard, put some gel in my hair, and looked at myself in the mirror from multiple angles, deciding I looked good.

KNOCK, KNOCK.

I turned around to find a fully dressed Jon standing in the doorway of the room, looking at me with his eyebrows raised. He looked like he had stepped out of a magazine, with perfectly styled, golden brown hair with blond highlights, flawless airbrushed skin, freshly trimmed beard, and a just-applied spray tan that his personal assistant had helped him with. He was wearing what was undoubtedly a very expensive outfit, with name brand everything, and plenty of flashy jewelry featuring his birthstone, which happened to be diamonds. He wore a beige vest over an ivory button down shirt, khaki cargo pants, and ultra high-end designer boots in a beige snake print. His watch was ultra luxury, with diamonds on the face, and he wore diamond-adorned rings on most of his fingers. His necklace was white gold with a huge diamond pendant, and several bangle bracelets, all white gold and one of them with diamonds embedded throughout. He was holding clothes in his hand.

"How do I look, Jon?" I asked hopefully. "YOU look perfect as always."

He stepped into the room, sighing. "How about I give you a makeover?" He suggested in a tone that was a touch too cheerful to be genuine in its kindness.

My face fell and I got that all too familiar sinking feeling in my stomach. Nothing was ever good enough for my snobbish best mate. "I take it you don't like my outfit?" I asked exasperatedly.

He smiled condescendingly. "Well, I mean, it's fine if you're going to the local watering hole with Daryl, but these people coming to the party are mostly models and actors, and I just want to make sure you fit in." His smile broadened. "So, I got this outfit for you to try on. The clothes are too big for me but..." He looked me up and down before continuing. "But they MIGHT fit you."

I clenched my teeth, determined to stand my ground. "You know what, Jon? I think I'm good. I'm comfortable wearing what I have on."

I saw Jon's jaw clench and his eyes narrow slightly as he stared at me in silence. It was obvious he wasn't pleased. Then his expression suddenly changed to one of pleasantness again.

"Tell you what," he said with a bright smile. "I will leave this outfit here for you, in case you decide to try it on." He placed the clothes on a nearby chair.

I nodded, already deciding I wasn't going to wear his outfit to the party. "Sure, Jon."

He smiled and patted me on the arm. "Good choice. I know you will like the outfit and that it will look great on you. I think you and I can BOTH agree you can do better than that cheap black shirt and ugly jeans." His nose wrinkled as he looked at my somewhat pricy silk shirt, which I thought looked rather classy. And the dark rinse jeans were NOT ugly. He was just trying to control me, per usual, with "helpful suggestions."

"Thank you, Jon," I said through clenched teeth. "See you downstairs soon."

Jon stared at me for a few more seconds, trying to intimidate me. "Mhmm."

Then he turned and walked out of the room, wasting no time calling to his brother. "Hey Daryl! Want me to give you a makeover?"

Daryl suddenly staggered past my room, wearing only his boxers. He was already stoned from the small amount of weed he had smoked. It was comical how low his tolerance was. "Sure thing, big brother!" He slurred.

Jon laughed, putting his arm around him. "Awesome! You know, Daryl, you're so much easier to get on with when you're high. You should smoke more often."

Daryl burst out laughing, as did Jon, and then the two blokes disappeared into the bedroom next door. I knew that Daryl was going to be Jon's new "favorite person" for the night, since he had given into his whims and agreed to be his puppet. I, by contrast, would be shunned for daring to assert myself.

I decided to try on Jon's outfit, if only to confirm it wasn't my style and that it didn't fit properly. I was right on both counts. The "winter white" shirt was too tight in the shoulders and made me look washed out since, unlike my bronzed best mate, I lived in the chilly northeast and therefore lacked any sort of tan by perhaps October. And the khaki pants were too tight in the thighs and bum. I simply had a different build than Jon, and also weighed around twenty five pounds more than him. Aside from that, I refused to let him "win." I put my own outfit back on, refusing to be his clone. I stepped out onto the balcony and had a smoke, relaxing before the guests arrived.

Lisa knocked on my door after perhaps twenty minutes to let me know the guests were starting to come in and to join the party. I thanked her then made my way downstairs.

There were a handful of well-dressed men making their way into the living room, exchanging hugs and greetings with Jon, Daryl, and Lisa. One of the guests looked a bit like Jon and was complimenting the décor, and expressed regrets at his boyfriend Steve's inability to come to the party. He was tall, broadly built, with dark hair and a dark beard, and wore glasses. He wore a black shirt like mine, and dark jeans. We could have been twins, I thought to myself. So much for me not "fitting in." I'm glad I had kept my outfit on. Jon could kiss my arse.

Daryl was standing next to his brother, looking pretty damn close to a carbon copy of Jon but with different coloring and broader build. His dark brown hair was gelled and styled in a similar look to Jon's, and his facial hair trimmed to look just like his brother's as well. He wore a beige colored outfit I never would have imagined him wearing before. He even had a subtle spray tan, which made his blue eyes pop. I figured he must have been pretty high to agree to wear said outfit, nevermind the flashy jewelry. I had to admit, though, he looked pretty good, like a super model version of his usual boy-next-door self.

As I approached the group, Jon turned his head and saw I was wearing my original outfit. His "perfect host" smile immediately disappeared, and he glared at me something awful. I could feel his blazing green eyes burning a hole through me as I got closer, and I simply did my best to ignore him.

"Hello, everyone," I said. "I'm Ken."

The men extended their hands one by one, introducing themselves. The Jon lookalike,, named Jesse, looked me up and down with a huge smile.

"Oh my GOD," Jesse said as he put his hand to his chest. "I love your shirt! Is that silk?" He began to feel the material.

I nodded with a smile. "It is."

The other men complimented me on my outfit as well, asking if I was a model. I had said no but explained I was a personal trainer and ran a gym with Daryl. They were impressed and one of them, Chris, the blond actor and model who I would soon learn did fire-breathing and would visit Jon after his motorcycle accident several years later, talked about how he thought of getting his certification. That was when Jesse commented on my "adorable" jeans and "cute" necklace.

"Jon, where did you find a friend with such fabulous taste?" Jesse asked with a smile.

Jon, clearly uncomfortable, shrugged. "I guess I'm a good influence," he said with a smirk.

The men laughed, but I wasn't laughing. The bastard had a lot of nerve, having just bashed my outfit a mere twenty minutes prior, and now he was taking credit for my "fabulous taste."

Just then, Nick arrived. Irony of ironies, he was also wearing a black button down shirt with dark jeans.

"Hey, buddies!" Nick exclaimed when he saw me and Daryl, giving us huge hugs. "Great to see you guys again!" He then exchanged hugs and greetings with Jon and Lisa. Nick then looked me up and down and smiled broadly. "We are twins!" Then he noticed Jesse dressed similarly. "Or should I say the three of us are triplets! How are ya, buddy?" He asked Jesse.

"I'm fabulous," Jesse said with a flourish and a giggle. "I'm SO excited for tonight! It's gonna be super. Jon always throws amazing 'par-tars!'"

Jon looked ready to explode but was holding it together. "I try. Hey I don't know about you guys but I could use a drink, so why don't we all head outside?"

Everyone agreed and I stifled a smirk, satisfied that Jon was in the minority in terms of what was considered an "acceptable" outfit. He truly seemed jealous that I was getting positive attention from an outfit he didn't like. He lit a cigarette and gave me dirty looks every chance he got. Perhaps karma was biting my best mate in the arse for his judgmental comments, because perhaps five minutes into his glare-a-thon, Chris looked down at Jon's ivory shirt, which happened to have a new hole in it and what appeared to be some cigarette ashes.

"Oh, no," Chris said as he pointed to Jon's shirt. "Looks like you burned a hole in your shirt."

Jon looked down, noticing the fresh hole and ash stains. "Aw, bloody hell," he mumbled. "Thanks for letting me know," he said with a charming smile as he made his way back into the house, being sure to give me one more dirty look as he did so. That was when I decided to chance it.

"Jon, just so you know, there's a spare outfit in my bedroom," I called out in a sarcastic tone. "I decided not to wear it."

His green eyes grew wide and his face turned red. He looked ready to kick my arse in front of his friends. The others looked on as Jon stood in the doorway, a vein popping out of his forehead. His hand formed a fist. Was he really going to cause a scene?

Just when I thought he was going to lose his shit, his expression broke into a smile and his fist relaxed. Somehow, Jon was always able to keep his cool in front of company, vain prick that he was. "Oh, yes," he called out. "I almost forgot about that outfit. Thanks for reminding me, mate! See you all in a few." Then he winked before disappearing into the house. Within seconds, my phone buzzed.

Unsurprisingly, it was a text from Jon. "You stupid fuck. That was completely unnecessary. If it weren't for the fact that it was Christmas and there was a party, I would tell you to go back home tonight. You just embarrassed the shit out of me. Stay away from me the rest of the night!"

I swallowed. Despite his unpredictable attitude, Jon didn't usually get this angry. But I was pretty annoyed as well, and tired of his overbearing behavior. I quickly wrote back a reply. "I will stay away from you for the rest of the night if you agree to stop trying to control me. I'm not your modeling clay. Stop pressuring me to dress like you, or look like you. I have my own look. Deal with it."

Jon's reply was a "middle finger" emoji. I laughed since it was so infantile. Then I replied, "Merry fucking Christmas to you, too."

Then he fired back, "I want you to leave first thing tomorrow. Fuck the sightseeing. Daryl can stay. HE actually listens to me sometimes."

Me: "Listens? As in, he let you be his bitch tonight after you got him high? I think it's sick that you need him to be your twin. You and I both know there's no way he would wear that outfit if he were sober. It's not his style."

Jon: "Well I'm sorry for trying to get you boys to look more put together, and less like a couple of low class hobos. You're a few short years away from living in a trailer park. I can see it now. But point taken. You're going to pay for this. Conversation over."

I was completely livid. In fact, I was tempted to throw my phone in the swimming pool but opted for ordering a strong drink instead. I got myself a Long Island and sat at the bar, fuming as I nursed it. After a few moments, I felt a hand on my shoulder. It was Lisa.

"You ok?" She asked sweetly. "You seem... deep in thought."

I sighed. "Jon is mad at me because I wouldn't let him give me a makeover. Then we had a fight via text and now he's saying he wants me to leave tomorrow."

She smiled sympathetically. "Aw, honey. So sorry. He just likes to try and help, but he gets a little... enthusiastic in his approach at times. I'm also pretty sure he's annoyed that one of his favorite shirts got ruined and took it out on you. I can talk to him if you like?"

I took a sip of my drink and shrugged. "As far as his opinion of me is concerned, it certainly can't get any worse, so if you want to talk to him, be my guest."

Lisa nodded and gave me a hug. "He loves you," she assured in a soft voice. "He actually raves about you to his friends when you're not around, telling them how you're such a hard worker, and how good looking you are. He's even said he wishes he had your butt." She giggled, as did I. "But most importantly, he said you're an amazing friend with a huge heart."

"No kidding," I said with a smile, not really believing what she was saying but desperately wanting to.

Lisa nodded. "It's true. But let me go inside and chat with him for a while." She squeezed my shoulder and headed into the house.

After a while, more people arrived, and Lisa reappeared. She was a lovely hostess. Jon was nowhere to be found in the pool area but I figured he was somewhere in the house. Daryl took a seat next to me,

looking delightfully sloshed. We talked for a while then music started to play and people started to dance.

"Let's boogie!" Daryl slurred and he encouraged me to join him. Hesitantly, I got up and started dancing with some of the other guests.

Daryl, Jesse, and I started dancing in a little circle, occasionally knocking back nips of tequila that the staff had set out on the tables for the party goers. At some point, I noticed the staff had changed their red uniform tops to black tops, and wondered if Jon had made them change. He was such a vindictive bastard at times.

Nick was ready to join us in the circle, to complete what Jesse called our "black shirt gang," when people suddenly began approaching him asking for refills on drinks and food. Being a softie, he didn't have the heart to correct people to let them know he wasn't a staff member, so he went around fetching cocktails and appetizers for others. Jesse and I started to feel bad so we took a break from dancing and decided to help him out. A short time later, the music paused and Jon's voice came over the speakers.

"Attention, everyone!" Jon began, holding a microphone in one hand and a cocktail in the other. He had changed his shirt to the winter white one he had initially suggested I wore. Aside from it being a baggy fit, it looked rather good on him. "Hope you're having a fabulous time! I just wanted to give a special shout out to Nick and Ken, who SO graciously agreed to serve all of you lovely people food and drinks for the rest of the evening, so the other staff can get a bit of a break! In case you don't know who they are, they're two tall, sexy blokes with dark brown hair,

and wearing button down black shirts. They will be happy to take your orders. Enjoy the party, everyone, and merry Christmas!"

Everybody cheered and clapped. My heart was jackhammering in my chest as I looked around me, noticing the staff had changed outfits once more. Their outfits no longer matched and they were mingling with the crowd, dancing and throwing back shots of booze. One of the staff members had patted me on the back, thanking me, and I was in too much shock to respond. Some time prior to Jon's speech, Jesse had taken off his black shirt, revealing a dark blue, fitted tee shirt, perhaps not wanting to be mistaken for staff himself. This was obviously a plot, Jon's way of getting revenge on me for refusing to change my outfit, and his staff was undoubtedly in the dark about what had actually happened. I was in such a state of shock that I couldn't move or talk.

Jon made his way through the crowd with a cigarette in his mouth, handing wads of money to the staff members, who now looked like all the other partygoers. He was telling them to enjoy their holiday bonuses. Nick took the situation in stride, and continued hustling to pass out drinks and food to others. Like Lisa, he was a chef and server when he wasn't doing modeling and acting gigs, so this all came natural to him. I, by contrast, was no service person and had no desire to be. Nor was I going to be forced to become one, much less at the hands of my scumbag "best mate."

I felt so hurt and exploited, and had to get out of there. My eyes filled with tears of humiliation and I ran into the house and up the stairs to my room to pack my stuff and get the fuck home as soon as possible.

The tears came quickly and plentifully as I packed up my belongings and began putting them in my suitcase and overnight bag. What a fucking asshole Jon was. This was the last goddamn straw for me. I was sick of his games.

KNOCK, KNOCK.

The door was shut for obvious reasons. I wiped my tears away and cleared my throat.

"Who is it?" I asked.

"It's Lisa. Can I come in?"

I sighed, rather relieved it was her and not Jon. I walked to the door and opened it.

Her expression went from cheerful to concerned as soon as she saw my tear streaked face. I generally kept my emotions in check so she wasn't used to seeing me crying.

"Are you ok?" Lisa asked sweetly as she put her hand on my shoulder. "Jon wanted me to check on you. He saw you run into the house and was concerned. He also wanted to apologize to you about before because he thinks he overreacted." She lit a cigarette.

I sighed and sat down on the bed, putting my head in my hands as I began to cry again. She put down her cigarette then wrapped her arm around me and took her hand in mine.

"What's going on, honey?"

I wiped my eyes. "I need to go home."

"Oh my goodness. How come?"

"That thing that happened back there with Nick and me being appointed the new 'help?' That was too much for me. I never agreed to do that. Looks like Jon gave the staff black shirts to wear so most of the guests would mistake me for staff, and before I knew it, I was waiting on people, and for FREE. I guess this was Jon's way of punishing me for not wearing the outfit he had suggested."

Lisa knew full well how Jon could be and was also good at handling him, so I felt comfortable telling her all this. She gasped.

"Oh my god, Ken! No, that's not what happened. It's a misunderstanding. It's no wonder you're so upset, though. I would be too. But that's not what happened."

I looked at her. "How do you know?"

"Well, Jon saw you and Nick serving guests and he wasn't sure why. I wasn't sure either. So he approached Nick and asked him about it, thanking him for helping but telling him he didn't have to, and to relay the same message to you. Nick insisted, saying it was no problem and that the staff needed a break anyway. So, Jon interpreted it to mean that you and Nick were volunteering to serve others for the night, and I had assumed the same up until now. Anyway, Jon wanted to make that announcement as a 'thank you,' and was going to give each of you guys a holiday bonus for your effort. Just like he had done with the staff. I had heard him talking about it to one of the other staff members.

"As for the black shirts, Dale told me that two of the staff had spilled wine on their bright red tops, and there weren't any more clean ones in that color, which meant all staff had to change tops and wear a different color. You see, Jon likes the staff to all have matching tops so people know that they are staff, and plus he thinks it's a professional look. They would typically all be wearing green as a 'backup color' since it's Christmas. But they didn't have enough green shirts for everyone so they opted for black, because that was the only color they had in the necessary quantity.

"Of course, I didn't get a chance to tell Jon this little detail about the color change, so there's no way he would know that you guys were being mistaken for staff due to wearing black shirts. And apparently Nick didn't think to tell Jon the guests mistook you guys for staff when he spoke to him. I had no idea that was the case myself, until you told me just now. I guess some details are important." She winked, then picked up her ciggy and took a hearty drag, holding in the smoke.

I sat there in silence for a few moments, digesting what she had said. It was a relief to know it was a misunderstanding, but given Jon's history of bullying and passive aggressive behavior, I couldn't always tell what his intentions were.

"I suppose that's a fair explanation," I said flatly. "It's just...he's hard to understand at times. I don't always know what to make of the things he says and does."

Lisa nodded sympathetically. "I know, and I'm so sorry this happened," she soothed as smoke trailed out of her mouth and nose. "Like I said, Jon loves you. He just gets a little ahead of himself."

KNOCK, KNOCK, KNOCK.

Jon was standing in the doorway with a guilty look on his face.

"May I come in?" He asked sheepishly.

I rolled my eyes and sighed. "It's your house," I muttered.

Jon sat in the chair across from me and looked at me with a gentle smile. "I just overheard the conversation with you and Lisa," he began in a soft voice. "I am so sorry for the misunderstanding, and for the way I

behaved, and for arguing with you via text over such a stupid thing. I admit I was very pissed that my shirt got ruined so I snapped at you, which wasn't fair. But...did you honestly think I would plot something like that to humiliate and hurt you? That I would make my staff members dress like you to fool the guests into thinking you were hired help?" He bit his lip, looking genuinely upset that I interpreted the events the way I did, and that I was in such pain as a result.

"I wasn't sure, to be quite truthful," I replied with a sigh.

He shook his head sadly. "No, Ken. As Lisa told you, I had no idea they had even changed their uniforms. I had just come outside after helping in the kitchen and spotted Nick running around juggling platters of food and trays full of drinks, and saw you doing the same thing at the far end of the pool area. I understand why you're so upset. And I'm sorry for the things I said about your outfit, it was petty of me. You should wear what makes you comfortable. And clearly, my concerns about you fitting in were unwarranted, because at least two other actor/model guests were wearing the same damn thing." He gave a light chuckle, as did I. Then his expression once again turned serious. "I was wrong. I fucked up, mate. I admit it." He looked at me with such sad eyes, it was obvious his words were sincere.

I nodded. "Yes you did, Jon," I muttered. "You fucked up big time. I was horrified. To the point I started packing my things." I motioned to the overnight bag and suitcase on the floor.

Jon took my hand in his and squeezed it. "I don't want you to go home early. I want us to celebrate Christmas together as best mates. Will you

stay, Ken? Please?" He looked at me with those lovely green eyes and sweet smile. The bastard was charming as all hell. So as tempted as I was to get the hell out of there, I began to falter.

I sniffled and ran my fingers through my hair. "Yeah. I suppose I will stay, but you need to stop picking on me for how I look and dress. This is not the first time. I'm a grown man, and it's my business."

Jon nodded. "Agreed. I want to make it up to you. Which is why I'm changing into a black shirt and jeans. AND I'm going to help serving the guests so the staff - both real and imagined - can get a break!"

I laughed. "You don't have to do all that."

He shook his head. "I want to. Now, I don't actually own a solid black shirt, but I do have black with white stripes, which should hopefully be acceptable. The dark rinse jeans and black boots aren't a problem. I will go change right now, mate. Be right back." He left the room to change his clothes.

I laughed once again, amused by the idea that Jon wanted to dress like me for a change, instead of trying to make me dress like him. I turned to Lisa, who was smiling sweetly at me. "Thank you."

She kissed me on the cheek. "Of course."

Within a few minutes, Jon reappeared, wearing a very classy ensemble that included a fitted black shirt with subtle white stripes, designer dark wash blue jeans in a flattering fit, and a gorgeous pair of black leather cowboy style boots that sported a slightly pointed toe and intricate embroidery along the sides. They undoubtedly cost a fortune, but they suited him. He had kept his jewelry, which added an even more high end touch to the outfit.

"What do you think?" Jon asked with a sexy smirk.

I tilted my head. "You can unbutton the shirt a wee bit," I said with a wink.

Jon tilted his head back in laughter. "I think that's a good idea."

My best mate loved to show extra skin whenever he could, so he tended to wear his shirts half-buttoned whenever possible. He would often pair this look with pendant necklaces that fell to mid-chest, thus calling even more attention to his pecs. The girls loved it, as did many boys.

Jon undid several buttons on his shirt and came in closer to me, then knelt before me as I sat on the bed. There was lust in his glowing green eyes. Slowly, he ran his hand up and down my front, savoring the feel of my silk shirt.

"Perhaps YOU could use some... unbuttoning," he said in a sexy whisper, a smirk on his face. Then he began undoing the buttons on my shirt one by one. As that was going on, Lisa unbuttoned and unzipped my pants, and began sucking on my nipples. My dick got hard very quickly. I began to moan. Then Jon pulled down my pants and my boxers, freeing my erect manhood from the confines of my black cotton knickers. He wrapped his strong hand around my cock, fondling me gently. I began to buck my hips.

"How about a little 'stocking stuffer'?" Jon quipped as he kissed the tip of my penis then slowly lowered his mouth onto it. I closed my eyes and lay back onto the bed, succumbing to the pleasure. As this was going on, Lisa continued to suck and bite my nipples, and occasionally kissed me passionately on the mouth. I fondled her full breasts, delighting in their shape and the softness of her skin. Between gorgeous Lisa devouring my upper body and letting me touch her tits, and Jon pleasuring my manhood as if his life depended on it, I began to have one of the most intense orgasms I'd had in months. I groaned and grunted as sweat covered my body, and within minutes, I ejaculated into Jon's mouth.

He abruptly lifted his head up and grabbed the back of Lisa's head. They exchanged a feverish kiss, and it was obvious he was feeding her my load. She swallowed without hesitation, smiling and licking her lips afterwards. It was so sexy and kinky.

"I'm craving a smoke," Lisa purred, then grabbed a pack of full flavored menthols from the nightstand, offering Jon and me one as well. We accepted and the three of us lit up. Jon and Lisa were such heavy smokers that just about every room in the house had a pack of ciggies in it just in case a craving hit, which, in their case, happened about every ten minutes. Between the two of them, it was common to go through a

carton a day. They smoked quickly as well; in the time it took me to smoke one cigarette, Jon and Lisa smoked two, lighting fresh ones with the lit end of the old, taking long drags and holding in the smoke for a minute or longer.

They helped me get redressed, smiling at me sexily as they did so. Within seconds, my shirt was rebuttoned and my undies and pants were back on. Jon rose to his feet and helped me up from the bed. We stood facing each other for a few moments. His eyes were calm, and his gentle smile sincere.

"You feel better now?" He asked as he placed his hands on my shoulders.

I nodded. "Yes, I do."

He smiled broadly and enveloped me in a warm embrace. "Good. I'm glad we kissed and made up. I love you."

"I love you too, Jon," I said as I backed away from him and turned to Lisa to give her a hug.

"We BOTH love you," Lisa said sweetly as she hugged me. Just then, Jon snuck in and wrapped his arms around us both.

"Group hugs are the best," Lisa said with a giggle.

"Agreed," Jon and I said in unison, and the three of us laughed.

"Now let's party!" Jon exclaimed with a huge grin as he held out his hand to me.

I eagerly took his hand, and Lisa ran ahead of us, giddy as a little girl. We both laughed at her level of enthusiasm. It always amazed me how quickly things could change when hanging out with Jon. It was like being on a rollercoaster. There was never a dull moment and sometimes things got pretty stressful, but when push came to shove, we always wound up having a blast.

The three of us rushed down the stairs like hyperactive school children and made our way back outside to the party. We hadn't been gone that long, but there were now a number of guests in the pool, and many others were shirtless or wearing bathing suits.

The music was playing louder than it had been at the beginning of the party, and the overall energy was very cheerful. There were about forty people in attendance, and Jon checked in with each one, making sure that everyone was well fed and taken care of in the drinks department. I saw him fetch cocktails and snacks for some of the guests, and at one time he knocked back shots with Dale, who looked more than happy to have a break from tending bar. One couldn't help but get swept away in the joyous mood, and before long, I was dancing and drinking like there was no tomorrow. And yes, MY shirt did wind up coming off!

Daryl was completely shitfaced but was having a great time. He was now wearing swim trunks and was sitting at the edge of the pool with his legs in the water and a drink in his hand, occasionally splashing Jesse and Nick, who were horsing around in the shallow end.

Jon and Lisa stripped down to their swimsuits, so I decided to do likewise. Despite the fact my black knickers weren't swim trunks, they could pass for such, so I decided to say, "fuck it." I barely had a moment's peace before Daryl got up and stood behind me, swaying slightly but managing to remain upright. He had a goofy smile on his face.

"Guess what?" Daryl asked.

"What?" I replied.

Then he pushed me into the pool. I fell backwards and made a huge splash. To my surprise, the water was nice and warm, it felt great. I began to laugh and splash at Daryl, good naturedly calling him names as he walked back into the house to go to the loo. Then Jon pushed Lisa into the pool, jumping in after her as she squealed in delight.

A crowd gathered around the pool, and more people began jumping in, until everyone was elbow to elbow in the water. Women began taking off their bathing suits and men discarded their swim trunks, and this happened in AND out of the pool. I eventually ditched my own knickers and it wasn't long before I was swapping spit with random girls. I was literally elbow deep in tits and pussies, and I said a silent prayer to both

God and Father Christmas for making good on a wish that, up until that point, had only been a fantasy.

Things only got better when Lisa surprised me from behind, grabbing my bum and my penis at the same time. I turned around to find her naked, and became mesmerized by her hardened nipples. Jon and Nick looked on, encouraging us to continue as they fondled themselves in the water. She kissed me aggressively, and guided my hand down to her newly waxed vagina. I rubbed her smooth outer lips before slipping my finger inside her, pumping in and out. She moaned with pleasure, continuing to give me a hand job from beneath the water. I closed my eyes and enjoyed the feeling of being masturbated in the warm pool. It wasn't long before she wrapped her legs around me and lined up my manhood with her opening. I looked over at Jon, who smiled and nodded his approval. That was when we began shagging in the water, in front of forty people.

Our activities were more than a little "inspiring," because it wasn't long before half the party was engaging in either full intercourse or foreplay, both in and out of the pool. Jon started a sort of sex chain in the shallow end, with Nick at the front. Then Jon got behind him, fucking him anally, then Chris got behind Jon, and finally Jesse behind Chris. Despite not being especially attracted to most men, I couldn't help but find the impromptu foursome sexy. I began to kiss Lisa hard on the mouth and started to play with her arsehole, as my spare arm remained locked under her bum. She locked her legs around me more tightly, riding my dick in the heated water, to the point that we made literal waves.

The pool water became choppy as more and more people began to fuck in it, approaching orgasm within perhaps minutes. It was surreal witnessing dozens of people orgasming at approximately the same time,

almost otherworldly. I felt like I was inside a washing machine as bodies began climaxing around me and it wasn't long before Lisa was doing likewise. The sensation of her pussy gripping my dick in the throes of orgasm was enough for my own cock to explode. I pulled out at the last minute, took a breath, and ducked beneath the surface, delighting in the sight of my semen floating into the chlorine, a sea of naked bums serving as a backdrop. Lisa met me underwater, insisting on sucking out whatever she could from my still semi-erect member. Then she smiled and kissed me. We resurfaced together, laughing breathlessly at our shared rapture. I was ready to exit the pool to grab a drink and a smoke when suddenly I felt a tap on my shoulder.

"Will you blow me?" Jon asked with raised eyebrows. "I never climaxed. Nick's bum is too loose." He smirked.

Before I could answer, Dale handed me a martini, which I accepted graciously and guzzled within seconds. He laughed as he took back the empty glass, impressed. Little did he know, in order to suck off a man in front of a crowd of people, I needed some liquid courage.

I nodded to Jon. "Ok I'm ready now." Then I began to get out of the pool, ready to baptize one of the chaise lounges. He grabbed my arm, stopping me.

"No, mate," he said with a chuckle. "In the pool. Underwater. Understand?" He raised his eyebrows and his eyes got that familiar sinister look.

I felt my stomach heave, knowing damn well that sucking him off underwater would lead to him holding me under, refusing to let me come up for air until he climaxed. It was nerve wracking enough to deal with that shit one-on-one in a bathtub or jacuzzi, but quite another when a crowd was looking on. But the buzz from the martini spoke louder than my desire to keep my dignity, so I sighed and nodded.

"Ok, Jon," I said shakily.

Jon grinned at me sexily. Just then, Lisa swam up to him and whispered something in his ear. Jon's eyes grew wide and he looked legitimately scared, like a deer in headlights. The man had nerves of steel, so he rarely looked frightened or got nervous. In fact, I had only seen that look on his face once or twice in our 30 year long friendship. He forced a cocky smile and turned to look at her.

"Can we talk about it later, darling?" He whispered. "I'm just not ready to do that yet."

Lisa sulked but agreed. My imagination ran wild and I couldn't help but wonder what my seemingly fearless daredevil best mate could not be "ready" for.

I looked at Jon and wrapped my arms around his waist. Then I kissed him, doing my best to drown out the cheering and clapping around me. His body initially felt tense but then he melted against me, returning my kiss and my embrace. I ran one of my hands down his front until I had reached his penis, which was only semi-hard. I continued to jerk him off

as I kissed him, and his manhood eventually hardened. I began taking deep breaths as I left a trail of kisses down his front. I took one final deep breath before disappearing beneath the surface. I knelt down on the surface of the pool then grabbed his cock and began to suck him off, playing with his bum as I did so. His body was trembling and I wasn't sure whether it was due to fear from whatever Lisa had whispered to him or arousal, or a combination. I expected him to push on my shoulders, making it harder for me to resurface but he simply stood there and gently cradled my head as I fellated him. This surprised me but I was able to remain relaxed as I remained underwater for at least five minutes. His climax was rather wimpy, to where I almost wasn't sure if he had simply gone soft. I ascended to the surface, leaving another trail of kisses up his front until I reached his face. I could hear the crowd cheering and my name being chanted but I didn't dare look anywhere but straight.

My best mate once again looked panicked, like he had seen a ghost. He was shaking slightly and his breathing was rapid, more than it should have been, even for having orgasmed. He once again forced a smile and thanked me.

"You alright, mate?" I asked.

Jon nodded quickly, and it was obvious he was doing his best to appear more relaxed. "Oh yes. I think I had a touch too much weed. Happens even to seasoned potheads like me." He winked.

I hadn't seen him smoke pot in a number of hours but I also hadn't seen him every second of the party either, so I figured he was being partially

honest. I was pretty sure, however, that he wasn't telling me the entire truth about what was wrong. His whole countenance had changed after Lisa had whispered in his ear, so I had a feeling his frightened appearance was related to that. My suspicions would prove correct later that night.

It was getting late, and most of the guests took cabs home. Aside from me and Daryl, only a select few planned on spending the night: Nick, Chris, Jesse, and the staff. We made it inside, intent on getting high one more time before bed.

I walked inside the downstairs loo to take a piss, when I was greeted with a semi-conscious Daryl, lying naked on the floor. His clothes lay in a pile next to him. Alarmed, I knelt down and shook him.

"Daryl, buddy, you ok?" I asked as I draped a towel over him.

He opened his eyes and looked up at me sleepily. "I don't feel so good," he slurred. "I took off my clothes because I felt hot and I didn't want to throw up on Jon's outfit."

I rubbed his back. "It's ok, mate. You had a lot to smoke as well as drink. Do you want some water?"

Daryl nodded. "Yes, please."

Just then, Jon popped in the doorway and came into the bathroom. His expression was sympathetic. "Hey, little brother," he said soothingly as he knelt down. "I was wondering where you had disappeared off to. How you feeling?"

Daryl looked ready to cry. "I'm sick, Jon," he said with a reddening face. "I feel like I gotta puke."

"Aww, Daryl, I'm sorry," Jon said softly, pouring him a cup of water from the sink and holding it to his lips. He took tiny sips. "Well, if you need to throw up, it's ok. I'm not going to judge you. I admit, I egged you on tonight, I was a bad influence." He winked.

"Nah," Daryl mumbled, then lifted his head, finally noticing he was wearing a towel. "Oh, bloody hell," he muttered. "Thanks for covering me up, Ken. And I'm sorry I got naked, Jon. I just didn't wanna ruin the beautiful clothes you gave me in case I got sick. Plus I felt hot."

Jon nodded and smiled gently. "It's alright, brother. I'm here to take care of you. Ken is here too. You're in good hands. Besides, you saw me naked when you first arrived, so we are even." He winked.

Despite his discomfort, Daryl laughed weakly. "True. Hey I have a favor. Can you help me off the floor? I wanna... I wanna take a bath."

"I can do that," Jon said, and began to position Daryl's arm around his back. I acted as spotter, but Jon was able to hoist him to his feet. He was

about to collapse but luckily Jon and I caught him, and had him sit on the toilet while we filled the tub with water and bubble bath.

"Oh, shit," Daryl slurred as he began to wretch. "I need a bucket!"

I quickly grabbed a garbage can from under the sink and handed it to Daryl. He threw up in the garbage can several times, getting some of it on his chin and on the floor as he did so. I grabbed a towel and cleaning supplies and got to work, and Jon comforted his brother, who began to cry and apologize for the mess.

"I'm so sorry, Jon," he said through tears as he wiped his chin with a tissue. "I'm too old to be doing this. I'm a grown ass man, 25 years old. I shouldn't be puking myself."

"It's ok, Daryl," Jon said in a kind voice. "Everyone gets sick. Don't you remember who took care of you when you were sick from chemo as a little boy? This is no different. And it doesn't matter that you're 25 and I'm 30. No matter our ages, we all occasionally get sick and need to be looked after. You will always be my little brother and I will always take care of you. Now do you want some more water?" He rubbed his shoulder as he refilled the water cup and held it out to him, then grabbed a bottle of disinfectant to help me with cleaning.

Daryl sniffled and nodded. "Yes, thank you," and he took the cup, taking sips from it.

I piped up as Jon and I cleaned the floor and garbage pail. "If it's any consolation, I'm 31 years old and I've already thrown up on myself a number of times this year!"

Daryl laughed, as did Jon. The bathtub was almost full with water so I turned off the nozzle. After a few trips to the garbage can outside Jon's house, the bathroom was once again clean. We helped Daryl off the toilet and assisted with him getting into the tub, making sure to hold up the towel that he had been covered in, to protect his modesty.

"I feel like a toddler," Daryl commented with a chuckle as he carefully lowered himself into the sudsy water.

Jon smiled warmly. "No judgment here, little brother," he assured as he handed him a washcloth. "You're talking to a couple of professional drunks here. There isn't a single person in this room, or in this house for that matter, who hasn't been where you are right now. Sometimes we all need someone to take care of us, and that's alright."

Daryl nodded as he laid back in the tub, when suddenly he began to break down crying again.

Jon and I knelt down beside him, asking in unison what was wrong.

"I have nobody," Daryl said through sobs. "Since my wife and I divorced, I feel so alone. We got married too young, I think. 22 is too young. We should have waited but I loved her and she loved me, but not in the way

I wanted her to love me. Three years of marriage down the toilet. How was I supposed to know she was a lesbian? I had no bloody idea."

Jon placed his hand on Daryl's shoulder. "Aww, Daryl," He soothed. "This wasn't your fault. She simply didn't tell you certain things, and that's on her. And you were a great partner to her. With regard to sexuality, people go through what they assume is a phase and go on with their life like nothing is 'off,' and they deny themselves what turns out to be a legitimate part of their identity. Elizabeth's love for you was real, but things got to a point where she could no longer keep her sexuality a secret, and when the truth came out, it hurt. I know how hard it is to lose someone you love, to any number of circumstances. But you're lovable. And you're NOT alone. You have Ken, and mum, and dad...and you have me." Jon smiled warmly at his brother.

Daryl sat there sniffling, absorbing his brother's words. "Thank you, Jon," he muttered. "I appreciated when you flew out in August to comfort me after I called you up crying with the earth shattering news that Elizabeth was gay and wanted a divorce. I was so lost, I didn't know what to do with myself. But you really took the reigns, and helped me with everything from legal matters, to finances, to grocery shopping, and taking me out to get me good and shitfaced." He chuckled then looked at me. "And you, too, Ken. You were so helpful, taking care of the gym while I sulked at home for days, listening to me cry and moan, and bringing me my favorite beer."

I smiled. "You had done the same for me when I had lost my wife several months prior. And you had the displeasure of watching me try to drown myself, and then had to witness your brother nearly drown trying to save me."

Jon reached out and grabbed my hand, his eyes misted over with emotion. "I would do it again in a heartbeat," he said softly. "You're worth risking my life for."

My eyes filled with tears and I gave Jon a hug. Daryl smiled at the scene, wiping away fresh tears. It was nice to have this little bonding moment with my two best mates, and to see Jon's nurturing side come out once again. For all his flaws, he was a wonderful caretaker, and great in a crisis.

Daryl took a washcloth and a bar of soap and began cleaning himself, and the three of us started talking about plans for Christmas Eve as well as Christmas Day. The clock on the wall revealed it was after midnight, which meant Christmas Eve had arrived. After a few more minutes, Daryl rinsed the soap off his body and announced he felt better, ready to exit the tub. Jon and I stood by and held up the towel while he successfully got up from the tub, then took the towel to dry off. He let us help him step out of the tub, then once he had dried off, Jon gave him a robe that he put on. He seemed a touch more steady than before but still needed some help, so Jon and I each took one of Daryl's hands and began walking him up the stairs to his room.

Jon turned down the bed and I helped him to get situated, making sure he had a bottle of water next to him on the nightstand, and his cell phone near him in case he needed anything. Jon sat on the bed to talk to him.

"I just want to say, I'm very proud of you," he began in a soft voice. "I'm impressed with the way you run the gym with Ken and keep things organized even when your personal life goes to shit. You're one of the strongest people I know. And I don't always express it properly, or at all, for that matter, but I wanted you to know that, even though we argue a lot and have misunderstandings, I do love you." He smiled sweetly at his younger brother.

Daryl appeared shocked but also moved by Jon's words. "I love you, too, Jon," he whispered, sounding rather choked up. "But I have a favor. I might not remember much when I wake up, so can you record a video of you saying what you just said, and send it to me? Because I want to remember it. Also, this isn't like you, and I want to make sure what you're telling me isn't a drunken hallucination." He winked.

Jon and I both laughed heartily. "Sure thing," Jon said, and took his phone out of his pocket to record a video. Once finished, he texted it to Daryl. "There. Now you have proof."

Daryl laughed sleepily. "Thanks. I had fun tonight. Thank you for having me over, Jon." He then looked at me. "And thank you Ken, for being a great business partner and friend, and travel buddy."

I patted him on the arm. "Any time, Daryl."

Jon and I took turns giving Daryl a hug, told him goodnight, then I turned off the light next to the bed. Then Jon shut the door to the room. He looked at me, giving a relieved sigh.

"Now that that's all done, want to see what got me so scared before?" He asked with raised eyebrows.

I nodded. "Yes, I've been curious."

Jon walked down the hall and opened the door to the room he referred to as the "sex dungeon." It was painted a sensual deep purple, and was lined wall to wall with an assortment of chains, whips, knives, bondage rope, and so on. At the far end of the room was a king size bed with a black velour bedspread and matching satin sheets. The curtains were suitably black, and designed to blot out all light from outside. Candle holders were built into the walls, and there was a beautiful chandelier hanging from the ceiling. It was the middle of the room, however, that caught my eye.

There was a black cage, similar in style to a dog crate, that was situated in the very center of the room. It was large enough for two people. Jon walked to it and lay his hand on the top.

"This bundle of black steel is the source of many a nightmare for yours truly," Jon admitted. "You see, for all my daring ways, I'm claustrophobic. Lisa is, too, but not as badly as me. She has spent time curled up in this cage, and has worked her way up to three hours. I have spent time in it as well, but only lasted two hours before frantically breaking my way out. I injured myself doing so. I was home alone, and had asked Lisa to lock me in there before she went out with friends. Between bending the wire with my fingers, punching at the door with my knuckles, then kicking it open with my bare feet, I wound up rather

bruised and scraped up. But I had to get out of there. I felt like I was being buried alive, and that's my biggest fear."

I nodded sympathetically. "I can understand that. I'm not fond of closed in spaces, either. But what exactly did Lisa whisper to you earlier?"

"That's just what I was about to tell you," he said with a sigh. "She wants to spend the night in the cage with me. Now, she's told me she feels safer with me in there with her, but I don't feel safer with her in there with me. We had sex in the cage recently and she wanted to lay in there with me after, but I tell you, if you think it felt cramped with just me in the cage? It felt even worse with her there. I couldn't get air. I had to leave. So the idea of spending the whole night with her in this tiny metal box, trying not to panic in front of her, unable to sleep? I just can't stomach it."

I digested what he had just said. "Do you think it would help if you had someone outside the cage, who can let you out if you need? This is how my parents got me to sleep in a crib. It was my earliest memory: I would cry if I was left alone in there, but if one of them sat by my crib until I fell asleep, I was fine. My mum would occasionally hold my hand through the bars. Sometimes the idea of being able to escape is just as appealing as actually escaping. Anyway, this was just an idea I had. What do you think?"

Jon rubbed his chin. "I would feel like a bit of a pussy, needing a babysitter when I'm lying in a cage with my fiancée. But I might do that, especially if it's the only way I can last the night. The problem is, finding someone who is willing to do that for me."

I smiled and raised my hand. "We can do it as early as tonight, if you like."

Jon grinned broadly. "No shit! Thanks, mate! I best tell Lisa, and we can get started. I know she will be pleased. And I reckon I will need some chemical help to get through this."

I nodded. "Understood."

Jon and I left the "dungeon" and met up with Lisa, who was downstairs in the living room having a drink and smoking a cigarette in front of the TV. Nick, Chris, and Jesse lay on nearby sofas, dead to the world.

"We are all set for tonight," Jon said to Lisa as he fixed himself a drink. "We are spending the night together in the cage."

Lisa got up from the couch and gave him a big hug. "That's great! I'm so happy!" What made you change your mind?"

Jon swallowed. "Ken said he would stay in the room with me. It's the only way I can do it. Somehow the idea of having the option to escape gives me comfort, as does the moral support."

Lisa smiled at Jon then at me. "I think that's a great idea. Whatever helps you be more comfortable."

Jon quickly knocked back his drink then took a hit off his bong, and the three of us went upstairs. We washed up briefly then made our way to the dungeon. Lisa wasted no time undressing Jon, who did likewise to her. I ripped off my own clothes, and within seconds, the three of us were all over each other on the king sized bed, kissing and fondling each other until Jon and I were hard as rocks, and Lisa was as wet as a faucet. Jon had Lisa get on all fours, then he grabbed a straw, razor, and baggie of coke from the nightstand. He cut himself a line on Lisa's bum and looked at me with a smirk.

"The forecast called for a wee bit of snow," he quipped. "Who says you can't have a 'white Christmas' in Southern California?"

I chuckled at his joke, as did Lisa, who wasn't overly fond of Jon's cocaine habit, but tolerated it as long as he didn't use it too often. He happened to use coke almost daily but out of respect for her, he usually got high alone, and she was none the wiser. Jon quickly snorted the line off Lisa's arse, then offered to cut a line for me. I agreed, figuring it was a holiday. I snorted the line off her bum, quickly feeling a rush and also becoming incredibly horny.

Just then, Jon began choking Lisa from behind with one hand while pinning her arms behind her back with the other. I positioned myself on my back so she could suck me off while Jon fucked her doggie style. It was a glorious romp of the impromptu variety, and the three of us orgasmed at almost exactly the same time. After Lisa had swallowed my

load, Jon sucked the cum out of Lisa's pussy and fed it to me. I managed not to gag as he kissed me aggressively, forcing his tongue deep into my mouth.

Still breathless, Jon fetched the three of us cigarettes, which we smoked rapidly. Afterwards, he got off the bed and walked over to the cage, opening the door with a flourish. He looked at Lisa with a sexy grin.

"Ladies first," he said in a sexy voice.

Lisa nodded and crawled right inside. "Come join me!" She said as she looked up at him, bare breasts still looking perky, even as she crouched down in the cage.

Jon smiled sexily and I knew he was stalling for time. He walked over to the nightstand and opened the drawer, grabbing a blue pill, which turned out to be a benzo, and the bottle of vodka that sat next to the baggie of coke. He washed down the pill with a couple of hearty swigs then slammed the bottle back down. He must have finished a third of the bottle's contents.

"Woohoo!" Jon called out as he approached the cage. "Nothing like having a threesome with Bennie and Belvedere to go with my threesome with Lisa and Ken." The three of us laughed. "NOW I'm ready."

He ducked down and got inside the cage, cuddling with Lisa. I got comfortable in the bed, then turned down the lights. The dungeon was equipped with dimmer switches on all the lights, including the lamps on the nightstands, so as to create a sensual glow. I also figured Jon would feel less claustrophobic if the room wasn't pitch black.

I began to doze, when, after about a half hour, I noticed some snoring coming from the cage. I sat up, curious who it was.

"That's Lisa," Jon whispered with a chuckle, somehow knowing what I was thinking. "Once she's out, she's out."

I laughed quietly in reply. "I had a hunch it was her. How are YOU?"

Jon sighed. "Can you grab me my smokes?" He asked.

I chuckled, getting up to fetch him his cigarettes and an ashtray, then sat down on the floor next to him. "That good, huh?"

Jon smiled sadly, letting me put the ciggy in his mouth and light it through the bars. "It's gonna be a long night," he muttered.

"I'm here," I said as I took a drag.

"I know," he said with a gentle smile. "Thank you."

We smoked in silence for a bit, then when he was done, I took the cigarette from his mouth and put it out in the ashtray.

"Did you want me to leave a few cigarettes and a lighter in the cage with you?"

Jon nodded. "Yes, that would be great, and you can leave the ashtray outside the cage as well. I'm sure I will crave a smoke again by morning, and I don't expect to get much sleep."

I obliged then got back into bed. My body was so tired from the traveling and the events of the day that I began falling asleep rather quickly. But, as was typically the case after a night of drinking, my bladder woke me up within two hours of falling asleep. I got up and staggered my way to the loo, quickly taking a piss before returning to the dungeon. I stopped by the cage to check in with Jon, who, unsurprisingly, was still wide awake and had a pained expression on his face. I knelt down to talk to him.

"You doing ok?" I soothed.

Jon shook his head. "I feel like I've jumped out of a plane, free-falling towards earth, and I have no parachute," he whispered. "I want to scream, or break out of this glorified coffin, but I'm paralyzed. And I want to be brave for Lisa. It's so stupid because I've done so many bold

things - bungee jumping, BASE jumping, free diving, skydiving, mountain climbing with no harness, walking a tightrope between tall buildings. I've even worn a bloody wingsuit while flying above the pyramids of Giza, for God's sakes. When doing my acting gigs, I've done my own stunts. I'm no pussy. Until now."

I smiled sympathetically, then grabbed a blanket and pillows from the bed and arranged them on the floor in front of the cage, so I was right next to Jon.

"What are you doing?" Jon asked with an amused grin.

I lay in front of him, blanket draped over me, then slid as much of my hand as I could through the bars. "I'm going to be your parachute."

Jon smiled softly then gradually took my hand into his. We lay there in silence for a few moments, just gazing into each other's eyes. It felt comforting - two best mates, one in a cage and the other on the floor, keeping each other company in the dark on Christmas Eve. Jon fell asleep within minutes, and I followed not long after.

Christmas Day, back in the present...

I woke up with a start, still expecting to be in Jon's dungeon, but finding myself back in my own room, in my own house. I got up and walked into the living room to check on Anna, who was spending what would be the

first of seven nights in the cage. I knelt down, and I saw she was awake. She met my gaze, and I saw how scared she was.

Without any words, I grabbed some pillows and blankets and set up camp next to the cage. Then I held out my hand, and smiled at her. She smiled back, and took my hand in hers. Just like what had happened with Jon, she fell asleep quickly, finding my presence comforting.

Several hours later, on day one of slave week...

The sound of chirping birds woke me up. I rose from the floor slowly, feeling slightly sore in my low back and stiff in my neck. I packed up the pillows and blankets, returning them to the couch before going to the loo to take a piss. Then I went to the kitchen to cook breakfast for Anna and me.

As I made the eggs and French toast, I thought of what I would do to Anna for day one of slave week.I had tinkered with the idea of making her cook breakfast for me, but decided to surprise her with a nice meal since it was Christmas. Jon would probably argue that I was being too easy on her, that I should have awakened her by banging on the cage and demanding she cook a full breakfast. But I wasn't Jon. In fact, I believed my flashback dream was a reminder that it was important to maintain my own identity, and not give in to pressure from Jon to change the way I did things. I was ME. As for the infamous black shirt and jeans? I still owned them and decided to wear them for my Christmas outfit.

Minutes after finishing the eggs, I heard sniffling coming from the cage. Anna was awake. The food was piping hot. My mouth turned into a smirk as I got a depraved idea. I walked up to the metal contraption, her frightened face looking up at me.

Many hours later...

"I already feel like a fucking monster," I said as I sat in Jon's beautifully decorated living room, close to tears. There was a fire going in the fireplace and his home smelled like a combination of hot cocoa and homemade cookies, both of which he and Candy had made earlier. It was only ten degrees outside and was flurrying on and off, so they spent the holiday doing what Jon referred to with a wink as "cozy, indoor things."

Jon nodded, a concerned expression on his face. "I understand, mate."

"She's got burns all over her hands from me forcing her to eat boiling hot food from the frying pan, and even some burns on her stomach from where the grease dripped on her. I can't even get into what her bum and vagina look like after I used the grease as lube. I DID put ointment on her wounds and let her rest on my couch and watch tv as a sort of reward for handling herself so well, but I still feel like a horrible person. How in the hell am I supposed to make it the whole goddamn week? We know bloody well what happened to Amy last time. The experience weakened her so much that she wound up in hospital with dehydration, and got the flu not long after that. I don't think I can do this, Jon." My eyes filled with tears.

Jon put his hand on my shoulder as he looked at me with sympathetic eyes. "Go with your best instinct," he said soothingly. "Nobody is pressuring you to continue on with something that's unsafe, or that feels wrong. Do what you feel is right, mate."

I nodded. "No matter what I decide, I know this will be the longest week of my life. The longest week of OUR lives."

Jon nodded and lit a cigarette. "It will. But you will emerge stronger as a couple, trust me. You might want to give her an incentive to continue, something to look forward to as a reward? I did that with Lisa, promising her a spa day and picnic, and she loved that idea. It made her want to continue past the five day mark, despite my refusal to do so. I had told her she was still getting rewarded, that it didn't matter she hadn't made it the five days since I was the one to end things early, not her. You and I BOTH know what happened after that." He winked and pointed to his ring finger, then took a drag off his ciggy.

I chuckled. "Well, I'm certainly not ready for that leap, but maybe I can give her permission to...dominate me when this is all over? She hasn't done that yet, and I can tell she wants to."

Jon smiled broadly as smoke trailed from his nostrils. "I love that idea."

Just then, Candy entered the living room, wearing a beautiful red robe and a smile. Her blond hair was wet.

"Hi, Ken!" She said as she leaned down to give me a hug, which I returned. "Merry Christmas!" She sat on the recliner chair adjacent to the couch.

"Merry Christmas, Candy," I said warmly. "How is your first holiday in 'Casa de Mooré?'" I asked with a flourish.

Candy and Jon both laughed heartily. "It's wonderful," she said sweetly as she grabbed Jon's hand and kissed it. "He's very kind and generous, and a wonderful cook."

Jon smiled shyly. "And a gifted lover, let's not forget that," he said with a wink.

Candy and I chuckled. "Touché," she replied. "He surprised me with breakfast in bed, which I loved. And he got me this beautiful robe as a Christmas present," she said as she rubbed the sumptuous, velvety material. "And he also got me a luxury bath set that comes with this incredible bath oil and body wash, which I just had the pleasure of testing in the tub," she said with a wink at Jon. "He's even booked a two-day trip to New York to go sightseeing and watch a broadway show, along with dinner, dancing in a fancy club, and a stay at a five star hotel."

My best mate grinned and kissed Candy's hand. "Anything for my little angel. She gave ME some lovely little gifts, too. She got me a few bottles of my favorite wine, and new bling for my manhood." Candy and I giggled at his expression for his new jewelry. "AND she made me

another beautiful painting. Reminds me of the sunsets in California." He nodded at the far wall of the living room. It was a lovely watercolor of a beach sunset, dotted with palm trees.

"You're an amazing artist," I said to Candy.

She smiled and blushed, thanking me. Just then, she looked at my black shirt. "Speaking of amazing, I love your getup," she said. "Is that silk?"

I nodded. "Indeed it is."

Jon's eyes grew wide, finally noticing THE shirt. "Is that the same one you wore to my Christmas party four years ago?" He asked shyly.

I swallowed and nodded. "Yes."

His eyes filled with tears and he shook his head. "I was so mean to you," he whispered with a trembling lip. "I'm sorry for all the times I criticized you and tried to make you change. I was wrong."

I smiled and gave him a hug, which he eagerly returned. "It's alright," I soothed. "You've more than made up for it over the years."

Candy smiled broadly at us. "That's so sweet," she said sincerely.

Jon looked over at Candy. "My little angel has helped me soften up a wee bit," he said with a grin. "Her love has a healing power that can turn the hardest, most dominant bloke into a soft ball of mush." He winked at her.

Candy giggled. "I don't know about that, Jon. You were pretty hard earlier today!"

The three of us broke out in raucous laughter, before having quite a bit of wine and plenty of homemade fruitcake, both of which Jon packed up for me to take home.

"You wouldn't want your slave to miss out on the holiday goodies," Jon said with a grin. "Candy and I made this fruitcake from scratch."

Just then, Candy got a mischievous look on her face. She got up and walked over to the coffee table where some of the fruitcake was. Then she dug her hand into the fruitcake, picking up a nice handful. Next, she opened her robe, revealing her perky tits and shaved cunny. She quickly rubbed the cake all over her breasts and looked at both of us with eyes full of lust.

"Who wants seconds?" She asked with her eyebrows raised.

Jon didn't hesitate, getting up off the couch and rapidly lowering his mouth onto one of her breasts, devouring the cake that covered it. Candy looked at me and nodded, encouraging me to help myself to her other breast. I smiled and joined Jon, lowering my mouth onto her cake-encrusted tittie. My manhood hardened and I noticed Jon undoing his pants as he sucked away, revealing his own erection. I undid my trousers as well, at which time Jon began to fondle me, taking my hand and placing it on his cock so I could do the same to him.

Candy ripped off her robe then began moaning and fondling herself. Within moments, the three of us were naked and lying underneath the massive Christmas tree in Jon's living room, kissing and fondling each other. Jon had Candy get on her knees and spat on the head of his huge penis, which sported the new jewelry that Candy had gotten him for Christmas. He then began bum-fucking her, at which time Candy lowered her mouth onto my penis and began to blow me. It was a holiday surprise of the best kind, and, as I became closer to rapture, I momentarily forgot that I had a girlfriend waiting for me just five houses down.

"Oh, fuck!" I called out as I orgasmed in Candy's mouth. She quickly lifted her head and kissed me aggressively, feeding me my load. Before I had a chance to swallow, Jon withdrew from Candy and kissed me, sucking the cum from my mouth and swallowing with a sexy smile on his face.

"Good to the last drop," he quipped as he wiped his mouth and lit another cigarette. I lit up as well. The three of us lay under the tree, cuddling and chatting. It felt nice to be with my best mate and his little angel on Christmas, naked and completely relaxed with each other. It was a much needed reprieve from the guilt I had been experiencing at

home. We talked about plans for New Year's Eve, which involved Jon hosting a party at his house. I fantasized about all the fun things we would do, all the sex and debauchery that would inevitably take place...

After a while, I noticed the lateness of the hour and decided to get dressed and head back to my house, where I'm sure Anna needed me. Jon and Candy were still nude and both gave me hugs and kisses, assuring me I was a good person.

"You're no monster," Jon whispered with a wink. "You're my best mate, and one of the kindest people I know. And you're a great partner to Anna. Don't feel bad."

Candy nodded in agreement. "And we loved the gift basket you got us," she said sweetly. "I already finished half the cheese."

I smiled, assuring her it was no problem and was glad she enjoyed it. Then I thanked them both for a great time, leaving with the wine and fruitcake in tow.

As I walked the short distance to my home, I thought of how much Jon had changed in a few short years. Four years prior, he was still a cocky, narcissistic scumbag a lot of the time, and continued to be that way up until a year and a half prior. Once he had learned that he had raped me while blackout drunk, he began to change into a much kinder person. Of course, he had to go through hell to heal from so many traumas and most likely would have to deal with some issues for the rest of his life, but with Candy as his partner, he was in good hands. Perhaps I would

allow Anna to take care of me, the way Jon allowed Candy to take care of him? However, I had to get through slave week before I even thought about anything else.

When I arrived back home, Anna was in the kitchen, naked as the day she was born and cooking what appeared to be a sumptuous feast. The air smelled divine. The dining table was adorned with a poinsettia plant and several lit candles. I smiled and greeted her with a kiss.

"What is all this?" I asked, motioning to the kitchen.

"Christmas dinner, Master." Her smile was so sexy. "Chicken in wine sauce, along with mashed potatoes and mixed vegetables."

I nodded in approval, holding up the fruitcake and wine. "I've got dessert covered," I said with a grin. "Jon and Candy were baking earlier, and wanted to share. How are your burns doing?"

Anna shrugged. "I've experienced worse."

I kissed her on the lips. "That's my brave girl."

I poured us both a glass of wine and made a toast "to us," then I sat down at my usual place at the table while she finished in the kitchen. I sipped my wine as I watched her cook in the nude, wearing only her slave collar. It was so sexy, watching her make all that food, humming

under her breath, perfectly content, and seemingly oblivious to the fact that she was my captive, and that I had burned her merely six hours prior.

Buzz, buzz.

My phone went off in my pocket. I took it out and looked at the screen. Jon had sent me a video of himself, along with a text that read, "Super private. Watch this with headphones. Jonny is about to be a bad boy again. Mwahaha!"

I chuckled and grabbed my headphones from the end table next to the couch then plugged them in. I pressed play.

Jon's smirking face took up most of the screen. It was clear he was a bit drunk, but was at least happy. He exhaled a cloud of cigarette smoke at the camera then began to sing in his sexy baritone voice.

"Silver bells...silver bells. It's time to pierce Candy's titty...."

I raised my eyebrows and laughed heartily, shaking my head. Just then, Jon began to talk.

"Wish me luck, mate. First the titty, then the clitty. Will let you know how it goes. It might inspire you to do something similar to Anna? Anyway, Merry Christmas, Ken. Will see you in a few days, after we

return from New York for our little couples' getaway. Candy doesn't know yet, but the little dance club I'm taking her to has a 'lower level' for...horizontal mambo lessons. That's right, there's a top secret, underground sex club with every fetish imaginable: voyeurism, BDSM, partner swapping, and just about everything else you can imagine. This will be a big adventure for us, because we have been monogamous aside from the BJ you gave me on Thanksgiving and the the one she gave you today. Be well and say hi to Anna for me. I love you. Ciao." He winked and smirked sexily before ending the video.

My dick hardened as I took off my headphones and put down my phone. I began picturing my best mate banging Candy in front of random strangers in a sex club, then imagined him restraining her to his bed, forcing her to endure piercings to her nipples. The imagery made me incredibly horny. Thanks to Jon's video, I felt inspired to test my little slave after dinner. I had a homemade piercing kit, and now had every intention of using it.

One hour later...

Anna lay on my bed, her ankles and wrists restrained in leather straps. Her breathing was heavy and it was clear she was in distress. I crouched between her spread legs, needle in hand.

"Everything is sanitized properly," I assured her, having wiped down her skin as well as the needle with disinfectant, and had applied a mild numbing agent to help reduce her discomfort. "Just try to relax."

Anna closed her eyes as I pulled her nipple upward and began to line up the needle with the tender knob of flesh. For her piercing, I decided on a discreet, horizontal barbell made of titanium. Jon, however, had decided on a big, flashy ring made of 18 carat gold for Candy, and had texted me a picture not long after sending his video. It even had a small ruby embedded in it. He had included a caption to go with the photo: "Pain meds sold separately" with a "devil" emoji.

I knew poor Candy would have to deal with a fair amount of pain, seeing that it was a decent sized piece of jewelry, and would therefore demand a larger-than-average size hollow needle for her to endure. Also, Jon didn't use any topical numbing agents while doing body modifications and even refused to dispense any aspirin or ibuprofen, insisting it "took away from the full experience for both giver and recipient." Hence his caption about pain meds. The possibility of Candy dealing with preventable agony a few houses away was upsetting to me. The man had few inhibitions and no sense of subtlety, electing to go big and bold or not go at all, and whoever was close to him had no choice but to go along for the ride.

I took a deep breath and began pushing the fine gauge needle into her nipple. She began to whimper and hyperventilate, doing her best not to move or scream.

"You're doing great," I said, as I grabbed the barbell and slid it through the hollow needle that was embedded in her nipple, then removed said needle and finished putting the barbell together. Once I felt a "click," I knew the piercing was secure. Her left nipple now sported a small titanium "ball" on either side, and it looked rather classy. There was minimal bleeding, which I wiped away with cotton saturated in

disinfectant before placing the bandage over the area. Anna was breathing heavily but otherwise alright.

I undid the restraints and gave her a kiss, which she returned. "I would hug you but it's a fresh wound," I said with a grin.

Anna chuckled. "It wasn't as bad as I thought it would be."

"I'm glad," I said with a smile. "Well, it will take some time to heal and it's important to clean the area and change the bandage frequently, especially in the first few days. And it might take a few months to heal completely, which I might have mentioned before."

Anna nodded. "Understood."

I ran my fingers through her hair. "I'm very proud of you. This has been a great first day of slave week and a great Christmas. Thank you for dinner, and for being such a good sport."

She smiled and let me carry her back to the living room, where I let her watch tv on the couch with me for a while before it was time to go to her cage. She even let me take a picture of her nipple, which I planned on texting Jon in the morning. Before long, the timer on my phone went off, at which time she looked at me and kissed me on the lips.

"I guess it's my bedtime," she whispered.

I nodded, helping her up from the couch and letting her wash up in the loo. Once she was done with that, I walked her back to the cage, opening the door for her.

"Goodnight, Master," she said with a sexy grin.

"Goodnight, Anna." Then I closed the door, making sure the metal lock was in place.

Feeling satisfied about the day's events, I washed up and went to my bedroom, deciding to wind down with a book and some soft music. I fell asleep rather quickly, having a rather brief but vivid dream about getting my dick pierced by Anna.

Day two of slave week, early morning...

"Rise and shine!" I said as I banged on the cage, forcing my little slave awake. My veneer of kindness was mostly gone, and, as with Amy, I planned on being tougher with her from this point onward.

Anna looked up at me with frightened eyes, afraid to speak. I opened the door to the cage and she rapidly let herself out. Then she stood there, waiting for my instructions.

"You are permitted to use the bathroom and take a shower with me. Once we are done, I want you to cook me a full breakfast of scrambled eggs, bacon, toast, and fresh squeezed orange juice."

Anna nodded then walked with me to the bathroom. While she did her business on the toilet, I turned on the shower, making sure the water was nice and warm. I got in the tub and she joined me a few moments later, lathering me up. She started with my hair and worked her way down, taking the time to massage my scalp and nether regions as she did so. I did the same for her, being gentle around her burns and her nipple, which still had a bandage over it.

We stood under the water for a few moments, letting the soap rinse away from our bodies. Something electric passed between us as we looked into each other's eyes, and it felt intense yet pleasurable. Her slave necklace was still in place around her dainty neck, and her long red hair cascaded down her front in wet tendrils. My penis got hard, and I felt an irresistible desire to fuck her.

"Turn around and bend over," I growled as I fondled my hardening member.

"Yes, Master," Anna whispered, doing as I instructed.

I knew her vagina was most likely still tender from the hot grease I had slathered on it the day before, so I was rather gentle entering her. She moaned as I did so, holding onto the edge of the tub as she bent over.

"Take every inch," I spat as I pounded her, choking her from behind. The water poured over us like a waterfall. Between the feeling of the water and the sensation of her walls gripping my manhood, I climaxed within a few minutes, withdrawing abruptly.

As if on cue, Anna turned around and bent down, sucking me off like a good girl. I held her head in place, delighting in the sight of her gagging on my dick. Once she had done a respectable job, I turned off the shower and stepped out of the tub. She did likewise, and grabbed a towel to dry me off. I dried her off in return, then changed the bandage on her nipple.

We retreated to the bedroom, where I allowed her to dress in a robe. Then I got dressed in a comfy sweater and jeans. As I put on my clothes, she looked at me with such love in her eyes that I could have melted right then and there. Jon had told me about his own moments of weakness during slave week, where Lisa was so tender with him that he felt regret over his treatment of her. He got through it by avoiding eye contact with her and assigning chores that would put her out of his sight. Somehow, looking into Lisa's baby blues was enough for him to feel guilt, and I was getting the same feelings from looking into Anna's green eyes.

I rapidly looked away from her and scowled. "I'm getting hungry," I grumbled. "Go make breakfast."

"Yes, Master."

She scurried off to the kitchen to cook, so I decided to relax on the couch in front of the Telly. I lit a cigarette as I scrolled through the channel guide, finally deciding on a cooking show. Then I picked up my phone, wasting no time sending Jon a photo of Anna's nipple piercing. He replied within seconds.

"Nice work, mate," he wrote.

"Yes and she wasn't in too much pain afterwards," I replied. "How did it go with Candy?"

A few moments passed before Jon replied. "Not so good."

"What happened?" I wrote, taking a drag off my cigarette. He was typing a long reply, as evidenced by the three animated dots that appeared under my text and stayed there for several minutes. My heart rate quickened as I tried to imagine what had happened with him and Candy. I did my best to distract myself with the tv, while suddenly my phone lit up once more with his text.

"When I put that big needle inside her, she screamed in agony, begging for me to take it out. So I did. Then there was so much blood. She'd had a lot to drink, so I'm sure that was a factor in the bleeding. Anyway I need to rethink my 'no pain meds' policy. It broke my heart to see her in that much pain. All I could do was hold her as she cried, and I kept pressure on her nipple, waiting for the blood to stop. It was as bad as

that time I had pierced Lisa's clit. If we ever attempt this again, I want to bring her to a reputable parlor. Twice is too much to fuck up a DIY piercing, especially on a girl I love."

I swallowed, sad for Jon and Candy but also unsurprised. Body piercings plus alcohol was a bad combination. "I'm so sorry," I wrote back. "Do you think there's something you can do to make it up to her? Something special she likes?"

"Well we don't leave for New York until tomorrow, which would give us BOTH a little bit of time to heal." He includes a winking emoji.

I raised my eyebrows, curious. "Care to spill the details?"

"I'm letting her gun-fuck me."

My eyes widened. "No shit! I thought you were going to let her give YOU a piercing of some kind. Or that you were going to take her out shopping or to the spa, or dinner like you did with Lisa. But I reckon the New York trip already counts as taking her out. Wow. I was convinced after the incident earlier this year that you two had sworn off any kind of gun play."

Jon sent a laughing emoji then another text. "Nope. I trust her implicitly and am ready for a new challenge. She's the only one I would ever allow to bum fuck me with the barrel of a gun. I even told her it was alright to

load it, or to at least not tell me if it was loaded or not, so as to add to the suspense."

I shook my head and tried not to laugh, at once horrified and amused that Jon would allow this situation, one that was not only very uncomfortable but potentially fatal. "Only you, Jon," I wrote. "But do try to survive, and not get shot. It would be an awful way to go. Besides, who else would be able to host an amazing New Years party?"

Jon sent another laughing emoji, then one with a silly face. "I promise I will survive. I can even do a video chat with you, when we do it. And Anna can watch as well. What do you think?"

I agreed with a thumbs up then told him about Anna cooking breakfast for me, then we agreed on a time of 10pm to do the video chat and exchanged goodbyes. Then I put away my phone, looking over at Anna, who was just about finishing up and was setting the table.

"I can't wait to eat," I said with a smile, watching her fix me a plate, then fix one for herself. Within a few moments, she brought the food to me, then went to sit down in the cage to eat hers. I toyed with the idea of letting her join me but decided against it. In fact, I had a new challenge for her.

"This tastes terrific," I said with a smile, as I helped myself to a helping of eggs and French toast. "I hope you will feel replenished after this meal because we are going on a little trip to the center of town."

Anna looked at me with raised eyebrows as she ate. "Where's that?"

I smirked. "Well, since I saw how good you are with needles, I decided it was time for a new challenge. I think it's time for you to get inked."

Anna's mouth opened and her eyes grew wide. "A tattoo?" She asked in a frightened voice.

I nodded and gave her a sinister smile. "That's right."

Her face became pale. "I'm not sure."

I glared at her. "I wasn't asking you if you wanted to do it," I snapped, making her jump. Seeing that I had startled her, I softened my tone a bit. "I think you're ready, love. Besides, I will be there with you and I will get a tattoo myself, to support you."

Anna ate in silence for a few moments, perhaps realizing it was futile to argue.

Two hours later...

"Ouch, it hurts," Anna said through clenched teeth as the tattoo artist began to work on her lower right leg. She had chosen the outside of her calf for the tattoo, reasoning that it would be less painful than some other areas. I lay in the chair next to Anna, offering moral support and verbal encouragement to her, and doing my best to drown out my own discomfort.

I had chosen a spot on my lower left leg, picking a discreet, simple design for my butterfly, which was meant to represent an important part of my past: my wife.

My mind wandered as I lay there, trying my damndest to avoid thinking of the needle. I closed my eyes and fantasized about New Year's Eve at Jon's house, picturing all the horny people who would be there. Andre, Todd, Noelle, Mario, and Brittany were coming, as were Lisa and Nick. With those folks in attendance, wild and crazy sex was an inevitability. Despite my physical discomfort, I developed a semi-erection while in the tattoo artist's chair.

The timing couldn't have been worse as far as an erection was concerned, as I was unable to shift my weight or cross my legs without possibly ruining the tattoo. So I began to feel rather restless. Luckily, however, the artist was, at least by my standards, an unattractive male, who sported a bald head and a potbelly. In order to go limp, all I had to do was look at him for a few moments.

The tattoos were done rather quickly, and I could tell the experience had been a challenging one for Anna, who appeared rather pale and shaky. Still, the body art had turned out very well. It was amazing how

two simple letters could look so sexy on a woman's body. That's right: I had made her get my initials tattooed on her.

Later that night...

Anna and I sat on the couch with the laptop in front of us, a live-action scene of Candy and Jon in their bedroom taking up the screen. They were both naked. Candles covered the nightstand next to their bed and sensual music came from the speakers in their bedroom. Jon lay face down on his bed, while Candy knelt behind him, gun in hand. They both looked at the monitor to speak to us.

"Can you see and hear us?" Candy asked.

Anna and I nodded. "Crystal clear," I replied with a smile.

Jon smirked at the camera. "Let's get down to business," he said in a low, sexy voice before putting his head back down on the pillow and spreading his legs wider.

Candy positioned herself between his legs, then spread his arse cheeks and crouched down. She began tossing his salad, beginning at his crack and working her way down to his hole. He moaned sensually, struggling to lie still.

"Mmmm," Jon moaned as he moved his hips in subtle undulations. "Feels so fucking good. You have an angelic tongue."

Anna and I laughed at Jon's comment as we looked on with eager eyes at the laptop screen. Jon's phone was positioned in such a way that we were able to see everything - his shapely bum, his pristine looking crack, his pink colored arsehole, and Candy's eager lips and tongue... and it was glorious.

After a few minutes of eating Jon's arsehole, Candy backed away and lifted the gun until the barrel was lined up with his opening. Then she slowly eased the tip of the deadly steel tool into his bum.

Jon appeared to tense up considerably, and his heavy breathing was audible. He began to slowly buck his hips, at which time Candy began pumping the barrel of the gun in and out of his arsehole.

"How does it feel, honey?" Candy asked, as she began moving the gun in and out at a more rapid pace.

Jon hesitated before answering, doing his best to maintain his composure. "Uh...it's... intense," he panted. "Feels cold."

Candy smiled and interpreted his words to mean that it was ok to fuck him harder. So she sped up her movements once more, and forcing the barrel deeper into his backside.

Anna and I winced as we watched what appeared to be an increasingly uncomfortable situation for Jon, who began to shake and whimper, and grabbing at the sheets as if to brace himself. After a few minutes of this, I noticed something disturbing.

"Candy, he's bleeding," I pointed out. It was just a wee amount of blood, but still alarming to see.

Candy nodded and continued, her movements slowing down some. "Jon told me if that happened to just keep going," she said in a shaky voice. "Isn't that right, Honey?"

Jon moaned and grunted before answering. "Yeah," he gasped. "Don't stop. In fact, I want you to fist me...with the gun in my bum."

Anna and I gasped, as did Candy, who momentarily stopped pumping the gun in and out. "I'm not sure I'm comfortable doing that," she said. "I don't want to injure you."

Just then, Jon turned around to glare at Candy. "I didn't bloody ask for your opinion," he spat. "You might be the one holding the gun but this is still my show, and you're still my submissive. Switching roles for a short time doesn't change that. Now be a good little angel and do as I asked."

I shook my head and looked over at Anna, who also appeared nervous after hearing Jon's proposal. Anal fisting was risky enough without other objects inside one's bum, and the fact that said object was the barrel of a gun only made it more dangerous.

Candy sighed. Then, with the barrel of the gun still embedded in his arsehole, she spat in her opposite hand then positioned her fingers as if she were about to pick up a tissue. With utmost care, she slowly began to insert her hand into his bum. Her fingertips disappeared, then her fingers, then knuckles, then her entire hand, until only her wrist was visible. Jon's breathing was even more rapid than before, and he was clearly in some pain but lay as still as he could while this was happening.

"Now that your hand is inside me, make a fist," he panted.

Candy shook her head, looking about ready to cry. "I don't think that's a good idea," she said sheepishly. "You're already bleeding a good amount."

She let go of the gun handle then took the phone and moved it closer to Jon's bum, so Anna and I could see some of the blood dribble from Jon's backside as the barrel of the gun and her other hand remained inside him. It was painful to watch and I could only imagine how it must have felt for Jon. Despite his high pain tolerance, he must have been very uncomfortable.

"I told you, I don't care if I'm bleeding," Jon growled. "Make a fucking fist."

Candy sighed again. "But Jon-"

"DO IT!" He shouted, making her jump.

"Ok, ok," Candy replied anxiously, taking some deep breaths. After a few moments hesitation and plenty of wincing on her end, she closed her eyes and did what he said.

Jon's moans became grunts, which morphed into sobs, and he began to writhe and contort on the bed. It seemed he was punishing himself for what he had done to Candy with the nipple incident, and perhaps even the gun play debacle that had occurred many months prior.

"Oh, God," Jon cried as he forced himself to lie as still as possible. His body began to tremble and a sheen of sweat covered his back.

Candy's eyes filled with tears as she held her fist inside Jon's bum. "Are you alright?" She asked. "I really think we should stop."

Jon shook his head as his body trembled harder and he started to hyperventilate. "No," he gasped. "Don't stop. I deserve this for what I did to you and the boys tonight."

Candy looked at the camera with a bewildered expression. "The boys?"

"Todd and Andre," Jon panted. "Who else? So don't stop, Noelle."

Anna and I exchanged worried glances. I knew what was happening. I cleared my throat.

"Candy, I think Jon is having a flashback," I said in a shaky voice. "It's his PTSD. He needs reorienting. Ask him if he knows where he is."

Candy nodded. She had seen him experience flashbacks in the past, so wasn't entirely shocked. "Jon, do you know where you are?"

Jon panted and grunted as he grabbed at the sheets, forcing himself to endure the painful fisting and gun play. "Don't ask silly questions, Noelle!" He barked. "We are at the palace hotel in New York City! You must have snorted too many lines, my little virgin...." Jon began to writhe and buck his hips. "Ugh! Oh god! Oh fuck!" Just then, Jon's body tensed up something awful, and he let out a deafening scream.

"AAAAAAHHHHH!!!!"

In a panic, Candy abruptly withdrew the gun and her fist from Jon's bum, placing a towel against his traumatized opening to stop the blood. He curled up into the fetal position, clearly in total shock as he lay there shaking, sweating, and completely dissociated.

I leaned in closer to the screen to talk to Candy, prepared to head over there to help take care of my best mate. "Listen, Candy," I said in a steady voice to Jon's frightened girlfriend. "Just stay with him, alright? Keep him calm, and do your best to remain calm yourself. I am heading over there right now."

Candy wiped away her tears and nodded. "Ok," she said through sobs. "I'm afraid I might have really hurt him. It's so hard to see him like this."

I nodded sympathetically. "I know, sweetheart. I will be right over."

We exchanged goodbyes before ending the video call, then I turned to Anna. "I will be back as soon as I can," I said as I put on my shoes and coat. "You deserve some free time after today, so make yourself comfortable here on the couch, maybe have some wine, watch some TV, and so on."

Anna nodded and smiled sweetly. "Are you sure you don't want me to come along for moral support?"

I shook my head. "That's kind of you but not necessary. Jon might get overwhelmed and then he could act unpredictably. Plus I need to handle this myself. It's the least I could do, especially after all he's done for me."

"I understand," Anna said with a gentle smile. "See you later and give him my best."

I nodded as I opened the sliding glass door. "Will do." Then I stepped it into the cold night and began the short trek to Jon's house.

Ten minutes later...

"Jon, it's me, Ken. Are you hurt?" I asked as I sat on the bed and gently placed my hand on his shoulder.

My best mate breathed heavily and continued to shake and whimper as he remained curled into a ball, his eyes clamped shut. "Uh... I-I don't know. I don't think so," he stammered.

Candy tearfully removed the towel that she had been holding against his bum, and she and I both breathed a sigh of relief when we saw only a tiny bit of blood on the towel. After his loud scream, we were convinced he was severely injured.

To be more certain that he was alright, I took a look at his opening, going so far as to use the flashlight of my phone to get a better look at his bum, both inside and out. What I saw was encouraging.

"Well," I said, after I gently spread his arse cheeks and looked inside him as best I could, "I'm no doctor, but I've looked inside a fair amount of traumatized bumholes over the years, and it seems that you're alright. Although you might be a wee bit sore come morning." I crawled around

his front and once again placed my hand on his shoulder. As I did this, Candy took his hand and held it gently.

Jon's eyes remained shut as he cried quietly. I cleared my throat.

"Jon, can you open your eyes?"

Jon slowly opened his swollen, bloodshot eyes, looking at me with trembling lips as he whimpered.

"Do you know where you are?" I asked gently.

He looked around the room momentarily, then at Candy, before settling back on me. I said a silent prayer that he would know where he was, and that he wasn't stuck in a flashback.

"I'm, uh..." he began in a barely audible voice. Candy gripped his hand harder as she bit her lip, trying her best not to burst out crying.

I nodded and smiled gently, rubbing his shoulder as I did so.

Jon then sighed, and looked at me with a relaxed expression, the slightest smile on his face. "I'm home."

Candy's eyes filled with tears of joy, as did mine, and we enveloped Jon in a warm, prolonged embrace.

"So glad you're back in the present day," I said as I held him. "You were 'time traveling' for a while there."

Jon backed away with a sad expression, looking at me and then at Candy. "So sorry, little angel," he said shakily as his eyes filled with fresh tears. "Sometimes this happens to me. It's like I forget where I am and who I'm talking to. I truly felt like I was back in New York with Andre, Todd, and Noelle. I had a feeling the fisting would trigger me, bring me back to that moment in the hotel with Noelle and the boys, but I reckon I deserved some form of punishment after the nipple piercing mishap."

Candy nodded reassuringly and caressed his tear streaked face. "It's ok," she said gently. "I'm glad you're alright. I know that what happened in New York was intense. I mean, I can't imagine what it must have felt like for Todd to have made a fist BEFORE entering you, nevermind the fact you had a broken tailbone when he did it."

Jon shuddered and shook his head as he recalled that moment. "Yep, and let's not forget the fact that he did it with no lube and very little spit, or the fact that Andre was holding my head underwater while it occurred. The ball gag in my mouth had filled with water and I had nearly drowned. Hey, speaking of water, I feel like I could use a shower. How about you two join me?" He raised his eyebrows.

I nodded. "That sounds like a great idea," I said.

With those words, Candy and I helped Jon from the bed and walked him to the loo, where the three of us joined him in the shower.

Candy helped to lather him up, beginning with his hair and working her way down. When she got to his bum, she was extra gentle. It was beautiful to watch her take such good care of my best mate. I pictured Anna doing the same for me, shampooing my hair and washing every nook and cranny of my body with loving care. I smiled at the notion.

Once the three of us had toweled off and Candy had treated Jon's backside with disinfectant and first aid cream, Jon turned to me.

"Hey, Candy and I were talking earlier and we wanted to know if you and Anna would like to join us in New York? Our suite has a second bed, and I think the four of us would have a great time."

My eyes widened and I nodded eagerly. I so loved the city, and the prospect of going with Anna was too appealing to pass up. "Yes, absolutely!" I said.

24 hours later (End of Day 3 of Slave Week)

"Come on, my little angel! Breathe!"

I knelt next to a frantic Jon, who was doing CPR on his beloved Candy. It appeared she had gotten very drunk and had lost consciousness in the hotel suite's jacuzzi.

I had found her in the jacuzzi room, which was adjacent to the suite's living room. She face down in the bubbly water and there was an empty bottle of tequila on the floor. I had wasted no time pulling her out, only to realize she wasn't breathing. Her pulse was also very weak.

"Jon!" I had yelled as I began chest compressions. "Get in here quickly! Candy passed out in the hot tub and she's not breathing!"

Within seconds, Jon had come barreling from the suite's kitchen into the jacuzzi room, dropping to his knees and gasping in shock as he saw Candy very close to death. He had insisted on taking over with the CPR, intent on being the one to save his little angel.

I looked on with fearful eyes as I watched Jon cry and do his best to revive Candy, as Anna slept off her own drunken stupor in the next room. My best mate and I were both guilty of upsetting our respective girlfriends earlier in the evening, to the point that they wanted to go off and do their own thing, and one of those things involved getting incredibly shitfaced.

The day had been like a fairytale. We had arrived by late morning, having travelled by car to New Haven, Connecticut then taking the train the rest of the way. Our activities included everything from ice skating in Rockefeller center, to traveling to the rather crowded top of the Empire

State Building (where I convinced Anna to give me a hand job while Candy did the same to Jon), to going indoor sky diving, to having a quickie in the hotel elevator when it was just the four of us in there. Anna had taken a while to climax in the elevator, but, with Candy's blessing, Jon gave me a literal helping hand while I remained inside her, flicking at her clit with impressive speed while sticking his finger inside her bum. The combination had driven her wild and after perhaps two minutes of the dual penetration and clit flicking, she had squirted all over my cock and balls.

Dinner had been a high class affair at a five star restaurant in uptown Manhattan, and neither Jon nor I spared any expense on our girlies. It felt great to spoil Anna, although I still made sure she was my slave. She still had to wear a collar to dinner, and a shock collar at that. I made it so she had to endure electric shocks of various intensity throughout the meal. Jon had kept Candy on her toes by making her wear a remote controlled vibrating egg inside her bum. It was glorious to see my best mate's little angel do her best to cope with that contraption buzzing at random inside her arsehole, while enjoying a feast of escargot, lobster, and tiramisu martinis.

By the time we had arrived at the hotel from that amazing dinner, the four of us stopped at the bar adjacent to the opulent lobby, nursing stiff drinks. After about two hours of drinking and talking, the girls were mildly plastered. However, my best mate and I were more than a bit buzzed on multiple martinis, and therefore feeling dominant and mean.

Jon had texted me a "script" to use on Anna for our next shag session. The idea was to up the ante with regard to Anna's experience as a slave. She had been such a good sport during the week and I was running out of ideas as to how to challenge her. Jon was experiencing the same

issue with Candy and was trying to find new ways to push her, to really get under her skin. The physical stuff seemed to have minimal effect on our respective girls. So the next step? Psychological torture.

The trick was to get the submissive to question reality and create an emotional response that the physical challenges were failing to elicit. I knew firsthand how powerful a technique this was, having tested it on my wife many years prior. I had also seen Jon use it on Lisa, convincing her that his love for her wasn't real, that she was nothing more than a fuck toy. Of course, there would be plenty of nurturing aftercare, with verbal reassurance to go with physical pampering. The risk of this psychological play was that the submissive would remain in a fragile and traumatized state, not believing anything the dominant would say after the play had ended.

I opened the door to our room, forcing Anna to walk on all fours as I did so. Jon did the same with Candy, smirking at me knowingly as he closed the door to the bedroom next to Anna's and mine.

"Strip naked then get on the bed," I barked as I took off my belt, holding it menacingly. "Take off the collar, too."

Anna did ask I asked, knowing better than to question my authority. Once done, she lay on her back. I began to undress, then positioned myself on top of her. The knife lay next to the nightstand, so I grabbed it and held it to her throat, belt still in my other hand.

"Who's cunt is it?" I growled, as I drew back the belt.

Anna swallowed. "Yours," she whispered.

CRACK!

I slammed the belt against her right hip, making her scream. A red welt remained. I wasted no time in forcing her legs farther apart, spitting on the head of my penis, and entering her roughly. She moaned in pain as she tolerated my thrusts. As all this happened, I continued to hold the knife to her throat. Then I began to fuck with her, mentally.

"How does it feel?" I asked with a sexy smirk as I slowed down my thrusts and put down my knife. "Feel good?"

Anna nodded and smiled sexily, wrapping her arms around me. "Yes, Master," she moaned.

I did my best to remember the short script that Jon had texted me, and my countenance changed. My thrusts became more aggressive, and I placed my hand on her throat. The fear in her eyes made my dick harden all the more.

"Do you think this is real?" I growled.

Anna's brow furrowed. "What do you mean?"

I glared at her, thrusting harder still. "You think I actually care about you?"

She swallowed. "Yes. Don't you?" She asked shakily.

I began to chuckle in an evil way. "This is all just a game. You're a toy to me. Nothing more."

My eyes bore a hole through her skull as I glared at her shocked face. I felt rather guilty fucking with Anna's head like that, but wasn't sure how else to get a rise out of her. I pounded away as I did my best to push aside feelings of remorse.

Anna's eyes filled with tears as she did her best to tolerate the hard thrusting. combined with the "news" that our relationship wasn't real. I couldn't help but wonder how Candy was handling herself, after hearing the same words from Jon in the next room.

Just before I was about to climax, I pulled out of her and masturbated for a few seconds before climbing up about a foot and ejaculating all over her face and hair. Semen covered her red hair and her porcelain complexion, and her eye makeup became smudged. It was a rather large load, and I smirked at how much a little jizz had ruined her appearance. She trembled slightly, looking ready to cry. I resisted the temptation to gently clean her off, hold her in a loving embrace, and whisper reassurances in her ear that she was special to me and that I

cared for her. Instead, I swallowed and shook my dripping cock, watching the milky drops land on her soft skin.

Once I was confident that the last drop of cum had left my penis, I jumped off the bed grabbed a towel from a nearby chair, wiping myself off. Then I threw the towel at her.

"Clean yourself," I said coldly, then I put on a robe and abruptly left the room.

Jon was already sitting out in the living room, dressed in an identical robe and smoking a cigarette.

"How did it go?" He asked with raised eyebrows.

I sat next to him and lit up myself. "I feel rather guilty for lying to her, then for leaving so abruptly. It's clear she's in 'subspace' and could use comforting. I hope she knows I wasn't serious."

Jon smiled sympathetically. "It will be alright," he soothed. "I think both our girls need some time to process but they should be fine after we surprise them with a late night meal from room service, and plenty of cuddling and reassurance."

I nodded as I smoked. "Hope you're right."

"I AM right, mate." He winked, then lit another cigarette and picked up the phone to order room service.

One hour after the room service call...

"Can we come in?" Jon asked as he knocked on the door. "We got dinner for you girls." In addition to surprising Anna and Candy with room service, he and I had gone down to the hotel gift shop to buy them flowers, returning just in time for room service to arrive to our suite.

The scent of fresh seafood filled the air as Jon and I stood outside the door to the second bedroom, where Anna and Candy were hanging out, or, more accurately, hiding.

"We want to stay in the room for now," Candy called out in a shaky voice. "We need some time alone."

Jon and I exchanged worried glances. "Alright," Jon said. "I will leave the tray of food outside your door and you girls can take it when you're ready. Sound good?"

Slight pause, followed by mumbling. "Yes, that's fine," Candy replied.

I took one of the trays of food and placed it on the floor next to the door of the room, and placed the bouquet of flowers in vases, along with sweet, handwritten notes for each of the girls. Then I picked up the other food tray off the cart and looked at Jon. "Want to eat this in the other bedroom?" I asked.

Jon shrugged. "Sure, why not? We could use some long overdue 'bestie' time," he said with a gentle smile.

One hour and multiple drinks later...

"And then the little cunt said to me in her Russian accent, 'You forgot to bring me a drink.' So I whipped out my ten inch winkie and pissed in her face!" Jon slurred before breaking into raucous laughter. His robe opened part of the way as he leaned back on the bed, his flat stomach rising and falling with his cackles.

I was beside myself with laughter as I listened to my best mate share crazy sex stories with me. I had changed back into a robe as well, and reveled in the feeling of the soft material against my skin. We were both in need of comic relief after being shunned by our respective girlfriends.

Dinner had consisted of caviar, lobster, and asparagus with a dessert of gourmet chocolate truffles. We washed it down with a bottle of single malt scotch, which Jon and I had managed to polish off in a very short time. It felt nice to spend one on one time with Jon. It was almost like being in college all over again, when he and I would stay up late getting drunk and making each other laugh.

Once the laughter had died down, I stared into Jon's lovely green eyes, my smile melting into a look of admiration and lust. He looked back at me with a kind smile, and slowly sat back up from the bed.

"I've missed hanging out with you one-on-one," I said softly, as I picked up his hand and rubbed it. I moved in closer to him, until my face was inches from his.

Jon nodded with a sexy grin. "Ditto," he whispered.

Fueled by booze and longing for touch, I leaned over and kissed him on the lips. Our mouths remained locked for several seconds, then I opened mine wider, my tongue meeting his. Then I began to run my fingers through his soft, blond hair. He did likewise with my dark brown locks, and my breathing got heavier.

My mouth continued to devour his. His robe was wide open, revealing his pierced nipples, chiseled abs, and erect, diamond-adorned member. I ran my hand down his front, going lower and lower until my hand was grazing his penis.

He backed away suddenly, and cleared his throat.

"Um, sorry," Jon began shyly as he closed his robe. "I don't do anything sexual without Candy's knowledge."

I nodded and swallowed. "I understand," I said softly.

Jon smiled sweetly at me. "Thanks for understanding. It's just not something I want to do to her. But I WILL still hold and kiss you. We can comfort each other in that way. Just no sex."

"Sounds like a plan, Jon. I sure am impressed by how you have changed over the years," I said with a grin.

Jon laughed and shrugged. "Maturity, I suppose. Better late than never!"

We both broke into laughter, then briefly washed up in the loo and retreated to bed, holding each other tightly until sleep overcame us.

Two hours later...

Jon and I woke up from what had amounted to a drunken cat nap, and now we had a second wind. It was only 10pm, so the night was fairly young. Jon went to the kitchen to get a nibble and a drink and I went to the living room to grab a fresh pack of smokes, but not before popping my head inside the other bedroom and finding Anna sound asleep in our bed. I quietly closed the door, electing to let her rest. Then I grabbed and opened a new pack of cigarettes and grabbed my lighter. That was when I decided to take a soak in the jacuzzi. I opened the door to the

jacuzzi room, and that was when I saw Candy floating face down in the jacuzzi and tried to revive her, screaming for Jon as I did so.

The horrifying minutes ticked by as Jon did his best to breathe life into his girlfriend, who lay unresponsive. We both began to cry, convinced that she was gone for good as Jon did multiple rounds of CPR.

"C'mon, baby," Jon sobbed as he did chest compressions. "I just found you again after so many years. Don't leave me..."

I began to cry even harder as I placed my hand on Jon's back, horrified and heartbroken for him. What would he do if Candy was dead? What could I do to help him?

My best mate began to wail in despair, completely defeated as he continued to half-heartedly continue with chest compressions and mouth-to-mouth. It was so heart wrenching to witness. Just when I was about to call 911, a sound emanated from Candy.

Jon's and my eyes lit up as Candy began to gurgle then vomit up the water she had inhaled and swallowed. I turned her head so she wouldn't choke on the water, and Jon placed a nearby towel under her head to use as a pillow. Color began to return to her face as she regained consciousness.

Jon began to cry tears of joy, as did I. "Oh, my baby is back," he said through sobs as he held her. "You almost became a real angel! I was so scared, honey."

Candy coughed a few more times before talking, returning Jon's embrace. "I don't know what happened," she said hoarsely. "I had a lot to drink then went in the hot tub, and must have fallen asleep."

I chimed in. "I had found you passed out, face down in the water. So I took you out of the tub and discovered you weren't breathing so Jon and I did CPR. You're very lucky, Candy." I winked.

Candy began to cry. "Thank you both for saving me," she said.

I wrapped my arms around her tightly in a warm hug, then my best mate did likewise. We were both so relieved that she was alive and well.

After a few moments, Jon cleared his throat. "I didn't mean what I said earlier," he whispered as he backed away from her tear streaked face. "It was just role play, and it got too intense. I'm so sorry for messing with your head like that. It wasn't my intention. You are very special to me. What we have IS real, and I truly love you. Please know that. Ok?"

Candy smiled and nodded. "I was hoping you would say that," she admitted shakily as she ran her fingers through his hair. "I didn't know what to think, I was so confused and devastated. I love you too, Jon. So very much." Fresh tears formed in her eyes as she looked at her

boyfriend with an intensity that made it clear how much she adored him.

Jon began to cry again and wrapped his arms more tightly around Candy. My own eyes filled with tears at the beautiful scene. That was when I decided to talk to my darling Anna.

"Would you excuse me for a moment?" I asked, then got up and headed to the bedroom where Anna was sleeping.

I opened the door to the room and sat down on the bed, caressing her gently until she opened her eyes slightly, then looked at me sleepily.

"Hey, beautiful," I said softly as I ran my fingers through her hair. "I just wanted to say I'm sorry for before. I do care about you. What we have is real. You're my girl."

Then I leaned down and kissed her gently and she wrapped her arms around me. "It's ok," she whispered as she smiled gently.

Two hours later...

"What do you have to say for yourself?" I asked Anna, as she lay tied to the California king size bed. I grazed the knife down her front, delighting in her nervousness as the blade got closer to her exposed vagina.

The four of us had arrived at the club around midnight, deciding to start the night with some dancing on the top floor before retreating to the lower level, where an array of sensual delights awaited us.

The upstairs level had been stunning, with subdued lighting and incredible music. Jon had insisted in arriving by limo, so as to add to the luxury factor. Anna wore a gorgeous blue dress, and Candy wore a sexy red one. Jon and I both wore solid black shirts with matching pants and expensive leather shoes, as well as plenty of silver jewelry.

The sexual tension was overpowering in that club, and after perhaps a half hour of dancing and several rounds of tequila shots, the four of us retreated downstairs to the lower level.

The lighting was suitably dark and sensual, as was the decor. There was a scantily clad brunette gal who gave us a tour, and we were all very impressed. There were several rooms, each one with its own theme - voyeurism, partner swapping, fetishes, and, Jon's and my personal favorite, BDSM.

Anna looked at me pleadingly as the knife grazed her privates. "I'm sorry, Master," she mumbled.

Satisfied, I lifted the knife from her skin and smiled. "Apology accepted."

The crowd of naked people applauded, impressed with Anna's and my little performance. Jon and Candy stood closest to the bed, and were ready to join us for a foursome.

I freed Anna from her restraints then invited my best mate and his girlfriend to join us. Jon and Candy held hands as they climbed onto the bed, then exchanged a sweet kiss as they lay down side by side. Then Anna crouched between Jon's legs, and I got into the same position with Candy. Jon's and Candy's hands remained intertwined and their gazes locked on each other. This would be their first time being polyamorous aside from the blow jobs they had given me and the incident in the elevator with Anna, but it was clear that their bond, and their devotion to each other, were very strong.

"I love you," Jon whispered to Candy with a sweet smile.

"Love you, too," Candy whispered back with a wink.

Just then, Anna took hold of Jon's erect penis and began sucking. I spread Candy's pussy lips apart and buried my face inside her hole. Their moaning began instantly and I could feel the crowd getting horny around me. It was as if the temperature in the room increased ten degrees within seconds, and the voyeurs began pairing up with each other, some retreating to nearby beds or other rooms, and some electing to fondle, blow or fuck each other while watching our little sex show.

My best mate and his girlfriend orgasmed within minutes, panting and smiling as they did so. Anna kissed Jon on the mouth, making sure to feed him his load. I did the same to Candy, jamming my tongue down her throat so she could taste her juices. Then Anna and I backed away from them, retreating to the edge of the bed and exchanging a kiss. I was able to make out the taste of Jon's semen on her breath and felt my cock harden once more. I looked over at Jon and Candy who began kissing each other passionately, their hands traveling over each other's bodies with increasing enthusiasm. After a few moments, Candy straddled Jon and began to fondle him until he was once again erect. Then she guided his engorged penis to her wet pussy and started to ride him.

Anna and I cheered as we remained seated at the corner of the bed, as did the other people in the room. It was so sexy to watch the two of them fuck in front of an audience. Things got even sexier, however, when Candy wrapped her hand around Jon's throat and began to squeeze.

Jon smiled broadly and placed his own hands atop Candy's, intent on helping her choke him. He so loved a good round of erotic asphyxiation, and before long, half the people in the room were choking each other. Anna and I decided to do likewise, knowing full well that the majority of the others probably didn't know what the hell they were doing and would wind up fainting or causing injury. But it wasn't our problem. I closed my eyes and reveled in the sensation of my air supply dwindling, loving the way my head, AND manhood, felt.

"Hey, honey, I want to stop," Candy's frightened voice said. "You're going to hurt yourself. I don't want to choke you anymore. Let go of my hand."

My eyes snapped open and I saw Candy doing her best to free her hand from Jon's throat, but he held her hand there in a cast iron grip, his face a deep shade of red. It was clear he was trying to choke himself and wouldn't let up until he lost consciousness. I had seen him do similar with other girls, including Lisa. Anna and I promptly let go of each other's throats and I crawled up to Jon, doing my best to pry his hand from Candy's.

"Jon," I began calmly, "Let go of Candy's hand. She doesn't want to hurt you."

But my best mate wouldn't listen and tightened his grip even more. His face was purple by this point and his eyes began to roll back into his head. Candy began to cry, as did Anna, and the others in the room became concerned. Adrenaline coursed through my veins and I had to think of a way to stop Jon.

I grabbed the knife from the nearby table, the same one I had used for knife play with Anna, and held it to Jon's hand. Then, before anyone could stop me, I drew the blade along his metacarpals. Jon and Candy both gasped as Jon loosened his grip, and the wound began to seep blood immediately. Candy freed her hand from his throat, which was now bruised. Then she got off of her boyfriend, placing her hand on his shoulder to comfort him. I had gone deep enough to cause Jon pain but not deep enough to cause serious injury.

Jon looked at me with raised eyebrows as he licked the blood from his hand. His green eyes glowed with anger.

"You think you can stop me from choking myself?" He asked with a smirk. "You're wrong, mate."

Before I could react, he wrapped his uninjured hand around his throat and began to squeeze, then placed his other hand around his erect cock to fondle himself. We all sat in shock as my best mate masturbated with a bloody hand, while choking himself into an increasingly altered state. Within less than a minute, he lost consciousness.

I ignored the panic going on around me since I was used to this nonsense from Jon, so I crawled up to his face and checked to see if he was breathing. Thankfully, he was, even though his breathing was shallow. He had done a number on his neck, which sported several more bruises, and his hand would require disinfecting and bandages, but he would be alright. I began to talk to him.

"Come on mate," I whispered. "Wake up."

Candy and Anna joined me, appearing concerned as she waited for Jon to wake up. Within a few moments, he opened his eyes a crack and began to breathe more deeply. I gave him a hug, as did Candy, followed by Anna.

"That could have been dangerous," I said sternly.

Jon nodded as he rubbed his sore neck. "I know, mate. But I feel alright." He looked at Candy and ran his fingers through her blond locks. "Sorry I held your hand to my throat," he said sincerely, to which Candy nodded and assured him it was ok. "I just got carried away. Anyway, how about we check out the fetish room before heading back to the hotel?" He asked, looking at each of us with a sexy grin. "I heard there are some folks in there who are into food play." His smile broadened.

We all nodded excitedly and slowly got off the bed. I found some disinfectant and bandages on a nearby table and quickly cleaned and dressed Jon's wounds, then we got dressed before heading off to the fetish room.

The moment the four of us walked through the door, we could make out the smell of fresh baked cookies and brownies. Surely enough, a gorgeous brunette was lying naked on a bed while several people - men and women - ate baked goods off her naked body.

We all began to undress and approach the bed, grabbing a cookie from a nearby plate. Jon, always the bold sort, grabbed a brownie as well, then looked over at his darling Candy.

"Want to double team with me?" He asked his girlfriend. "Double decker cookie sandwich?"

Candy giggled then nodded, and the two of them joined several others in placing baked goods on this lovely girl's naked body. Jon placed the brownie just above the girl's pussy, while Candy placed her cookie

between the girl's breasts. Then they lowered their mouths to the delectable treats, using their tongues on the girl's flesh as they ate. It was so sexy to watch. After a few moments, Anna and I joined in and the four of us were devouring sweets off this sexy stranger.

Once the sweets were gone and the only thing left to devour were the girl's intimate areas, Jon and Candy locked eyes. Then they nodded at each other with a smile and held hands.

"I love you, Candy Girl," Jon whispered. "Remember, I belong to YOU."

Candy winked. "I love you, Jonny Boy. And I know you belong to me. I belong to you, too."

The two of them kissed. Then Candy lowered her mouth to the girl's breast and Jon began eating the girl's pussy. They continued to hold hands as they pleasured the girl. It was the first time either of them had done anything sexual with a stranger, but, as with the session with Anna and me, it was clear that they were still very connected to each other. Anna and I decided to branch out as well, and decided to play with a girl on a nearby bed, who happened to be a blonde. We grabbed fresh cookies and ate them off of our new friend, who moaned at the sensation of our tongues lapping away at her pussy and tits. It was glorious.

By the time we were done with the fetish room, we had all eaten at least six cookies apiece and at least one brownie. Between the four of us, the "pussy count" was around three per person, and the "dick

count" around two. Sleep came quickly that night in the hotel, and I dreamed about Anna and what I would do to her for the remainder of the week.

Day two in the city, and day four of slave week...

The second day in the Big Apple was just as much fun as the first. Despite the festivities, I still made it clear to Anna that she was my slave, and, as a new challenge, had made her wipe my bum after I had gone to the loo that morning. We then ordered room service for breakfast and I had Anna feed me by hand, while wearing nothing but her slave necklace. After breakfast, the four of us had a spa day, with massages, manicures, pedicures, hair cuts, and a gourmet lunch. Then we headed to a broadway show.

Jon, having lived in the city for a year before heading to California, bumped into some old friends from his theater days. That's right: Jon Moore was a broadway star before going after his dream of becoming a Hollywood actor.

Whilst at Brown university, Jon had majored in theater arts with a concentration in dance, and, by junior year, had wound up landing a weekend gig as lead dancer for a show that played at one of Rhode Island's biggest venues. It was for a production that featured several styles of dance, with Irish step dancing at the forefront, and Jon was the biggest star of the show. Within months, Jon was dubbed "the Michael Flatley of Providence," and by the middle of his senior year, he got invited to New York to audition for a broadway production and totally nailed it. Once he and Lisa had graduated, they packed their bags and

moved to a beautiful apartment in downtown Manhattan. Lisa began a successful career as a fashion model, and Jon got to be an even bigger star than before, performing in sold out theaters for a year straight. He even wound up on the front page of the New York Times, the headline for which read, "From Britain, to Brown, to Midtown: London born 'triple-threat' makes it to Broadway." (In show business, a "triple threat" is the term for someone who can sing, dance, and act.) Below the headline was a photo of Jon doing an airsplit on stage, a huge smile on his face.

Fast forward to present day: Jon's old theater friend bumped into him in the theater's lobby. His name was Danny, and he was with his boyfriend Dave, both of whom happened to have seats in the same aisle as we did. They were both gorgeous. Danny had medium brown hair and hazel eyes, sporting a slim but chiseled physique. Dave had reddish hair and green eyes and was slightly taller and more broadly built than his friend. Danny had starred in the same performances as Jon, but unlike my best mate, hadn't been "front and center," and was more of a backup dancer. Jon had slept with Danny many times, along with almost everyone else who had starred in the show with him.

"Jonny!" Danny called out from across the lobby.

Jon turned around, as did the rest of us, and we all exchanged greetings and pleasantries. Danny continued to live in the city with his boyfriend, and he worked as a bartender while he wasn't busy acting and dancing. Dave worked in finance, and went to Danny's performances every chance he got, sometimes meeting him backstage for a quickie. They seemed like a cute couple, and I was happy to be able to meet some old friends of Jon's.

"Oh, my God, it's Jon Moore!" A random woman shouted excitedly in the lobby. Within seconds, hordes of people were coming up to my best mate and asking for his autograph as well as selfies. Anna, Candy, and I got plenty of attention as well, and Jon's fans were more than eager to meet his girlfriend as well as his best mate, and best mate's girlfriend. I was in awe of Jon at that moment, as people's camera flashes went off nonstop, and strangers came up to him giving everything from handshakes, to hugs, to kisses on the cheek. Several people recognized Danny as well, and posed for photos with him. It was quite amazing, and Jon handled the ambush with ease and grace, and took the time to make Candy feel included in the spotlight, as well as me and Anna.

Then, as quickly as the people came, they dissipated, and either made their way outside or into the theater to enjoy the show. We followed behind the crowd, excited for the performance. Jon led the way through the dark theater, and it turned out we were in the front row. With the best seats in the house, we all felt like royalty. Better yet? Our respective girlfriends were both dual penetrated with vibrating eggs, and he and I held the remote controls.

Four hours later...

"Oh my fucking GOD!" Danny exclaimed as he got pummeled from behind by Dave. Slapping noises filled the air as sexy auburn haired Dave pounded the shit out of his sexy, hazel-eyed boyfriend.

The four of us lay on the king sized bed, naked, drunk, and in full on "voyeur mode," as we watched Danny get bumfucked by his boyfriend.

Our tummies were pleasantly full with dinner we had ordered from room service. The broadway show had been incredible, and Jon and I had kept both our girlfriends on the edge of their seats - literally and figuratively. The vibrating eggs had gone off at random in their pussies and bums for the better part of the performance. Anna had actually experienced an orgasm toward the finale, doing her best to keep her moans and grunts quiet. Watching her squirm and squeal in her seat had been quite the "curtain call."

Now we had another little show happening right in our hotel room, and it was glorious to watch. Dave was so delightfully rough with Danny, whose moans were the result of pleasure interspersed with pain. His thick cock moved in and out of his boyfriend's tight ass with increasing speed and it was only a matter of time before he would climax.

"Oh, Danny!" Dave grunted as he ejaculated inside his boyfriend's bum. Then, once he had finished climaxing, he ordered Danny to lie down on his back. He did as Dave told him, and then closed his eyes tightly. Just then, Dave squatted over him, took his penis and pissed all over his boyfriend's face and torso. Danny giggled as he got covered in urine, and the rest of us laughed and cheered at the kinky, crazy scene.

After the two boys had washed up in the shower, the six of us got into the jacuzzi to get high and make love in the water. It had been a while since I had smoked pot and was looking forward to getting stoned. Danny and Dave were chainsmokers like Jon and me, and in between bong hits, the four of us enjoyed smoking one cigarette after the other.

The bong full of weed and bottle of booze got passed around until there was nothing left but empty vessels, and what happened next was nothing short of an all-out orgy in that jacuzzi. Jon went down on Candy underwater, impressing everyone with his ever-improving breath holding skills, and I did the same to Anna. Whilst down there, I had decided on what I wanted to do to her for the next two days of slave week.

Words could make a serious impact on a sub, as evidenced by Anna's reaction to my mindfuck game the night before. However, silence was often just as powerful, if not more so. For that reason, I decided to enforce a "no talking" rule for the final 2 days of slave week. Anna would have to communicate by writing things down, and if she spoke, there would be consequences.

My lovely redheaded slave climaxed after 8 minutes, not long after I had blown bubbles into her cunny. Candy, by contrast, had taken over 13 minutes to orgasm, and Jon had to be a regular Houdini. It was so sexy watching my best mate's girlfriend climax in that hot tub, and to watch Jon resurface breathlessly. The idea of near drowning to give someone an orgasm has always turned me on, even as a young lad.

Danny and Dave spent the night in our suite, falling asleep on the couch, in each other's arms. The four of us fell asleep in the same bed, naked, drunk, and happy.

Day five of slave week...

Jon and I stood side by side in a jewelry store on Madison Avenue. We had stopped there on impulse, after I had caught Anna and Candy looking through the display window at some lovely necklaces. We encouraged the girls to go to the cafe next door to grab a coffee while my best mate and I browsed for something special for our respective ladies.

It wasn't long before Jon and I had found what we wanted, and even though the jewelry had cost a pretty penny, the girlies were worth it.

Anna was doing well with remaining silent, having awakened to a handwritten note next to her pillow that instructed her to refrain from speaking to me for 48 hours and to communicate either by text or by writing down notes on a piece of paper. Her reaction had been a thumbs up and a smile, and she had even put on her slave collar herself. I would reward her handsomely for her compliance at the end of slave week.

The ride home was predictably quiet, aside from Anna and Candy making small talk and giggling. Jon and I dozed on and off on the train ride, content but exhausted from all the activity over the previous couple days. By the time we got to my Mercedes, we were all ready for a nap but luckily the drive from New Haven to Rhode Island went by quickly.

Two days later...

It was New Year's Day, around 4am. Jon's party had been an epic affair, with many people in attendance. I sat next to my best mate on the couch, and we marveled at the state of disarray in his living room. Party guests were fast asleep on the floor, and many of them were naked. Bottles of booze littered the floor, and empty trays of food were scattered about the kitchen and dining area. There had been plenty of dancing, drunken sex, and incredible music. Party guests had shagged in the sauna, pool, jacuzzi, and just about every other room in the house. I got to see so many friends, both old and new. The best part of the evening, however, was kissing Anna at midnight.

She had been relieved to take off her slave collar and talk to me again. I had promised her a reward for surviving the week. I was going to allow her to dominate me. But until I was able to think of that, I was going to think of the jewelry box I held in my hand.

Jon and I opened up our respective boxes, studying the contents. It amazed me how something so small could represent something so big. My best mate and I looked at each other.

"I think I want to ask Candy on the first of May," Jon began. "That will make a year for us, if you count the months I was away. How about you?"

I nodded. "I'm not sure," I said sincerely, as I held the jewelry in my hand. "I haven't even told her I love her yet."

Jon smiled sympathetically. "Baby steps, mate."

My best mate had decided on a spectacular 2 carat princess cut ring in white gold, with 2 rubies on either side of the diamond. Anna had simple tastes when it came to jewelry, so I had purchased a one carat marquis cut stone with a yellow gold band. That's right: Jon and I had gone out and bought engagement rings.

Chapter 7: "Some Things Never Change"

"Come on, mate," a 17 year old Jon chided as he pulled down his knickers with a smirk and revealed his massive cock in front of a crowd of our friends and acquaintances, who looked on with either curious or horny eyes. "Give it a kiss."

The drugs, alcohol, and sex were nonstop that night. Beer cans, assorted bottles of liquor, red plastic cups, candy dishes full of pills, boxes of half eaten pizza, condom wrappers, and overflowing ashtrays dotted the landscape of what was normally a pristine living room. Conveniently, Martha and Jon Sr. were on vacation, celebrating their wedding anniversary. Little did they know how much their firstborn was destroying their house while they were gone. Lisa was sound asleep in the den, having pre-gamed with her beloved Jonny hours before the first guest had arrived. As for 12 year old Daryl, he was in his bedroom, most likely engrossed in a video game, and knowing better than to get involved in his elder brother's questionable "activities."

It was a school night, and the first day of the last month of our junior year of high school, and my best mate had insisted on having a huge party at his house. Dozens of kids had shown up, and even some "adults." Jon was so popular that he had friends who were in college. By "friends," I meant people who were old enough to legally supply booze. Several of them dealt drugs as well, including "hard" ones like cocaine, ecstasy, psychedelics, and just about anything else Jon or his other friends craved.

I sat there, feeling uncomfortable and exploited, as Jon exposed himself to me, pressuring me to give him a blow job in front of dozens of people. Granted, the majority of the party guests were either gay or bi,

and very open minded. In fact, a number of them had fucked or engaged in foreplay in the living room, pool, jacuzzi, or kitchen at some point in the evening. However, I still felt that it was my right to refuse to suck my best mate's cock. Sadly, the only one who had an issue with this refusal was my best mate.

"Jon, I don't want to do this in front of everyone," I said in a mousy voice, trying to bargain with him. "I want these moments to be special and private. Just us blokes."

Jon glared at me, continuing to fondle himself. "But this is a party with our friends, and they don't care if you suck me off. I will do you after you do me. What ya say, hmm?" He raised his eyebrows and moved closer to me.

My heart pounded in my chest but I stood my ground. "No, Jon," I said firmly. "I'm not doing this now."

Jon's green eyes grew wide and a vein popped out of his forehead. Without taking his hand off his penis or his eyes off of me, he lit a cigarette, and took a deep drag. He held in the smoke for a solid minute, staring at me without blinking. Then he leaned in close to me, and blew a cloud of smoke right in my eyes. Out of defiance, I did my best not to flinch at the burning sensation and met his angry gaze.

"You'll be sorry." His voice was low, almost demonic, in tone. I had no doubt he would make me pay for refusing to give him a blowie on command.

I nearly pissed myself but pretended to play it cool. Jon could be so fucking intimidating.

True to his word, he did "make me sorry" later that night, when he waited until I was sound asleep and tied me to his bed. Then he face fucked me, going so deep into my mouth and down my throat that I threw up all over his dick and wound up choking on my vomit. I thought that was the end of me. I truly couldn't breathe. He quickly released me from my restraints after he had seen I was about to die due to his antics, and wound up giving me the Heimlich maneuver. He had been very apologetic after that, helping me clean up in the loo, then holding me and letting me know how much he loved me as I fell asleep in his arms. He had even made me breakfast in the morning.

I had believed Jon, had fallen for his expression of remorse and declarations of love. He was so nice to me that summer, taking me on shopping trips and even a family vacation. But of course, it would only be a matter of time before he would slip back into his controlling and predatory behavior.

In fact, Jon wound up coercing me into fucking him anally at the epic "senior year" party he hosted that September. I had tried to refuse, until he had threatened me privately with a switchblade. Later on, he had tried to pass it off as a joke, insisting he would never cut me but simply wanted to "add a challenge" of some kind. He had succeeded, in that I'd had a horrible time getting it up, and when it was all over and all our friends were cheering at our little sex show, I had excused myself to the loo and remained there for a solid half hour, crying and shaking.

After dragging myself out of the bathroom, I had made a beeline for Daryl's bedroom. Jon's younger brother had been surprised to see me pop my head in the door but was delighted to hang out with me. We wound up spending hours laughing, eating popcorn, sipping hot cocoa, and playing video games until we had fallen asleep on the floor of his room, game controllers in our hands. Somehow, hanging out with Jon's wholesome little brother was the perfect antidote to the sordid activities I got pressured into, and I found his innocence to be a true breath of fresh air. It was this trait, among others, that made me want to get closer to Daryl over the years.

Nearly two decades later, I still had nightmares about what Jon did to me, and this particular night in January was no exception. First, there was the flashback to the party where he had tried to pressure me to blow him, then the harrowing incident with the switchblade. As an added bonus, I had a dream that was luckily fictional but felt incredibly realistic, where Jon dragged me onto a big stage, with hundreds of people in the audience. He tied me to a bed, put a knife to my penis, and began sawing it off in slow motion. Blood went everywhere. The crowd cheered at my agony, and my darling Anna was in the front row, a sadistic smile on her face. Sitting next to her was my wife, and she was cheering along with the crowd. The pain, betrayal, and humiliation had felt real, so much so that I had screamed myself awake.

"Aaaaahhhh!!!" My eyes shot open and it took a moment to realize where, and when, I was.

Anna woke up with a start, placing her arm around me in the bed. She looked so scared.

"Are you ok, Ken?" She asked. "Did you have a nightmare?"

I nodded as I returned her embrace. "Yeah, it was about Jon. It was awful. He had tried to cut off my penis." I shuddered. "Prior to that, I had flashback dreams from when we were in high school, back when he had pressured me to do sexual things in front of our friends."

Anna looked at me sympathetically. "He was pretty mean to you back in the day, huh?"

"He was," I said with a sigh as I took a sip of water. "But he's gotten so much better over time."

Ding!

My phone had gone off, and I looked to see who had texted me.

"Speak of the Devil," I said with a grin. "It's Jon."

I read the message. "Good morning, mate. Hope you and Anna had a pleasant sleep. Where did you want to go for dinner this evening?"

Jon had invited Anna and me on a double date with him and Candy. Back in the day, my best mate would have never let me pick a restaurant OR a movie, always having to be in charge. I quickly thought of a nice Italian place nearby, one that my wife and I used to go on date nights. Oh, how I missed my butterfly...

"How about 'Bella?'" I texted.

Jon sent a smiling emoji followed by another text. "I knew you were going to pick that place. Brilliant choice, mate. Will pick you up at 6."

I replied with a thumbs up, then devoted my attention to Anna. She was so beautiful, the way she lay there with her red hair fanned out on the pillow and her perky bare breasts and shaved pussy just begging to be kissed and sucked. My manhood hardened as I took in the sight of her. I crawled down to the foot of the bed and kissed her inner thighs. She instinctively spread her legs and moaned, inviting me to devour her cunny.

"I want your cunt for breakfast," I growled, then lowered my mouth to her womanhood.

Anna moaned and squealed with pleasure as I ate her snatch, tasting the faint coppery hint of blood that let me know she was about to get her period. I fondled myself as I stuck my tongue deep inside her hole, swirling it around and occasionally blowing air into it. My thoughts traveled to an upcoming event that got me rather nervous. By the end

of the month, I was going to let Anna dominate me. I was going to give her free reign to to anything she wanted to me, sexually.

My lovely redhead climaxed within minutes, squirting all over my face as she did so. Without even having to ask her, she licked my face and stubble clean, reveling in the taste of her own juices and kissing me feverishly on the lips after. It was so fucking sexy!

Later that night...

"Mmmm..."

The sound of Candy's moans were audible over the din of the restaurant as Jon stuck his finger in her pussy from underneath the table, pumping in and out with a sexy smirk on his handsome face.

"Bella" was a classy, oceanfront establishment with a five star reputation. It was the type of place that sported white tablecloths and played classical music over the speakers. The menu was appropriately upscale, and the wine list was extensive. Most of the patrons dressed up, with most of the men wearing button down shirts and the majority of women wearing skirt sets or dresses. Incidentally, Anna and Candy both wore dresses...minus underwear. We were lucky enough to score a table that was in a rather private area, so we could engage in certain depraved activities without being seen.

Due to the easy access of their respective vaginas, Jon and I got to enjoy pussy for our appetizers, delighting in sneaking under the table to finger our girlfriends. The best part, aside from hearing them moan, was licking our fingers clean. I had nearly creamed my knickers when a good amount of blood appeared on Jon's finger, and he admired the sight before shoving it in his mouth.

"How does it taste?" I asked Jon, who appeared in heaven.

"Like candy," he quipped as he sucked the tip of his finger. "Even her period tastes sweet."

With those words, he leaned over and kissed Candy hard on the mouth, undoubtedly forcing her to taste her menstrual blood. It was so sexy in its depravity.

Candy backed away from Jon's mouth with a mischievous smirk on her pretty face. "Tell me, Jon," she began in a teasing tone. She opened her legs wider. "How many girls have you tasted or fucked during their periods?" She asked boldly, as she began to finger herself.

Jon raised his eyebrows as he studied his girlfriend. "Hundreds."

His voice was suitably low as he stared her down. My best mate didn't fuck around when it came to pussy. Or dick. Or arse, for that matter. He was a true sex connoisseur, and knew what he liked.

Candy smiled sexily as she masturbated beneath the table. "How many have asked you to cut your penis? You know, so it bled?"

I gasped in shock at Candy's question, as did Anna. Jon, true to type, sat there stone-faced, as if he was expecting this mind fuckery from a woman who, more and more over time, seemed to be his only true "equal."

Jon sighed before answering, as he unzipped his fly. "None. Unless, of course, YOU'RE asking me to do that?" He asked teasingly, as he picked up his steak knife and twirled it in his hand slowly.

Candy nodded. "Yes," she breathed as she stuck her finger more deeply in her pussy. "I want you to cut yourself so you have your man-period." Then she took her blood covered finger and stuck it inside her mouth, taking the time to suck and lick it suggestively. I instantly sported an erection.

Jon tilted his head back and let go a sultry laugh for a solid thirty seconds, before nodding his head. "Ask, and ye shall receive, baby."

With those words, he freed his erect penis from the confines of his designer underpants, then lowered the knife down to his member.

I tried not to flinch as I saw Jon hold the blade to the flesh of his manhood and apply enough pressure for it to start bleeding. If he was in any pain, he didn't show it. His expression remained as calm and neutral as if he were cutting a piece of steak. Candy and Anna looked on in equal parts horror and fascination as Jon sliced his dick with the sharp instrument. After a few more uncomfortable seconds, he took the bloody knife and examined it. Then he licked it clean, a sexy smirk on his face. His other hand grasped his wounded cock, which was bleeding moderately but not as heavily as I had expected, and the cut appeared modest in size. He placed the knife down on the table and looked at Candy with raised eyebrows.

"Satisfied now, Princess?" Jon growled as he waved his bleeding penis, as if to taunt her with it.

Candy swallowed and nodded, clearly surprised and impressed, but somewhat disturbed by what Jon had just done. "Yes, but...didn't you feel any pain?" She asked with concern.

Jon shook his head. "Not at all. Can't say you will be able to say the same after we go home and I bite your nipple hard enough to draw blood."

Candy's eyes grew wide. "Why would you do that?"

"Quid pro quo," Jon said with a smirk, wrapping several paper napkins around his penis before pulling up his knickers and pants. "I did

something for you and now you will do that little something for me. Nothing's free, doll."

Before she was able to respond, the waiter arrived with our entrees. Anna and I had ordered pasta dishes, and Candy had salmon. Jon had only gotten a small salad and a cup of soup. Every time my best mate ordered a light meal, I got concerned he was relapsing with his eating disorder.

"Is that all you're going to eat?" I asked Jon in as casual a tone as I could muster, placing my arm around Anna.

Jon stared at me for a few moments, his expression somewhat annoyed. He took a sip of his wine before answering. "Who are you, mate?" He said in a low voice. "Hmm? My mum? My shrink? The food police?"

I sighed. "Jon, of course not. Don't be silly. I was just-"

"What?!" He barked as his hand formed a fist. "I'm not a child. I know how to feed myself. Mind your business."

Then he grabbed the fork and began stabbing at a piece of tomato in the salad, using more force than necessary, then shoved it in his mouth. He chewed angrily and avoided my gaze. Candy looked over at me with sympathy, mouthing "I'm sorry." She knew how defensive Jon could get with regard to his eating habits and ongoing struggles with his body image, and knew better than to bring up the subject to him.

I winked at Candy and took a bite of my pasta, savoring the flavor. Then I turned to Anna and smiled as she took a bite of her own food. "How does it taste, sweetheart?" I asked.

Anna nodded and smiled. "Amazing. This was a good idea."

I smiled and kissed her on the cheek as I took a sip of wine, happy that she was enjoying her pasta dish.

Just then, Candy took a bite of her salmon and made a face as she chewed. Then she turned to Jon.

"Honey, this salmon tastes a little off to me," she began. "Maybe it's just my imagination. Would you taste it?" She put some on a fork and held it up to Jon, who nodded.

"Sure, doll," Jon said. "Wise idea to make sure it's not poison." He winked then opened his mouth, allowing Candy to feed him.

I stifled a smirk, knowing full well what Candy was up to. Several months back, she had confessed to me that she used little tricks to get Jon to eat more, and among them was occasionally having him taste her food, to make sure it wasn't stale or otherwise inedible. Another trick she used was to sneak more food onto his plate when he wasn't looking, doing it while sending him to the kitchen to fetch her a drink. These

tactics seemed to work rather well, and Jon's weight had remained fairly stable since his return from treatment back in November.

My best mate chewed the salmon and shook his head as he swallowed. "Tastes alright to me," he said. "Perhaps try cleaning your palate with some of your wine? Remember, the last thing you consumed was blood from your vajayjay, so I would imagine that would leave a bad taste in your mouth... literally."

Candy roared with laughter at Jon's comment, as did Anna and me. Then she took a hearty sip of her wine before taking another bite. Satisfied, she smiled. "Tastes better now. I guess it's not poison. But would you take another bite for me? It's kind of weird, but I like the way your kisses taste after you eat fish." She blushed and giggled at her admission.

Jon laughed heartily and let Candy feed him a generous forkful of salmon, which he devoured within seconds. It made me happy to see my best mate with a woman who knew just what to say and do to help him stay well. Once done with the piece of salmon, he kissed Candy passionately, caressing her breast as he did so.

"Fishy enough for you, Candy Girl?" He asked after he backed away from her lips with a sexy smile.

Candy laughed and nodded. "More than fishy enough, Jonny Boy."

The two love birds gazed admiringly into each other's eyes as they held hands. Something electric passed between them they made it evident how in love they were with each other. It was so beautiful to see. I looked at Anna and took her hand, and felt the same sensation looking at her that I got from looking at my best mate and his twin flame. When you met your true match, it felt like the ultimate high.

The four of us spent the next hour and a half in total bliss - talking, laughing, drinking, and eating to our hearts' content. Anna and I shared a dessert, as did Jon and Candy. My best mate and I so enjoyed feeding our girlfriends by hand, scooping up dainty spoonfuls of creme brûlée and gently slipping the spoons into their pretty little mouths. I got hard as I envisioned Anna licking dessert off my junk. Perhaps when we got home, I would cover my dick in whipped topping and have her clean me with her tongue...

Things were going amazingly well, when suddenly I spotted what appeared to be a dead ringer for my wife. She was several yards away with a group of other women, and, with the dim lighting of the establishment, she was a carbon copy. Same long, wavy, black hair, same caramel skin color, same height, same curvy build. Even her posture was similar, as was her bouncy walk. It was hard to make out her facial features from so far away and with such inadequate lighting, but the overall resemblance still impressed me. My jaw dropped. The others noticed.

"Ken, you ok?" Anna asked as she rubbed my thigh, her mouth full of creme brûlée.

My best mate and his girlfriend looked at me as well, concerned expressions on their faces. I slowly nodded.

"Yes," I said tentatively. "It's just, I saw someone who looked just like my wife."

Anna smiled sympathetically, as did the others. They looked over in the same direction as I did, to see what the woman looked like. Jon nodded.

"Very similar," Jon said as he studied the woman, who was now seated. At one point, the woman turned her head and looked around the restaurant, and it was easier to see her face. It turned out she looked a great deal different from my wife, and had more Asian features. If I had to guess her background, I would have said she was Filipina, unlike my wife, who was Hispanic. We quickly averted our gazes, to avoid looking creepy.

Somehow, knowing what she looked like made it easier for me to relax and I laughed, as did the others.

"The face is different for sure," Jon said with a chuckle. "But upon first glance, it's easy to see the similarity. It's going on five years, is it not?" He asked with sympathetic eyes.

A lump formed in my throat as I nodded. "Yes."

Jon reached across the table and placed his hand on mine. "I'm sorry, mate," he said softly, and with utmost sincerity. "I know it's hard. And I'm sorry I snapped at you before, when you asked about what I was eating. I know you were just looking out for me because you care." He smiled gently.

I smiled back, and squeezed his hand. "Not a problem," I assured. "Speaking of food, I don't know about the rest of you but I want to get some extra desserts to go. This is the best fucking creme brûlée I've had in my whole life!"

Everyone laughed and agreed. When the waiter came to our table, we requested some of the delicious desserts to go then asked for the check. Then the four of us discussed what we planned to do once we got to Jon's house. It seemed "food play" was an activity everyone could agree on.

On the ride to Jon's, Anna and I sat in the back seat of the Tesla. She rested her head on my shoulder and we cuddled in silence, relaxed but also excited for the activities to come. From the front seat, Candy was doing her best to encourage Jon to "branch out" and engage in full intercourse with either me or Anna, insisting she wouldn't get jealous and would find it arousing. My best mate still had yet to go "all the way" with anyone but his girlfriend since they had made their relationship official a little over a year prior. It seemed he had become accustomed to a more monogamous arrangement compared to years past, and wasn't quite ready to do more than foreplay or oral sex with anyone.

Aside from Jon wanting to explore what he called "modified monogamy," I knew that the main reason he hesitated to have full intercourse with anyone else is because he worried that Candy WOULD get jealous if she saw him do that, especially with another girl. He admitted this to me a few months prior. This concern came from the fact he had witnessed this jealousy in Lisa back in high school, when they'd had their first "two-girls/one-guy" threesome with one of Lisa's cheerleader friends. Jon's ex had been fine with him sleeping with me or any other bloke, but seeing him fuck another female made her quite envious. In fact, Lisa had been heartbroken and their relationship suffered for a long time, to the point they almost didn't make it. Jon didn't want history repeating itself, especially with the girl he considered his true soul mate.

"Let's play it by ear," Jon said with a sweet smile as he placed his right hand on Candy's thigh.

Two hours later...

"Oh, Ken..."

Jon moaned as I bumfucked him for the first time in a year and a half, when we had been in New York for the oh-so-eventful weekend with Noelle, Todd, and Andre. Only this time, I didn't need to pretend it was someone else I was fucking in order to remain hard. Nor did I need to be under the influence of psychedelics or inordinate amounts of other drugs. In fact, I was rather sober and was able to look right into his beautiful green eyes. AND I had an audience. It was amazing how much

easier it was to enjoy sex when I was actually ready to do so, and didn't feel pressured or bullied into anything.

Candy held his hand as he lay on his back, letting me make love to his lean body. She locked lips with him periodically, exchanging "I love you's" and similar affirmations as I rode him missionary style. He wrapped his legs around my waist, moaning periodically and caressing my back. A sexy smile spread across his face as he gazed into my eyes.

"This is so fucking beautiful," Jon panted with a sexy smile as he propped his legs onto my shoulders, allowing me to penetrate him more deeply.

I leaned down and locked lips with him passionately, noticing my lovely redhead's lustful expression as she sat on the opposite edge of the bed as Candy. She fondled herself as she watched me and my best mate make love.

The encounter had started not long after the four of us had knocked back several shots of tequila. Then Jon and I had locked eyes with each other, our faces getting closer and closer until we were kissing passionately and undressing each other in a frenzy. Candy had begun to cheer us on, as did Anna, and they began to undress as well. Jon and I had laughed with delight as we saw the two girlies begin to kiss and suck each other's breasts, and occasionally pulling each other's hair. Both Jon's and my cocks had gotten so hard so quickly, and I had wasted no time climbing onto my best mate's naked body.

After exchanging more kisses with me, he had turned to Candy and took her hand in his, gazing soulfully into her eyes as he recited the mantra that had become their custom before engaging in sexual encounters with third parties.

"I'm your Jonny Boy, and I belong to you," he had said breathlessly.

Candy had leaned down more closely to her boyfriend's face. "I'm your Candy Girl, and I belong to you."

Then they had exchanged "I love you's" and gentle kisses.

SMACK!

I had spanked Jon on his right buttcheek, making him gasp in surprise. Then I had smiled sexily and began to slowly guide the head of my penis to his opening. He opened his legs and began to breathe heavily with desire. His green eyes glowed as he panted.

"Put it inside me, Daddy," he had whispered as a smile spread across his gorgeous face.

A half hour later, back in the present...

"Oh, Ken," Jon breathed once again, his grip tightening around Candy's hand as he approached orgasm. He turned to his girlfriend. "When he comes inside my bum, I want you to be a good girl and suck it out of me," he said with a smirk.

Candy kisses Jon's hand and nodded. "I will do that for you only if you agree not to bite my nipple until it bleeds," she said with raised eyebrows. "Quid pro quo, remember?"

Jon's eyes grew wide before he began to laugh, his legs wrapping more tightly around my waist as my thrusts quickened. "Aren't you a feisty girl. Alright, it's a deal. BUT, you mustn't gag or spit it out, or else the agreement is null and void."

Candy giggled and nodded. "Understood."

Anna watched in amusement from the other side of the bed, touching herself sensually. I winked at her as I thrusted more and more quickly, pounding the hell out of my best mate. He and I both began to moan as I approached orgasm, our bodies covered in sweat. My manhood began to spasm and I looked intensely into Jon's green eyes.

"Tell me how much you love my dick inside your tight arse," I growled as I pounded him harder and harder.

"I fucking love it!" He panted as his own cock began to explode. The sight of him ejaculating triggered something in me, and within seconds, my own manhood let loose with a generous amount of semen.

I grunted loudly as I came deep inside his tight bum, leaning down to kiss his sweaty face before backing away from him and embracing Anna, who was still masturbating. Candy wasted no time leaning down and sucking the cum out of his bumhole, then quickly swallowing the contents. Without missing a beat, Jon sat up and kissed Candy passionately, as a puddle of his own semen ran down his stomach. Like me, my best mate recovered quickly from orgasm, so even though he had just ejaculated, his dick was hardening once again.

"That was good. You're one filthy little bitch. Get on your hands and knees, you dirty cunt," Jon growled, as he took a fistful of Candy's blond hair and pulled roughly. "I want to fuck you doggie style, like the animal that you are."

Candy nodded and did what she was told, getting on all fours. Her round arse was deliciously exposed, and, despite the fact that I had just ejaculated, I felt my dick harden. I held Anna more tightly and began to kiss and fondle her, still keeping my eye on Jon and his girlfriend.

Just then, Anna looked at me with such love in her eyes it made me almost want to cry. But I held it together, closing my eyes momentarily in case they filled with tears I wasn't yet ready to let her see.

SMACK!

Jon broke me out of my love lorn stupor when he spanked Candy's arse, making her yelp in pain. Then he held onto her hip, lined up his hard cock with her wet pussy, and quickly entered her from behind. The laceration on his member was luckily very tiny, and had long since stopped bleeding. Candy's tits shook as Jon pounded the hell out of her. As my best mate fucked his girlfriend, Anna took my penis and wrapped her dainty hand around it, smirking at me as she did so.

"I want some of this," she whispered sexily as she moved her hand up and down the length of my rock hard shaft.

I nodded with a grin. "You don't have to ask twice, sweetheart."

Anna lay on her back and spread her legs wide, revealing a pussy that was bleeding slightly. I bent down and licked some of the blood from her womanhood, becoming even more aroused after having done so. The veins popped out of my cock, and I wasted no time slamming into her.

On the nightstand next to my bed lay a blunt full of high quality weed, which had been a Christmas gift from one of the gym members (who was also a drug dealer). It had been a while since I had gotten high, so I decided on a fuck-and-bake. While still inside Anna, I reached over and grabbed the blunt as well as my lighter and lit up the bad boy, taking a hearty hit.

"Sharing is caring, mate," Jon panted with a smirk as he continued to fuck Candy. "Mind if I take a hit? I haven't smoked pot in almost a month, not since New Years, so I'm sure a little with go a long way."

Still holding my breath, I nodded and handed the blunt and lighter to my best mate, whose hard thrusts continued as he re-lit the blunt and took a huge hit, inhaling as deeply as he could and holding it in. Then, after ashing it, he began to move the lit end more and more closely to Candy's left hip. My eyes widened, and I became nervous for her. Anna looked over as well, her face appearing alarmed. As tempted as I was to speak up, I decided against it, and watched in awe as Jon burned his girlfriend with the cherry end of the blunt.

"Ughhh!" Candy grunted as the lit end of the blunt made contact with her flesh for a split second. "That hurt. What was that?" She turned her head as she remained on her knees.

Refusing to exhale the smoke, Jon held the blunt up to her face. Candy looked down at the burn on her left hip, which was luckily mild. I had been expecting a bigger reaction from her, perhaps a loud scream or more of a flinch than was the case, but Jon's girlfriend was a trooper and had simply made a groaning noise.

"I guess since I avoided getting my nipple bitten, I had to pay the price some other way," Candy reasoned as Jon continued to plow into her. "I know how you operate, Mr. Moore." She giggled softly.

My eyes widened and my heart raced as I waited for Jon's reaction to Candy's feisty comment. Anna caressed my face as we made love, perhaps in an attempt to keep me calm. I expected my best mate to either burn her more severely or beat the crap out of her. But neither happened. Instead, he let go of the breath he had been holding and burst out laughing.

His loud, wheezing cackles were contagious, and before long, all four of us were in stitches. It felt good to have some comic relief, considering how serious the situation could have become.

"Oh, Candy," he said as he continued to laugh. "You tickle me! Oh, dear me. You DO know how I operate! That's why I love you. Well, one of many reasons." His thrusts slowed down, and he gently cupped one of her breasts. Before long, he was soon making gentle love to her, eventually withdrawing from her to kiss and lick her womanhood while she remained on all fours. After a few moments of this, she turned around on her back, a sexy smile on her face. What she said next startled me.

"Would you do the butterfly?" Her voice was low and sexy, and slightly breathless. "I love that position."

I swallowed as I continued to make love to Anna, who, along with Jon, knew that word was a source of anxiety and sadness for me. As I have mentioned, "Butterfly" was my wife's nickname as well as the name of her favorite sex position, and readily conjured up feelings of grief for yours truly. This was why I used it as a safe word. I did my best to

remain erect as I thrusted, holding my darling redhead a little more tightly.

Jon smiled sympathetically at me for a brief moment before turning his attention back to Candy. Then he got up from the bed and stood at the foot of it, bringing his girlfriend closer to him until her legs were resting against his front. Then he smirked sexily and entered her gently, holding her legs to him as he did so.

While my best mate was making love to his girl, I once again devoted all of my attention to Anna. The words "I love you" were at the very top of my tongue. For all my boldness, however, I couldn't say it to her. Not yet.

"Mmmm…" Jon moaned as he made passionate love to Candy. "I love you."

Candy smiled as he rubbed her hands up and down Jon's chiseled abs. "I love YOU," she said with a giggle.

A lump formed in my throat as I gazed into Anna's green eyes. I leaned over and kissed her, thinking of the words as I made love to her mouth with my tongue. We switched positions a number of times, reveling in the feel of each other's bodies. There were several times I had no idea what was happening around me, we were so increasingly enamored with each other and the sensations going through us that we might as well have been alone. Within perhaps a half hour, she and I approached orgasm at the same time. Afterwards, we lay on the bed holding each

other in silence, locking eyes and exchanging kisses frequently, blissful smiles on our flushed faces. Hopefully she knew how I felt about her without my having to say it aloud. I prayed. I hoped.

Two hours later...

"Can you see a future with me?" Jon asked sheepishly.

I knew it was rude to eavesdrop through the door, but my curiosity got the best of me and I pressed my ear to the door of my bedroom, keen on listening to my best mate's conversation with Candy. A few minutes prior, I had heard what sounded like the beginning of an argument, and had gotten up from the bed to listen in. As usual, my best mate's tone was reasonable. Candy's tone, by contrast, was flustered. It was hard to make out the words from my bed or even through the walls, but once I placed my ear to the door, the dialogue was crystal clear. Anna lay sound asleep on the bed, covers draped partially over her naked body so her left breast was exposed. Her chest rose and fell with her deep breathing as she snoozed.

"Um," Candy hesitated. "I think so. It's just so new to me, all this. I do love you, and I love being with you, as well as living with you. But it's just so hard for me to see more than a month or two ahead. I wish I had a more definitive answer for you. Sorry." Her voice was quieter than it had been moments prior, and sounded a little sad.

There was a pause, followed by what sounded like liquid pouring into a glass. I reckon Jon was pouring himself a shot, and was feeling rejected, if not outright traumatized.

"Well," Jon began, "I wish you had a more definitive answer for me as well, Miss Klein." His voice shook slightly and I knew he was close to tears. "Little know fact about me? When I'm all in, that's it. I don't hesitate. You and I have been connected since we were children. Even though we went two decades without seeing or talking to each other, I never felt like we lost touch. At least that's my experience. I can see us spending the rest of our lives together. I, uh…"

Jon's voice trailed off, like he was trying to keep his emotions in check. He cleared his throat before continuing. "I…. I feel like you and I are soulmates. I thought you felt the same way?"

Candy sighed. "Jon, I do. It's just… This is so overwhelming, that's all. So new. I'm still used to living alone, to BEING alone. I've never lived with a boyfriend before, much less a roommate. I want to continue to be with you and to live together, but I don't know what the future holds yet. I want to play things by ear, let things develop naturally. Unplanned. You're not disappointed, I hope? I don't mean to break your heart. I'm just being honest."

Some sniffling followed by the sound of more liquid pouring. "I don't want to say anything in the heat of the moment that will bite me in the arse later," Jon said shakily. "Let's sleep on it, hmm?"

"You ARE disappointed, aren't you?" Candy insisted.

Long pause. "I reckon you already know the answer to that question, darling," he said in a sad voice. "Goodnight, my love." His voice cracked as he uttered that last sentence.

"Why are you going to Ken's bedroom?" Candy asked in a voice on the verge of tears. "Aren't you going to sleep with me in the guest room?"

Jon sighed, then sniffled. It was clear he was beginning to cry. "I just...need to think. I'm sorry. I love you. Goodnight."

I backed away from the door in a hurry as Jon opened it and walked into my room, looking completely defeated. There were tears in his eyes.

"Did you hear any of that?" He asked with a look of total despair.

I nodded sadly. "Yes, I did. I'm so sorry."

Just then, Jon's lower lip trembled and he began to sob. I wrapped my arms around him and let him cry into my shoulder.

Sometime in the middle of the night...

My best mate slept in my bed that night, along with Anna, having fallen asleep crying in my arms. It felt good to be there for him in his time of need. I had a hunch that, despite outward appearances, Candy WAS in it for the long haul and was simply being cautious due to past traumas. She was used to being single and living alone, so this was a whole new experience for her. I admired how open Jon and his girlfriend could be with their feelings, exchanging "I love you's" regularly and having deep conversations. As for my relationship with Anna? I had to work up the courage to open up to her, and tell her I was in love with her.

That night I dreamed about my wedding day with Anna, with all my friends and family there. Then time sped up and I saw us with children, pushing strollers and playing games with them on a blanket in a park. The final part of the dream took place far into the future, and showed Anna and me as a gray haired couple at holiday time, with what I assumed were our adult children and their kids, OUR grandkids. They were opening presents in front of our Christmas tree. I had awakened with a huge smile on my face, my arm around Anna. She looked so peaceful as she slept, her long red hair flowing freely down her chest. I took a deep breath.

"I love you."

I whispered it under my breath as she slept, just as I had a few months prior. Except this time, my whisper was louder.

"That's great, mate, but maybe tell her when she's awake."

I jumped, not realizing that Jon had heard me. I turned on my other side to see him smirking at me, his eyes half open.

I laughed quietly then playfully slugged him in the arm. "I was practicing," I whispered with a wink. "Hey how did that whole discussion with Candy start anyway? I only made out the tail end when you had asked if she saw a future with you."

Jon sighed. "Let's have a smoke on the deck and I will tell you about it. It's pretty mild out tonight, especially for January."

I nodded then grabbed my cigarettes, and put on my robe, as did Jon. Then I quietly opened the sliding glass door that led to the deck outside my bedroom, closing it behind me so any potential draft wouldn't awaken Anna.

Jon lit up and sat down, and I did likewise. "An engagement ring commercial appeared on the telly and Candy laughed, then made a comment about how she's not sure that she's marriage material, much less girlfriend material. I asked her what she meant. She said she didn't mean anything by it and had intended it as a joke, and was referring to her history of singledom as well as her failed relationship and would-be engagement to Mario. But the joke made me feel like she wasn't really serious about our relationship. I got insecure, so I questioned her about it some more. So she got upset and began defending herself. Then it got even worse when I asked if she saw a future with us. I put her on the spot. I should have kept my mouth shut, mate. I should have laughed it off, and seen it as the self deprecating joke that it was. Instead, I got

upset, and got HER upset as well. But after our discussion, it seems that she isn't as committed as I thought, or hoped, she was."

I sat there in silence for a few moments, and took a drag off my cigarette before replying. "I can understand why you feel that way, especially after buying an engagement ring. But I think Candy just needs a little time. I doubt she's going anywhere. You two have a magical chemistry. I'm sure she's processing a lot of changes. Between the two of you reconnecting and becoming an item, then you leaving for four months, then your return home, and then her moving in? It's a lot of transition."

Jon exhaled a cloud of smoke and nodded. "Makes sense. I just love her so much and want things to work so badly, I would hate to have scared her off by putting her on the spot like that. It's just... well... You know me, mate. I'm a planner. I always like to know where I'm going and what I'm doing, sometimes years out. It helps me feel more efficient. I'm driven. It's the 'Aries' side of my personality." He chuckled softly.

I laughed. "Well, luckily, you have enough Taurus traits to help you stay patient and calm while working towards your dreams. Things will work out. I have a good feeling."

My best mate smiled gently. "You always know what to say to me to help me feel better. Thanks, mate."

I nodded and took a final drag off my ciggy. "Anytime. Speaking of planning, I just have to think of a good time to talk to Anna. I feel

ashamed of myself for not being able to tell her how I feel about her. How long has it been since I started to fall in love with her? A year? It's ridiculous how long it's taking me."

Jon placed his hand on mine. "Don't put pressure on yourself like that. Some things really are better left unplanned. I suppose that's a lesson I can learn from Candy, and from her conversation with me. Every once in a while, things should just happen naturally. You and I had a similar chat last year, and I had told you that you will know when the time is right to tell Anna you love her. And look on the bright side: you've managed to say 'I love you' out loud while in her presence, and now you just have to master saying the words while she's not asleep!"

We broke out in hearty laughter, doing our best to be quiet so as not to awaken Anna. After having one more cigarette apiece and making small talk, we exchanged hugs and retreated back inside the house. Jon decided to risk going to the guest bedroom, intent on joining his darling Candy. Since it was once again just Anna and me, I decided it was a good idea to wake her up for some good old fashioned lovemaking at 3am.

I removed my robe and got up behind her, pressing my erect penis against her arse crack. She began to stir then woke up with a sexy moan.

"Fuck me, Master," she whispered sexily.

She didn't have to ask twice!

The following day...

"How do you like your eggs?" Anna asked me, as she stood naked in the kitchen, a sexy smile on her face.

I sat on one of the barstools at the kitchen counter in my robe, sipping the coffee she had made for me. "Fried, sunny side up, and preferably eaten off your naked body," I quipped with a smirk.

Anna giggled and got to work in the kitchen, humming to herself. She and I had slept in after having marathon sex at 3am. As for Jon and Candy, they were still in bed, and I had a hunch that they weren't sleeping.

While my lovely redhead was cooking, I tiptoed over to the door of the spare bedroom. Their moans were audible through the thick wood, and I smiled to myself as my best mate and his darling Candy made passionate love.

"Oh, Daddy!" I heard Candy cry out as slapping sounds filled the air. Jon must have been pounding the shit out of her.

"That's it, my little angel," Jon panted. "Tell Daddy how much you love getting fucked in all your holes. And after this, you get to use Daddy's body as a canvas, using blood from your no-no place as paint."

"Yay! I love painting, Daddy!" Candy panted in a high pitched, little girl voice. "I will make a nice picture for you."

"You better, or I will punish you," Jon warned. "I will make you taste your period blood and force you to go out in public with no panties."

I bit my tongue to keep from laughing at the dialogue of this particular age play session, while suddenly Anna called out to me to let me know breakfast was ready. I scurried back to the kitchen and sat on the barstool, where a plate of hot, homemade food awaited me.

Anna stood in the kitchen, looking at me sexily with her long red hair cascading over her bare breasts and her shaved cunny delightfully exposed. I stared at her like she was a T bone steak and got a lovely idea.

Ten minutes later…

"Ahhhh!"

Anna moaned and squealed as she lay atop the kitchen counter on her back, legs spread wide. She was managing to reach orgasm as I sucked spicy home fries out of her pussy, a first for me. My experiences with food play typically involved more solid things, such as pieces of chocolate or fruit; but semi soft foods such as potatoes presented a new

challenge, one that involved some serious tongue action and sucking power. The fact she had her period made it all the more enticing, and I loved the way the salty taste of her blood intermingled with the savory flavor of the seasoned potatoes.

"Mmmm," I moaned as I sucked and ate the contents of her womanhood. "Your cunt is so delicious. Best fucking potatoes ever!"

Anna laughed as she squirted all over my face. I licked up her juices like a rabid dog, loving the way she tasted. I began to masturbate as I lapped at her cunny some more, occasionally biting her clit. Her squeals made me all the more excited. I picked her up from the counter and dragged her over to the couch, where I forced her onto her belly and quickly penetrated her pussy. Within perhaps a minute of wild thrusting, I came inside her, my entire body shaking as I did so. Just then, the door to the second bedroom opened, and out came a sweaty, blood-streaked Jon with a cigarette in his hand and a satisfied smirk on his face.

He walked up to us and did a 360, allowing me and Anna to admire the artwork that Candy had done on his stomach and bum. She had painted hearts and flowers using her menstrual blood as a medium. The rest of his body was covered in a light glaze of the red fluid, and it mingled with his sweat. Even his hair and face were covered in it. The sight was kinky as well as depraved, and I couldn't help but chuckle. Anna joined me, covering her mouth as she did so.

"Yes, I am one kinky fucking bastard," Jon said with a giggle as he took a drag of his ciggy and made his way to the kitchen. "My little angel is

thirsty, as am I, so I'm fetching us some drinks. We have been fucking nonstop for hours and need replenishment."

He took two large bottles of electrolyte sports drink from the refrigerator, then began to scurry back to the bedroom. I cleared my throat.

"Hey, Jon? I assume everything is ok with you and her now?"

Jon smiled and nodded as he took another drag off his cigarette. "Oh, yeah. She was just feeling insecure and needed some reassurance. I will tell you about it later. But for now, I must take care of my darling little angel." He winked then opened the door to the room. "Daddy's back with bottles of juice, baby!" He announced gleefully before closing the door behind him.

Anna and I broke down into more laughter, deciding to take a bath together before I headed to the gym to meet a client for personal training.

Three hours later...

"Are you serious?" I asked Daryl, who was doing curls with dumbbells at the gym, a cocky smirk on his face. As for myself, I was working my chest and triceps so was doing mostly bench presses and push-ups. My form as typically flawless when doing push-ups, but after what Daryl had just told me, I had nearly fallen to the floor.

"I'm dead serious," Daryl admitted as he continued his reps. "I let Tracy peg me. Mind you, the strap on wasn't very big but considering my bum was a virgin up until two nights ago, size did NOT matter!"

We both broke into laughter at that one. I was shocked. Even though Daryl had become more adventurous in the bedroom, it was still out of character for him to engage in anything involving his back door. In fact, he was notorious for sticking to what he called an "exit only policy." This aversion to anything involving his bum was so strong that when he had to get a prostate exam at the doctor's, he had needed to down several shots of vodka prior to his appointment in order to relax.

"Did you tell your lovely brother about this?" I joked, as I began resuming push-ups.

Daryl tilted his head back and laughed heartily. "Hell, no! It's not his business! And I'm sure he would taunt me like crazy, anyway."

I got up from the floor and picked up my cellphone from a nearby bench, then began to write a text to Jon. A huge smile spread across my face.

"What the hell are you doing?" Daryl asked as he dropped his dumbbell and got up from the bench. An amused smile was on his face.

"Nothing," I insisted, as I typed.

"Let me see," Daryl insisted, as he began to take the phone away from me. I turned away as I hit the "send" button. Daryl began to play-wrestle me, eventually succeeding in taking my phone from me.

"You little bastard," he joked. "Let's see what you sent my arsehole brother."

I had sent a short but sweet message to Jon: "Your baby brother got pegged by Tracy." Then I had added a smiley face and a hotdog emoji.

Daryl laughed incredulously. "You bastard!" He said with an amused smile. "He's going to harass me so badly, I know it."

Surely enough, Jon replied within seconds. First, he sent a link to a song, specifically "Peg" by Steely Dan. Then he sent an animated message with a dancing pickle that read, "Congrats!" with confetti. Last but not least, he sent a cartoon of a giant hot dog, with a caption that said, "It's better with butter on the bun!" For the grand finale, he FaceTimed Daryl.

By this point, Jon's younger brother and I were in stitches, and it took a few rings before Daryl was coherent enough to reply. When he did, Jon wasted no time breaking into song. His ditty of choice? The "Oscar Meyer Wiener" theme song.

Daryl and I cackled as his elder brother serenaded him. His voice was resonant and enthusiastic, and he even finished with a little dance. When he took a bow, we both clapped.

Jon cleared his throat and smiled broadly. "Welcome to the club, little brother," he said with a wink as he took a sip of beer then lit a cigarette. "I never thought you'd have it in you… literally!"

Daryl blushed and laughed at his brother's words, shaking his head. "You're a jackass!" He said through peals of laughter.

"I say what's on my mind," Jon corrected. "So I must ask: Did it hurt?" He inquired as he took a drag off his ciggy.

Daryl nodded. "It did at first. But after a while I began to relax and I actually…I-I climaxed."

Jon's eyes widened and he grinned ear to ear. "WOOHOO!" He exclaimed. "Isn't it amazing what happens when you broaden your horizons and take a risk? I'm so proud of you, brother. For taking a chance and allowing yourself to be vulnerable. And to find love again. I'm sure it took a lot for you to get to this point."

"It did," Daryl admitted. "But I trust my sweet little Tracy. It's impossible not to feel comfortable around her. I feel like I can tell her anything. I'm so in love with her." He smiled gently.

Jon nodded and took a sip of his beer. "That's wonderful," he said with a grin. "I feel that way about Candy."

I chimed in. "And I feel that way about Anna," I said with a wink as I popped my head into the phone's camera frame. "It's about bloody time the three of us found lasting happiness on the 'love' front. We have all struggled a ton."

Jon nodded. "I'll drink to that!"

Daryl grabbed his water bottle and held it up. "Me, too!"

I grabbed my bottle of electrolyte drink, clinking it against Daryl's water bottle. "Me, three!" I quipped.

The three of us laughed and made plans to meet for dinner and drinks that night. It had been a while since we'd hung out together, just us blokes.

Later that night...

"The three musketeers, together again!" Daryl announced as he held up his beer. "Here's to friendship and brotherhood."

Jon and I laughed and clinked our beer mugs together then we took hearty sips. We had met at our usual bar, treating ourselves to wings and IPA on tap. It was a much needed boys' night out. The topics of discussion included everything from sports, to the gym, to politics, to (surprise, surprise) sex.

Daryl's elder brother wasted no time talking about all the depraved shit he did with Candy, describing in graphic detail everything from covering himself in her period blood to tossing her salad while underwater. Of course, Jon's little brother blushed a ton and appeared rather embarrassed but was at least interested, and even expressed a desire to do some of these kinky things to Tracy.

"Have you ever gone down on Tracy during her period?" Jon asked with raised eyebrows, as he sucked on a chicken wing. Then he began to dart his tongue in and out of his mouth as he licked the sauce from the wing. It almost looked as if he was performing cunnilingus, and Daryl and I couldn't help but laugh.

"No I haven't," Daryl admitted, "but I have had sex with her during her time of the month."

Jon nodded and began to eat the chicken wing. "Next time, make her suck your dick after it's been inside her bleeding pussy," he said with a sexy smirk. "And make her kiss you right after. When you do that, you

must make it seem like her period blood is the best thing you have ever tasted. After you kiss, go down on her and suck the blood right out of her juicy cunt. Let your face get covered in it. Tell her it tastes like honey. Or anything else that's sweet. Then suck on her clit. She will fucking love it and squirt all over the place. Trust me."

Daryl's face was beet red by this point, and he was doing his best to play it cool as he listened to his sexually uninhibited elder brother say filthy things. It made me laugh, watching Jon talk so easily about bleeding pussies while his shy, modest brother sat there tongue-tied and nervously sipping beer.

"I know it's a lot to process," Jon said with a gentle smile as he took a sip of his drink. "But it will be worth the effort if you want Tracy to be your queen. Do you?"

Daryl looked at Jon with a confused expression as he took another sip. "Do I what? Want her to be my 'queen?' You mean, my....my wife?" He raised his eyebrows.

Jon nodded and grinned.

Daryl blushed again as he thought for a moment. After a few seconds of silence, his lips formed a shy smile. "Yes. In fact, I, uh... I bought an engagement ring last week."

"Woohooooo!"

Jon and I both spontaneously cheered at the news, hugging Daryl and patting him on the back. "You dirty dog, you!" Jon exclaimed as he gave Daryl a bro-hug. "That's brilliant news, little brother. I reckon you haven't proposed yet?"

Daryl shook his head. "Not yet. I need to find the right moment."

That was when Jon and I took out or cellphones to show Daryl the rings we had bought our girlies. His blue eyes opened wide.

"Wow!" Daryl exclaimed. "So I guess this means all three of us are getting engaged?"

"Ideally," I said jokingly. "We haven't proposed to our girls yet. Let us see YOUR ring."

Daryl smiled shyly and took out his phone, then showed us a lovely, square cut diamond ring with a white gold band. Tiny emeralds adorned either side of the diamond. Emerald was Tracy's and Daryl's birth stone, so it made sense for him to have picked that accent color.

"It's so beautiful," Jon commented. "You did well, Daryl. Some of my good taste must have rubbed off on you!"

Daryl laughed as he took a sip of his beer. "Thanks a lot, Jon!" He teased.

Just then, I felt a tap on my shoulder. I turned around and saw Amy smiling at me. Next to her was Eugene. They both looked incredible. Jon and Daryl saw them and smiled broadly, greeting them enthusiastically.

"It's great to see you," I said as I stood up and hugged Amy, then gave Eugene a handshake. Daryl and Jon did likewise, and invited them to sit with us.

It had been maybe a month since I had seen my ragdoll and her ginger haired boyfriend, since they were among the guests at Jon's New Years party, but it seemed like longer. There was a part of me that still wondered about Amy and me, and how things might have been different between us. As much as I loved Anna and our life together, the overthinker in me still fantasized about "alternate realities," so to speak. Aside from thinking of Amy, I caught myself fantasizing about my wife, and how my life would be if she were still in the picture. I missed her so. If I concentrated hard enough, I could still smell her scent, and feel the softness off her hair...

"Yo, Ken! Did you hear me, mate?" Jon asked as he waved his hand in front of my face.

I jumped as I broke out of my revelry. "No, sorry! I was, uh, daydreaming," I said with a blush.

The others laughed good-naturedly at my absent mindedness. Jon nodded and leaned in closer.

"I asked if you wanted to go outside and join me for a smoke," he said with a gentle smile, as he put on his jacket.

I nodded, grabbing my own jacket and walking with him to the restaurant patio. We both lit cigarettes, taking deep drags as we took in the fresh air. The winter wind blew softly, creating a breeze that was rather pleasant.

"I wanted to tell you about what happened with Candy," Jon began, as smoke poured out of his mouth and nose.

"Yes," I said as I took a drag off my ciggy. "I've been curious."

Jon took a deep breath. "Not long before Candy's and my argument where I had asked her if she saw a future with me, her well-meaning cousin Irene planted some seeds of doubt in her head, as far as whether my intentions are pure. Mind you, Irene has never met me and is making judgments based on my social media accounts and random articles on the internet. She's also seen some commercials and movies I've been in.

"Anyway, Irene told Candy that rich, actor/model types usually prefer other rich, actor/model types, so she worries that I might not be serious about the relationship, that I might be using her. Or fooling around with others behind her back. Hearing these ideas made Candy feel like she wasn't good enough for me, that she wasn't rich, glamorous, or successful enough for me. She compared herself to Lisa, saying she couldn't hold a candle to her."

Jon paused to take a drag. "Well, I opened up to her about my relationship with Lisa. I told her that just because Lisa was a wealthy actress and model doesn't mean that we were a good match. Also, all the money in the world can't make up for the fact that Lisa was abusive towards the end of our relationship, and had a drinking problem. Now, I was careful with my wording, because I still want Candy to like Lisa, but I was detailed about what I had to endure from my ex during her blackout drunken rages. I told her about the time Lisa hit me in the head with a cast iron skillet, as well as the time she threw broken glass at me. Then there were the multiple bouts of slapping, hair-pulling, clawing at my face with her long nails, and at least 2 incidents where she had given me a black eye."

My eyes widened. "Oh my goodness," I gasped. "You never told me about the cast iron skillet incident. That's horrible."

Jon's eyes filled with tears at the memory. "I had dropped to my knees when that had happened, had nearly passed out. She had snuck up behind me when I was in the kitchen doing dishes. I had wound up with a concussion. It had taken hours for my head to stop bleeding, and weeks for it to stop hurting. So painful to think about. Aside from the incidents with Lisa, I also told her that most of my actor and model friends are exceedingly troubled, with drug issues as well as eating

disorders and mental health problems to go with their fame and fortune. Candy was shocked by the information about Lisa, but she also felt more secure, especially after I assured her that she was indeed good enough for me and showed her a list I had made of all the things I loved about her. After she had read it she began to cry and apologize. I held her in my arms as she wept, and I told her that I love her for HER, not what she owns or what she does for a career. And I told her she should feel free to let her cousin know this."

I smiled sympathetically, patting Jon on the shoulder. "I'm sure once Irene meets you, she will see you for the kind, generous soul that you are. She just seems very protective of her cousin. Probably because she loves her and doesn't want to see her hurt."

Jon nodded. "You're right. Candy has mentioned that about her, how she's always looking out for her and making sure she doesn't get burned. Makes sense, especially since Candy is an only child. Irene is more or less a surrogate sister to her."

"Candy doesn't have much in the way of family," I said as I finished my cigarette. "That must be tough."

"It can be," Jon admitted. "It's one of the reasons I got her into age play. See, after our little talk, I held her in my arms and asked her if she would let me be her daddy and she could be my baby girl. She had thought it was silly in the beginning, and had laughed a ton, but the ten hour sex-a-thon wound up being a real bonding experience. And I actually wound up feeling more protective of her, almost paternal. It's nice, because I felt like I was able to take care of her as a way of thanking her for taking

care of me a little over a year ago, when I was still recovering from my traumas and on those meds that made me a shaky mess. She had really mothered me."

"I recall that," I said with a smile. "That was when I knew Candy was a keeper. Your story makes me want to do something similar with Anna. Maybe she can be my 'mother?'" The thought gave me an erection.

"Hmmm..." Jon said with a smirk. "I actually think Anna should be your Master, and you her slave. It would be a complete role reversal, and very hardcore. In fact, I see pegging in your future."

My heart sped up. "I'm not sure about that," I admitted. "Perhaps I should start with a pinky first and see how I do."

Jon chuckled. "Of course. Baby steps, right? That's the only way to do it."

The mere thought of being dominated and pegged by Anna made my anxiety level skyrocket. I had a hard time sitting still through dessert, and wanted to get home so I could get drunk and try to work up the courage to let Anna do anal play on me. Surely, if Daryl could handle it, I could. Right?

Once we were finished with dinner, I invited Eugene and Amy to my house for drinks with me, Anna, Jon, and Candy. Daryl elected to go home to his lovely Tracy, who was waiting in bed for him. As for the six

of us? We all wound up getting completely and utterly shitfaced, and, inevitably, the clothes came off.

One hour later...

I lay on my stomach, the bed covers feeling soft underneath me. I did my best to keep my breathing steady as I opened my legs wider. Anna began to caress my bum, her hands nice and warm. Her finger teased my crack, and I willed myself not to tense up as she got closer to my hole.

"Let me know if it's too much," she said soothingly, as she began to slowly insert the tip of her finger into my arsehole.

The others looked on, drunkenly kissing and cuddling as they did so. The fuckfest had been a wild experience, with nonstop orgasms and partner swapping. Eugene got to experience a blow job from Anna as well as Candy. Jon, still having yet to engage in vaginal sex with anyone but his little angel, went down on Anna and let her toss his salad afterwards. As for me? I had eaten Amy's pussy. It had felt so bizarre going down on Amy, seeing that the last time we had been intimate was over a year prior and had occurred on the night she had broken up with me. I reveled in the taste of her womanhood and the memories of us as a couple as I lay prone, forcing myself to stay relaxed while Anna violated my back door.

Jon remained in the periphery, chain smoking ciggies as he sat in a chair against the wall of my bedroom, a sexy smile on his face. Candy

remained at his side, kissing and caressing him at random as she masturbated. He wrapped his arm around her, occasionally kissing and nuzzling her. They both watched me with eyes at horny half-mast, but spent a lot of time gazing into each other's eyes, suggesting they were more into each other than their surroundings.

"Ugh," I grunted, as Anna slipped her index finger into my bum hole. I had decided against starting with the pinky, on account of possibly appearing like a pussy in front of the others. At least starting with a bigger finger gave me a valid excuse to wince in pain.

"Pump your finger in and out," Jon suggested to Anna with a smirk as he lit a fresh cigarette with the end of the old one.

My heart beat faster as Anna began to pump her finger in and out of my backside. I actually began to relax, when I heard the sound of a phone buzzing.

Candy grabbed her phone and looked at who had texted her, a smile on her face. Jon looked on with raised eyebrows.

"Nick again, hmm?" Jon said as he took a drag, undraping his arm from Candy and positioning himself farther away from her. "You two seem awfully chummy lately."

Candy's face fell and she looked immediately guilty. "Nick's just a friend," she assured. "He sent me a funny cartoon, that's all."

Jon scoffed as he exhaled a cloud of smoke. "The man IS a funny cartoon. A bloody caricature of a human being who has a penchant for stealing everything from styles of dress, to hobbies, to sports titles, to girlfriends. He even cut his hair in a similar style to mine and grew a beard. YOU saw him at my New Years party, we could have been fucking twins. I didn't love the way he was dancing with you, either...and eyeballing you all night long. You would think he forgot he's married to Lisa. I'm surprised he hadn't tried to kiss YOU at midnight. He had pulled similar crap the year before, at the casino. That New Years dance party had been the first time he had ever met you, and I'd seen him laying his paws all over you and whispering stupid jokes in your ear. Bastard needs to get his own life and stop copying from mine. AND he needs to stop flirting with you. I see what he's trying to do. 'Tricky Nicky' is at it again. I best call him."

With those words, my best mate got up and stormed out of the bedroom, cigarettes and cellphone in hand. Candy got up and followed behind, gently closing the door behind her.

I was able to see why Jon was jealous, since, aside from Nick's flirty behavior at the New Year's Eve parties, Jon was barely recovered from Lisa having left him for the bloke. It hadn't even been two years since they had ended their 20 year relationship, so the wounds were still somewhat fresh. And, despite Nick and Jon being close friends, Nick HAS always sort of imitated him, if not intentionally then at least on a subconscious level. I knew it was because Nick saw my best mate as his idol. In fact, Nick had told me as much, but Jon interpreted his behavior as predatory, and an attempt at stealing from him. Aside from idolizing him, however, Nick was somewhat wary of Jon, and didn't completely trust him. Per a conversation that took place about a year and a half

prior, Nick felt that Jon had a very violent streak that needed to be kept in check, one that went beyond hardcore BDSM play. He truly felt that my best mate had it in him to kill someone in cold blood. I hadn't disagreed.

The conversation between Candy and Jon was barely audible through the door, so we decided to carry on with our own little activities. Eugene and Amy sat naked on the chaise lounge next to the bed, cuddling as they watched Anna pump her finger in and out of my arsehole. Without warning, she added a second finger, forcing me to yelp. I did my best to breathe deeply and not clench up, focusing my thoughts elsewhere.

This charade continued for the better part of a half hour, until she was able to get three fingers inside me. By that point, Jon and Candy were back in the bedroom, cuddling and happy after having spoken, and had applauded when they saw it happen. Eugene and Amy joined in on the applause. I grunted a ton and was only able to handle a few moments before using the safe word, but decided that if I was able to handle four fingers inside my bum, I just might be able to handle being pegged.

"Well done, mate!" Jon said as he climbed onto the bed and gave me a bear hug along with a kiss on the lips. Candy followed, as did Amy. It felt so good to get so much love from several friends at once. As for Anna? She grabbed the back of my head and kissed me hard on the mouth, shoving her tongue to the back of my throat. In turn, I grabbed her arse, digging my fingernails into her flesh as I did so. The others cheered on at our aggressive display of affection. My arse felt a wee bit sore but that was alright. I had done better than I thought I was going to do.

Half an hour later…

"What do you think?" Jon asked Anna and me, as the four of us sat in the living room, dressed in robes and sipping wine. Eugene and Amy had just gone home, so it was just me, Anna, Candy, and Jon.

The proposal was a surprising one, and I didn't think Jon would have been open to such a thing due to his jealousy issues, but Candy had mentioned it a few times and thought it would be fun. "An adventure" is the term she had used. For all Jon's dominance and need for control in the bedroom and other parts of his life, he was a true softie when it came to his little angel. So naturally, it hadn't taken much effort to convince him that partner swapping on Valentine's Day with Lisa and Nick, followed by an orgy with all six of us, would be a great activity.

"We can't deny the sexual tension that exists among us," Jon began, "and I think the only way to ease that tension is to have one on one time with different partners. This means going on separate dates and having sex in separate rooms, perhaps even separate houses. Then we would all meet up at the end for a six-way." Jon winked and lit a cigarette. "See, every 'swapping' activity we have done so far has been as a group. We have all been in the same room, looking at each other, making comparisons, and so on. But rather than bring us all together, I think it's created feelings of envy. I can see it. That's why I think Candy is onto something. Now, Lisa and Nick are visiting for Valentine's weekend and they are more than a little bit on board with this idea, kinky freaks that they are…" We all laughed at Jon's comment.

I spoke up, already fairly confident of the answer to my question. "Who goes out with whom?"

Jon smiled sexily. "I was thinking that you go out with Lisa, Candy goes out with Nick, and I go out with Anna." He looked at my girlfriend with a seductive smirk on his face.

Anna and I nodded and smiled, agreeing it was a good idea. As for Jon's answer? I had guessed correctly. I had never hung out with Lisa unless we were with others, nor had I slept with her one on one, so I was curious to see how that experience would be. As for Anna, I know she has always wanted to go on a date with Jon just once. And it was already clear how Nick felt about Candy. So this would be a good way to satisfy everyone's curiosity, and potentially calm any jealous feelings.

Later that evening, I had asked Jon if he had actually called Nick. He had said yes but that he was polite to him, and simply wanted to get an idea of what Nick's feelings were towards Candy. Nick admitted he was attracted to her but would never cross a line, out of respect for Jon and also out of his love for Lisa. This pleased my best mate, and made him want to go along with Candy's proposal to swap partners for Valentine's Day. Nick had been very surprised but also delighted by the prospect of having a date with Jon's girlfriend.

In terms of sexual fetishes, it seemed we all shared an affinity for water and enjoyed dressing up in costumes, but we each had our unique preferences as well. I loved food play, whereas Jon had a thing for knives and razors. Candy loved her gun, Anna had a thing for shock collars and was developing a bit of an anal fetish, and Lisa loved to

choke, scratch, and bite. That left Nick, who, aside from being a full blown masochist, had a fascination with fire. Whether it was wiping alcohol on his cock and igniting it with a lighter, holding the lit end of a cigarette to his ballsack, or lying in a tub full of boiling hot noodles, Lisa's husband loved the sensation of being burned. Lisa, being more of a sadist, was happy to go along with this kink. Knowing Candy and her tendency towards dominance, I had a feeling she would also be a good fit for Nick, sexually. As for the idea of group sex at the end? I couldn't help but get hard at the idea of all of us fucking the shit out of each other.

That night, I had fallen asleep with a hard-on and awakened the same way, having frequent dreams about fucking Anna, Candy, and Lisa all at the same time. My wife had made a surprise appearance during one of these dreams, and I would be lying if I said I hadn't awakened with tears in my eyes from that one. I couldn't believe that it would soon be five years without her...

Valentine's Day eve...

"Hey, buddy!" Nick exclaimed from the front porch as I opened Jon's front door, holding a large bottle of wine and a rolling luggage cart.

He and Lisa came through the door, looking amazing as ever in designer winter garb, and reeking of both marijuana and cigarettes. I could practically see a cloud of smoke form around them as they walked inside my best mate's palatial home. They each gave me a hug as we exchanged enthusiastic greetings. I practically got a contact high from the fumes coming off their clothes. They were both chimneys, smoking

as many blunts and ciggies as Jon did at his drug-addicted worst. When they weren't smoking cigarettes or pot, they enjoyed cigars, vape pens, and even pipe tobacco. In addition to that, they consumed insane amounts of food and alcohol; yet, they were both incredibly athletic and had perfect bodies.

"So great to see you!" I said with a smile as I helped them with their luggage and bags as well as the wine, and hanging up their jackets. "Jon is just finishing up in the loo, he wanted to tidy up a bit before you arrived. But of course, he takes forever to get ready." I winked.

"Same old Jonny," Lisa said with a chuckle as she ran her fingers through her blond curls. "Some things never change! But I also know we got here a little earlier than we said we would. Hey, where's Candy?"

"Yeah, where's my date for tomorrow?" Nick said with a smirk and a giggle. Lisa smiled broadly and playfully elbowed him.

I laughed. "She's tidying up as well. But I have a feeling she will be done before Jon is." We all exchanged a chuckle. "And Anna is coming in about twenty minutes."

"Was just about to ask about your lovely, redheaded lass," Nick said with a grin as he placed his arm around Lisa.

BOOM!

The three of us jumped at the loud thud that emanated from upstairs. I told Nick and Lisa to make themselves at home in the living room while I decided to go upstairs to investigate. They did just that, lighting cigarettes and getting comfy on Jon's luxurious leather sofa. A decanter full of single malt scotch sat atop the coffee table along with several glasses, and they poured themselves drinks.

I was halfway up the winding staircase when I saw Jon and Candy arm in arm and staggering their way down the hallway, ready to descend the stairs. Jon mumbled something about being a "bloody falling down drunk," which made Candy giggle. They were dressed in upscale winter clothes, complete with designer scarves, and they looked close to perfect aside from being completely inebriated, their faces flushed and sweaty from what had clearly been a shag session fueled by alcohol. My best mate looked particularly impaired, with his eyes bloodshot and his hair a post-coital mess.

"Well, well, WELL!" Jon slurred at top volume, as he held onto the banister and made his shaky descent down the steps. I discreetly acted as his "spotter," prepared to catch him if he fell. "If it isn't Tricky Nicky and his Lil' Lioness! Welcome back to my castle!"

"Heeey, great to see you, Buddy!" Nick said cheerfully as he put down his cigarette and rose from the couch to greet Jon. Lisa got up as well, a huge smile on her face.

Just then, Jon stumbled and nearly fell, breaking down into drunken cackles as he did so. Candy began to laugh as well, and caught up to him

on the steps. The rest of us joined in on the laughter, relieved Jon was ok. We all exchanged hugs and greetings.

"I'm just a silly drunk," Jon announced. "Candy and I decided to pre-game before the party. You must have heard that 'bang'? Well, that was me, unsuccessfully trying to put on my pants after fucking! I put both feet through the same pant leg and landed on the goddamn FLOOR! Can ya fucking believe it?!"

We were all laughing hysterically by that point, knowing full well how hard it was to get dressed after a drunken session of power-fucking.

"Perhaps we should ALL get silly with a few drinks?" I suggested with a grin, as I gently took Jon by the arm and helped him to the couch. Candy followed behind, and began to pour drinks for us, electing not to have any herself. Jon also waved away a glass, insisting he wanted to be a wee bit more sober before going out to dinner.

We sat in the living room, smoking, sipping scotch, and making small talk, while I heard a knock at the door, followed by the sound of footsteps. My lovely redhead had arrived. It was officially time to party!

Two hours later...

"Ohh God!" Lisa howled as she lay naked atop Jon's coffee table as Nick went down on her. The remaining four of us sat in the nude on the living

room sofa, fondling and kissing each other as we watched the impromptu sex show.

On a whim, we had decided on delivery for dinner, our philosophy being that Chinese food tasted so much better when enjoyed naked in Jon's living room. Aside from that, we were all incredibly intoxicated and the sexual tension was getting very intense.

As was typical for them, Nick and Lisa had brought some of the "good" weed, along with some psychedelics. Once dinner had arrived, the two of them were tripping balls on a combination of magic mushrooms and multiple hits from Lisa's designer bong, with expensive champagne in place of water. The rest of us had refused the shrooms but had taken a modest hit from the bong, mostly out of curiosity about the combined effects of high-end bubbly with strong weed. It provided a rather mellow high with a nice head rush, a perfect combination for getting dicks hard and pussies wet. Within minutes of getting high, we were ripping off our clothes and eating piles of lo mein off each other's privates.

Nick had insisted on Lisa microwaving the noodles so they were extra hot, and he had nearly gotten burned when the contents of the bowl had landed on his junk. Still, he had insisted on Lisa giving him pain, and seemed to get off on it. Also, the two of them had ordered multiple quarts of wonton soup for a top secret "finale" to the sex show. I found it sexy how Lisa and her husband had gone thorough the trouble of planning this, and was curious what the "final act" entailed.

Lisa began to moan and squeal as Nick devoured her cunny, burying his face so deep inside her that it was clear he was going without air. The minutes rolled by as he made her have one orgasm after the other, not bothering to take a breath as he did so. Her moaning became louder as the orgasms intensified, and she began bucking her hips and writhing. The rest of us began to pant and masturbate each other, our horniness becoming more pronounced as we watched Lisa cum so hard she began to squirt all over Nick's hair. With how long he had been at it, he must have been close to drowning in her juices.

When he finally backed away panting from Lisa's vagina, his face and beard were caked in blood. The sight of it turned me on to no end, and judging from Jon's growing erection, I wasn't the only one!

Lisa wasted no time sitting up and licking Nick's face clean. She even took the time to lick some of her juices out of his hair. He knelt patiently like the obedient catholic school boy that he was raised to be, his eyes closed as Lisa lapped away at her menstrual blood with her long tongue. It was so unbelievably sexy, I thought I would cream myself right then and there.

After a few more moments of licking Nick's face clean, Lisa lit two cigarettes and handed one to Nick, who began taking greedy drags. "That was the longest I've gone without a cigarette all day," he said with a grin as smoke poured out of his mouth and nose. "But worth it, because I made you climax."

Lisa smiled and kissed him on the cheek as she went to the kitchen. She came back seconds later with a large pot that was full of wonton soup.

She placed it on the floor then stood above Nick with her eyebrows raised.

"You know what to do," she purred as she took a drag.

Nick looked up at her sexily with his bright blue-green eyes, taking a long drag off his cigarette before putting it out in the ashtray. He began to caress Lisa's upper thighs, gradually working his way to her labia. Then, without warning, he spread her pussy lips and shoved his right hand inside her, making her moan. After a few seconds, he took his blood-covered hand out and appeared to be holding what turned out to be a small cup designed to hold period blood, and it was filled to the brim with the crimson fluid. Nick emptied the contents of the cup into the pot of soup, turning it a bright red color. After that, he exhaled the smoke he had been holding in his lungs and licked the cup clean, as well as his hand, appearing to savor the taste of the blood before placing the clean cup on a nearby table. Lisa quickly leaned down and kissed him hard, intent on sucking her blood out of Nick's mouth. Then she picked up the strap-on with a smirk. My jaw dropped, as did the others.' I had to place my thumb atop the opening in my dick to keep from spraying myself with semen.

"Put on the collar and get on all fours," Lisa ordered as she lit another cigarette and fastened the strap-on to her lithe body. Nick obeyed, placing the leather slave collar around his neck, which sported a long chain for Lisa to pull on so she could choke him. He positioned himself in front of the pot of soup, which was piping hot and merely inches from his face.

Lisa spat on her hand and wiped the spit onto the large dildo attached to the strap on, then lined herself up with Nick's arsehole. She took a drag off her cigarette, held onto his hip, and eased her way inside him.

"Oh, my goodness," Nick breathed as he endured Lisa's hard thrusts. "This feels so great. Don't stop, baby."

Lisa sped up her thrusts and grabbed the chain attached to Nick's collar, pulling slightly. His face turned pink and he began to pant as his wife restricted his air supply.

Jon began to chuckle softy as his eyes got that sinister look, appearing to derive pleasure from Nick's discomfort. He wrapped his arm around Candy and began to fondle himself, his erection revealing the extent of his arousal. Candy looked down at Jon's member and decided to help him out, wrapping her hand around his. She smiled sweetly at him and kissed him on the lips. The chemistry between them was so lovely that I felt compelled to be more affectionate with Anna, so I began to run my fingers through her long red hair. She, in turn, rubbed my stubble. I got tingles down my spine as I planted a kiss on her cheek. Oh, how I loved her and wanted to tell her as much...

"Aahhh!!!"

My "love stupor" was suddenly broken by the sound of Nick crying out. Lisa was holding the lit end of her cigarette to her husband's left buttcheek, burning him as she continued to thrust. After a few seconds, she lifted the cigarette from his blistered flesh and took a drag.

"How did that feel?" Lisa asked in a sexy voice as smoke escaped her mouth and nose in thick bursts.

"Exhilarating," Nick panted with a smile. Just then, he made eye contact with Candy, who appeared rather awestruck at his level of pain tolerance. His smile morphed into a flirty smirk and he winked at her. Candy, being the gracious type, returned the sentiment. Jon glared at Nick something terrible at this point, his eyes glowing with jealous anger.

"Hey, Daddy?" Lisa said to Jon, perhaps noticing the tension in her ex's face. Her thrusts remained steady and she began to caress Nick's back.

"Yes, my lioness?" Jon replied with a kind smile and raised eyebrows.

"Do you think the soup is a good temperature?"

Jon grinned ear to ear, knowing full well what Lisa and Nick had in mind. He rose from the couch and placed his finger in the pot of soup, which still had steam coming off of it. He nodded.

"Nice and hot," he confirmed, before looking at Nick, whose eyes were scared. "You'll love it."

Nick blinked as he continued to endure his wife's rough sodomy. "Really?"

Jon nodded. "I assure you. Try it yourself."

Nick reluctantly placed his hand inside the pot, holding it there for what must have been about thirty seconds before taking it out. His skin was pink. "It's hotter than what I'm used to, but I think I can handle it."

Jon sat back down on the couch and lit a fresh cigarette as he wrapped his arm around Candy. "I suggest preparing with deep breathing now," he said in a low voice. "Put those freediving skills to good use."

Nick nodded. "Good idea," he said. "But I think I need some weed first!" He giggled.

We all chuckled at his comment. The bong and lighter were on the table next to me, so I grabbed them and handed them to Nick, who took a generous hit and held in the smoke. He offered some to Lisa, who refused but I agreed to take a hit, as did the others.

I looked over at my darling Anna, who was pleasantly stoned. She leaned over and kissed me tenderly on the lips, running her fingers through my hair as she did so. My hand slowly traveled from her breast to her womanhood as we locked lips, savoring the taste and feel of each other. I couldn't wait until later, when we got to fuck like bunnies and fall asleep in each other's arms...

"Heavenly Father, thank you for the bounty you have set before me…," Nick mumbled as he bowed his head and placed his hands together in prayer, pot smoke trailing out of his mouth as he did so. The rest of us respectfully sat in silence, letting him offer words of praise to a higher power. Lisa stopped thrusting, then lovingly placed her hands on Nick's shoulders as he prayed.

For all his decadent ways, Nick was still a devout Catholic, doing his best to attend church at least every other week, and praying before every meal as well as before bed. In fact, after he and Lisa had eloped in Las Vegas, he had convinced his new wife to have a more traditional ceremony at the Catholic church they both belonged to, with only a few local family members in attendance. Jon found it rather silly that Nick felt the need to stick to a religion that seemed to be at the root of a lot of his problems growing up, including temporarily being shunned by his own father for being bisexual. But Nick saw religion as a way to remain faithful to his roots and maintain a moral code that he felt made him a kinder person. Aside from drugs, chainsmoking, and what his religion might consider "sexual deviance," Nick was rather wholesome, rarely using profanity and dedicating himself to charity work when he wasn't working as a chef or doing modeling and acting gigs.

"In the name of Jesus, I pray. Amen." With those words, Nick made the sign of the cross and began taking slow, deep breaths. He opened his eyes once more, looking at Candy with a gentle smile, which she returned. Then he took as much air into his lungs as he could and lowered his head into the pot of hot soup.

Lisa resumed thrusting as her husband went without air. One minute turned into two, which turned into three and counting. I couldn't imagine how difficult it must have been for Nick to keep his head submerged in a pot of soup that, only moments ago, had been close to boiling. The fact that he was being pegged at the same time only made it more challenging, as did the fact that the top of his head occasionally hit the side of the pot due to the force of Lisa's thrusts. Jon once again seemed to enjoy watching his longtime rival endure discomfort, chain smoking his ciggies and sipping scotch with a satisfied little smirk on his face.

"How's the soup, Nick?" He asked sarcastically as he took a drag and placed his arm around Candy. "Still nice and hot, yes?" Candy looked at him with an amused grin, shaking her head.

Still remaining submerged, Nick gave a thumbs up. He had just passed the four minute mark. I couldn't help but sprout an erection as I saw Nick's body break into a fine film of sweat as he forced himself to hold his breath, all while taking it up the arse by his gorgeous, but sadistic, wife.

Just then, Jon whispered something in Candy's ear, and she responded with a nod and a smile. "You sure that's ok?" He asked in a gentle voice with raised eyebrows, to which Candy nodded again, kissing him on the cheek. They exchanged the "I belong to you" mantra and a passionate kiss, followed by "I love you's." After that, Jon took a long drag from his cigarette and put it out, then rose from the couch and walked over to Nick and Lisa, a sexy smirk on his face.

"Hey, Lisa, mind if I have a turn with Nick?" Jon asked sweetly, running his fingers through her blonde hair as smoke poured out of his mouth.

Lisa nodded excitedly, slowly withdrawing from her husband. "You know I love seeing you two boys together," she cooed. Then she retreated to the loo to freshen up.

Jon eyeballed Nick like he was a piece of meat, then knelt down to whisper in his ear. Despite being submerged in hot soup for nearly five minutes, he had yet to let go any bubbles or show any signs of discomfort aside from the sheen of sweat covering his body.

"It's your buddy," Jon whispered sexily as he caressed Nick's back. "I want to be inside you."

Nick reached behind him to touch Jon, caressing his arm. My best mate returned the favor, kissing Nick's shoulder and leaving a trail of kisses down his back until he was level with his bum. He knelt down and tossed his salad for a few moments, fondling himself as he did so. Then he spat on his hand and covered his erect penis in a fair amount of spit, then eased his way into Nick's backside.

Jon's cock was a fair amount larger than Lisa's strap-on, so I wasn't surprised when Nick let go some bubbles. Jon saw this and smirked, thrusting harder. The top of Nick's head hit the side of the pot and some of the soup splashed out. I shook my head, feeling somewhat annoyed. It was clear that my best mate was making Nick "pay" for his upcoming date with Candy. Why couldn't he have simply refused to the partner

swapping if it was going to make him jealous and act in a vindictive way?

Just then, Lisa returned from the bathroom and made her way over to Nick's head, caressing his shoulders as she knelt down. Jon continued to fuck him as he smiled at Lisa. She returned his smile and gave a wink. I looked at the clock and saw that 7 minutes had passed since Nick had lowered his head into the soup.

"Want to come up for air, honey?" Lisa asked.

Nick nodded slightly as he resumed submerged.

"Well, you know what to do."

Nick gave a thumbs up then began to masturbate. His large cock began to grow in size as he touched himself. It was clear that Lisa wasn't going to let him come up for air until he climaxed. Meanwhile, the rest of us were getting horny as we watched Nick fondle himself, taking it upon ourselves to fondle each other. Candy pleasured herself with one hand while grabbing Anna's right breast, while I grabbed her left and slid my finger inside her pussy. This excited Lisa and Jon to no end, and they cheered us on. Jon's thrusts sped up, which in turn made Nick run his hand over his dick that much faster. Lisa began to masturbate as she knelt near her husband's head, ready to push it back down into the pot of soup if he dared to try and get air before climaxing.

The next few moments were tense, with Nick letting go some bubbles every few seconds while running his hand up and down his shaft, trying to reach orgasm so he could breathe. Jon was determined to make Nick struggle, having lit a cigarette and holding the lit end to his buttcheek for a second. This made Nick let go even more bubbles, and I could imagine that he was nearly out of air and forced to hold a vacuum as he remained submerged. His body began to shake and his sweating increased as he frantically choked his cock, perhaps silently praying for a climax. Just when I thought he was going to come up for air prematurely, his manhood exploded and he lifted his head out of the soup, gasping for breath after more than 8 minutes of torture. We all applauded, impressed by his stamina. His face was unsurprisingly bright pink from the heat of the soup.

Lisa had a towel at the ready and draped it over Nick's head, congratulating him on a job well done. Jon withdrew from his backside, taking the time to shake Nick's hand and give a congratulatory kiss as Lisa dried him off, feeding him one of the wontons as she did so.

"Mmm," Nick uttered as he ate the wonton. "Tastes even better with the blood added to the soup. Try one." He plucked a wonton from the pot and fed it to Lisa, who eagerly devoured it. Then she went right for his hand, licking the semen off of it while her mouth was still full of food.

The rest of us were about ready to cream ourselves as we watched those two. Jon quickly freshened up in the loo, then marched over to Candy with a huge smile on his face and a massive erection. He began kissing her passionately, and I did the same with Anna. Within moments, my best mate and I were shagging our respective girlfriends right there on the couch. Nick and Lisa became inspired by our

impromptu fuckfest and were at it again, this time baptizing the loveseat that was perpendicular to the couch we were on, and smoking pipe tobacco as Lisa rode her hubby cowgirl-style. Per Nick's request, Lisa dropped piles of hot ashes on his stomach and chest, even forcing him to eat some of the ashes. Candy, Anna, and I all looked on in horror as Nick gagged and choked, while Jon smiled sadistically, urging him to chow down.

"Finish your supper like a good boy," Jon taunted as he piledrove into Candy, whose face reddened and contorted into a grimace from the strenuousness of the sexual position.

Nick forced the ashes down, nearly throwing up as he did so. Little did he know, things would only get more bothersome for the bloke. That's right, my best mate would see to it that the rest of Nick's visit would be an exercise in endurance. Despite his apparent generosity and willingness to go along with the partner swapping, Jon was determined to let Nick know there was no such thing as a free lunch...or free Candy for that matter.

The next morning, Valentine's Day...

"Honey, have you seen my rosary and my St. Christopher pendant?" Nick called from the living room as he rummaged through one of his overnight bags.

"No, I haven't," Lisa called from the kitchen as she lit a cigarette and poured herself a coffee. "Maybe try the front compartment of the rolling luggage cart?"

"I checked there, but I can check again."

I sat at the kitchen table next to Anna, and noticed Jon stifle a smirk as he stood at the counter, chopping up vegetables to put in the omelettes he was making for all of us. Candy sat opposite Anna, and was looking at her phone. She and Nick planned on going to Connecticut for their date, deciding on the casino for their destination. As for the rest of us? Jon was taking Anna to Boston for the day, and I was taking Lisa to Newport. As should be the case for Valentine's Day, it was ladies' choice.

Nick never traveled without his rosary or his antique white gold pendant, believing that both items keep him from getting into accidents. In fact, the one time he had forgotten them at home, he'd gotten rear ended by someone. St. Christopher is known as the "patron saint of travelers," and many Christians carry a token of him in their travels because they believe he protects them from harm. As for Nick's rosary? It had been his great-great grandmother's, and was made of rose quartz. He hung both of these prized items from the rear view mirror of his car at home, and did the same thing with rental cars when he traveled abroad. At least three times, I had seen Jon yank these items off the mirrors when getting behind the wheel of Nick's car and carelessly tossing them aside, insisting they "distracted" him. Despite not being terribly religious, I had always considered Jon's gesture to be disrespectful and borderline sacrilegious, and would take care to lovingly replace the items back on the rear view mirror once Jon was done driving. One time, my best mate had caught me replacing the

pendant and rosary where they belonged and had asked me what I was doing.

"These items are important to Nick and I think he would be upset if he saw them tangled and balled up in the backseat, so I'm putting them back." Jon had rolled his eyes, then the following day placed a battery operated menorah with bright, flashing electronic "candles" atop the dashboard of my car, sarcastically insisting he needed it for "protection."

Jon's mum was Jewish and had raised both her sons as reform Jews, making sure they'd both had bar mitzvahs. However, she was very lenient and did her best to make the experiences fun. She had also encouraged them to make their own decisions about religion and to learn about Christianity, since their father was a Christian. As a result, the Moore family celebrated both Jewish and Christian holidays, and attended church as well as synagogue. Jon had referred to this childhood ritual as a "double helping of bullshit."

Aside from the annoyances of these religious rituals, Jon rather enjoyed learning Hebrew, visiting Israel, and discovering delicious Jewish food. But the only other positive, according to my best mate, was that my family attended the same church as his family, so it would often double as a social activity for him and me. In fact, if there was a day I didn't go to church, Jon wouldn't go either. Anyway, after sitting through one too many boring lectures at both places of worship, witnessing rampant homophobia among worshippers and clergy alike, and hearing about Nick's nightmare of a Catholic upbringing, Jon had written off organized religion for the most part, identifying as agnostic by early adulthood. As such, he hadn't attended a religious service since his early twenties. Daryl, by contrast, was a touch more observant, and found that liberal

Christianity suited him better than Judaism. While not nearly as religious as Nick, Jon's younger brother attended church on Easter and Christmas at bare minimum, and prayed somewhat regularly.

As a final act of protest against what Jon referred to as an "invisible form of mind control in the sky," he had, at age 22, accepted Nick's invite to midnight mass on Christmas, but had no intention of taking the service seriously. In fact, the first 20 minutes of what he referred to as a "brainwashing seminar with music," he had convinced Lisa to have sex in the church bathroom. When ejaculating in her mouth, he had called it "the new way to take communion." That was also the night he had delivered what I considered his most memorable quote regarding his beliefs: "Holidays are nothing more than a bloody excuse to eat whatever, drink whenever, and fuck whoever." He'd spent the remainder of the service getting drunk on the vodka he had smuggled into the church, throwing communion wafers at the backs of people's heads, and mumbling "a-hole" in place of "amen" during prayers. Nick had been fully engrossed in the service as well as the music and was even moved to tears during a rousing rendition of "O Holy Night." He hadn't seemed to notice anything my jackass best mate was saying or doing. Jon had topped off the evening by urinating on the statue of the Virgin Mary located outside the church. Luckily, none of the other patrons had seen him do it. My immature 20-something self had found his antics to be very funny, but my evolved 30-something self found it insensitive, immoral, and rude.

Fast forward more than a decade later, and Jon was a bit more accepting of Nick's religious beliefs but still had what I privately called his "overgrown frat boy" moments. While he was far past the point of pissing on a religious statue, pelting worshippers with communion wafers, or shagging in a church toilet, he still found sneaky ways of

making his opinions known. At this moment, it manifested in the contents of a kitchen junk drawer.

Jon opened the drawer and took out two small items, placing them on the kitchen counter. A sly little grin spread across his face.

"Hey, Nick?" Jon called out. "I found your rosary and pendant!"

Nick came barreling into the kitchen with a flushed face, clearly flustered from searching for the two items he probably cherished more than his wedding band. He grabbed the rosary and pendant and gave Jon a big hug, appearing close to tears.

"Thanks so much, buddy," he said in a choked up voice. "I would have cried my eyes out if I had lost those. They're so precious to me."

Jon backed away and smiled condescendingly. "They were tucked away in the junk drawer for some reason," he said with what sounded to me like blatantly fake innocence. "Must have happened when I was cleaning the counters last night. I must have put them away and forgotten." He turned around and flashed me a smirk that made it clear he had misplaced them on purpose just to fuck with Nick and make him panic. Unamused, I glared back at him.

Nick was so sweet and gullible that he didn't suspect for a moment that Jon had pulled one of his nasty tricks on him. He simply thanked him once more and sat down next to Candy, exchanging warm greetings

with her and lighting the first of what would be multiple cigarettes. Lisa quickly got up and poured him a cup of coffee, which he graciously accepted, kissing her on the cheek.

"Sorry about the sauna incident last night," Lisa said in a soothing voice. "It must have been terrifying being locked in there for so long. That could have been dangerous."

Nick shrugged and chuckled. "I had asked you to lock me in there," he admitted as he took a drag. "It wasn't your fault you had fallen asleep and didn't hear me yelling for help."

Lisa giggled softly. "That's right, it's Jonny's fault because he was the one who convinced me to knock back extra shots of vodka with him. He knows that stuff puts me to sleep!" She playfully stuck her tongue out at Jon, who laughed shyly.

"Now why would I EVER be a bad influence?" He said with a wink, once again looking at me with an expression that once again made it obvious he had been up to fuckery. I shook my head at him then decided to ignore him. I picked up my phone and looked at the weather and traffic report.

"Looks like the weather is clear for today," I said to Lisa. "45 degrees and sunny. No traffic delays, either. So, it looks like our trip to Newport will be rather pleasant. I haven't been there in ages. Great choice."

Lisa smiled broadly and lit another cigarette, taking a deep drag. "I'm so excited!" She said as she placed her hand on mine. Even though Jon's ex had a history of problem behavior, she was a very sweet girl and incredibly sexy. As I stared into her lovely green eyes, I got the beginnings of an erection.

Candy looked up from her phone and turned to Nick, smiling at him. He returned her smile, placing his arm around her.

"You ready for an epic casino trip?" Nick asked as he took a drag.

Candy nodded. "I'm feeling lucky," she admitted with a giggle.

"YOU'RE feeling lucky?" Nick asked with a wolfish grin as smoke escaped his nose and mouth. "I'm going on a date with a blond haired, blue eyed angel. Doesn't get any luckier than that."

They looked into each other's eyes with lovestruck smiles. In that moment, I felt that if Jon and Lisa weren't in the picture, Candy and Nick would be a great match for each other.

Bang!

We all jumped. Jon had dropped a dish in the sink, and I had suspected he had done it on purpose to break Nick and Candy's connection.

"Whoops, sorry!" Jon said cheerfully through clenched teeth and a squinty smile. "Hey, Nick, what did you want in your omelette again? I can't recall."

"Avocados, roasted peppers, cheddar cheese, and tomatoes, please," Nick answered. "With home fries, sausage, and whole wheat toast on the side. But no bacon. I'm giving it up for lent." He lit a fresh cigarette with the end of the old one. "I really should be giving up tobacco for lent, but I like it way too much!" He chuckled and took a long drag, inhaling the smoke deeply and holding it in.

On a typical day, Nick smoked between 80 and 140 unfiltered cancer sticks a day, and 3 blunts of weed. He used a vape while at work and in other places where he couldn't smoke, stealing drags off his pen whenever he could. The cigars and pipe tobacco he tried to limit to his days off, but wasn't always successful. This habit began at age 7 and, similar to Jon and Lisa, got worse over time. These days, he smoked constantly, even while eating and bathing. Lisa wasn't much better than him and lit up almost as frequently, and with full flavor menthol 100's, no less. Like Nick, Lisa's smoking habit had started in first grade, and by age 12 she was smoking 2 packs a day.

Jon rolled his eyes at Nick. "You and your lent," he grumbled as he turned back to the counter to chop veggies. After a few seconds, he stopped chopping and took a small jar out of the refrigerator. He made eye contact with me, once again getting that look on his face.

I squinted at the jar and saw the green contents as well as the telltale Japanese characters adorning the side. It was wasabi. The infamously spicy Japanese garnish. I bit my lip as I saw my best mate scoop a very generous amount of it onto Nick's eggs, humming as he did so. Nick loved spicy food, but the amount of wasabi that Jon was piling on there would surely be excessive, even for a spice lover. I kept my mouth shut and sipped my coffee in silence, knowing damn well that there was no reasoning with Jon when he got like this.

Just then, Anna rested her lovely head on my shoulder, providing a welcome distraction from Jon's passive-aggressiveness. I ran my fingers through her long red locks, taking the time to bury my nose in her sweet smelling hair. Meanwhile, the kitchen began to fill with the delicious scent of home fried potatoes and various other breakfast items that Jon was cooking up, and I felt my mouth watering.

Within the next few moments, Jon began piling platters of delicious food onto the dining table, figuring it was easier to serve everyone "family style," than to load everyone's plates separately. The table was already set, and we each took turns filling our plates and passing the dishes around when needed. Before long, we all had heapfuls of delicious eggs, potatoes, and toast on our plates, and glasses full of fresh squeezed orange juice.

"Valentine's Day breakfast is served," Jon said with a flourish as he removed his apron and sat at the head of the table, perpendicular to Candy and Anna.

Nick exhaled the smoke he had been holding for what had been several minutes, and took another drag before having us all join hands in prayer. Jon grudgingly obliged but kept his eyes open and refrained from saying "amen" at the end of it.

"Smells delicious," Nick commented, as he dug into his eggs, still holding his cigarette in his opposite hand as he did so.

Jon smiled cheerfully at Nick, clearly pleased with himself for dumping so much wasabi in his friend's eggs. "There's a special ingredient in there," he said in a voice dripping with sweetness.

Nicks eyes widened and a smile spread across his naive face. "Let me guess… is it love?" He scooped up some eggs onto his fork.

Jon bit his lip to keep from laughing then quickly recovered. "Yes, Nick, of course!" He replied in a voice better suited for young children and not a thirty something adult.

I rolled my eyes and began to eat my toast, noticing how Jon kept his eyes glued on Nick as he shoveled a large forkful of the wasabi laden eggs into his mouth. It would be a few seconds before the spiciness would kick in, after which point, Nick would most likely be in some agony.

"How's the nipple?" Jon whispered to Candy, who blushed slightly.

"Sore," she replied with a wink as she ate her potatoes.

I noticed Nick sneaking a wary glance in Jon's direction. It was clear he knew how sadistic my best mate could be and felt protective of Candy.

Jon nodded and placed his hand gently on his girlfriend's shoulder. "I figured that would happen after I bit hard enough to break the skin. I can put more ointment on it before you leave?" His tone was soothing.

Candy nodded and smiled sweetly. "Sounds good to me."

Just then, Nick began to moan. "Mmmm," he said as he chewed his eggs, taking a sip of his juice as his face turned pink.

Jon's eyes perked up. "How are the eggs, Nick?" He asked in the too-sweet voice again.

"They're amazing," Nick said as he shoveled a big piece into his mouth. "You put extra hot sauce on it, didn't you? Along with wasabi? So good!" Just then, he grabbed the hot sauce off the table and poured more of it over the eggs.

Knowing Jon had been defeated, I stifled a laugh. My best mate sighed as he stabbed at a piece of egg on his plate, clearly not thrilled that his plan to fuck with Nick had failed miserably.

"Glad you like it," Jon said in a flat tone as he scowled, dejectedly shoveling food into his mouth like a bratty little kid whose mum just told him he couldn't watch TV before bed.

Anna kissed me on the cheek just then, before turning her attention to Jon. "I'm excited for our trip to Boston," she said with a smile.

Jon looked up at her and returned a sexy grin. "As am I," he crooned as he took a sip of his coffee. "And we are going to have a great time, I assure you. Lots of fun little things planned."

Nick lit yet another cigarette while his mouth was still full of food, and Lisa did the same. "Are you guys going to Quincy market?" He asked excitedly. "Last time Lisa and I went to Boston, we spent hours there. Great place to shop and lots of incredible food choices."

Jon smirked. "Well, we sure as hell aren't going to church," he snarked. "As for you, I'm surprised you agreed to the casino, considering how 'sinful' gambling is."

Nick chuckled good naturedly at Jon's sarcastic remarks. "Hey, I'm the one who got married in Vegas, remember? Besides, God loves us as we

are. None of us are angels. Well, MOST of us aren't." He looked over at Candy with a wink, who blushed and winked back.

Jon cleared his throat, appearing irritated. "Yeah, Nick, you got married in Vegas but you still wanted a 'chaser' ceremony at your Catholic Church, because you didn't believe that a wedding officiated by a skydiving Elvis was legitimate in the eyes of 'your' god."

Lisa chimed in, noticing how flustered Jon was getting. "Hey, Jonny, I know how you feel about religion," she began in a soothing voice. "But for some, it can be a source of comfort."

Jon took a breath and appeared more calm. "That's fair comment," he said quietly, as he ate some more of his eggs. "It's just... my experience has been different from yours."

Nick piped up, as he took a drag off his ciggy. "Hey, why don't you try going to mass with us while we are in town?" He asked cheerfully. "It's changed a lot since we were younger. It's more progressive. Maybe we can ALL go?" He gestured around the table to include the rest of us. Despite the fact that I hadn't attended church in several years, I was open to the idea of attending mass but knew better than to say so at that moment.

Jon scoffed. "'Progressive'? As in, they wait until your second visit before they make you sacrifice a young homosexual?" Candy placed her hand on Jon's shoulder, perhaps in an attempt to pacify him, but he kept on. "Nick, how about this: you keep religion in your way, and I keep

it in mine, hmm?" With a red face, he shoved a large serving of food into his mouth and stared angrily at his plate.

Poor Nick looked ready to cry at that moment, biting his lip as he looked down at his plate. Lisa, who sat at the opposite end of the table as Jon, reached diagonally across the table to touch Nick's shoulder. She knew of Jon's bad experiences with religion, specifically the homophobia he had witnessed, and the allegations of child molestation by at least one of the clergy members at the Catholic Church that Nick had taken him to. Having been molested himself as a boy, Jon had felt very triggered and retraumatized when he learned of the incident, hence his rebellious attitude at midnight mass that one Christmas.

Jon's history of bullying Nick goes all the way back to when he and I had moved to the states in the second half of fifth grade, and met the bloke for the first time. As I have mentioned, Nick was the first male friend we had made after moving to America, and since he was originally from Montreal, we had all bonded over the fact that we were immigrants. Nick was fluent in French, and my multilingual best mate enjoyed having conversations with him, especially when they were in public and didn't want others to know what they were saying.

Nick's wholesome, happy go lucky personality, religious leanings, and Canadian accent occasionally made him an easy target for teasing, as did a learning disability that made his parents put him in private school for a short time. However, he managed to become more popular once he proved himself to be not only a class clown but also a talented athlete, and got "image coaching" from Jon. My best mate had treated him to a new wardrobe and several "makeovers" over the years, and Nick, being the easy going boy that he was, went along with it. He was always grateful for Jon's "help," seeing that it landed him more

modeling and acting jobs. He never once considering the possibility that my best mate was grooming him, and making it so he was "cool enough" to be accepted into Jon's group of friends. Nick's muscular physique, kind personality, and what Jon called "pasty Irish and Canadian good looks" with his jet black hair and light green eyes, got him a lot of positive attention from the girls, and even some boys who, at the time, had the good sense to keep their sexuality a secret... at least until high school.

The year following the pivotal wrestling match that ended Jon's winning streak, Nick switched schools and joined our school's wrestling team. Being Jon's teammate, however, didn't entirely change my best mate's feelings of resentment towards Nick. While Jon was often helpful towards Nick and even tutored him with his school work, he took advantage of our friend's naïveté and, not long after taking his virginity, began to bully him even more. If he wasn't making him his personal servant during parties and calling him names, he was going after him in the school locker rooms after sports practice. Things came to a head when, one day, Nick and I were taking showers in the boys' locker room and Jon came in, naked and with a fully erect cock.

He'd had that look on his face that made it known he was in a predatory mood. I closed my eyes and played it cool as best I could while he picked the shower directly between me and Nick and lathered up, his soapy hand lingering around his bulging penis as he stood under the stream. I jumped as I felt his hand touch my back, knowing better than to fight him when he lathered me up with his bar of soap.

"Why are you so tense, mate?" He had asked sexily in my ear as the bar of soap made its way to my butt crack. "Relax."

I had taken deep breaths and made sure to keep my eyes shut as his hand made it around my front, reaching my penis. I had simply pretended that he was a girl, and was able to relax somewhat as he did things to me that I didn't want him doing. Playing this game helped me feel less guilty about not putting up a fight.

Just when I had thought he was going to try and pressure me into giving or receiving a blow job, he had let go of my member and kissed my shoulder then walked over to Nick, who, like me, did his best to be cool. UNLIKE me, however, Nick was ok with being on the receiving end of anal sex, and Jon was about to take advantage of this.

"Hey, buddy," Jon had crooned, using Nick's preferred term of endearment as a way of mirroring him so he would let his guard down and be more willing to submit sexually. He moved in close to Nick and began masturbating him from behind. Nick tensed up initially then began to moan as Jon got down on his knees and gave him a rusty trombone. After a few minutes, Jon got to his feet and violently bent Nick over, entering him roughly.

Nick's face had contorted in pain as he endured the brutal sodomy, the water cascading over his frightened, trembling body as he did so. All I could do was watch, knowing that if I intervened, Jon would hurt him worse. The slapping sound and subsequent moans echoed off the locker room walls and as much as I wanted to walk away, my feet remained planted on the wet tile, and my head under the spray. After what seemed like an eternity of pounding the shit out of Nick, Jon began to choke him from behind, not letting up until his legs gave out and he fainted.

When Nick's body had crumpled to the tile floor, Jon's entire countenance changed and within seconds, he went from an aggressive bully to caring friend. I knelt down and turned off the water that was raining down on an unconscious Nick. Blood trailed from his bum as he lay there. Jon had really hurt him.

"Come on, Nick," Jon said shakily, as he cradled his friend's head in his hands and lowered his own to Nick's mouth and nose to make sure he was breathing. He appeared relieved that he was, even if the breathing was shallow. Bruises had already begun to appear on his neck from where Jon had mercilessly choked him. I said a silent prayer to god as I begged Nick to open his eyes. Jon bit his lip, barely managing to keep himself from shedding tears that rarely fell due to his emotionally repressed nature. After several more horrifying moments, Nick opened his eyes and began to cough, clutching his sore neck as he did so.

"Oh, thank God you're alright," Jon had said as he held his friend close. Nick lay there weakly, his eyes at half mast as he regained consciousness. As this happened, Jon kept whispering "Thank you, God," occasionally looking upward as he did so. It wasn't lost on me that my best mate went from "borderline atheist" to "believer" when there was a crisis. While Jon held him, I had gotten up and grabbed some water for Nick to drink, as well as a towel for him to hold against his bleeding backside. When we had finally gotten him to his feet and helped him get dressed, he had needed paper towels to shove inside his boxer briefs, so he wouldn't bleed through them. Jon had felt terrible for hurting him, apologizing for being too rough and assuring him he loved him but got carried away. As was typical, Nick had been a good sport and made jokes on the bus ride home, talking about how he had his "man period." We'd laughed until our bellies hurt.

The next several hours had been spent pampering Nick, who, despite persistent rectal bleeding, had insisted on skipping a trip to the hospital. "I can't let my parents know what happened," he had said as he sat on a bag of ice in my bedroom. "My dad will kill me if he finds out I'm bisexual." Jon and I had both agreed that it was cruel of Nick's father to be so judgmental about his only son's sexuality, but understood the desire to be discreet. Thankfully, the ice stopped the bleeding and the antibiotic cream had helped prevent infection. Jon had given him makeup lessons as well, showing him how to cover up bruises with concealer. The three of us blokes stayed at my house that night, deciding that was the safest place to be since Jon and Nick both had fathers who were overbearing and strict. Also, my sister Bridget and brother Lawrence were both away that night so we had more "alone" time. We had spent hours in my room, talking and watching the telly. My parents had been very nice to Nick that evening, ordering pizza and giving us our privacy. I'd appreciated how nobody asked questions when we had retreated to my bedroom with bags of ice for Nick's bum. As for the antibiotic cream? I'd already had 2 tubes of it in my bedroom, from when I had done anal on a girl and had made HER bleed.

Fast forward to present day, and Jon was once again acting like a locker room bully, and it would only be a matter of time before his behavior would catch up with him for the hundredth time.

After Jon and Nick's little episode, conversation gradually returned to normal and we were all making friendly small talk over breakfast. Between Nick and Lisa lighting up constantly, the air got rather thick with smoke, even with Jon's advanced air purifier to help. Craving a cancer stick myself, I lit up one of my clove ciggies and brought up an idea that had occurred to me while having sex with Anna the night

before. She had been riding me cowgirl style and I recalled feeling very turned on by it. I was so used to being in charge and "on top" that a change of pace felt good. So half way through my second cup of coffee, I made my suggestion.

"I have an idea," I began. "When it comes to having sex with our respective dates, how about a little role reversal? As in, 'tops' become 'bottoms,' and 'bottoms' become 'tops?'"

Everyone instantly became excited, agreeing wholeheartedly with the idea. Nick was especially vocal about it.

"Lisa almost never lets me dominate," he said teasingly. "So this would be a change of pace for sure! As long as Candy is up for it." He turned to look at Jon's little angel, who nodded enthusiastically.

"I'm in a similar boat," Candy said as she stuck her tongue out at Jon, who laughed good-naturedly.

"Naturally, this means that lovely Anna gets to tie me up and have her way with me," Jon said as he gazed sexily at my darling redhead and winked. Anna blushed and giggled. When I envisioned her dominating my best mate, I couldn't help but get aroused.

Lisa piped up. "And Kenny will let me peg him!" she chirped.

My heart immediately began to race at Lisa's words and I became mortified. Lisa didn't know of my aversion to being fucked up the arse, much less the fact that I was barely able to handle 2 fingers up there. But I simply chuckled. My best mate looked at me sympathetically before directing his attention to Lisa.

"Ken doesn't do anal," Jon said, as he lit a cigarette. "He doesn't like it. But he does like being choked." He winked at me.

I nodded in agreement. "Jon's right," I admitted, taking a sip of coffee. "I can't handle more than a finger in my arse but I love when a girl wraps her hands around my throat."

Lisa smiled sexily. "I will keep that in mind."

Just then, Anna ran her fingers through my hair, making tingles run down my spine. Between my lovely redhead caressing me and that little lioness smiling seductively, I got a huge erection. I so wanted to fuck them both. Breakfast couldn't end quickly enough!

By the time we were done eating and were getting ready to go on our respective trips, Jon became unusually sweet towards Nick. Initially, I had thought it was because he felt guilty about snapping at him about religion, but something he said made it clear there was something else. Something he was plotting.

"Hey, buddy," Jon whispered to Nick before he and Candy got ready to head out the door to the casino, "There's a little something in the guest bedroom that will spice things up a wee bit for you when you sit in the jacuzzi. It's on the nightstand."

Nick smiled gratefully. "Thanks! I can't wait. And I appreciate you letting me use your bedroom."

Jon nodded. "Of course. Just make sure you clean the tub afterwards. I know you probably plan on turning it into a giant vat of noodle soup and I don't want ramen or spicy seasoning to clog up the filter." He winked.

Nick laughed heartily. "You know me too well! And yes I will definitely clean it, from top to bottom."

Jon's comment about "spicing things up" had me more than curious, so I began to sneak my way up to the bedroom that was next to the master. Once I opened the door, I went over to the nightstand and saw a blue plastic bag with handles that were tied in a knot, and writing on it in big bold letters that read, "Just use a wee bit in the jacuzzi! Contents are rather hot!"

I untied the knots and opened the bag to see what was inside. The moment I did that, my eyes began to water, my nose began to run, and my throat began to burn.

"Bloody hell!" I gasped.

Many hours later...

"Oh, fuck me, Mistress..."

My voice came out in gasps as Lisa bounced up and down on my cock, her short, sexy red nightgown billowing around her. The tablet sat atop my nightstand and we were able to watch the split screen sex show as we fucked.

It had been Jon's idea to turn our partner swapping fuckfest into an x-rated "zoom" meeting, and we had all found the idea to be incredibly hot as well as innovative. However, I knew my best mate and could read him like a book, so I knew that the reason he wanted to do this was to keep an eye on what Nick was doing with his beloved Candy.

Incidentally, Jon's little angel and Nick were both wearing a pair of green fairy wings, and Nick was running a magic wand up and down Candy's naked body. She lay atop Jon's bed with her legs spread, as Nick grazed her clavicle, nipples, navel, and labia. Eventually he turned the wand around and inserted the handle into her pussy, pumping in and out. "I want to sprinkle fairy dust on your garden," he said sexily. Nick enjoyed referring to women's intimate parts as "gardens" or "flowers," deciding that it was more respectful and poetic than more vulgar terms. He slowly took out the handle of the wand and picked up a shimmery plastic container, holding it closer to the video screen. "Edible glitter." He smiled and sprinkled some of the silvery substance onto Candy's breasts and mound, then bent over and began licking the contents off her body. She squealed and giggled at the sensation. Nick occasionally

stuck out his tongue and laughed, happy to show off the glitter to both his fairy partner and the audience. We all chuckled, more than a bit amused at Nick's silliness.

Before long, the glitter was gone and Candy had climaxed when he had gone down on her for a few short minutes, letting his lips and tongue go wild inside her. It was all very sexy in an other-worldly, hippie kind of way. I couldn't help but applaud, and my best mate joined in.

In their spare time, Nick and Lisa frequented renaissance fairs as well as Cosplay parties, where they enjoyed dressing up in everything from fairy outfits, to parasols and old-fashioned suits, to pirate costumes. However, they favored the fairy look, describing the practice of wearing wings as "freeing." Some of the outfits were racy and came with edgy accessories like fishnet stockings, barely-there codpieces, or ultra-high heel shoes, making them especially suitable for bedroom fun.

As that was happening on the left side of the screen, the right side revealed a smiling Jon, who was in the bedroom of the in-law apartment at his parents' house and was being dominated by my darling Anna. He was sitting in a chair fully clothed while Anna did a strip tease for him. She was wearing a black bra and underwear with patent leather high heels, and she was grinding on his lap. Her long red hair flowed freely as she moved. It was beyond sexy to watch. Then she began slowly unbuttoning his shirt, then his pants, and eventually freeing his cock. She then got on her knees and sucked him off. He lit a cigarette then looked at the tablet and winked before tilting back his head in rapture.

Lisa lit a cigarette as she continued to ride me. She took a deep drag and held in the smoke. After at least a minute, she leaned over and blew a cloud of smoke in my face before kissing me hard on the mouth. Out of the corner of my eye, I noticed the monitor. Nick was leaning over Candy and kissing her passionately for a few moments before picking her up, carrying her, and pinning her against the wall. Her legs were wrapped around his waist. He had one muscular arm under her bum while using the other to line up his huge cock with her pussy. Then he thrusted up into her over and over, his fairy wings bobbing up and down as he did so. It was so arousing, and even Lisa enjoyed the view of her husband in "fairy mode" and fucking another woman silly. As for Jon, his eyes remained riveted to the tablet screen, perhaps doing his best to put aside any feelings of jealousy.

My date with Lisa had been lovely. We had arrived in Newport by 9am and had a spa day complete with a fancy lunch and plenty of sight seeing. During one of our 3-way video chats, I had kissed her in my car, being sure to massage and taste her breasts as I did so. Her pierced double d's had been so much fun to suck on. I also took her shopping and got her a few cute accessories, fashionista that she was. I made sure to get something for Anna as well. That's right, after we were done shagging our "partners for the day," we were going to meet up at Jon's house to exchange Valentine's gifts with our real partners and have a wild and crazy six-way. I could hardly fucking wait.

After a few more minutes of fucking Candy against the wall, Nick hooked both arms under her arse and, still burrowed inside her, fucked her in mid-air. Nick was naturally strong as an ox, and managed to keep his athletic physique despite only working out once or twice a week. He's always claimed that cigarettes have helped him stay lean, along with eating copious amounts of protein. Steak was one of his favorites and he would eat a huge sirloin at least three times a weak, with a side

of ribs and asparagus. He would enjoy the feast with 2 blunts of weed, 3 martinis, and two packs of cigarettes, preferably clove, which he has said makes the steak taste that much more delicious. "Dessert" was either a hash brownie or a triple espresso with whipped cream and several shots of rum, typically enjoyed with a Cuban cigar. Personally, I had always felt that, like Jon, Nick was a freak of nature, whose vices should have caught up with him by 30, giving him at least a chronic cough and high blood pressure if not an outright heart condition or a weight problem.

While in the casino, Candy and Nick had video chatted with us as well. During the chat, Candy had laughed about how high energy Nick was. Aside from physical strength, his stamina was legendary, rivaling mine as well as Jon's. Between his singing in the car (while chainsmoking), playing air hockey in the arcade for an hour with no break, dancing with Candy to live music for another hour nonstop (and fast dancing, no less), and visiting practically all the damn shops in the mammoth structure that was the casino, Nick was a force of nature. He had kissed Candy for the first time while on camera, and it had been a sweet kiss. They had been sitting at a restaurant table, away from others so he could sneak hits off his vape. Candy was about to dig into a pile of cheese fries, while he suddenly leaned over and locked lips with her. Nick was a very wet kisser but also very gentle, only getting rough after verbal encouragement. Jon's kisses, by contrast, were often smothering and felt like being gagged, swallowed alive, or bitten by a damn vampire. His hugs felt like being crushed. It took effort for Jon to "reign it in," so to speak. As I had put it years ago to a friend who hadn't met Jon but had met Nick, "If Nick is a teddy bear or pussy cat, then Jon is a python or boa constrictor."

As for Jon and Anna? They'd had an amazing time in Boston, hitting up Quincy Market for shopping and lunch, as well as a five star spa and

salon in downtown Boston. While there, Jon had treated her to a haircut and blowout, along with a manicure/pedicure, massage, and body treatment. He had done similarly for himself, and bought an array of skin, nail, and hair products for Anna with no expense spared. Then, true to his bold personality, he had kissed her in the middle of Quincy Market on a busy street, twirling her around as he did so. Several people had recognized Jon from commercials and movies he'd been in, and had asked for autographs and selfies with him. Always unfailingly polite to fans, my best mate had been very gracious and took the time to write a nice, heartfelt message with his name written in his trademark, back-slanting cursive.

Fast forward several hours, and it was clear that Anna was the bold one. After sucking off Jon for several minutes, she got up and ordered him to lie down on the bed, at which point she tugged down his pants. He was now totally naked and smiling at his lovely, red haired dominatrix, who picked up a giant dildo. Anna spat on the end of it and smirked at Jon, who spread his legs with glee. She wasted no time shoving the silicone penis inside Jon's tight bum. He cried out in pleasure, a huge smile on his flushed face.

Lisa smiled broadly at the scene of her ex getting arse-fucked by a huge dildo, and began teasing my nipples with her long nails. Her hips grinded against mine, and I felt myself grow even harder inside her. I loved the way the juices from her aroused pussy mixed with her period blood, making for an incredibly slippery ride that was messy in a sexy, depraved way. She pinched and twisted my nipples for a few moments then her hands glided their way up to my throat. While still thrusting, she began to squeeze. My manhood nearly exploded right then and there.

"Uhhhh!" Jon moaned as Anna continued to violate his bum with the dildo, going at a faster pace. Nick and Candy glanced at the screen, smiling as they watched Jon and me getting dominated by our respective dates. Just then, Nick carried Candy over to the bed and had her lie on her back at the edge, at which time he butterflied her.

"Your flower feels so good against my magic wand," Nick said between thrusts with a sexy smile as he caressed Candy's legs, which rested against his front. "I could stay in your lady garden all night."

Laughing from Jon ensued. "Nick," he began through chuckles as Anna began to eat his arsehole, "For the love of all that is holy, no pun intended, call it a cunt! Or at least a pussy!"

We all broke into laughter, and Nick actually said "pussy" at one point, perhaps rationalizing that it also meant "cat." He AND Lisa were always proper and respectful when it came to sex talk, and sometimes even poetic. It was never "fucking;" it was "making love," "two becoming one," or "walking through a garden." A clit was a "rose bud," and a penis was a "wand" or a "sheath." Anal sex was the "back yard" or "dessert." Many years prior, I had asked Nick why he referred to sex acts and private parts in such proper terms, his explanation had been very mature and evolved. "I believe that sex is a beautiful thing, and that the body parts associated with it deserve to be referred to with utmost respect, since they were created by God. Every time we refer to a woman's vagina as the 'C word' or a penis as the 'D word,' we are degrading and devaluing these instruments of pleasure. We're not appreciating them for their inherent godliness and beauty, or their potential to create feelings of ecstasy." I had agreed, and added words like "copulation," "womanhood," and "maleness" to my vocabulary when shagging, much to my wife's delight... and Jon's laughter.

Lisa suddenly held the lit end of her cigarette to my nipple, making me cry out in a mix of pain and pleasure. The others looked at the monitor with fascination, followed by horny smiles. It seemed that everyone was getting off at the sight of me getting off on pain, and the thrusts only got harder and faster.

Anna began to fist fuck Jon, who howled in delight. Our eyes remained fixed to the screen as my best mate got fucked up the arse in a most hardcore way. Nick decided to compete for kinkiness, lifting and holding Candy's bum off the bed as he continued to butterfly her. Jon had told Candy that, like himself, Nick loved an acrobatic partner, so she brought her legs back until she was able to put both feet behind her head. Nick smiled broadly and decided to climb up onto the bed, letting himself fall onto her over and over again in a contortionist version of the pile driver position.

"I see you've been doing your yoga," Nick panted as he fucked the hell out of the world's sexiest pretzel.

Candy giggled as she did her best to tolerate Nick's pounding, her body remaining folded in half as she did so. "Jon makes sure I stay nice and limber," she quipped.

"One of the benefits of having him for a partner," Lisa said with a wink as she lit another ciggy with the end of the old one. "Nick ALSO loves a flexible woman, as does my sexy Ken!" Then, while still riding my dick, she opened her legs super wide until she was doing a split. My cock nearly exploded right then and there as I lifted my hips higher and

grabbed her luscious tits. A mixture of blood and pussy juice covered my lower abdomen and public area, and dripped down to my taint and arsecrack. Just then, I noticed the screen.

Nick was giving a thumbs up to Lisa. "Well done, honey!" He said with an applause. Then he got in close to a still-folded Candy and whispered in her ear. She smiled and nodded then took her feet out from behind her ears, got off the bed, and got into a handstand position while Nick held onto her legs. Then he began wheelbarrowing her. All this was happening whilst both of them were still wearing fairy wings, and I found the sight all the more arousing, as did Jon who was still getting fisted up the arse by Anna.

"I love watching my little angel get piledriven and wheelbarrowed," he crooned as Anna's fist disappeared up his arse up to her wrist. "We're still working on her letting me fuck the shit out of her while suspended from hooks going through her skin, but that won't happen until she can tolerate getting a body piercing."

Everyone became still at that moment, shocked at Jon's comment. It seemed that, despite his overall level of sensitivity and compassion improving, his hardcore sadistic side was still alive and well. Lisa was the first to recover, grinding against me slowly as she cleared her throat.

"Jonny," she began in a motherly tone, "You know how tough the 'suspension' was for me to get through, even after many years of BDSM. I had been in a ton of pain and I had actually passed out twice, remember? You and Candy have only been together a short time, so it

may take a while for her to graduate to such an extreme level of edgeplay."

Jon nodded and lit a ciggy as he began to masturbate, smiling at Anna as she fisted him at a faster pace. "This is true, my little lioness," he admitted with a wink. "But can you do me a favor? Can you do a demo for Candy, as far as your level of pain tolerance goes? So she can be… inspired?" He raised his eyebrow.

Lisa nodded, and Nick let Candy come up from her wheelbarrow position to look at the monitor. Then Lisa took the lit end of her cigarette and held it to her left nipple for ten seconds, not flinching or appearing in any form of discomfort. The sound of her flesh sizzling was nothing short of cringeworthy but I still got aroused, as did Candy, Nick, and Anna. As for Jon, he smiled proudly and nodded in approval.

"That's my girl," he said with a huge grin. "I made her the force of nature she is today. When she and I first met, she was so soft. So sensitive. And now? She's practically superhuman."

We all laughed at Jon's comment. Lisa began to move her hips at a more frenzied pace, edging me towards orgasm. The others followed suit, with Anna masturbating Jon with one hand and fisting him with the other, and Nick pounding the shit out of Candy's back door as he guided her back into a handstand position. It was very sexy watching Jon's little angel get fucked anally while inverted, and while wearing a pair of fucking wings.

"Oh, God!" I shouted as my cock exploded inside Lisa's cunny. Within seconds, the others climaxed, letting themselves go with various levels of vulgarity. Nick preferred breathlessly uttering "Oh, boy," while Jon favored grunting "Oh, fuck!" As for the women, they moaned and panted without words, their facial expressions being sufficient proof of their rapture. Before I could fully recover from an amazing orgasm, Lisa sat on my face, nearly smothering me as I sucked the heady cocktail of period blood, natural secretions, and semen out of her pussy. I got turned on by the fact that her juices tasted and smelled like a combination of tobacco and weed, with a slight hint of tequila. Jon's ex was a wild one, but, despite her occasional erratic moods, she was a lovely gal. And she was married to one of the nicest blokes I had ever met.

Incidentally, Nick was enjoying what appeared to be his second orgasm, as was Candy, who remained inverted and was panting with pleasure as he fucked her in the arse.

"May I plant another seed in your back yard, my darling?" Nick asked as he continued to go balls deep in her bum, holding onto her legs as he did so.

"Cum in my ass!" She blurted with a smile as her arms began to shake. We all roared with laughter.

"As you wish, milady," Nick panted, then he began to moan and breathe heavily. Candy grunted as she began to climax, and Nick once again sped up his thrusts until he was covered in sweat and breathing very heavily. After a few moments, he let go a heavy sigh and offered praises to God

as he let go a second load into her tight arsehole. Then he bent down and sucked the contents out of Candy's bum, swallowing it without hesitation.

Lisa and I applauded at Nick and Candy's epic climax, as did Jon and Anna, who were taking a smoke break. I decided to do similarly, lighting myself a ciggy.

Loud music suddenly emanated from the tablet. Candy, who was finally right side up, had turned on the stereo in the room and was filling up the jacuzzi with water. Nick wasted no time adding packets of ramen noodles to the water, doing a little dance as he did so. He glanced at the bag with the writing that warned about "hot contents," and I noticed Jon appeared apprehensive on his side of the screen, absentmindedly fondling himself while Anna got up to use the loo. Once the water in the tub was at a high enough level, Nick removed his fairy wings and climbed in. Candy picked up the bag with the writing on it and opened it, then, with Nick's encouragement, emptied all of the contents into the jacuzzi.

Jon began to visibly panic, placing his hand over his mouth as his eyes widened. Then he began to shout at the screen, doing his best to address Candy and Nick. But the music was too loud for them to hear and Nick continued to "cook" in the jacuzzi tub-turned-pot of soup.

Ghost peppers, when chopped up and cooked in large amounts, can be dangerous for the eyes and lungs, causing blindness as well as breathing issues. Hence the warning Jon had written on the bag to use sparingly. Nick, spice lover that he was, had insisted on Candy using the entire

bag's contents. Little did Jon know that, when I had snuck into his room earlier that day, I had replaced the ghost peppers with the much milder red bell peppers I had spotted in his refrigerator.

"Jon, relax," I said into the screen as I fondled Lisa's titties. Jon's ex looked suitably alarmed, and also curious as to what had just happened. "Candy and Nick are ok. See?"

His eyes still the size of pie plates, Jon leaned in closer to the screen, amazed that they were both enjoying themselves and not suffering. Nick was sitting in the hot tub, smoking and singing, while Candy did a sexy dance for him at the edge of it and occasionally threw pieces of vegetables into the hot tub. Both of them would have succumbed to the effects of the peppers by that point, with stinging eyes and possible respiratory distress. Jon had obviously not intended for his beloved Candy to handle the contents of the bag, fully expecting masochistic Nick to do the honors. But, like the peppers themselves, there had been a change of plans. In this case, the change was a positive one.

Jon smiled gently, feeling relieved that they were alright and turned his head to look at a naked Anna, who had just returned from a quick trip to the loo and was eyeballing my best mate like a steak.

"Shall I ride you rawdog?" She asked with one eyebrow raised as she put her hands on her hips.

Jon grinned ear to ear at Anna's words, then he nodded as he began to fondle himself. "You shall. And perhaps smack me around a wee bit if you like."

With those words, my lovely redhead jumped atop Jon's lap and guided his huge cock to her clean shaven womanhood.

More than ready for round 2 and once again hard as a rock, I smiled at Lisa, who began to ride me once more, this time in reverse cowgirl position. As for Nick, he was happily sweating buckets as he reveled in the fantasy of being a dumpling in a giant pot of soup. He handed Candy a large dildo to play with, then took some deep breaths and disappeared beneath the surface of the boiling hot jacuzzi.

One hour later...

The six of us fucked like bunnies on crack in Jon's master bedroom, which he had decorated luxuriously just for the occasion. The light coming from the chandelier was set to a sensual glow, the room darkening curtains were drawn, and lit candles sat atop the end tables and wall shelves. Rose petals were scattered about the floor as well as the bed, and sultry music played from the high end sound system. The bedding was a dark and sensual velvet, with coordinating satin sheets.

I pounded the hell out of Jon's back door as he ate Candy's cunny. As the was happening, Candy was fingering Anna, who was blowing Nick, while he was getting his salad tossed by his darling Lisa. This was the

last of several variations on the epic six-way we had all been looking forward to.

The girlies had all loved their Valentine's gifts, which included a variety of jewelry, flowers, and gourmet chocolate. It felt great to spoil our respective partners, and I couldn't help but fantasize about Anna, and our future together. Until then? It was time to fuck, and to get drunk and high.

Nick had spent more than ten minutes underwater while in the jacuzzi, emerging breathlessly with a smile on his red face as Candy had greeted him with a cocktail in one hand and a pussy juice covered dildo in the other. He had licked the toy clean then had downed the cocktail in five seconds flat. It had been only the beginning of what would turn out to be a drug and alcohol fueled shag fest that would culminate in a number of unexpected events, some more pleasant than others.

"I'm ready to do a line," Nick gasped as he climaxed, ejaculating into Anna's mouth. "My nose is getting hungry." He chuckled, then he lit a cigarette, rose from the bed and made his way over to the nightstand, which had a cosmetic bag situated on it. He opened it up and took out a baggie of white powder, as well as a razor and straw, then began emptying some of the contents onto the table's granite surface. Then he cut himself several lines with the razor.

The rest of us froze and stared at him, rather shocked that someone as pure as Nick Trudeau had picked up a cocaine habit. The most any of us had ever seen him do was drop acid or eat magic mushrooms for what he called "spiritual reasons," but he was mostly into pot and booze, or

perhaps an occasional benzo. Lisa looked particularly upset, which wasn't surprising, considering how much she had despised seeing Jon do coke. Like me, she had witnessed firsthand what the drug did to my best mate's personality, and had experienced the displeasure of watching his nose bleed uncontrollably. It had been a rather pitiful site. I shuddered at the memory, and felt a wave of PTSD wash over me as I watched Nick snort the powder up his nose.

"Anyone else want some?" Nick asked with a smile as he rubbed some powder onto his gums and sniffled a few times, looking more at me and Jon than at the girls since he knew my best mate and I had a history of cocaine use. "It's the high grade kind. Gets you so euphoric, you can feel God's presence. It's like being in heaven."

We all collectively declined, deciding to take a break from sex and refill our drinks instead. Jon, Lisa, and I lit cigarettes, then Lisa spoke up.

"Nick," she began in a motherly tone as she placed her hand on his back, "If you're not careful, you will wind up in heaven for good. You know how dangerous this stuff is." Her expression was that of a caring and concerned wife.

Nick smiled reassuringly as he sniffed and took a drag. "I'm careful with it," he said as he caressed her face. "Don't you worry. I have God on my side. He won't throw anything at me that I can't handle, and the same goes for those I love."

"Oh, for fuck's sake," Jon snapped as he sprang up from the bed and stormed out of the room, slamming the door behind him.

I couldn't blame Jon for being incredulous, especially after seeing how cocaine affected his health. He knew from personal experience that faith in God alone wasn't enough to prevent someone from going down a long rabbit hole. He had needed to go to rehab and spend hours in therapy to train himself not to use his favorite drug. The spirituality component only came after months of detoxing, relapses, and emotional struggles, at which point Jon was ready to give up. But meditation and prayer helped him get through the pain of withdrawals as well as the unpleasant side effects of the meds he took for depression. Unbeknownst to Nick, my best mate had begun praying regularly about a year and a half prior, but was very private about it. In fact, the few times I had caught him on his knees saying prayers under his breath, he had rapidly made it look like he had been doing yoga or looking for something on the floor.

"Would you excuse me for a moment, sweetheart?" I asked Anna, who nodded and smiled sweetly. Then I got up and walked out of the bedroom to talk to Jon.

Fifteen minutes later...

"Get off him, Ken!" Jon shouted as I strangled Nick, who struggled against me as I straddled him. But my best mate couldn't pull me away. My rage was at full throttle. "Tricky Nicky" had crossed a line with me as well as with Jon, and I wasn't about to let it go.

Not long after I had gone out and joined Jon in the living room couch to chat with him, a coked out Nick came down. His wild eyes gave away his level of aggression and when he spoke, it was clear he was out of his mind with cocaine induced psychosis. He immediately accused me and Jon of trying to steal Lisa from him. Jon's reaction was one of incredulous laughter, and I joined in as well.

"It's not funny," Nick said with clenched fists, his blazing blue-green eyes widening. "I know you're both plotting something." Beads of sweat formed on his brow.

Jon took a drag off his ciggy, smirking. "Did the, uh... invisible man in the sky give you this information? You know, the one you pray to?"

Nick's face turned red and he walked closer to us as we sat on the couch smoking. "Yeah well, the invisible man you speak of at least inspired me to marry Lisa properly in a church, rather than the snooty, godless, black-tie affair at the Bellagio you had tried to pressure her into."

More laughing from Jon. "You little arsehole," he said through chuckles. "That 'snooty, godless, black tie affair' was something she and I had BOTH wanted, and had planned together. Unlike your joke of a church ceremony. And in case you forgot, YOU stole her from ME!" Jon rose from the couch, his face a mask of rage.

Nick walked in closer to Jon, a vein popping out of his forehead. "Actually, I didn't steal her, she had come to me for comfort when you were too busy banging chicks left and right while filming your little

movie overseas. And the straw that broke the camel's back was when you were unreachable for five days during her time in the hospital. She had almost bled to death. She still has nightmares about that incident, as well as the miscarriage. Also, she has nightmares AND flashbacks about her sexual experiences with you. We BOTH do. You traumatized us. You probably traumatized Ken, too. And countless others."

I swallowed, being able to relate to Nick and his issues with the nightmares and flashbacks. Jon had been a monster back in the day, and it seemed we all had some form of PTSD from the stuff he had done. Still, I didn't care for the way Nick was dropping all these bombs on my best mate due to being strung out on coke. Because of this, I decided to say something.

I cleared my throat and stood up. "Nick, perhaps it's not the best time to discuss this sort of thing. It's a holiday. So why don't we all retreat to the bedroom and talk about it in the morning, hmm?"

Nick shook his head, the expression on his normally kind face nothing short of scary. "You don't get to tell me what to do."

Then he shoved me. Hard. And I saw red.

"YOU SON OF A BITCH!" I screamed as I charged at him, knocking him to the ground. I wrapped my hands around his throat and squeezed, my strength amplified by my rage.

Nick was as strong as I was, but was completely unprepared for the ambush and, as such, had one hell of a time trying to pry my hands free from his neck. His legs kicked wildly and his face turned deep red as he fought for air, his windpipe close to being crushed.

Jon began to try and pull me away, urging me to back off. "It's not worth it, mate!" He cried as he did his best to drag me off of Nick. But I ignored him and kept on. What finally broke me out of my blind rage was the sound of a fully dressed Lisa running down the stairs in a panic, cell phone in her hand. Candy and Anna followed behind, and they were clothed as well.

"Ken, please!" Lisa begged as she grabbed my right shoulder, with Jon at my left side doing likewise. "There's an emergency! Nick's grandmother is dying."

It took a few seconds for reality to kick in, and I slowly let go of Nick's throat. He sat up, choking and slightly dazed. The next several moments passed in a haze of emotion and confusion, and we all entered autopilot as we got ready to accompany Nick to County Hospital, where his grandmother was on life support after having suffered a massive stroke.

Nick had been very close to his nana on his mother's side, especially after coming out as bisexual and being temporarily disowned by his own father. In fact, he had lived with her for a while before things died down at home. She had always been very kind, never once judging her grandson for his sexuality.

As for my outburst, I knew that it was out of a deep seated anger I had towards Nick for using his religious beliefs as an excuse to make poor decisions with impunity. Seeing him snort cocaine to feel "closer to God" had been the final straw for me, and it had become clear to me why Jon had lost patience with him many years prior. It was hard enough watching him brainwash pagan-leaning Lisa into full blown Catholicism, but hearing him compare hard drug use to a spiritual experience was one line of bullshit too many. Still, annoyances aside, I felt for the bloke, and any feelings of frustration would have to go on the back burner. It was time for me and Jon to be there for our friend while he said goodbye to one of the most important women in his life.

The next few hours melted into days of grieving, and paying respects to a sweet, Irish woman who had loved her grandson like an actual son. Lisa didn't leave Nick's side, nor did I, and nor did Jon. Perhaps out of guilt and a desire to repair things, my best mate was a model friend to Nick, accompanying him to church, praying alongside him in the hospital chapel, and even reading out loud from the Bible while sitting at the grandmother's bedside. She was a devout Catholic and had gone to church every Sunday up until she had fallen ill. One particularly sad day, Nick had begun to cry while reading psalm 23, and Jon had lovingly taken the Bible from his hands and had begun to read in his resonant voice. While that happened, I had held Nick's hand, letting him shed tears silently.

Inevitably, the day came for nana to pass away. It happened in the early morning on a Sunday. A funeral was planned and scheduled, and almost everyone in Nick's large family had come to say goodbye to her. Some of our mutual friends had shown up as well, including Mario, Brittany, Amy, Eugene, Daryl, and Tracy. The ceremony had taken place on a gorgeous sunny day, and, despite the somberness of the affair, it had been a beautiful event, complete with music and several touching

speeches. The highlight, however, was hearing Jon sing "Amazing Grace." I had the honor of playing the organ while his voice carried through the place of worship, and there wasn't a dry eye in that church by the end of the song. Even Nick's father, who was typically unemotional and very strict, had tears in his eyes. Nick himself was, unsurprisingly, bawling his eyes out, and Lisa held him close as she cried. At the end of the song, Jon and I exchanged tearful hugs with Nick, telling him we loved him.

Afterwards, we all went to lunch at a nearby restaurant, discussing memories of the grandmother as well as random stories about our respective families. Some of these stories were rather comical, and it felt good to learn about Nick's family a bit more. Perhaps the hardest part of the funeral was being reminded of my own losses, specifically my wife. Unlike my traumatic dreams about Jon, I rather enjoyed when she came to visit me.

Speaking of my best mate, he and I actually got to have a discussion about the nightmares Nick had talked about. Jon was horrified to learn that Nick, Lisa, and I had been suffering for years from bad dreams about the things he did to us sexually. He apologized tearfully, and we exchanged a prolonged hug, during which I had assured him that it was alright. Jon and I had been through a lot together, and for all the bad shit that had happened, there was plenty of good. We were best mates, and that would never change.

Nick and Lisa left for California several days after the funeral, taking the time to relax and unwind with all of us before returning to their daily grind. It also gave Nick a little extra time to continue detoxing from coke. He hadn't used since that fateful Valentine's night, but, despite suffering from mild withdrawals and cravings, he was determined to

give it up. In an especially bold gesture, he had insisted on Lisa, Jon, Candy, Anna and me watch him pour the contents of the baggie down the toilet. We had cheered and congratulated him, proud of his decision to stop using cocaine.

As a parting gift, Nick gave me and Jon pieces of jewelry that had belonged to his nana. Jon got a sterling silver cross pendant with a small diamond in it, and I got a black rosary. It had been such a touching gesture, made more so by the fact that both items reflected our styles. Jon loved diamond jewelry, and I loved anything black. We had thanked him profusely and promised to wear the items proudly.

"Thanks for being such great friends to me," Nick said as he stood at the doorway of Jon's house, his arm around a smiling Lisa.

"Of course," Jon and I had said in unison, exchanging hugs. Candy and Anna were next, wishing them safe travels and promising to keep in touch until we all met up again.

That night, I had a pleasant dream about Jon, and my wife was in it. In our dream, we had a threesome and Jon had ejaculated on her face, making her laugh. I awoke with a massive erection, a smile on my face, and Nick's rosary on the nightstand next to my bed. I picked it up and fidgeted with the jewelry for a few moments before carefully placing it back down. Then I looked over at Anna, once again whispering "I love you" before turning over on my other side. I loved Anna, this was true, but I still loved my wife. Some things never change.

Chapter 8: Training Wheels

"Will you marry me?"

His timid voice barely registered on the phone's video as he knelt in the sand before his beloved girlfriend, who stood crying tears of joy as her long blonde hair flowed behind her in the breeze. It had been a gorgeous evening in late March and the sunset cast a lovely hue on the beach, making the atmosphere all the more romantic. The ring was a beautiful combination of emerald and diamond, with a dainty, white gold band. His hand trembled slightly as he held out the ornate velvet box that held the piece of jewelry. He had been dreaming of this moment for years, and, after purchasing a ring several months prior, had finally gotten up the courage to ask her.

"Yes!" Tracy exclaimed as tears streamed down her pretty face.

Daryl smiled broadly as he began to cry and got up from a kneeling position, his 6'5 frame contrasting adorably with his now fiancée's 5 foot tall one. He placed the lovely ring on her finger with a trembling hand then kissed her passionately, wrapping his strong, muscular arms around her tiny waist. She returned the embrace as she kissed him through tears, her long, flaxen locks flying wildly in the wind. Just then, Daryl picked her up and twirled her around, making her giggle and squeal with delight. They exchanged tearful I love you's and more hugs, before a smiling Daryl walked up to the phone he had placed in a nearby beach chair and picked up the phone so his handsome face was looking directly at the camera lens.

"She said yes," he stammered as fresh tears of joy spilled from his blue eyes. Then the video ended. Daryl blushed and put down his phone, a shy smile on his face.

We all cheered and clapped at the video, congratulating Daryl and Tracy on their engagement, which was now two and a half weeks old. Being a quiet and shy bloke, Daryl had wanted a simple and somewhat intimate gathering to celebrate the event, and Tracy was fine with that. So Jon and I had gone halfsies and rented out the top floor of Daryl and Tracy's favorite restaurant, which happened to be on a harbor in a nearby town. It was a modest sized venue with a small dance floor. It was also tastefully decorated and had a lovely view. Also, their food was to die for.

I had my arm around Anna as we sat down at our table, along with Daryl, Tracy, Jon Sr, Martha, Candy, Jon, Amy, and Eugene. There were a number of other people there, including some colleagues from the gym as well as some friends and extended family who had made the effort to travel for the event. Nick and Lisa had flown in once again, more than happy to celebrate Jon's little brother getting engaged to his longtime crush. All in all, there were perhaps 30 people, which was at the upper limit of what Daryl considered comfortable. But he was a trooper, taking the time to socialize as well as get drunk and stoned... thanks mostly to me and his bad boy older brother.

"Don't be a pussy tonight," Jon and I teased in unison as we fed Daryl shots at the bar and snuck him hits from Jon's new marijuana vape. "You're such an altar boy," Jon added as he knocked back a shot of tequila. Nick's diamond cross necklace hung from Jon's neck, providing a subtle shimmer to his upscale, earthtone ensemble. "It's bloody time you stop being so wholesome!"

"Hey, I call bullshit," Daryl said with a sly grin. "I'm not as wholesome as you think. In fact, I got a collar for Tracy and she even talked me into ordering a sex swing."

Jon's eyes widened, as did mine. We both patted him on the back and congratulated him on his decision to invest in what was arguably the most fun piece of furniture a couple could purchase.

"Brilliant, mate," I said. "Now do you plan on actually fucking on it or using it as playground equipment?" I asked with a smirk.

The three of us laughed raucously at my wisecrack, while suddenly, Tracy and Amy came up to us with smiles on their faces. "We wanna do shots with you guys!" Tracy exclaimed with a grin, her arm around adorable Amy.

The four of us knocked back shots, then Anna, Candy, and Eugene joined us, getting comfortably hammered. The music became louder in volume and some of the party goers began to dance. After a few more shots, we decided to join them. I took Anna's hand and smiled as I pulled her out onto the dance floor.

As I twirled my lovely redhead around in time to the music, I thought of our relationship and how much I loved her. Daryl inspired me, because if a shy guy like him could get up the courage to propose to Tracy, it seemed reasonable for a more outgoing bloke like me to say the three little words I had been dying to say to her for over a year.

"I love you!!!"

I spun around and was greeted by a shitfaced Daryl, who was already succumbing to the effects of a few shots of tequila and a modest hit off Jon's vape. He wrapped his arms around me and led me in a drunken dance while others cheered us on. I began to laugh and join him in his antics, even lifting him up once or twice. Several guests took pictures and videos with their phones, including Jon, who was beside himself with laughter. It was a riotous good time.

The alcohol continued to flow, with most of the party guests knocking back shots. I even spotted a few people taking pills, and vaping what I assumed was marijuana. After a few more moments of drunken dancing, Daryl eventually found his way back to Tracy, who was getting as inebriated as he was. As for Anna? She was soon dry humping me like she was ready to shag right then and there, and I wasted no time discreetly feeling her up as we danced.

Jon surprised me with a tap on my shoulder, a shit eating grin on his face. He opened his mouth and stuck out his tongue, revealing a blue pill. He quickly knocked it back with a swig of beer, and smiled broadly.

"What was that you just swallowed?" I asked with a smirk as I danced with Anna, who was pleasantly drunk.

"Something that will keep my dick awake all night long, as well as yours," he slurred, before handing me one. "It's prescription, and it's amazing. I already gave one to my brother. He's gonna be as hard as a fucking rock in no time!"

My eyes widened. "I've always wanted to try Viag-"

"Shh!" Jon said with a smile before leaning in to speak into my ear. "You want Anna to think a huge erection lasting for hours is a natural phenomenon, don't you? So you best keep it to yourself."

I laughed and nodded. "This is true!"

Jon patted me on the back. "That's my boy! Now I must get back to my darling Candy. Afterparty at my house, yes?"

"I wouldn't miss it for the world!" I said as I twirled Anna around, quickly and discreetly popping the pill into my mouth and swallowing it without anything to drink.

My best mate gave the thumbs up and ran up to Candy, picking her up and spinning her around in circles. She laughed raucously at the horse play, kissing him passionately once her feet were back on the ground.

Within perhaps a half hour of dancing and occasional drinking, I felt the stirrings of a massive erection forming in my knickers.

Three hours later...

"Oh my fucking God..."

Daryl panted as I sucked him off on the swing set in the park. He sat on the swing with his pants around his ankles as I knelt before him in the sand, taking as much of his ten inches into my mouth and down my throat as I could without gagging. He was probably the drunkest I had ever seen him, and the fact he had begun to grope and French kiss me moments before was testament to that. He identified as heterosexual,

having only consented to a kiss on the lips from me once before, and on an evening when he and I had been marginally more sober.

It hadn't been part of our original plan for all of us to stagger several blocks down the road to a playground, but we weren't quite ready to go to Jon's afterparty just yet. In fact, between the drunkenness, the talk of sex swings, and the blue pills working over time, we needed to fuck... and soon.

Jon was busy pounding the shit out of Candy, who was bent over a mini jungle gym. He moaned in ecstasy as he repeatedly plowed into her, seemingly unaware of what was happening to his younger brother several yards away. Tracy and Amy sat in the sandbox, fingering each other and looking on with horny eyes at Daryl getting blown by his best mate. Eugene lay on a nearby park bench, drunk out of his mind with his hand down his pants, his eyes half open and an intoxicated smile on his face as he watched the scene. An equally sloshed Anna lay next to him, recovering from having been fucked by yours truly on an old school merry-go-round several moments prior, with Jon and Daryl taking turns spinning it. I had nearly lost my lunch after that mess but had managed to keep it together, holding onto the metal handles for dear life.

Fast forward twenty drunken minutes later, and I was sucking off a self-proclaimed straight male, and we were both enjoying it. Months earlier, Tracy had mentioned to Daryl that she considered it hot to picture him having sex with another male, and he had blushed and chuckled softly, shaking his head as he insisted he "didn't fancy blokes." All that went out the window the night of his engagement party, and I had the honor of providing him with his first - and most likely last - sexual encounter involving yours truly.

"Hey, Daryl!" A familiar voice called out, along with girlish giggling. "How's it going, bro?"

Daryl drunkenly opened his eyes to see who was calling his name and several of us turned around. Nick and Lisa hobbling up to us with tipsy smiles on their faces. From the looks of their clothes and hair, it appeared that they had already fucked.

"Hey, it's my brother from another mother and his darling wifey!" Daryl slurred, causing most of us to laugh. I continued to suck him off, feeling self conscious and therefore not quite ready to reveal what I was doing, much less to whom.

"Ooh, it's an after party!" Lisa said with a chuckle as she noticed Tracy, Amy, Eugene, and Anna, all of whom exchanged drunken greetings with them. Jon and Candy were a bit too far off in the periphery to be seen by Lisa and Nick. My other best mate and her girlfriend also seemed to be in their own little world, not appearing to notice the new guests as they shagged. Lisa held onto Nick more tightly, trying not to fall over as she walked on the grass in her high heels.

As Nick and Lisa got closer, they realized what was happening to Daryl and that was when they noticed me sucking him off. Daryl once again had his eyes closed and his head tilted back as he sat on the swing getting blown.

"Oh wow," Nick commented with a horny smile. "Ken, I didn't even see you until now. I thought you were a shadow." He knelt down to me with a sexy smirk on his face. "He must be pretty impaired, seeing that he's been straight as an arrow ever since I've known him...but he seems to be enjoying himself."

"Don't stop," Daryl slurred as he pushed on my head. I laughed and ran my hand up and down his shaft, giving myself time to breathe.

"Would it be alright if I gave him a 'bro job?'" Nick asked with a raised eyebrow. "I've always wanted to do that, and this might be my only chance," he said with a chuckle.

I giggled myself and shrugged. "I don't see why not, but you might want to ask him." I got up from my knees and let Nick kneel down directly in front of Daryl, who wasted no time running his fingers through Nick's full mane of dark hair.

"Mmmm," Daryl moaned. "Suck my dicky, Tricky Nicky," he slurred.

We all broke out in wild laughter at Daryl's words, and then Nick went down on him. As this was happening, Lisa was opening her blouse and lifting up her bra. She positioned her exposed tits to Daryl, who began grabbing and sucking on them. It was a delightful scene. Tracy looked particularly turned on at the sight of her fiancée branching out; whether he would recall anything in the morning was a matter of debate.

"Ughhh!"

Multiple yards away, Candy cried out as Jon pounded the hell out of her, his thrusts making slapping sounds that echoed through the crisp outdoor air.

"Take it like a big girl," Jon growled. "And I expect you to swallow my load, too."

I sauntered over to Jon and his girlfriend, fondling myself as I witnessed her being raped while bent over a piece of playground equipment. It brought me back to the time that my wife and I had visited a playground after hours many years ago...

She had been sitting outside on our deck, smoking. Her long dark hair blew in the breeze and her caramel skin glowed in the evening dusk. Her yellow bikini hugged her curves. Sunset was merely minutes away. I got an erection the moment I saw her. It didn't take long to convince her to take a drive with me to the kiddie park several miles away.

The place was already deserted, so we ran like giddy school children onto the jungle gym. After a few minutes of climbing and horsing around, our eyes locked and we began to kiss. I wrapped my arms around her sexy body as she leaned against the bars of the jungle gym. Then she pulled up her skirt and dropped her bikini bottoms, exposing her shaved cunny. I wasted no time pulling down my own knickers then abruptly lined my stiff cock with her opening. I locked my arm under her

bum as I entered her, making her moan. Within seconds, we were fucking on the jungle gym.

"Hey," she panted after a few minutes of wild and crazy coitus. "Let's baptize the merry go round!"

I chuckled and picked her up, carrying her over to the merry go round, giving it a good spin before jumping aboard. She squealed as her bum hit the metal surface, but I barely gave her a chance to recover before I entered her again. The structure remained spinning for quite a while, making the sex that much more intense. At least once, I had forced her to remain bent over one of the metal handles, occasionally jumping off to give the equipment a fresh "spin." The best part was getting her to hold onto the bottom of the metal handle while I wheelbarrowed her, which was not easy to do while the merry go round was spinning. Yet I managed, as did she.

I was on the brink of climax, when I heard what sounded like a person approaching. So we quickly got dressed. However, upon further examination, I saw that it was a harmless deer. The wife and I began laughing heartily, delighting in the presence of such a lovely animal that seemed completely unfazed by us. In fact, we were able to get close enough to pet the creature. It was such a crazy and surreal experience, going from fucking in a deserted playground to encountering a deer, and one who seemed to enjoy people, no less.

The animal eventually walked away, eventually seeming more interested in finding something to eat. My wife and I looked on in awe

as we waved goodbye, watching it exit the park the same way it had come in. We turned to each other once again. Lust was in her eyes.

"Where were we?" I asked with a sexy smirk.

We wound up shagging on every piece of equipment in that playground, leaving the swing set for last. I had climaxed on that swing while my wife straddled me, and it had been a very intense orgasm. The best part was seeing the deer reappearing, this time with her babies in tow. We had laughed breathlessly at the notion of having woodland creatures for an audience, and wondered aloud how often animals got off on watching humans fuck. Anyway, when we returned home that night, I purchased a sex swing, but not before convincing the wife to sport a pair of antlers while fucking her doggie style (or "deer style") on the couch.

My pleasant trip down memory lane abruptly ended when I heard the all too familiar clanking sound of handcuffs against metal. I looked more closely at Candy and saw that she was handcuffed to the jungle gym and was unable to escape Jon's hard thrusts, or his overall roughness with her. The sight of it both turned me on and unnerved me.

He pulled her hair as he continued to impale her from behind with his manhood, nearly snapping her neck. She gasped in discomfort and wriggled her wrists inside the handcuffs in a futile attempt to free herself from the cold, metal restraints that cut into her flesh.

"You've been a naughty girl," he growled as he pounded her, continuing to yank her blonde

locks as well as choke her. "Not following simple instructions. Being insubordinate. I think you need a lesson. You need to see how a REAL submissive behaves. When we get to my place, I'm going to dominate Lisa and you are going to watch. You need to take notes. And practice, practice, practice."

I smirked as I saw Candy close her eyes and tolerate what was undoubtedly a difficult situation. The girl was so poised. AND dominant. She was a veritable wolf in sheep's clothing, matching my best mate's alpha-ness. Despite my desire for dominance, I had always had a thing for strong women. They provided a challenge that submissive types often lacked. My wife was a perfect example, and she had kept me on my toes from day one with the way she wouldn't give me the time of day, making me earn her affection. As for Anna? She was more complex. I sensed a storm was brewing inside her, one that was ready to overtake her normally sweet and docile façade.

My wife had taught me that the BDSM world was nuanced and multifaceted in its ability to leave "marks." The physical cuts, bruises, and scars left behind from whips, chains, knives, floggers, and fists were only the beginning; the impact that words left behind were often much greater. The evening's events, as well as some future events, would be testament to that.

From several yards away, Daryl groaned his way to orgasm as he sucked on Lisa's double D tit. Tracy looked on with horny delight as her new fiancé succumbed to rapture. Nick's head moved up and down at a more rapid pace and eventually stopped, swallowing what must have

been a rather large load. Daryl had revealed to me during a drunken conversation that he didn't climax every time he had sex and rarely masturbated. His elder brother, by contrast, wrapped his hand around his own cock at least twice a day and orgasmed every time he fucked, which was at least once a day.

"Oh, Nick," Daryl panted with a drunken smile as he lay slumped in the swing, still fondling Lisa's breasts with his hand. "That was beautiful."

Just then, Tracy walked up to her fiancé and planted a kiss on his lips. He pulled her onto his lap, and which time he nearly fell off the swing but managed to remain upright as they giggled. Nick and Lisa exchanged sexy smiles then kissed each other passionately, then Amy went over and sat on Eugene's lap as he lay semi-comatose on the bench, wrapping her arms around him and swapping spit. Last but not least was my darling Anna, who rose from the bench and jumped into my arms with a squeal of delight, at which time I anchored my arms under her bum and twirled her around.

Clank! Clank! Clank! Clank!

The insistent metallic sound echoed through the park and became faster and more intense as Jon pounded away at Candy, groaning as he reached a frenzied orgasm. Candy followed after him, breathlessly moaning her way towards a climax that doled out equal parts pleasure and pain. Then, just as quickly as the sound of their animalistic fucking and accompanying sounds had begun, it stopped. And the only sound that remained was their heavy breathing and the faint chirping of crickets in the background.

Jon undid the handcuffs long enough to free Candy from the confines of the jungle gym but quickly placed her hands behind her back, clicking them closed once more. She bowed her head down in shame as he pulled up his pants and pulled down her skirt in a single, efficient motion, then led her through the park's entrance that doubled as an exit.

When Jon was in full "dominant mode," he didn't notice much of what was happening around him, and most likely didn't know what Daryl had been up to. He hadn't even noticed when Lisa had shown up at the park with Nick. I understood firsthand how it felt to have tunnel vision as a result of being in "top space;" it was a unique experience, one that eliminated distractions and made me feel more powerful.

Just then, a stretch limousine pulled up, ready to take us to Jon's house for the afterparty. Several of us helped Daryl get situated, pulling up his pants and half-carrying him to the shiny, upscale black vehicle.

Jon, having already helped Candy into the limo, was rather surprised by Daryl's disheveled appearance and began to laugh good-naturedly. "How's my baby brother doing? Having a fabulous time, yes?"

Daryl nodded and hugged his elder brother warmly. "Best fucking party ever!" He slurred. "Thanks, big brother!"

Jon chuckled and returned the hug, helping him get seated. "Any time, mate. And there's more fun to be had at my house."

I let Anna go inside the limo before me then entered the vehicle myself. The others followed suit, talking and laughing drunkenly. Music began to play and the smell of marijuana filled the inside of the vehicle. Jon was using his vape, as were Nick and Lisa. Aside from the fact that they were passing them around so we could all have some, it was hard to avoid getting stoned with the windows rolled up. However, the vape provided a nice mellow high when combined with the booze that also flowed freely throughout the limo. In fact, less than halfway through the 20-odd minute trip, we were all pretty fucked up. Daryl and Tracy, who sat across from me and Anna, were half asleep and rested their heads on each other, drunken smiles on their faces. As for Amy and Eugene? They were seated in a separate row, and we all placed bets as to whether they were sleeping or fucking.

My best mate and I spent a majority of the ride whispering filthy things in our respective girlfriends' ears. Anna blushed and laughed at most of what I said to her, whereas Candy appeared more serious. It got to where Jon asked if she was alright.

"I have a headache," Candy replied as she avoided his gaze.

Jon placed his hand on her thigh and smiled sympathetically. "I'm sorry, doll. When this is all over, I will pamper you. I promise." Then he kissed her on the cheek and rested his head on her shoulder, taking occasional hits off his vape. Nick, who sat directly across from Jon and had his arm around his wife, looked at my best mate warily, knowing as well as I did

that Candy was less than thrilled with Jon's plans to "teach her a lesson," which, unbeknownst to Nick, involved watching him dominate Lisa.

I looked over at my lovely Anna, who appeared in high spirits and was singing along to a song playing from the speakers. The limo had a good sound system with plenty of bass. It was a catchy hiphop tune and before long, most of us were singing and rapping along. At some point during the song, Jon leaned over to me with an all too familiar sinister look in his eyes.

"I think it's time to bring out the clothespins and duct tape."

Half an hour later...

"You best lie still or I will cut off your air supply again." Jon's voice was a low growl. Anna and Candy watched from the periphery of the room, equal parts frightened and intrigued, and knowing better than to intervene.

Lisa fidgeted uncomfortably on the bed, lying spread-eagled as Jon tightened the bondage rope around her breasts. As he did this, I tightened the leather straps around her ankles and wrists. She still had a pink imprint surrounding her mouth from where the duct tape had been, as well as marks on either side of her nose from the clothespin. That's right: for the last five or so minutes of the ride home, my best mate had forced his ex to go without air. In a show of support, Nick had

insisted on going without air as well, pinching his nose closed as he held his breath and holding Lisa's hand as he did so.

Years of being with Jon had resulted in Lisa being in impressive physical shape, with plenty of stamina and strength despite her vices. Like Jon, she was already a natural athlete at a young age, participating in a number of sports. Smoking, drinking, and drugs did little to ruin her performance and she managed to win multiple awards in swimming as well as cheerleading. Lisa, Jon, Nick, and I were known to be the heaviest cigarette smokers in both middle school and high school, yet were incredibly athletic; we could outrun most of our peers and hold our breaths for very long periods of time. Lisa, however, had the distinction of being the only female athlete in school who smoked heavily. This reputation of hers took on a newer, more sordid meaning in sophomore year of high school, when she had chainsmoked an entire pack of cigarettes at a pool party then had given Jon an underwater blowjob, remaining underwater for four minutes. After that, her new nickname had become "the Little Mermaid," and it became the inspiration for a small tattoo of a mermaid on her right ankle.

Throughout their relationship, Jon continued to push Lisa to the breaking point, creating new challenges for her that made her pain tolerance go through the roof. Cutting, branding, underwater bondage, whipping, caning, choking, body piercing, electrocution, being locked in a cage with no food or water, and forcing her to hang from hooks by her skin were some of the methods of torture that Jon had used to challenge Lisa for their edgeplay sessions. Sadly, despite my best mate's efforts to comfort her with copious amounts of aftercare and pampering, she still suffered PTSD and nightmares from all the things he did, as did the rest of us. I had done many of these things with my wife, but only after she had encouraged me to do them. She had been more

of a "top" than a "bottom," and her boldness had been one of the things I had loved about her.

"Jonny, it hurts," Lisa said breathlessly as she squirmed.

SMACK!

We all jumped as Jon backhanded her in the face. He picked up the clothespin and roll of duct tape, then held the items in front of her frightened eyes.

"You think this hurts now? Just imagine how much more painful it will be if you can't breathe. Now, shut up. We have done this routine many times before. And don't call me 'Jonny.' I'm 'Daddy.' As for your darling Nick? He can't help you right now because he's passed out in the other room with an equally comatose Daryl and Tracy, so you may as well suck it up. Do those visualization exercises I taught you. And the breathing exercises. We must show our little audience how a REAL submissive behaves." He glared at Candy as he said that last sentence. Candy, knowing better than to argue, lowered her gaze.

Lisa whimpered then nodded. "Ok, Daddy."

Jon took off his shirt then removed the rest of his clothes until he was completely naked, his pierced manhood fully erect. Then he lit himself a cigarette and took a long drag, holding in the smoke. He then knelt on the bed, situating himself between Lisa's spread legs and exposed

cunny, where he began to play with her clit piercing, pulling on it gently and then more roughly, making her squirm. He smirked at her discomfort, then brought the lit end of the cigarette closer to her clit. I couldn't help but wince at the sight of it; similarly, Anna and Candy appeared rather horrified, perhaps imagining how painful it would be to have their vaginas burned with the lit end of a cancer stick. Lisa would soon find out what it felt like firsthand, and experience backlash for resisting.

Lisa couldn't help but moan and writhe, truly fearful for what was about to happen. Tears filled her eyes. Jon continued to hold the cherry of the ciggy close enough to her labia for her to feel the heat of it and looked at me with that evil look in his green eyes, exhaling the smoke through his nostrils so he looked like a mean dragon.

"The bitch is already making too much noise," he growled. "Put duct tape over her mouth."

I sighed then did as Jon said, reasoning that it was better than him ordering me to put a clothespin on her nose at the same time. Although, knowing Jon, I could never be sure WHAT he would say or do.

Lisa tried to be quieter, breathing heavily through her nose and clamping her eyes shut, perhaps in an effort to calm down and maybe even do some visualizations. Jon inched the lit end of his cigarette even closer to her clitoris, perhaps only a centimeter away.

"Get ready," he breathed.

Anna and Candy held onto each other as they looked on with pained expressions on their faces. I smiled sympathetically at the girls so they would understand that I knew how they must have been feeling.

"AAAAAAAAHHHHH!!!!"

I had done a half assed job applying the duct tape, so it wasn't any surprise when it didn't stick to her mouth, which opened wide when she screamed. The sound was deafening as Jon burned her clit with the cigarette. She strained at the ropes restraining her and continually cried out, begging Jon not to do it again. The ropes cut into her flesh, leaving red welts that were ready to bleed. Anna and Candy placed their hands over their mouths in horror, doing their best not to react... lest they make Jon angry.

"Please, no more, Daddy!" She said as tears streamed down her face. "It hurts so much! You've never done that to me before. It's torture! It feels like it's on fire! I need ice, and some pain reliever!"

Jon nodded and put out his cigarette, grabbing an ice cube from the mini refrigerator and burn ointment from the night stand, applying one and then the other. He also removed the duct tape from her face. Lisa sighed and began to cry tears of relief. Jon and I were always prepared for edgeplay scenes, having first aid implements on hand for injuries that would inevitably occur during these hardcore sessions.

"We aren't finished yet," Jon warned as he finished putting the ointment on her clit. "Your bum is still serviceable even if your vajayjay is not. I'm sure you've missed being fucked up the arse while being restrained with rope. I even got some roach clips to place on those lovely nipples of yours. Nicky-poo certainly wouldn't do any of that, pussy that he is."

Lisa wriggled inside the restraints once more. "Why roach clips? Why can't we just use regular clothespins?"

Jon smirked and lit another cigarette before answering, taking a deep drag. "Because I only have one clothespin, and that will be on your nose," he explained as smoke poured out of his mouth. "Since you made so much noise when I burned your clit, you lost your breathing privileges."

Anna, Candy and I looked at Jon disbelievingly. It seemed that, even after so many years of BDSM and edgeplay, he kept finding new ways to torture people. Oxygen deprivation with anal play and rope restraints was challenging enough, but when combined with nipple torture? It was agony. I had only attempted it once before with my wife, who had worn a special mask over her face to restrict her breathing, but she was still able to take in some air. What Jon was doing wouldn't allow for that... especially if he was the one to put the duct tape on Lisa's mouth. The fact Lisa was also dealing with a second degree burn on her clit certainly added a whole other dimension of pain that I couldn't imagine.

Jon spat on his hand then smeared the saliva over the head of his dick. After that, he took several drags off his ciggy and crouched onto the bed

so he was once situated between her spread legs. He put out the cigarette then grabbed the duct tape, placing several pieces over her mouth to ensure that she couldn't speak or breathe through her mouth. Finally, he took the roach clips off the nightstand and clipped one to each nipple, using more force than necessary. She let go a muffled groan.

"Take some nice deep breaths, my little lioness," he said with a sadistic grin as he picked up the clothespin. "It might be a while before you breathe again. Let's hope I climax quickly, because I won't let you draw a breath until I have an orgasm."

Lisa began to breathe deeply and slowly, doing her best to calm herself. As for my own anxiety levels, they had been steadily climbing since the burn incident, so I lit myself a much needed cigarette. Anna and Candy looked rather apprehensive as well. Jon, noticing this, smiled sympathetically at us and took a hit off his marijuana vape, then graciously held it up to Lisa's lips. She took a greedy drag, needing to settle her nerves. Then Jon offered a hit to us. I said yes and took a hit but the girls declined. A scowl formed on Candy's face as she looked at Jon, who smiled gently at her in an attempt to placate her.

"I'm your Jonny Boy, and I belong to you," he said in a soft, loving voice as he began to line himself up with Lisa's bum, cock in one hand and clothespin in the other. He looked at her expectantly.

Rather than offer the reciprocal line of, "I'm your Candy Girl and I belong to you," Candy remained quiet, her nostrils flaring as she kept her arms folded across her chest.

Jon's lip trembled and his eyes looked sad; he wasn't used to this kind of behavior from his little angel. But in an attempt to stay in dominant mode, he scoffed and rolled his eyes. "Ok, fine, have an attitude," he grumbled as he turned his attention back to Lisa.

Lisa took several final deep breaths before filling her lungs with as much air as possible, at which time Jon put the clothespin on her nose. At the same time this was happening, he slowly entered her back door. The thrusts started out gentle and graceful, almost like dancing. His ten inch, diamond-adorned member glided in and out of her tight arsehole, and his hips moved in sexy figure eights. I couldn't help but sprout an erection as I saw him fuck his ex, and the fact that she was restrained and going without air made it all the more sexy to me. Then I got an idea.

"Hey, Jon," I began with a sly smile.

My best mate turned to me as he continued to thrust into Lisa, eyebrows raised. "Yes, mate?"

"Why don't you undo the straps on her ankles so you can lift up her bum more? And pound her harder?" I took a drag from my cigarette.

Jon smiled sexily and nodded. "I like that idea. But would you do it for me so I don't have to break rhythm?"

I agreed and got up from my seat, quickly undoing the restraints on Lisa's dainty ankles. Unsurprisingly, she didn't try to move away and was a compliant sub.

Jon wasted no time picking up her legs and placing them so they rested against his front, then lifted her up slightly so her bum was raised off the bed. Then he began to pound her. Slapping sounds echoed off the walls as he went balls deep into her arse. It was clear she was in some distress, and was beginning to struggle. The clothespin on her nose slipped but not enough for her to really get any air. Her face turned pink. But this didn't stop Jon from continuing to push her limits. He began to bite at her lower legs, leaving red marks. At least twice, he bit hard enough to break the skin, forcing Lisa to thrash around in the bed. He licked at the tiny bit of blood that seeped from the wounds, smiling at the taste as he did so.

"Keep taking it up the arse like a good girl," he growled as he plowed into her, holding onto her legs more tightly and digging his nails into her flesh, in a more sadistic version of the "butterfly" sex position. "We must teach these girls a lesson in humility and submission. They both like to top from the bottom. Especially my little angel, whose halo is rather crooked lately." He shot Candy an icy look. She simply looked back with a blank expression, arms still folded stubbornly across her chest. I sensed she was ready to lose it on Jon, to tell him something that was becoming harder and harder to keep to herself.

I wrapped my arm around Anna, who also seemed a bit on edge as she watched the tense scene. Perhaps five minutes had passed since Lisa had drawn a breath, and she appeared rather uncomfortable, squirming around on the bed in a futile attempt to adjust her body as Jon pounded the shit out of her. His breathing sped up and sweat formed on his brow

as his thrusts got harder, then within perhaps another thirty seconds, he pulled out of Lisa's bum and ejaculated all over her stomach. His sensual moans echoed off the walls and he smiled, rapidly licking the semen off her belly.

He took the clothespin off Lisa's nose, then removed the duct tape from her mouth. Lisa gasped for breath, taking in the precious air that had been denied her for roughly six minutes. While Jon did this, I undid the arm restraints and unbound her breasts. With the semen still in his mouth, Jon marched over to Candy and grabbed the back of her neck, forcing her to kiss him and swallow his load. She tried to move her head away but he was too strong. What happened next was a long overdue retaliation for what seemed to be rather insensitive behavior from my best mate.

"Ahh!" Jon gasped with surprise as he pulled away from Candy, holding his hand to his bleeding lip. "You fucking bit me."

Candy nodded and glared at him. "I know."

Jon licked the blood from his lip and leaned down until he was an inch from her face, green eyes blazing with anger. "That's going to cost you, honey. You've been walking a fine line with me for a while now. Did you not learn anything from what just happened to Lisa? I would love to see YOU try to hold your breath for six minutes. You best learn your place."

Candy sat there with an indignant look on her face, and it felt like a classic battle of wills. Jon scoffed and walked back to Lisa, holding up one of her legs and pointed to a tattoo on the back of her lower left calf.

"Come here and read this," Jon barked to Candy, who warily got up and walked over to Lisa and looked at the tattoo, written in bold, black cursive. "What's it say?"

Candy sighed. "'Property of J.R.,'" she grumbled.

Jon nodded. "That's right. My little lioness got that tattoo at my request. It was many years ago. A nice reminder that she belonged to me. And she always will. I expect YOU to do the same one day. And I will pick the design, as well as the location." He turned to Lisa. "I'm surprised you didn't get it removed," he said with a gentle smile. "I half expected you to put Nick's initials there."

Lisa shrugged and lit a cigarette. "Well, Nick is also a 'junior,' so I felt like it was still appropriate," she admitted.

Jon's face fell slightly as he lowered Lisa's leg. "I forgot the little weasel is a 'junior.' So much for carrying on my namesake." He sniffed and lit a cigarette himself.

Lisa sat up and placed her hand on Jon's shoulder. "Aw, Jonny," she soothed. "Don't be like that. There's a part of me that will always belong to you."

Jon took a drag and smiled sexily. "Once a fuck slave, always a fuck slave, I suppose."

We all laughed with the exception of Candy, who sat back down in a huff. Anna smiled sympathetically at her, patting her leg.

Knock, knock

Nick came through the door, a big smile on his face and a cigarette in his hand.

"How's everyone doing?" He said with bright eyes. "I just got up from a nap and I'm ready for the after party! Who's in?"

We all nodded and agreed to more partying, especially after seeing such an intense scene.

Lisa smiled. "Oh, I'm down, baby," she cooed. "What about Daryl?"

"He's getting his bearings and so is Tracy," Nick said with a wink as he rubbed Lisa's leg, when he noticed the bite marks on her leg and her inflamed clit. "Oh, dear. What happened to you?"

Jon piped up. "I happened to her, Nicky," he said with a smirk. "I'm afraid it's back-door sex only for at least a few more days until her bean heals. Things got a little... heated before."

Nick's eyes widened as he stared at Jon, then looked back at Lisa, once again rubbing her leg. "Are you in a lot of pain?"

"No, baby, I'm ok," Lisa assured as she took a drag off her cigarette. "It's just a burn. Jonny wanted to demonstrate a hardcore edgeplay session to Anna and Candy, so they can become better subs." She smiled sweetly.

Candy scoffed. Everyone directed their attention to her. I swallowed and held onto Anna's hand, perhaps sensing that there was about to be an explosion.

Jon glared at his little angel. "What's your malfunction, missy?" He growled.

Candy got up from her seat and walked closer to Jon. Her face was a mask of anger. "How do you live with yourself?"

Jon tilted his head back and laughed heartily. "Excuse me?"

"You heard me," she said as her hand formed a fist. "Just because you suffered trauma in the past doesn't give you the right to brutalize and

torture people. What makes it worse is that you get off on it. I mean, what kind of a monster are you?"

There was a collective gasp of shock in the room, followed by dead silence. I bit my lip, half expecting Jon to tie her up and beat the crap out of her. But he just stood there, eyes the size of pie plates. He truly had no idea what to say or do.

After a few more moments, tears filled Jon's eyes and he began to breathe heavily. He had never broken character during edgeplay, much less in front of his ex girlfriend. It was heartbreaking to see him crumble like that, someone who, just moments ago, was so strong and assertive, the epitome of "dom." And now? He looked every bit the fragile young man I had witnessed nearly two years prior, when he was in hospital and recovering from PTSD, depression, and an eating disorder.

He looked at Lisa in horror, having a crisis of conscience as he realized how depraved the situation was. It WAS rather over-the-top of him to sodomize, burn, asphyxiate, and bite his ex in front of Candy, especially without Nick's knowledge or permission. He lowered his head and sniffled as a tear fell from his eye and spilled down his face. His voice trembled when he finally spoke.

"I, uh... I guess I AM a bit of a monster, aren't I?"

With those words, he burst into tears and left the room, closing the door behind him. His sobs were audible as he walked down the hallway.

The room felt like all the air had been taken out of it as we all tried to process what happened to Jon. Lisa was the first to speak.

"I've never seen him crack like that," she said with a sad expression on her face. "In all my years, he's never broken character while in dominant mode." She turned to look at Candy, who was looking more than a bit guilty. "I can tell he feels terrible about the way he acted, and the way he talked to you. He loves you." Nick nodded in agreement with Lisa's words, as he held his wife's hand.

Candy nodded as tears formed in her eyes. "I had assumed he would know I was just playing along with the scene and, while I was a little frustrated with him and things were going a little too far for my liking, I don't want him thinking I don't love him." Her lip began to tremble and she began to cry. Anna placed her arm around her to console her, then Nick and Lisa went up to her to do the same, hugging her and telling her how good she was for Jon.

I cleared my throat. "I should go talk to him," I suggested. "He's my best mate and I think he just needs some reassurance that he's not an evil monster. This was simply a scene that went too far, and it got uncomfortable." The others mumbled in agreement. I turned to Anna. "I will be right back, sweetheart." I kissed her on the cheek then placed my hand on Candy's shoulder. "Don't worry," I assured her in a soft voice. "It will be ok. Just give us boys a few moments alone." Then I made my way out of the room and walked down the hall to the master bedroom. I opened the door and popped my head inside. Surely enough, Jon was curled up into a ball on his enormous bed, facing away from the door as

he cried quietly. He was wearing a black velour robe that Candy had given him for Valentine's Day.

Knock, knock

I rapped on the wall gently before closing the door behind me. "Hey, mate, it's me," I said softly. Jon remained turned away from me, sniffling and sobbing. "Can I keep you company, and chat for a while?"

Jon sniffled a few more times before replying. "As long as y-you don't mind being in the company of a... a monster," he stammered through tears.

I swallowed and climbed up onto the bed, lying behind him with my arm draped around his waist. "Oh, Jon," I soothed. "You're most certainly not a monster. Candy was just talking about it and felt terrible that she had hurt your feelings. She had assumed you knew that she was role playing."

Jon shook his head, remaining turned away from me. "But it's true, mate. Even if she was playing along with the scene, it doesn't change the fact that I've behaved like a sadistic bastard. All the awful things I did over the years to my subs? Traumatizing them to the point they have nightmares and flashbacks? And now Candy had the displeasure of watching me torture my ex? It's no wonder my little angel got uncomfortable. I feel so bad..."

His voice cracked and his body shook with fresh sobs. I wrapped my arm around him more tightly, doing my best to console him.

"Sometimes the lines between reality and fantasy become blurred," I began in a soothing voice. "You taught me this. And that's partly why we need aftercare. These intense scenes call for pampering, and for reassurance that we care about those whose limits we push. And let's be honest: words can hurt far more than a whip or a belt, or even fire. Emotions run so high that it's hard to remember that it's just a game. Everyone here knows you're a good person, Jon. As for Candy? She loves you. And she knows you love her."

Jon nodded and sniffled. "I could still tell she was upset," he admitted. "She was trying so hard to be a good sport and tolerate the scene but it was so clear to me that she'd had enough. So I've decided that, from now on, I'm not going to wait to hear the 'safe word,' or to hear that someone wants to end the scene. I'm going to pay better attention to body language. There's no way it was all an act with Candy. I mean, you saw the way she was in the limo, so quiet and withdrawn. She was afraid to speak up, mate. 'Sub' or not, I don't ever want her to feel like she can't say what's on her mind. Edgeplay is about communication. Without that, it morphs into something closer to psychological abuse."

I held Jon in silence, digesting what he had just said. He had a point. After so many years of edgeplay, I had become skilled at reading body language, to the point that I simply KNEW when to stop. My best mate, however, had a tendency to develop tunnel vision, only stopping when there was an emergency or a blatant request for things to end.

"I agree it's wise for you to pay more attention to body language," I said as I cuddled with him. "And encouraging communication is a good idea as well. But part of it is on the other party. If you've done all you can to encourage someone to speak up and they're still too nervous to do so, that's not on you."

Jon sniffled again. "I just want Candy to love me," he said through fresh tears. "I don't want her thinking I'm a monster..."

Knock, knock

I turned around to see who it was. Candy opened the door a crack and popped her head in. I nodded for her to come in. She walked slowly over to the bed until she was standing in front of Jon, then knelt down before him. She took his hand.

"I'm your Candy Girl and I belong to you," she whispered as tears formed in her eyes. "I love you. I'm so sorry for the things I said. I didn't mean it. I was going along with the scene, and didn't think you would take it seriously."

Jon sniffled. "So you don't think I'm a monster?" He asked shakily.

Candy shook her head and climbed up onto the bed. She ran her fingers through his hair as she gazed into his eyes. "No, I don't think you're a monster. You're my Jonny Boy." She leaned over and kissed him passionately. They held each other tightly as they locked lips.

I smiled broadly, getting off the bed and stepping out of the room to give them a bit more privacy. Unsurprisingly, Lisa, Nick, and Anna were all standing in the hallway, curious as to how Jon was doing. Lisa had since put on clothes, her deep v neck dress doing little to cover up her luscious tits.

"He's alright," I assured, as I placed my arm around Anna. "Turns out that Candy was doing some role playing of her own."

Lisa placed her hand on her chest and breathed a sigh of relief. "Thank goodness," she said. "I'd never seen him break down like that during a scene. In fact, I think I've seen him cry maybe twice in all the years I've known him. So glad he's ok."

Just then, Daryl, Tracy, Amy, and Eugene came hobbling down the hallway, having awakened from drunken naps. We all greeted them enthusiastically.

"When is the afterparty?" Daryl slurred as he came up to me and gave me a hug.

I chuckled as I returned the embrace. "It's right now," I said. "We were just waiting for the four of you to wake up."

Jon and Candy then emerged from the bedroom, eyes bloodshot from crying but smiles on their faces. Everyone took turns hugging Jon, assuring him he was loved. Daryl was especially enthusiastic when it came to telling his elder brother how he felt about him.

"I fucking love you so much," Daryl slurred as he held him tightly. "Best big brother ever!"

Jon chuckled through fresh tears. "You're not so bad yourself! But I must get dressed in something besides this robe before we continue the party."

Daryl backed away from his brother, noticing the tears falling from his eyes. "Oh, dear me," Daryl gasped as he looked at Jon. "Are you crying?"

Jon nodded and chuckled as he wiped his eyes. "It happens on occasion."

"I didn't know you had it in you," Daryl joked as he patted his brother on the arm. "I think I've seen you cry maybe twice in my entire life."

Lisa chuckled. "I had said the same thing," she said to Daryl as she patted Jon on the shoulder.

Jon shrugged and smiled. "I think I've become more emotional with age," he admitted with a wink.

At that moment, the doorbell rang. Per Jon's request, I went down to answer the door. Mario and Brittany had arrived. In Mario's hand was an acoustic guitar. It was time for round 3 of partying!

One hour later...

It was around 1am and the afterparty was still in full swing. Mario and Jon had played several duets with their respective guitars and were now dancing up a storm to the techno music playing from Jon's deluxe sound system. The rest of us followed suit, dancing, singing, and drinking as if our lives depended on it. I was having a grand old time sucking vodka off Anna's breasts, and taking hits off Jon's marijuana vape. As for Daryl? He had started out dancing drunkenly with Tracy and loudly singing along to the songs his brother and Mario were playing, and was now doing a striptease atop one of Jon's couches. It was rather hilarious watching him, seeing that he was ordinarily such an inhibited, modest bloke. For not being a dancer, his moves were rather impressive. His chiseled physique, combined with the fact he wore skimpy boxer briefs, made it all the more entertaining. At one point, Tracy put several dollar bills down his underwear, and we all cheered.

"Come on up on this couch with me!" Daryl slurred at Tracy, who drunkenly obliged. They began dancing sexily atop the couch, and within a few minutes, Tracy removed her shirt and began dancing in her bra. We all cheered. Amy in particular looked especially thrilled at the sight of her best friend dancing with no shirt and began to hoot and

holler. Daryl leaned down and began sucking and licking her breasts, much to Tracy's and the crowd's delight.

"Get a room!" I shouted out with a chuckle as I took a swig of beer.

"Sure thing, mate!" Daryl shouted with a grin.

With those words, he picked up Tracy and began his descent from the leather couch. He lost his footing, however, and stumbled, falling straight on his arse on what was luckily the soft leather surface of the couch and not the floor. He hadn't let go of Tracy, who was in his lap and laughing raucously.

Jon rushed over to his dazed younger brother and I followed suit, helping him and Tracy to an upright position. "You both alright?" He asked.

Daryl began to cackle as he stood wavering, no longer carrying Tracy in his arms. She was marginally more steady, holding onto Jon's hand for support. "You're such a good brother, Jonny!" He slurred as he ran his hands through Jon's hair.

Jon laughed good naturedly as he put his arm around Daryl. "I try. Now would you and Tracy like to continue the party or do you wish to go to bed and sleep it off?"

Daryl scoffed and laughed as he put on his shirt. Jon helped with his brother's pants, then I helped Tracy with her shirt. "The night is young yet! And I'm newly engaged! No point in being a pussy! So bring on the tequila!"

Tracy laughed, as did the rest of us. "That's right, dammit!" She slurred. "More partying!"

Daryl and Tracy began to dance drunkenly together, taking Jon's advice to position themselves by the couch in case one of them fell. As they did this, I reunited with my darling Anna, and Jon with his beloved Candy. Nick and Lisa began to make out on the loveseat, occasionally taking hits from their bong as they did so.

I knocked back a few shots of tequila then, emboldened by the booze and the pot I had smoked earlier, I lifted Anna and began to twirl her around. Her long red hair cascaded behind her as she squealed with delight. I began to envision a future with her, imagining what our wedding day would be like as well as what our children would look like. I thought of the marriage to my first wife and how magical the day had been. We had gotten married on the beach in Cape Cod, and the weather had been perfect. I pictured Anna and me on the beach, but in a more tropical setting, surrounded by palm trees and bright blue water, her red hair flowing freely in the breeze. My fantasy came to a halt when I felt someone spank my arse.

SMACK!

I dropped Anna and spun around. Daryl was there with a huge grin on his handsome, drunken face.

"May I have this dance?" He slurred as he held out his arms.

I laughed and nodded. "Of course!" I turned to Anna. "I will be but a moment, sweetheart. I just want to dance with my inebriated friend for a bit!" I kissed her on the cheek and she returned the sentiment.

"Not a problem, I'm thirsty anyway!" she said with a giggle as she grabbed my arse playfully then retreated to the kitchen to grab a drink.

Daryl wasted no time twirling me around as he cackled and occasionally stumbled over himself. Everyone cheered and clapped, encouraging us to continue. I was about to break away from him to refill my drink while, suddenly, he planted a passionate, open mouth kiss on me.

I was tempted to pull away but the softness of his lips and the sheer spontaneity of the moment kept me where I was. The crowd gasped in surprise and wonder, since everyone knew full well that Daryl was heterosexual. Jon looked particularly shocked but also rather delighted for his brother, hooting and clapping as we locked lips.

"It's about bloody time you branched out!" Jon said with a chuckle as he watched us swap spit. By this time, Anna was back from the kitchen with a new drink and was smiling broadly at the scene. She had always

gotten turned on by the sight of me with another bloke, and this time was no exception.

My lovely redhead sat on the couch and watched Daryl and me make out as she sipped her drink. Tracy sat next to her, and, like Anna, she also appeared turned on by the sight of her fiancé kissing me. I found myself developing a huge erection as I kissed my wholesome friend, suddenly wanting to do more than just suck him off. I began fantasizing about him sucking my cock, and getting bum fucked by yours truly. I toyed with the idea of asking him if he would be down for more than just kissing, but he beat me to it.

"Let's go upstairs," he slurred in between feverish kisses. "I want you to go down on me again, then I wanna go down on you. And you can fuck me in the arse. Tracy and your lovely Anna can watch, and whoever else is interested."

My eyes widened in shock at Daryl's proposal, and I couldn't help but laugh in disbelief. But I could tell from his face that he was serious. He began to rub my bulge, looking at me with lust in his soulful blue eyes.

Jon was even more shocked than I was, but nodded in approval. "Go for it, mate," he said with a sexy smirk on his face as he put his arm around a giggling, inebriated Candy. "I reckon he won't recall anything by morning anyway!"

I chuckled and looked back at Daryl, caressing his face and grabbing his crotch. Then I held onto his hand and began walking him across the

palatial living room and up the stairs. Tracy and Anna followed behind us, giggling drunkenly. I could feel all the others watch us - Candy, Jon, Amy, Eugene, Mario, and Brittany all looked at Daryl and me with awe. Even Nick and Lisa had stopped fooling around on the couch to watch me and Jon's sweet-natured brother ascend the steps. They had all seen the two of us kissing before; despite my alcohol-fueled tunnel vision, I was able to make out the gasps, hushed comments and random cheers.

Daryl wasted no time stripping naked once we had reached one of the guest bedrooms. I did likewise, and within seconds, he and I were kissing passionately on the bed and groping each other's cocks. Tracy and Anna snuck inside, making themselves at home on a nearby chaise as they drunkenly looked on. Several minutes later, Nick and Lisa joined, followed by Amy and Eugene. Mario and Brittany were the last to arrive, and appeared to be in post-coital disarray with their clothes half on and their hair messed. It seemed nearly everyone wanted front row seats to the Daryl show. Jon and Candy remained downstairs, the slaps of their hard fucking and accompanying moans audible through the thick walls, along with Jon growling something about an enema. I smirked to myself as I imagined him shoving a bulb of hot water up Candy's tight arse and fucking her afterwards, causing a mess and a subsequent need for "discipline."

Without warning, Daryl stopped kissing me and rolled on top of me, then began crawling down the length of my body until his mouth was level with my erect penis. Then he took my member in his hand and, ever so gently, began kissing the head of my engorged member. I moaned as I ran my fingers through his soft mane of dark hair, encouraging him to suck me off. After a few more seconds, he lowered his head until most of my shaft disappeared into his mouth and down his throat.

I moaned sensually as Daryl fellated me. Tracy and the others looked on with horny eyes, taking the time to pleasure themselves or each other. At one point, Tracy reached over and held Daryl's hand, encouraging him to continue pleasuring me. Nick and Lisa both lit cigarettes as they masturbated, occasionally locking lips as they did so. It became harder to resist climax as he sucked me off, the strong grip of his hand contrasting nicely with the gentle but consistent pressure of his mouth and lips. For an inebriated first timer, Daryl was great at giving head. However, I didn't want out overture to end. I slowly backed away from his mouth and cleared my throat.

"Let me have my way with you," I said in a low, sexy voice. "What do you say, hmm?"

Daryl lifted his head and smiled, his eyes at drunken half mast. "Yes, please."

With those words, Tracy graciously let go of her fiancé's hand and we switched positions. I crouched before his open legs and took hold of his erect cock. Then I began to suck him off gently, occasionally using my teeth. He got even harder, as did I, and I felt myself approaching orgasm. I delayed it as best I could, however, intent on making it to the grand finale. While still going down on him, I grabbed the bottle of lube that lay on the bed and squirted a generous amount onto my penis. I began to imagine how Daryl's tight arsehole felt...

"Uhhh..." Daryl moaned with a drunken smile on his face. "Feels so bloody good."

Tracy stumbled over to her fiancé with a mini bottle of vodka, a sexy smile on her face. "Drink this," she urged.

Daryl wasted no time taking the bottle out of Tracy's hand and knocking back the contents. He coughed slightly then smiled broadly. "Mmmm, good to the last drop," he slurred.

At that moment, I decided it was time to do something I had fantasized about for a long time. I spat on Daryl's arsehole then crawled up to his handsome face, where I began to kiss him. He returned my kiss and opened his legs wider, allowing me better access to his bum. I began to finger him with one hand as I masturbated with the other, my lubricated cock growing in size as I did so. While still kissing him, I began to tease his bum with the head of my manhood. He began to moan sensually. I continued to kiss him, gradually penetrating him more. His arsehole was so deliciously tight, and it was obvious he hadn't experienced more than a modest size strap-on. In fact, he was so tight that it almost hurt ME, and I decided to refrain from penetrating him more than perhaps a third of the way.

Daryl backed away from my face, his eyes closed. Thanks to the small bottle of vodka Tracy had given him, he appeared even more drunk than he had before. "Oh, dear me," he breathed as he bucked his hips, grabbing my arse as he did so.

I thrusted gently, deciding to go slightly deeper into his bum. I slowed down a bit when I felt him tense up. The others looked on with eager

eyes, mesmerized by the sight of Daryl being on the receiving end of anal sex with a real penis for the first, and most likely last, time.

"Oh, Tracy," Daryl breathed with his eyes clamped shut. "You're using a bigger strap on tonight, I reckon…"

At that moment, my eyes widened and my penis went limp. There was a collective gasp in the room. It was immediately clear that Daryl was so inebriated that he had no idea who was fucking him. Guilt consumed my thoughts. I gradually pulled out. Then I saw all the blood.

The next few minutes rolled by in a state of panic and autopilot as I rushed to get ice and first aid ointment for his bum. As I fetched these items, Tracy held him tenderly, speaking loving words to her barely coherent, half-awake fiancé. I debated on going downstairs and telling Jon what had happened but he was still balls deep in Candy and engaging in what sounded like an all-out torture fest, complete with the sound of whips, paddles, and his girlfriend's screams echoing off the walls of the living room.

I placed some towels underneath Daryl's bum and began to use the ice to slow the bleeding. The others provided moral support and helped with supply replenishment as well as cleanup. Luckily the bleeding had stopped quickly and Tracy expertly applied ointment to his traumatized bum hole. I said a silent prayer that Daryl was shitfaced enough to avoid recalling anything when he woke up the next morning.

Once he was all cleaned up, he began to snore. It was clear that, in his condition, all he could manage to do was sleep. Tracy and I put a robe on him and placed a blanket over him, deciding it was best to let him continue to rest. She decided to join him in bed herself, suddenly feeling wiped out from the day's events. As for the rest of us, we decided to call it a night, too, so we all exchanged goodnight hugs and kisses. Anna and I retreated to our room, as did the others. It had been a long and crazy night, but also a fun and memorable one.

I fell asleep to the sound of Jon and Candy fucking downstairs, the slapping sound of their bodies and moaning providing a nice soundtrack for sleep when combined with the sound of chirping crickets outside. There was an occasional whipping sound, along with muffled cries that I couldn't tell were from my best mate or his girlfriend. I know they enjoyed switching whenever possible, with Jon starting out as the "dom" and then ending as the "sub," so anything was possible. I envisioned Candy pounding the shit out of Jon with a huge strap on, and the notion got me hard. As I drifted off, I wrapped my arm around an already sleeping Anna, and wondered how long my best mate and his little angel had been at it, as well as what could possibly be going on. I would find out a LOT more by morning…

Some time in the middle of the night…

"How dare you do this to me?!"

Daryl's typically meek voice was loud and thunderous, and his body language uncharacteristically aggressive. I stood there frozen, not knowing what to say or do.

"I'm not gay!" He insisted as his hand formed a fist. "You waited until I was drunk to have your way with me? You AND Nick?"

I took a deep breath. "Daryl, you initiated-"

"I don't wanna hear it!" He barked, cutting me off. "You and Nick are disinvited from my wedding! I was going to ask you to be my best man but I will ask Jon to fill that role once again, like he did at my first wedding. I don't want to work with you anymore, either! You can work at Jon's gym. I know HE swings. You two can be 'butt buddies' all you like!" His lower lip trembled and he looked ready to cry.

My eyes filled with tears. "Daryl, can't we talk about this later, after you've cooled down? I understand why you're so upset and I'm sorry."

"Sorry won't cut it. You betrayed me. Don't talk to me again!"

With those words, he walked out of the room, slamming the door behind him.

At that moment, I heard as well as felt a loud bang, and I woke up from my dream.

My heart beat so quickly in my chest as I sat up, getting my bearings. Anna lay next to me, dead to the world. At that moment, I decided it was best not to tell Daryl what happened, because I suspected his reaction would be very similar to what had occurred in the dream. I didn't want to risk losing him as a friend, or have there be any awkwardness between us.

I wanted to investigate what happened to cause a bang (that may very well had been a dream induced hallucination) but felt too drained to get up from bed. So I simply wrapped my arm back around Anna and fell back to sleep.

The next morning....

"Scrambled, fried, or an omelet?" I asked Anna as I stood in Jon's kitchen, making breakfast for my lovely redhead as well as myself.

She sat at the kitchen table, tilting her pretty head to one side before making a decision. "Scrambled, please." She smiled sexily as she sipped her juice.

"Coming right up," I said with a wink as I began to cook eggs.

Everyone else was sleeping off the debauchery from the night before, but I had awakened bright eyed and bushy-tailed...and determined to keep Daryl in the dark about what had happened.

Knock, knock.

I turned around, and saw Tracy with a big smile on her face, and behind her was Daryl, looking more than a little hungover and walking with a slight limp. I stifled a laugh as the lovely couple sat down and exchanged good mornings.

"How you two feeling this morning?" I said with a smirk as I poured and served each of them a cup of coffee.

"I'm great!" Tracy chirped. "Can't say the same about my poor fiancé here. He's got a headache."

Daryl nodded as he rubbed his temples. "I reckon some other body parts are sore, too, but I won't get into that over breakfast!" He quipped with a chuckle as he looked at Tracy with a wink.

We all laughed, and I felt a wave of relief that Daryl didn't suspect a thing with regard to who had violated his backside. I had been tempted to tell him the truth the night before, but after that nightmare I had, I decided against it.

Amy and Eugene joined us, looking adorable in their matching baby blue pajamas. Amy's long dark hair was arranged in pigtails and she had her arm around a blushing and smiling Eugene, whose red hair was

scattered every which way. They sat down at the table and we all exchanged greetings. I felt a twinge of nostalgia and perhaps jealousy as I thought of my ragdoll and how in love with her I had been just a short time ago, but I was happy for her.

Nick and Lisa came into the kitchen not long after Amy and Eugene, cigarettes in their hands and tired smiles on their faces. They greeted everyone cheerfully and sat at the table, making small talk as they smoked.

My phone dinged just then. Jon had texted me.

"Good morning, mate. I won't be making it to breakfast this morning because I will be literally tied up, thanks to Candy...but you can join us in a few hours. I'm letting her do whatever she wants to me. And I mean ANYTHING. Also, Mario and Brittany snuck off late last night so they could fuck on the new memory foam bed she got yesterday. How romantic. Anyway, tell everyone I decided to 'sleep in,' haha. I will text you once my little angel and I are ready for company. Be good!"

I chuckled and shook my head, replying with a laughing emoji and a thumbs up before resuming cooking.

After a few more minutes, breakfast was ready and I placed an array of food on the table so everyone could help themselves. I made sure Anna got her scrambled eggs, of course. I sat down and filled my plate with some sausage and fried eggs, ready to fill my stomach with yummy goodness.

The others did similarly, chatting away about a variety of things as they piled food on their plates. I couldn't help but wonder what Candy was doing to Jon upstairs and my manhood hardened as my imagination ran wild. It was time for Anna to dominate me, to let her do whatever she wanted with my body, including my semi-virgin backside. The only issue was getting over my fear of that very thing. Suddenly, a wave of nostalgia passed over me as I thought of how skilled my wife had been at convincing me to let her do things to me that I never thought I would let any woman do...

She tied my wrists and ankles to the four poster bed with satin straps, her long black hair covering her luscious bare breasts as she did so. The air was thick with pot smoke and I enjoyed a lingering high as I lay naked on my back, watching the ceiling fan move in lazy circles. Once the straps were secure, she grabbed the blindfold off the nightstand and slid it over my eyes, tying it in a secure knot behind my head. I now had nothing to go on but my sense of touch. My heart beat more quickly, and I wondered what she would do. Just then, I felt something cold and wet on the soles of my feet and I did my best not to flinch or yelp, knowing it would earn me some discipline if I did.

She ran the ice cube up my legs until she had reached my cock and balls, lingering around that area for the fun of it. I chuckled and squealed as the coldness enveloped my member, only to melt quickly. She licked the area dry with her tongue, then moved onto something that felt like a feather moving up and down my arms, legs, and torso. But it wasn't a feather at all; in fact, she removed the blindfold and revealed that she was holding a giant butcher knife. Knowing better than to panic, I swallowed and took some deep breaths as she gracefully glided the weapon over my flesh. We had done this charade countless times

before but it never failed to cause me anxiety. But the thrill, and subsequent orgasm, were well worth the nervousness the knife play caused me.

Once done with the knife, she smiled broadly and straddled me, guiding my rock hard member to her wet womanhood. She rode me cowgirl style for a while, occasionally getting into acrobatic positions. She was very flexible and knew I enjoyed watching her do splits and put her ankles behind her head. And when she bounced on my cock, I loved the way her large breasts bobbed up and down. She knew just how to move, and her curvy hourglass figure was beyond sexy to stare at as well as touch. Her caramel skin was so soft and had a lovely sheen and her long dark hair was so full and luxurious, and even after so many years together, there wasn't a single day that I didn't appreciate her beauty. I was still just as much in love with her as I was when we had first made our relationship official. She was my one and only "butterfly."

"How about some syrup?" She offered with a seductive smirk.

"Yo, Ken! Can you pass the syrup?"

I jumped as I returned back into present day, Daryl's voice shocking me out of my memory.

"Yes, of course," I said with a chuckle, as I grabbed the maple syrup next to me and handed it to him. "Sorry, I was just daydreaming." I winked as I placed my hand on Anna's thigh.

I continued to fantasize about my wife as I ate, while still very curious about what was occurring upstairs with Candy and Jon. I would soon get a very clear idea, and it would be rather memorable and more than a bit depraved.

Several hours later, after the others had left...

"May I please have some dessert, Mommy?"

Naked as could be, she crawled up to his face and sat on it, making sure her wet womanhood was lined up with her "baby's" hungry mouth. He sucked eagerly, lapping away at her juices. He had just been spoon fed breakfast, being unable to feed himself on account of Mommy tying him to the bed. His apple juice had been given to him in a baby bottle. Tiny cuts, bruises, and scratches covered his body from many hours of discipline at the hands of his mommy, but remained happy as could be, thanks to being bumfucked with a strap-on and sucked off multiple times, and having unlimited access to her pussy, tits, and arse.

After all these years, Jon still loved age play, especially when he got to pretend to be a little boy. Candy, being a motherly type, was very much on board with it. Sometimes he played the role of a nonverbal, thumb-sucking infant who was completely dependent on a mum figure for everything from toileting, to bathing, to dressing, but he preferred being toddler aged, since it was easier - and more fun - to communicate using words.

I had asked Jon years ago what the hardest part of age play was, and I'd assumed he was going to say it was the toileting part. Wrong.

"Nope," he had said with a smirk. "I rather enjoy pissing the floor and getting away with it. For me, it's going without cigarettes. But I manage, because it's a bit inauthentic to act like a 3 year old boy while chainsmoking."

To stave off withdrawals, Jon often wore a nicotine patch during age play and this time was no exception. Despite cutting down a bit, he still smoked and vaped very heavily so he needed a patch to "take the edge off," as he put it.

Anna and I cuddled in the nude on the chaise lounge opposite Jon's bed, thoroughly enjoying the fuck fest. We were rather inspired by what we were seeing, and I thought of how sexy it would be for Anna to be my little girl, or, better yet, for me to be her little boy. I did my best to picture myself acting like a baby while being waited on by a hot MILF, being fed juice from a bottle, feeding on her breasts, and being "disciplined" when I misbehaved. My cock hardened as I pictured it, and was once again reminded of my wife, who had loved being my "mama." What great memories....

"I can still breathe, Mommy," Jon panted as he turned his head away from her pussy to talk. Candy was still sitting on his face but wasn't putting her full weight on him, figuring he would want at least some oxygen. She was wrong.

"Do you want mommy to smother you?" Candy asked reluctantly as she stroked Jon's flushed face.

Jon nodded. "Yes, please."

Candy sighed then positioned herself so her womanhood was once again aligned with his mouth. "Take some deep breaths, little one."

"Ok, Mommy."

He did as he was told, breathing deeply for a few moments before Candy lowered herself onto his face, sitting in such a way that cut off his air supply.

Anna and I both lit cigarettes as we watched in awe, completely and utterly aroused by the sight of Jon being smothered by Candy's pussy. My manhood hardened as I fantasized about my lovely redhead doing similar to me. Per a conversation at breakfast, Daryl admitted to letting Tracy tie him up at least twice, teasing him with everything from feathers to ice cubes, but had yet to try the face sitting. Being asthmatic, Daryl tended to shy away from anything that restricted his air flow, becoming rather panicked by such. Tracy, on the other hand, was more than on board with being choked and otherwise smothered, and encouraged her fiancé to engage in breath play whenever possible. Daryl was not a sadist by nature but enjoyed watching Tracy get off on being dominated, and was becoming more sexually assertive as a result. Jon and I had given him plenty of tips, most of which made him blush something awful but ultimately helped him become a better "dom."

Candy rode Jon's face, watching his body for signs of either struggle or unconsciousness. Between the chainsmoking, underwater swimming, and erotic asphyxiation, my best mate was used to going without oxygen so I knew it would take a while for him to become uncomfortable. I tried to imagine what it might feel like for Jon, being completely suffocated by the weight of his girlfriend, unable to breathe and all but drowning in her juices.

Speaking of juice, I glanced at the baby bottle full of apple juice sitting atop Jon's nightstand, and was immediately reminded of the day I had experienced near-suffocation at the hands of someone else for the first time. It was also the moment that made me develop an ever bigger fascination with breath play.

It had occurred when I was in hospital for an appendectomy seven years prior, and I was served apple juice with my first post-surgery meal of tasteless chicken and rice. My wife had visited me as quickly as she could, bringing balloons, homemade baked goods, and a smile, determined to be at my side as much as possible. Daryl had also popped by as soon as he was done with work, armed with some of my favorite snacks to make up for the bland hospital food. As for Jon? He had been in full on "douche" mode, arriving in my semi-private room wearing sunglasses, a leather jacket, and a smirk. He had been completely drunk on tequila, stoned on weed, and high on coke, his arm around an inebriated Lisa. Despite knowing it was unwise for me to drink while recovering from surgery, my best mate had insisted on smuggling a bottle of single malt scotch as a gift, cleverly placing it in a designer handbag. My mind traveled into the past as I recalled that day...

My head and torso throbbed as I lay in the hospital bed recovering from an appendectomy. I had developed acute appendicitis and needed surgery straight away. The procedure had gone well but I still felt rather weak and groggy. Thankfully, my lovely wife had popped by with some little gifts and a sweet smile.

She and I chatted for a bit as we watched tv in my semi-private room, which was luckily empty aside from myself. The room had a nice view, and I had the bed that was closer to the window so I was able to see outside. This made me feel like less of a prisoner as I recuperated. Not long after the wife had arrived, Daryl came with several bags of chips and a container of mixed nuts. Brother Lawrence came perhaps a half hour after Daryl, and had brought me several magazines that he knew I liked. The four of us talked and laughed for a while, discussing everything from the godawful food selections to the itchy gowns. I couldn't wait to be discharged so I could try the new choke collar I had gotten for the wife and I, kinky crazies that we were. Little did I know that my other best mate, good old Jon Moore, was en route along with his girlfriend Lisa, and ready to liven things up. It would be an experience I would never forget.

I was able to hear him long before he arrived through the door of my hospital room, his deep and resonant voice reverberating off the walls of the facility. It was clear that he was flirting and cracking jokes, and I heard the chuckles of hospital staff in response to nearly everything he said. Mr. Moore was the ultimate charmer, this was for sure.

Knock, knock.

"Heeeey, how's my bitch?"

Jon Moore staggered through the doorway, wearing designer sunglasses and an equally designer outfit, his leather jacket hugging his slim, athletic frame like a second skin. He had his arm around Lisa, who was nearly as tipsy as he was, and she wore a lovely sun dress in a flattering shade of navy. The smell of pot, cigarettes, and alcohol filled the room the moment they walked in. My wife exchanged enthusiastic greetings with them. Daryl and Lawrence, however, were less than thrilled by Jon's arrival, but they both got on well with Lisa, who they treated much more warmly.

My best mate wasted no time leaning over and hugging me, also taking the time to kiss me on the lips and grab my crotch. He handed me a designer handbag that had a bottle of my favorite scotch in it. Lisa followed, giving me a gentle hug and a box of my favorite chocolate from the gift shop. I thanked them profusely and told Jon I would drink the booze as soon as I got home.

"Pussy," he scoffed as he sat down. Lisa made a home for herself on his lap.

"I'm not supposed to drink when on my meds," I explained. "Sorry."

I could tell Jon was glaring at me through the sunglasses he refused to take off despite the darkness of the room. After a few tense moments, his expression changed and he flashed me his brilliant smile.

"Quite alright, mate," he assured me with a smirk. "Or I could always... spike your apple juice with it?" He raised his eyebrows and nodded towards the cup of juice on the table next to my hospital bed.

Daryl scoffed and mumbled under his breath and Lawrence shook his head.

"Problem, boys?" Jon asked with a sneer as he glanced over at our respective brothers.

Lawrence got up from his chair. "I think it's best I leave," he grumbled, looking ready to fight Jon, who smirked up at him. Lawrence looked at me and gently touched my shoulder. "I will be back later," he said softly. "I just can't be here when he's here. You understand, I'm sure."

I nodded, knowing full well how much my elder brother despised Jon. "That's fine."

Lawrence then waved goodbye to everyone, making sure to avoid eye contact with Jon, who sarcastically waved goodbye to him.

"Don't let the door hit you in the arse on the way out!" Jon quipped as he waved exaggeratedly. I couldn't help but chuckle, and my wife had joined in. She generally found Jon funny, if not occasionally annoying.

Lawrence glared at Jon and flipped him off before walking out. Daryl then got up and decided to "stretch his legs," which I knew was code for him needing a break from his brother.

"Already being a whiny little shit, are we, Daryl?" Jon snarked as he took out his vape pen and took a hit, blowing a cloud in Daryl's direction.

Daryl coughed and waved at the vape cloud, walking towards the exit in a huff. "You know I can't fucking breathe around that shit, Jon! I'm asthmatic!"

Jon tilted his head back in sinister laughter. "Daryl, pumpkin, it's fucking VAPOR. It's not the same as smoke. Your asthma inhaler probably has more harmful crap in it. In fact-"

"I don't care!" Daryl interjected. "It still irritates my lungs." He turned to me with an apologetic look. "I have to get out of here for a bit."

I winked. "I totally understand, mate."

Daryl then left, as did my wife, who had to go to work and gave everyone a hug and kiss before she left, promising me she would be back as soon as she could. Despite the fact that Jon had created chaos merely minutes before, he was once again Mr. Charisma, cracking jokes and telling hilarious stories that had me and Lisa laughing until our bellies hurt. As much as my elder best mate made me nervous and was a bit of a bully, he never failed to make things more fun and exciting.

Jon took a long hit off his vape, held his breath for 60-odd seconds, then exhaled gently through his nostrils. "How is it that I can go through at least four packs of ciggies a day, smoke weed all day long, use a vape, AND enjoy Cuban cigars but can still run a mile in under four minutes and hold my breath for ten? But my pussy brother starts wheezing if he walks too quickly from the refrigerator?" Jon snort-laughed at his own wise crack. "Makes no bloody sense."

Lisa's eyes widened and she got up from her boyfriend's lap. "Jonny," she scolded with her hands on her hips. "That was so mean what you did to Daryl before. Call him and apologize."

Jon looked up at Lisa with raised eyebrows. "Seriously?"

Lisa nodded. "Yes. He's your younger brother and he has asthma. He looked so upset when he left." In a huff, she snatched the vape from Jon's hand and took a deep drag then held in the vapor. I never saw her exhale. Despite weighing 120 pounds soaking wet, that girl could out-smoke most men, Jon included.

Jon smirked for a few moments then sighed as he took out his phone. "Fine," he grumbled.

I was always amazed at how different Jon was around Lisa. It was as if she was the only one who could manage to intimidate him. I would

learn later in the visit just how much she had control over my best mate...

He simply sent Daryl an apology text, due to what he claimed was poor cell service in the hospital, but I also figured that he didn't want to give in entirely to Lisa's demands. I couldn't blame him. For all Lisa's charm, she had a scary temper when drunk, and I had suspected for years that she had gotten physically violent with Jon on at least a few occasions.

After sending the text, Jon sent Lisa on an errand. "Would you be so kind as to go to the vending machine down the hall and fetch me a can of iced tea?" He asked sweetly as he handed her money.

Still holding her breath, Lisa nodded and walked out of the room. Once she was out of sight, Jon opened up the top of a poison ring he wore on his right ring finger. White powder lined the inside of it. Before I could ask questions, he put the ring up to his right nostril and snorted the contents, pinching his nose shut afterwards for a few seconds.

"Lisa detests my coke habit," he said with a smirk. "So I best keep it secret. Anyway, I hope she will want to go with me to visit the nursery later. I love looking at the babies. It's just hard convincing her that having kids would be so much fun. I so want to be a dad..."

His voice cracked, and he lowered his head in a mix of sadness and perhaps guilt at allowing himself to "feel." For the briefest of moments, I saw the "real" Jon - a soft hearted, young man with dreams of fatherhood, who lived a life of fame, decadence, and incredible wealth

but that lacked the emotional depth he craved. Suddenly appearing uncomfortable with his uncharacteristic vulnerability, he cleared his throat and straightened his stance, chuckling softly and shaking his head. "Whatever," he muttered with a smirk. Then took out a flask that was hidden from the inside pocket of his leather jacket and took a swig, then handed the flask to me.

I shook my head. "I told you, I shouldn't drink on my meds. But thank you for offering."

Jon scoffed, then grabbed my cup of apple juice, pouring some of the contents of the flask into the cup. "A wee bit won't hurt you. Plus it's tequila. The one thing I know that doesn't give you a hangover." He thrust the cup at me. "Just take a fucking sip. Don't be a bitch. Bitch."

I chuckled as I took the cup from him. He knew my weakness for tequila, especially when mixed with juice. I put the cup to my lips and took a modest sip. I nearly spit it out. It was so incredibly strong but I forced myself to swallow the concoction. Thanks to the meds I was on already, I felt the alcohol take effect within moments.

Jon applauded. "That's my boy! And just so you know, I crushed up an ecstasy pill in the booze before pouring it into my flask so if it feels like it has a little extra 'kick,' that could be why." He took a hit off his vape pen.

My eyes widened. "You serious Jon?! It's bad enough I'm drinking with my meds, but ecstasy? Are you trying to kill me?"

Jon smirked and shook his head, exhaling a vape cloud in my direction. It smelled like cotton candy. "No, silly, of course not. It's just a tiny amount. You will be fine. I promise. Plus if anything does happen, you're in a fucking hospital. And don't forget, you have ME as your nurse." He smiled sexily and placed his hand on my crotch again, rubbing my penis which, despite my annoyance, was becoming hard under his touch. He then held the vape pen up to my lips. "You and I BOTH know you are craving nicotine. Treat yourself."

I sighed then took a hit off Jon's vape pen, my head immediately swimming with the luscious sensation of nicotine entering my bloodstream. I took another, longer hit and held in the vapor.

Jon grinned sexily as he took another drag himself. "It's the strong kind, too. High nicotine content. The strongest kind they make at the vape shop, in fact. AND the most expensive. Why settle? Life is fucking short."

Just then, Lisa arrived, gently letting go of the breath she had most likely been holding since she had taken a drag off the vape, which was around five minutes prior. She wasn't even slightly winded and even took another hit off the vape when she sat down. She had a can of iced tea for Jon and a bag of peanuts that she wound up sharing with Jon and me. My head began to swim with the combination of chemicals, and after a while I noticed that hard rock music was playing as well as what appeared to be flashing disco lights. Jon had begun to play music from his phone and had actually plugged a usb-powered disco ball into the charging port. That's right: my best mate had managed to turn my plain, semi private room into a bloody nightclub.

He closed the privacy curtain so that anyone looking in wouldn't be able to see what was going on. Then he began to strip, doing a sexy dance as he did so. Lisa cheered and clapped, jokingly holding out dollar bills. I couldn't help but laugh and get turned on at his little performance. First he took off his jacket, then his shirt, then his boots, and pants. Before long, he only wore his sunglasses and his red silk boxer briefs, his erection clear as day. His ten pack abs looked all the more pronounced due to his golden tan, and his skin sported a sexy sheen that was partly body oil and partly sweat.

"Take off your sunglasses," I said with a smile.

Jon hesitated briefly then removed the eyewear. That was when I saw the bruise and cut on his left eyelid. I gasped.

"What happened to your eye?" I asked.

Jon shrugged and smiled, appearing nervous all of a sudden. Lisa lowered her head, in what appeared to be guilt. "Lisa and I were play fighting a few days ago. My little lioness got me good! She overdid it with the vodka, but it was all in good fun. She didn't mean it. Right love?" He said with a shy smile.

Lisa nodded and bit her lip. "Yes," she said sheepishly. "I just wish I was able to remember what had happened, I don't like that I blacked out. And I'm so sorry I hurt you."

Jon grinned sweetly. "It's ok, darling, it happens." Then he walked up to her and started giving her a lap dance. The music filled the little room, as did the lights from the mini disco ball. Lisa took occasional hits off her vape pen, passing it to Jon, who took a drag, then passed it to me. It was amazing how the room had transformed in a matter of minutes. I drank more of the tequila, apple juice, and ecstasy mixture, allowing my senses to become more delightfully distorted.

Jon continued his lap dance, kissing, fondling, dry humping, licking, and basically doing everything but fucking Lisa outright. Eventually, Lisa pulled down Jon's knickers and began sucking his erect cock, much to his delight. He especially enjoyed holding her head to his junk, refusing to let her breathe. She had no gag reflex and, like her boyfriend, was able to go a long time without air, so the breath play and vigorous face-fucking continued for quite a while. Jon, always the disciplined bloke, was able to pull out before climaxing. He kissed Lisa's makeup streaked face as he fondled her breasts. Then he made his way over to me, a sinister smile on his face. His green eyes glowed with a combination of lust and mischief.

"Ready for the thrill of your life, mate?"

Before I could answer, he grabbed a plastic grocery bag from one of his jacket pockets and placed it over my head. Since it wasn't an overly tight fit, I was able to breathe somewhat, but that was about to change. I felt Jon's strong hand around my cock and was able to make out Lisa's perfume. My best mate went to town on my dick, giving me a hand job to end all hand jobs, and his girlfriend began to suck and bite my nipples. My breath quickened and the bag began to stick to my mouth. I

did my best to blow the plastic away and move my head to get some more air flow, but the more I blew, the more condensation formed on the inside of the bag. I had marginally better luck breathing through my nose but even that was difficult with all the moisture accumulating on the inside. My heart raced as I began to panic, desperately wanting more air but unable to get any.

Jon's grip intensified on my cock as Lisa bit down harder on my nipples. I did my best to keep my breathing slow but was so hungry for air that it was a difficult thing to do. The bag tightened suddenly, and I knew I was going to have to go without oxygen. I did my best to focus on other things besides lack of air, trying to listen to the music playing and doing my best to enjoy the pleasurable feeling of having my dick rubbed. I thought I was doing rather well until I felt Jon go down on me. The sensation made me go wild and I so badly wanted to climax, but just when I was about to, he would let up. Since I couldn't talk, much less breathe, I was at his mercy. This edging charade continued for some time and before long, I began to hallucinate colors and shapes that looked like fireworks. I knew I was going to lose consciousness soon...

I fought against the rising tide of oblivion as waves of pleasure ran through my manhood, until I was met with absolute blackness and seemingly no way out. I heard Jon and Lisa calling my name as I drifted away on a raft of nothingness, my climax and loss of consciousness happening simultaneously.

The next voice I heard was my nurse's, begging me to open my eyes, and the first thing I saw when opening them was a bright light. I was able to make out Jon and Lisa's concerned faces in the background.

"He's coming around," the nurse said with a reassuring smile. "You gave us quite a scare, Mr. Smith! But you're alright, thank goodness. Your friend Jon said you had been drinking juice and suddenly passed out."

I nodded weakly, feeling rather altered and unable to determine how much of what had happened was a medicine induced hallucination. Jon then hugged me and smiled gently, relieved I was ok. I glanced around the room and saw that everything looked normal - no disco lights, no music, and no sign of alcohol or any other substances. I sighed with relief, rather confident that what had happened was some delirium from the meds and after effects of anesthesia.

After the nurse had taken my vitals and was confident I was stable, I decided to get up to use the loo. Once in there, I saw the contents of the garbage and my heart nearly stopped. There were several empty plastic cups that smelled like tequila as well as a shopping bag, the same color one that had been over my head. It hadn't been a dream after all. When I had finished doing my business, I went back to my bed with my heart in my mouth, feeling rather defeated and wishing to do nothing but sleep.

Jon and Lisa had stayed a while longer, happy that I was alright and apologetic for getting carried away. My best mate felt particularly remorseful, and he cuddled with me on my hospital bed for a while, his eyes misted over with emotion he rarely displayed.

"I know I can be a bit of a jerk at times," he admitted as he held me gently. "But I do love you, mate. And I'm so sorry that things got out of hand. I never like to see you hurt."

I nodded and placed my hand on his shoulder. "It's alright, Jon. It had its pleasurable moments. I had an orgasm, remember?"

Jon chuckled. "This is true. It was just scary seeing you like that, losing consciousness and not breathing. But I'm so glad you're alright." He ran his fingers through my hair and kissed me on the lips. Lisa joined us on the bed, spooning my best mate. I noticed Jon's body tense up when she got behind him, as if he were rather afraid of her presence. I had a conversation with Jon the following day, during which he revealed that the "play fighting" he spoke of was an actual attack by Lisa, who had gotten angry-drunk and had taken it out on him. As for visiting the hospital nursery? Jon told me he had wound up going on his own, looking at the newborn babies through the clear glass with tears streaming from his sunglasses-covered eyes, while Lisa waited outside smoking a cigarette.

After that adventure in the hospital, I decided that I wanted to experiment more with asphyxiation using plastic bags. Despite feeling somewhat taken advantage of by Jon, I had enjoyed the earth shattering climax, which, for the record, had been the most intense one I had experienced to date. When I was discharged from the hospital the following day, I stopped at the grocery store for a few items, making sure to keep the bags. They would come in handy that evening when I would have my wife put one of them over my head...

"Come on, Jon, breathe," I gasped as I did CPR on my best mate. Candy had called for emergency services, who were on their way. Anna waited downstairs for the paramedics to come.

Not including the time I had been trying to save him, Jon had gone approximately 15 minutes without breathing. At some point during the face sitting, he had stopped moving his hands and his body had gone limp. Candy had immediately climbed off him, only to see his lips were blue and that he was unresponsive. When I had pried his eyes open, his pupils had been completely enlarged. His heart beat had nearly been undetectable. I had hurried in, doing what I could to revive him while Candy called 911.

My heart raced as I did my best to help him, wondering what in the hell I would do if he died. I felt somehow numb, almost like my mind and body were going into survival mode and before long, I was outside myself and observing what I was doing. Then suddenly, I heard Jon's voice whispering to me.

"I'm going to be alright, mate," his voice said.

Somewhat shocked by the sound of his disembodied voice, I snapped back into my body, looking down at a still-comatose Jon who, in that moment, was quite incapable of speaking.

The next few minutes went by in a haze, with emergency workers at the ready with life saving equipment. Candy and Anna stood crying in the corner of the room, watching them work on bringing him back to life. I sat on the floor with my mouth hanging open, in shock at what was happening.

Then, just as quickly as the drama had started, it was all over, and my best mate began to breathe again. Color restored to his face as he took multiple labored breaths. Everyone in that room applauded, including myself. Once the ambulance worker was done taking his vitals, Candy rushed up onto the bed to hold him, crying apologies for something that wasn't her fault. He held her back, whispering reassurances and loving words in her ear and rocking her gently as he did so. It was a touching scene.

Crying tears of relief, I joined in on the embrace, which Jon eagerly returned. Candy got up and grabbed some water for Jon, who reassured the paramedics that he was alright and didn't want to go to the hospital.

"I'm here to stay," he whispered in my ear as we held each other.

The next several hours, Jon, Candy, Anna, and I sat on Jon's balcony talking at length about anything and everything. The subject of my wife eventually came up, as did the time I was recovering from my appendectomy.

"Your wife was always so attentive and kind," Jon noted as he lit a blunt. "She was so good to you when you were sick. I especially recall the time you had your appendix removed, and she had brought you that epic balloon arrangement, along with other random little gifts and homemade cookies. Meanwhile, I was a bit of a dick and pressured you to drink and vape while you were still doped up on meds, and not fully recovered from the surgery. Then the icing on the cake was when I had nearly suffocated you to death with a grocery bag." He shook his head and laughed bitterly. "I was such a prick, mate. For fucking years. I wish I

had a time machine so I could go back and be nicer to you, and be there for you when you really needed me to be. I'm sorry." His eyes filled with tears as he ashed his blunt and took a drag. Candy put her hand on his back as she looked at him sympathetically.

I shook my head and placed my hand on his shoulder, smiling reassuringly. "You have always been there when I needed you," I said in a kind voice. "You've had your 'dick' moments, but you've always had a big heart to make up for it. I've lost track of all the times you have supported me through all kinds of situations. You've cared for me when I was sick and/or drunk, you've helped me pick out clothes for everything from dates, to weddings, to dances, to fun nights out. Whenever I've had to deal with a major crisis, I could call you and you would be there, even if it meant driving to my place half awake and hungover, or flying across the country. At the very least, you would spend hours on the phone with me, listening to me grumble, yell, and even cry, and you always made me laugh and gave me great advice. You've even saved my life, and others' lives. I love you, Jon. You're a great friend. And I'm so glad you're still breathing." I winked at him as I became choked up.

Tears spilled from Jon's green eyes as he leaned over to give me a bear hug, which I eagerly returned.

Anna and Candy joined in for a group hug to end all group hugs. After several moments of stillness, hands inevitably moved south, and everyone's breathing began to quicken. I closed my eyes as visions of Anna's mouth on my dick filled my head. Someone's nails dug into my back and I felt a hand grab my crotch. After a few more moments of ever-increasing sexual tension, we decided to migrate back inside to the

master bedroom, where we all began feverishly kissing, and undressing each other.

A spontaneous four-way hadn't been part of the plan, but after the near-death experience that had occurred before, emotions were running high and we all needed a release. Orgasm was the most sensible solution.

The four of us lay on the black satin clad California king sized bed, taking turns kissing and groping each other in various combinations and positions. After a while, Candy began to feverishly kiss Jon as she put on a humongous strap-on dildo, much to everyone's delight. As this was happening, I went down on Anna, devouring her cunny with the ravenousness of a starving man. Jon wrapped his hand around my manhood while this was occurring, and Anna began to choke herself. Jon backed away from Candy's lips and repositioned himself on all fours, continuing to stroke me as he did so. I became lightheaded with horniness as the blood rushed from the head atop my shoulders to the head between my legs, and I panted with anticipation of what was about to take place.

"Ugh!"

Jon grunted in pleasure mixed with pain as Candy entered him roughly - and completely dry - with the giant strap-on, wasting no time pounding the hell out of him. It was surreal seeing my best mate struggle under the force of Candy's thrusts. She even seemed to be getting off on it, a tiny smirk forming on her face as she dug her nails into Jon's back and pulled his hair. His arms shook as he remained on all fours, taking every

inch inside his bum, which was being stretched beyond its usual limits. He was undoubtedly in some agony.

A depraved lightbulb went off in my head as I looked over at Anna, who was still masturbating me with her soft hand. Aside from the one time Jon had forced the tip of his penis inside me almost 2 years prior, I was an "anal virgin," in the sense that I had yet to experience real, consensual intercourse of the back door variety. I made up my mind right then: I wanted my darling Anna to fuck me with a strap-on. It's one of the few things my wife hadn't gotten the chance to do to me. Simple "domination" wasn't enough for me anymore; I wanted to be completely overpowered. The question was, would Anna be up for it?

"Have you had enough yet?" Candy teased as she fucked the shit out of Jon's arsehole. Slapping sounds filled the air as she violated him from behind, as did Jon's moans.

"Keep fucking me," Jon panted as he arched his back, clamping his eyes shut as the dildo tore him up. "Don't stop, Mommy!"

My best mate's body jolted repeatedly from the hard thrusts. He grabbed handfuls of the satin blanket that lay atop the bed as he groaned and grimaced, occasionally burying his face in the pillow.

Perhaps sensing my state of arousal, Anna lowered her head to my cock and began sucking me off with reckless abandon. I let myself fall backward onto the bed, pushing the top of her pretty little head as she deep throated me. It took enormous amounts of willpower for me to

avoid climaxing but I did my best, occasionally looking over at Jon being raped with a strap-on but having the good sense to look away before my dick exploded.

Not long after Candy had dug her nails into Jon's back, marks appeared on his skin and began to seep blood. A sheen of sweat appeared on his body as he trembled, taking the strap-on up the arse with the skill of a porn star. I noticed his face contort in pain, and tears formed in his eyes as he let Candy impale him repeatedly. I know a part of him felt guilty for torturing his girlfriend the night before. Prior to the ill-fated age play session, Jon had told me about the things that he had done to her whilst I was upstairs sleeping. He had done everything from shooting blanks at her at fairly close range, to holding her head underwater, to whaling her in the arse and low back with a cane, which is something she had found excruciatingly painful. She had even urinated blood at one point, perhaps due to being hit in the kidneys. In his mind, a little role reversal was the least he could do to even the score. Therefore, the name of the game for Jon was asphyxiation to the point of near-death, and sodomy with a 12 inch strap-on that even the most seasoned "anal connoisseur" would have trouble tolerating.

I held out my hand to a struggling Jon, who eagerly took it. In fact, he nearly crushed my hand. That was when I noticed some blood trickle down his inner thighs. I decided not to say anything, knowing full well that my best mate didn't want to stop until he climaxed. In fact, he used his other hand to fondle himself.

Candy paused his thrusts. "Turn over onto your back, son," she ordered.

Jon nodded, letting go of my hand as he flipped himself over onto his back and spread his legs. Candy noticed the blood and was momentarily taken aback before reentering her boyfriend and thrusting wildly. Once situated, he used his left hand to hold onto mine and took a hold of his cock with his right. As this was happening, Anna continued to suck me off, occasionally teasing the outside of my arsehole with her finger as she did so. The sensation drove me insane and it took even more willpower to avoid climaxing. As for Jon, he was shaking like a leaf and whimpering as he choked his member. The entire bed shook with the force of Candy's thrusts, and Jon's blood began to spread onto her inner thighs as it mixed with their combined sweat.

"Oh, Mommy!" Jon cried out as he began to sob, tears rolling down his face. "I'm cumming! Ughhhh!" He howled as his cock exploded all over his stomach and down his sides. Candy orgasmed not long after him, after which time she withdrew from his arsehole and removed the strap-on. The she crouched between Jon's legs and proceeded to lick and suck the blood from his bum and surrounding area until everything was clean, saving the cum covering his torso for last. Then she crawled up to him and held him, letting him cry into her shoulder, as she did the same. This all happened within a few minutes time, and the sight of it was what finally sent me over the edge. I came inside Anna's mouth, eyes rolling into the back of my head...

Several hours later...

"On Memorial Day weekend, I'm asking her to marry me," Jon said as he downed a shot of vodka and lit a cigarette. It was just him and me by that point, chilling outside on my deck while Anna and Candy went for a walk on the beach.

My jaw dropped in excitement. "Really?"

Jon nodded with a grin as he exhaled a plume of smoke out of his nostrils. "Yes. That's the perfect time to propose to her, I think. Mario and I will be playing a gig at Seaside Park in Westchester that Saturday. I wanted to do it even sooner, BUT I sort of overheard a phone conversation Candy had with her cousin Irene a few weeks ago. She had told her how she loved being serenaded, and that she fantasized about being proposed to in front of a crowd of people. So that's what I plan on doing. First, I'm going to sing a song in her honor. Then? I'm going to call her onto the stage, get down on one knee, and ask her to be my queen." His emerald green eyes had stars in them as he smiled.

I smiled broadly as I took a sip of my drink. "Bravo!" I said as I patted him on the shoulder. "I can't want to see that. It sounds very romantic, and very epic."

"I try," Jon said with a chuckle. "Any girl who can make me cry during orgasm is a girl who has my heart forever," he said with a wink. "Even Lisa wasn't able to do that to me, mate. But Candy?" He smiled and shook his head. "She's really special. I mean, uncanny. She's had my heart since day one. IF I'm being honest."

"She's so perfect for you," I said. "Have you thought of the kind of wedding you want?"

Jon shrugged. "I'm open to just about anything," he admitted as he took a drag. "Whatever makes her happy will make me happy. And I will spare no expense to ensure that happiness. I admit I don't fancy myself a traditionalist, nor does Candy, so I doubt that we would wind up doing the 'church and reception hall' thing. And a Vegas wedding might bring back some sad memories for yours truly. But we both love the beach, so I can see us doing something on the water, preferably in warm climate. Perhaps a destination wedding of some kind?"

I nodded excitedly. "The Caribbean would be incredible, or maybe the Bahamas. Actually, I know a girl from the gym who got married on the beach in Bermuda, and she said it had been like a fairy tale. Pink sand, and it was at a resort that had a panoramic view of the water."

Jon grinned from ear to ear and he got a faraway look in his gaze that made it clear he was picturing his wedding day. "That actually sounds quite magical," he said in a soft, lovestruck tone of voice.

"I know it doesn't compare to proposing marriage," I began hesitantly, "but I've decided it's time to tell Anna I love her. My goal is to tell her by the end of this month."

Jon's eyes widened and he smiled ecstatically. "That's fucking wonderful! Long overdue, I reckon. I was beginning to think you were never going to tell her. But I understand you had to be ready."

I lit a cigarette and nodded. "With the anniversary of my wife coming up, I've been in a bit of a funk. Just a lot of memories popping up, but I'm trying to move on."

Jon smiled sympathetically and placed his hand on mine. "I understand, mate."

My thoughts traveled to my wife, and back to Anna. Aside from my plans to tell Anna I loved her, I had plans that scared me just as much, if not more. I was going to let her peg me.

I spent the next several days training my back side with an "anal trainer" that Jon had purchased for me as a random gift.

"It's like training wheels for your arsehole," my best mate had quipped crudely with a smirk when he gave it to me, making me laugh.

I also practiced using an anal douche, which provided a sensation that was more pleasurable than I had thought it would be. I knew the hardest part of all this would be giving up any sense of control, and being at Anna's mercy.

Speaking of Anna, she gradually spent more and more time in "dominant mode," first blindfolding me, then tying down my arms with silk scarves. I even let her graze a dull knife over my flesh at one point. As for anal play, I had graduated to having 2 fingers inside me. This was

still a far cry from a strap-on penis, but still progress. At that point, I was only 2 weeks away from the big day...

Chapter 9: "Her Name Was Melody"

"Are you ready?" Anna asked as she stood at the foot of the bed, dressed in a sexy leather outfit. She held a whip in her hand and wore a

sexy smirk on her face. Her lips were a deep shade of red. Whatever trace she had of her usual "girl next door" self was all but gone.

I lay naked on the bed, smoking a joint to settle my nerves. I nodded as I exhaled a plume of smoke. "Yes, mistress."

After several weeks of rumination and procrastination, I decided on a particularly overcast and dreary day that it was time for Anna to make me her bitch. My bum was capable of taking a modest sized dildo by this point and I no longer experienced heart palpitations at the mere thought of my lovely redhead fucking me up the arse.

She crouched between my legs and began to suck me off, gently caressing the crack of my bum as she did so. I developed goosebumps on my flesh as she touched and sucked me, and I moaned with pleasure. I laid back on the pillow and took another greedy drag off the joint, finishing it. I inhaled deeply and held in the smoke. My head swam with rapture as I reveled in the sensation of her touch which, by this point, was becoming less gentle.

My heart rate accelerated as I noticed her putting on the strap-on penis, and I began to wonder if I had made a mistake. Perhaps I was still not ready. Perhaps it was best to wait a wee bit longer, or stick to just fingers inside my bum. But Jon, and Anna herself, had insisted I was more than ready. So I exhaled the smoke I had been holding in my lungs and decided to go with it. After all, what was the worst that could happen?

"Get on all fours," Anna ordered with a sinister expression on her face.

I swallowed and nodded, positioning myself so my bum was exposed to her. I willed myself to stay relaxed as she teased my opening with her lubricated finger, pumping in and out. After warming me up with 2, then 3, fingers, she began to ease her way inside me with the strap on. The tip of the silicone device went inside of me inch by painful inch, and it took all my willpower to avoid clenching up.

My thoughts traveled to places that were as long ago and far away as possible. I thought of the first time I had spotted my wife. It had been the summer before I had started college. Jon, Daryl, Lisa, and I had gone to our favorite amusement park in Massachusetts. At Jon's insistence, the four of us had decided to go on one of the scarier rollercoasters, one that had recently made it to the news when it had malfunctioned and resulted in someone becoming seriously injured. My cocky best mate told us not to be pussies, assuring us it was a fluke and wouldn't happen again. Unfortunately, it did, and about midway through the ride, the safety bars intended to hold passengers in their seats had become loose, flying open at random, and the riders had to hold onto the bars for dear life to keep from being ejected out of the seats.

The seatbelts had helped some, but it had still been a harrowing experience. Lisa's vagina had wound up becoming injured from Jon's fingering, and, at one point during an especially violent part in the ride, his fingernail had scraped her cervix, making her bleed. As for Daryl? He had wound up having an asthma attack on the ride, and, as his seat mate, I had done my best to keep him calm, managing to hold the inhaler to his mouth with one whilst holding the malfunctioning safety bar closed with the other.

With all the commotion and screaming around us, I had been convinced we were all going to die. But Jon, who occupied the seat in front of us and was doing his best to comfort a hysterical Lisa while white-knuckling his own safety bar, consoled us calmly. He had turned around to look at me and his horrified brother, and had said with utmost confidence, "Things will be alright. Just hold on." His words had stuck with me. And he was right. Once the ride grinded to a creaky and long overdue halt, we all stepped off on shaky legs. Jon had been very apologetic for guilting us into going on the ride, and took the time to comfort the three of us. He then took Lisa to a secluded area to get her cleaned up while I sat with Daryl and made sure he was recovered from his asthma attack.

All the passengers had made it out in one piece, traumatized but otherwise alright with little more than minor injuries. Most had looked disheveled, but there was one girl who didn't. In fact, she had looked remarkably unfazed, and was comforting what had turned out to be a friend of hers, who was shaken up. Her poise had impressed me, as did her exotic good looks. Her long black hair had a sexy wave to it and her caramel skin glowed. She had a round bum that I had wanted to sink my teeth into. I had so wanted to go up to her and introduce myself, but she had disappeared into the crowd with her friend. I had vowed to meet her at some point, feeling a strong attraction to her. Merely 2 months later, I would meet her at a college party, where it would turn out that she attended the same university. And the rest, as they say, would be history...

Thinking of that story made me want to take Jon's advice and "just hold on," and it also inspired me to remain as poised as my wife had been

during that debacle at the amusement park. So I gritted my teeth and endured what Anna was doing to me.

"You're just a toy to me," Anna growled, an unfamiliar bitterness in her voice. "Nothing more than a plaything."

A lump formed in my throat as I tolerated her thrusts, trying to remind myself that she was role playing. Still, hearing those words stung, and I began to worry that she had meant what she said.

"I don't really care about you," she continued as she pounded me. My insides throbbed and my eyes filled with tears as I grabbed handfuls of my bedspread. I knew better than to speak, not that it was possible for words to get past the lump in my throat. How could I address my growing feelings of hurt? It seemed all I could do was pretend all was well and let myself free fall into subspace. As I did that, however, my mind began to spiral into very dark places, and, before long, I found myself longing for my wife. I began to feel her presence very strongly, and suddenly tinkered with the idea of joining her a bit earlier than intended. After all, if Anna didn't really love me and saw me as nothing more than a fuck toy, what was the bloody point of continuing on?

The idea of an actual attempt at my own life wasn't quite appealing to me in that moment, but I was open to "rolling the dice," so to speak. Meaning, if the man upstairs wanted to take me sooner, I was alright with that. So I decided at that moment that, after this torture fest, I would get blind drunk and knock back some sleeping pills for good measure, then take a nice hot bath. I was bloody done existing with a hole in my heart that only my wife was willing to fill, so if it was my

time, so be it. I was done grieving nonstop, with nothing but pain and suffering that was occasionally relieved by well meaning people who couldn't compare to the love of my life.

"Mistress, it hurts," I grunted as she pounded me. By that point, I knew I was bleeding. Still, she kept on.

"Suck it up."

Tears fell from my eyes at the sound of her cold voice. Oh, how I wish Jon had been there to run interference, to give her a taste of her own medicine and provide some comic relief with his sarcastic jokes. What I wouldn't do to have a beer with him at that moment...

What WOULD Jon do in this situation anyway? I did the best I could to stop crying and tried to think of a way to channel him, so I could regain control of the situation, to once again be a "top." My bum was getting torn up to the point that I began to worry I was injured; aside from that, I could no longer mentally handle being the submissive one. My best mate was tough and brave with a pain tolerance that was off the charts, and I had told him as much following a hardcore edgeplay session several years back. His response to my comment had stuck with me.

"Well, that might be true, but sometimes being tough and brave means knowing when to end things, mate. It's not about tolerating unnecessary agony." His words had been accompanied by his confident smile. There was a fine line between being a "bottom" and suffering

needlessly, hence why it was important to know one's limits. I had reached mine.

"Butterfly."

I croaked the safe word as best I could, the sound of it instantly making me cry again. Anna paused, holding still inside me before roughly pulling out. I could instantly feel the blood trickle out of my bum and down my inner thighs. She got up from the bed and threw a towel in my direction. Then she left the room, slamming the door on her way out. Just like that, I was all alone.

Typically, the participants in role play break character after a scene has ended and the safe word is spoken. But every once in a while, it's difficult to switch gears and return to normal. I found this phenomenon to occur most commonly in people who are new to BDSM and role playing in general, but it can happen to those with more experience as well, myself included. Despite my understanding of the situation and my veteran status as role player, I very much felt like a victim and, without aftercare, I was falling deeper and deeper into subspace with every passing minute.

My body began to shake and I felt dizzy. My ability to cry was no longer there, despite wanting to. I craved warmth, whether from a body or a cup of hot tea. But the room and overall mood was so cold, and so unfeeling. Where was Anna? Why wasn't she coming back? I hugged my pillow and held out a bit of hope that any second she would come through the door with a cup of something warm and a smile. My hopes

were destroyed when I heard the back door of my house slam shut, along with the sound of her car starting then driving away.

I could have called Jon. I SHOULD have. He would have been over in minutes, happy to take care of me and help me get into a healthier frame of mind. But I lacked the fortitude to find my phone, much less dial his number. I looked at my nightstand, and saw that my phone wasn't there. A bottle of sleeping pills, however, was there, as was a handle of vodka. Did I dare go down that rabbit hole?

Tempting as it was to take the entire bottle of pills, I decided on a double dose, rationalizing that I simply wanted to take the edge off and not overdose on them. After all, the last thing I wanted was to wind up in hospital. I opened the pill bottle then unscrewed the cap of liquor, reveling in the strong smell that I knew would transport me to a state of oblivion. Then I took out six pills and placed them on my tongue. After a moment's hesitation, I put the bottle of vodka to my lips then tilted my head back, swallowing the tablets.

The liquid burned as it traveled down my throat and I felt that all too familiar and comforting sensation of lightheadedness. The pills slid down my throat with ease. I took another swig. Then another. I smoked a cigarette and managed to finish most of the vodka. Once feeling a decent buzz, I decided to get up from the bed, intent on taking a bath. I no longer gave a shit about the blood seeping from my arsehole and going down my legs. Who fucking cared? After all, I was headed to the loo to clean up anyway.

More blood dripped onto the floor as I exited my room, and I lacked the motivation to clean it up. In fact, it took every bit of energy I had just to stagger to the kitchen to grab my phone off the counter. I glanced at it. No fucking calls or texts. Nobody gave a shit about me. I slammed it back down on the counter, screen side down. On impulse, I hobbled farther into the kitchen and grabbed a bottle of tequila and a highball glass, then poured myself a drink. I needed something besides the plain vodka to dull my senses, so the complex, herbal taste of tequila was the perfect compliment to the harsh booze. I knocked back the contents quickly, then refilled the glass. Drops of blood dotted the linoleum floor, but I couldn't have cared less. I was about to draw myself what would probably be my last bath.

I was so drunk after slamming the tequila that I could barely walk, but I forced myself to, intent on making it to the loo for my bath. I decided to take my glass with me, figuring I could sip from it while bathing. Unfortunately, I slipped and fell on my way to the bathroom, dropping the highball glass, which broke to pieces. Tequila spilled everywhere. I felt a pain in my left hand, and realized I had cut myself with the broken glass, having landed on it when I had put my hand down to break my fall. Blood poured from it and when I tried to get up, I slipped again, this time landing on my knees. I elected to crawl to the bathroom, leaving a heavy trail of blood behind me. The bathroom light was already on, so all I really had to do was crawl my way into the tub. The pristine bathroom turned into a bit of a crime scene as the blood from my hand and arse covered the floor. I kicked the door shut then got onto my scraped knees, locking it. Then I crawled to the tub and hoisted myself into it, landing with a thud. I turned on the shower and, despite being unable to stand, did my best to clean myself. Once finished, I took a nearby rag and made a bandage out of it, wrapping my hand as best I could. My arse, at least for the moment, had stopped bleeding.

I closed the drain and turned on the faucet, wanting very much to take my bath. I even added some of my favorite oil and bubble bath. If I was going to either bleed or drown to death, I wanted to at least do so in style. As luck would have it, I found an open bottle of champagne and a box of chocolate next to the tub. Even fucking better. I was already drunk and dizzy as I could fucking be, but I uncorked the bottle of bubbly and put it to my lips, tilting my head back as I sat in the rapidly filling tub. I choked down a piece of chocolate, letting it dissolve in my mouth briefly before chewing and swallowing. My hand throbbed something awful and I might have even needed stitches, but I didn't give a shit anymore. And my bum was a lost cause.

I felt so torn up down there that I was pretty confident I would wind up incontinent for the rest of my life. I choked back tears as I assessed the direness of my situation: no more wife, no more parents, no more girlfriend, no more use of my hand (at least not for a while), and most likely no more being able to hold the contents of my fucking bowels.

"Fuck this," I grumbled through fresh tears as I finished the bottle of champagne, silently praying for death. My eyes grew heavy as I lay in the hot water, the color of which was turning a darker shade of red with every passing minute. I was definitely bleeding from my arse once again but didn't care. I held out my injured hand, examining it. The blood had seeped through the bandage a wee bit. I decided to remove the wound dressing, deciding that I would risk bleeding out. Sure enough, the blood seeped from the cut at a slow but steady pace. I let my arm fall into the water. The wound stung for a brief moment but after a minute or so, I wasn't able to feel anything.

I closed my eyes and felt myself drift away, barely conscious and wanting to sink as far down into a state of numbness as possible.

Perhaps God would take me, and that wouldn't be such a terrible thing. Granted, dying naked in a tub full of blood-water wasn't my preferred way to go, but it was far more appealing than continuing to live a life without anyone to love.

My mind traveled back to the day I had lost my wife…

"Put the blindfold on me," she said as she smiled sexily up at me, her pregnant belly sporting a bump that made her all the more irresistible. She wore a matching black bra and panties set, and her caramel skin shone like a goddess's. I wanted to fuck her so badly. But first? Foreplay.

We had been trying for a while to have a baby, and after about two years, had finally succeeded. She was five months along and had decided to wait until the day of delivery to find out the gender of our child. The suspense of not knowing if we were having a boy or girl was equal parts maddening and exciting, for both of us.

Not long after finding out she was expecting, she had, after many years, finally succeeded in weaning herself off the pain pills she had been taking for back pain resulting from a sports injury, and had also quit smoking. Detoxing was a task she had found daunting but she made it through. In support of her, I had also given up tobacco, deciding it was best for her health and the baby's health, as well as mine. Who knows? Maybe once the baby came, we would remain cigarette free, and only smoke weed on occasion instead? At any rate, the future seemed bright, and the possibilities endless.

I placed the blindfold over her eyes as she lay on the bed in that sexy lingerie. She smiled sexily. My manhood hardened as I envisioned what would come next.

"Shall I tie you up before going to the kitchen to make the nibbles?" My little butterfly always liked food play at the start of things, delighting in being fed random snacks while blindfolded. After feeding her, I would graze objects of random textures and temperatures over her body. Some of these items were edible and some were not; the point was to create the element of surprise.

"No, that's ok," she cooed with her eyes covered. "I will lie here like a good girl."

"If you say so," I said with a chuckle before closing the door and heading to the kitchen to make her some food. I decided on mozzarella sticks and an assortment of fresh fruit with whipped topping. I preheated the oven then took the box of mozzarella sticks out of the freezer, humming to myself as I did so. As I waited for the oven to heat up, I got some fruit out of the refrigerator along with a cutting board from the drawer and began cutting strawberries and melons into pleasing shapes. I developed an erection as I imagined eating the pieces of fruit off her lithe, naked body.

Once the oven was ready, I placed the mozzarella sticks on a baking sheet and placed them on the middle rack, closing the oven door with a flourish. I masturbated as I sat on the bar stool, watching the food cook and thinking of all the naughty things I would do to my butterfly in a few short moments. The timer went off after perhaps fifteen minutes, and I

took the yummy, piping hot snacks out of the oven. My mouth watered as I arranged the cheese sticks on a large plate with the cut up fruit, creating a little floral design with the food. I grabbed the whipped topping and a bottle of water from the refrigerator then headed back to the bedroom.

I opened the door and saw her lying on the bed with her blindfold sitting above her closed eyes. It appeared that she had fallen asleep. I smiled warmly and placed the plate of food next to her on the bed as I climbed up next to her, caressing her face.

"Wake up, sleepyhead," I cooed into her ear as I ran my fingers through her long, black hair. "It's playtime."

She lay motionless. I began to shake her gently then more vigorously and still nothing happened. My heart began to race as I leaned over to take her pulse and check to see if she was breathing. The next few minutes turned into the ultimate nightmare...

With numb hands and an ever racing mind, I dialed emergency services on my phone, doing my best to revive her with what little first aid skills I had. This couldn't be happening. Surely there was a solution, a quick fix that the paramedics could take care of? My butterfly couldn't be dead. She was too young.

"Come on, baby," I panted as I did CPR, sweat emanating from my brow. An ambulance arrived within minutes, and I stood by while the EMT's did their best to bring her back to life. At one point, I crouched down

onto the floor to grab a pillow that had fallen, and that was when I saw what was underneath the bed.

There were about 2 dozen or so empty or near-empty syringes on the floor under our California king. I grabbed several of them to see what they were. Several EMT's glanced at the syringes, and one of them took one out of my hand and looked at me sympathetically. I stared at the label in disbelief and began to mumble.

"No, no, no , no, no," I babbled through tears as I stared at my wife and then at the syringe. One of the emergency workers pointed to what appeared to be faded track marks on the inside of her arm. How had I not noticed? The unthinkable had occurred: my wife had accidentally overdosed on fentanyl.

I recalled screaming for her to wake up and falling to the floor in a fit of despair when she did not. After having this conniption, I started feeling like I was out of my body, going through the motions of indescribable grief. At once, I was mourning the loss of my wife as well as my unborn baby.

I managed to deal with the necessary death related stuff, like talking to the coroner who arrived not long after the paramedics had tried - and failed - to save her. Then I somehow had the wherewithal to call members of her family, most of whom lived in Puerto Rico. Afterwards, I called Daryl to tell him I wasn't going to make it into work. He had begun crying when I told him, insisting on closing the gym early and coming by to provide comfort for me. Brother Lawrence was next on my list, and he showed up not long before Daryl did, letting me cry into his

shoulder. I also called the local funeral home to make arrangements. Last on my call list was Jon, who I hesitated to contact because he was on holiday at the Bellagio in Las Vegas and had plans to elope with Lisa. The last thing I wanted was to ruin his trip and delay his nuptials. But I was losing my mind and could barely function, and I knew my older best mate was brilliant in a crisis. If there was ever a time I needed him, it was now.

At 1AM Eastern Standard Time on an especially dreary night, I decided I couldn't take it anymore. So I drunk-dialed Jon to tell him the awful news, doing my best to stop crying as I did so.

Jon's phone rang four times before he picked up, panting. I was able to make out the sound of slapping in the background, along with a woman's moans.

"This better be fucking important, bitch," he panted into the phone with a chuckle. "I'm balls deep in Lisa's bum as we speak. What the FUCK do you want, pussy?!"

I could hear Lisa's giggles in the background, along with gentle scolding for Jon to "be nice." Somehow, I wasn't able to talk and simply began to cry. I heard the slapping sounds get quieter and stop altogether.

"You there, mate?" Jon asked, his tone changing to one of concern. "You alright?"

My sobbing continued. "N-no," I stammered. "I'm sorry to interrupt your getaway but... my butterfly...she's...she's dead, Jon." I choked on my words as I sobbed uncontrollably.

Stunned silence permeated the air for a few seconds while my best mate processed the news. Then he sighed shakily before speaking.

"Oh, my god," he whispered, sounding choked up. He had been good friends with my wife, and so had Lisa. "I am so, so sorry. I'm here for you, mate. How did this happen?"

Through hysterical tears, I told him the awful story of the overdose and other unpleasant things I'd had to deal with, specifically a paralyzing depression that made it impossible for me to work, eat, sleep, or take care of anything. Leaving the house was out of the question. Daryl and Lawrence did what they could, but I felt like I needed another set of hands so those 2 blokes wouldn't become burned out. Also? Jon had a higher tolerance for stress than anyone else I knew, and I felt that his stability would be especially beneficial to me at this time.

"I am flying out there as soon as I can," Jon said in a steady voice. "I just checked the airline website on my phone while you were talking to me, and I can get a red-eye out of LAX after Lisa and I drive home tonight. I should be in Rhode Island by late afternoon, if not earlier. Will you be ok until then?"

Jon's velvety, deep voice was soothing to me. "Yes I will," I assured. "Daryl and Lawrence have been keeping me company, both together

and in shifts. Those poor boys need a break. Aside from those two, you're the only one I can really trust to handle this. Thank you, Jon. And I'm so sorry to bother you while you're on your trip." I began to cry again.

"Nonsense," Jon soothed. "We were headed home early anyway because Lisa got food poisoning and we are both coming down with something. A cold, or some bullshit virus. So we were going to delay our nuptials until later this year, or maybe even do something bigger the following year. THIS is more important, mate. You need me now."

"Thanks, Jon," I said tearfully. "I know Lisa will be devastated when she finds out. Unless she overheard any of this?"

"No, she hasn't," Jon said quietly. "She doesn't know yet. I actually retreated into the loo to talk to you because I knew it was serious when you began to cry. Sorry for the rude way I answered the phone, by the way. I had no idea you were calling with such tragic news and I was just being my usual sarcastic self. Anyway, you know I love you. We will get through this together, hmm?"

I began crying with a mix of relief and renewed sorrow. "Yes, yes we will."

"That's my boy," he crooned. "I will be sure and pop by the store to get some groceries for you before I arrive, because I'm sure that shopping is the last thing on your mind right now."

I chuckled for the first time since the wife died. "That's an understatement!"

We both laughed. "Alright, well, I will see you tomorrow, mate. Don't drink too much, tempting as it might be. It is a depressant after all." Jon was often very fatherly when someone was in a crisis. It was rather endearing.

"Yes, Dad," I said wryly. "I love you, mate. See you tomorrow."

We said our goodbyes and hung up. I managed to fall asleep not long after our conversation, relieved that my "rock" was going to help me get myself together...

I slept for twelve hours before waking up with a headache. Daryl and Lawrence knew to let me sleep, knowing it was my only escape from the grief and sadness I was experiencing. When I hobbled out of my room, Daryl was on the couch watching the telly and greeted me with a smile.

"Hello, mate," he said warmly. "I made breakfast for you earlier. It's in the refrigerator. Lawrence gave his regards and had to leave for work but said he would be around this evening after 8 if you needed him. Also, Jon called me to tell me he had talked to you last night, and would be flying in this afternoon sometime. How are you feeling?"

I shook my head and began to cry, sitting diagonally from him on the recliner. "Terrible," I sobbed. "I still have no appetite, and I can't think straight. I'm so glad Jon is coming. You and my brother can get a much needed break. I'm sorry I'm such a mess."

Daryl placed his hand on my shoulder. "It's alright, Ken," he soothed. "This is a rough time. Hey, do you want some orange juice?"

I sniffled and nodded. Daryl got up and poured me a glass then handed it to me. I took tentative sips then lit myself a cigarette, crying quietly as I stared blankly at the TV screen. I had yet to shower or eat since she had passed. I lived in my robe. Simple walking hurt my body and I experienced almost constant vertigo. My butterfly's memorial service, which was going to be an intimate gathering with only family, was scheduled for 3 days from that point, and I had no fucking idea how I was going to function for that event. I wanted to join her. I wanted to put an end to my suffering. As I sat smoking, I began to think of ways to end my life...

Knock, knock.

Daryl got up to answer the door. Jon had arrived. He was carrying several bags of groceries as well as his luggage. The two brothers exchanged greetings. I was able to make out Jon's words, when he quietly asked Daryl if I was holding up alright. His brother shook his head, making it clear that I wasn't doing so well. I slowly rose up from my couch to greet him, my tears starting all over again. He dropped his bags on the floor the moment he saw me and wrapped his strong arms around me in a tight embrace. I let myself cry into his shoulder, my

entire body shaking with the force of my sobs. The comforting scent of his designer cologne filled my nostrils and I reveled in the feel of his soft, white cotton tee.

"I'm here, mate," he whispered soothingly as he held me, rocking me slightly. "It's going to be alright. Just let it out."

I had no idea how much time passed as I stood there sobbing into his shoulder but it felt so good to be held by Jon. He gave the best hugs and was a calming presence during emotional moments. Daryl put away the groceries as we held each other, and I noticed him wipe away an occasional tear as he did so. Jon's younger brother was more outwardly emotional than Jon was, but was still a great support and very giving. I don't know what I would have done without the two of them at a time like this.

"Let's go over to the couch, yes?" Jon suggested as he walked with his arm around me to the living room and handed me a tissue, which I accepted as I wiped my eyes and my nose. Daryl brought over glasses of water for the both of us, then retreated to the kitchen to make some tea.

I sat on the couch next to Jon, who cuddled with me as I continued to cry. He looked at me with such love and concern that I knew I was in good hands. He didn't pressure me to talk or do anything, he simply gazed at me with those kind green eyes and a gentle smile, occasionally rubbing my hand or running his fingers through my hair. In that moment, I felt more like his son than his best mate. But in that moment of vulnerability, I needed parenting.

"You don't have to go through this alone," he said softly as he gently rubbed my back.

I began to cry harder as I used his slender, muscular body as a pillow. He held me more tightly with his tattooed arms and rocked me slightly. I didn't give a fuck if I looked like a pathetic toddler; I was in pain and needed to let it out. My wife and baby were gone, and never coming back.

Jon began to hum quietly as we embraced, which is a trick he learned to calm Daryl when he was panicked or otherwise upset as a young lad. He would climb into bed with his little brother and let him cry into his shoulder as he would hold him, humming everything from lullabies to familiar songs until he fell asleep. Occasionally, he would sing to him, making sure to keep his voice low and soft.

Just then, Daryl cleared his throat. "Um, the tea is ready." He brought over 2 cups of earl grey, setting them down on the coffee table. "Are either of you hungry?"

Jon shook his head. "I'm not hungry, thank you." He backed away from our embrace and gazed at me lovingly, wiping away my tears. "I already know you haven't eaten in a number of days," he began, "but do you feel up to trying some food? It might help you feel better."

I sniffled and continued to cry as I backed away from Jon's shoulder, noticing his t shirt was soaked with my tears. "I don't know if I can keep anything down," I said in a trembling voice. "I have no appetite, either."

Jon smiled sympathetically. "Well, why don't we at least try, hmm?" He suggested in a soft voice. "What do you say, mate?"

I sighed. "I suppose it can't hurt."

"Brilliant," Jon said as he took a sip of his tea.

Daryl, overhearing the conversation, volunteered to reheat the breakfast he had made me, and I agreed. After a few minutes in the toaster oven, the food was once again warm and he brought it over, along with a fresh glass of orange juice.

I simply stared at the plate, not unlike a baby incapable of feeding himself. I thought of my wife making me breakfast in bed perhaps two weeks prior, a smile on her face as she hand fed me a strip of bacon. Once again breaking down in tears, I attempted to pick up the spoon but found that my hand was shaking too badly. Jon, seeing my struggle, gently took the utensil and, with his steady hand, piled some of the home fries onto it, then held the spoon up to my lips.

"Take a bite," Jon whispered. "Just a wee bit. You can do it, mate."

I opened my mouth and allowed about half the contents of the spoon into my mouth, my taste buds cringing at the onslaught of flavors. After holding the seasoned potatoes in my mouth for a few moments, I tentatively began to chew, and eventually swallow. It was difficult getting that small mouthful past the lump on my throat, but I managed.

Both my best mates smiled broadly. "Good boy," Jon said softly. "Doesn't it feel good to have something solid in your mouth? Something besides tea or juice?" He scooped up more potatoes onto the spoon and held it to my mouth.

I nodded, taking another bite. "Now I just have to make sure I keep it down," I half-joked.

Daryl and Jon chuckled. "I tried to add just the right amount of seasoning," Daryl said as he sat down on the recliner with a cup of tea. "I know you like onion powder as well as paprika."

"You did great, Daryl," I assured him as I chewed.

For the next ten or so minutes, Jon hand fed me small spoonfuls of potatoes, cottage cheese, and eggs, and I finished most of what was on the plate. It had been my first meal in days, and I felt I had a bit more energy. But I still felt horribly depressed. I continued to have crying spells throughout the day and into the evening, and my two best mates did a great job taking care of me. At some point, Daryl went home because he had to open the gym early the following morning, and

needed some rest. He thanked Jon for flying in, and gave me a brotherly hug before taking off, assuring me he would be back after work.

Once Daryl left, Jon turned to me with a smile. "Looks like it's just us, mate." He placed his hand on my shoulder. "You want to watch a funny movie? Maybe play cards or something? It may help to keep your mind busy."

I sighed. "I definitely don't have the mental energy for a game, but I would fancy a movie."

Jon nodded and smiled. "Let's do that, then."

After a few minutes of scrolling with the remote, my best mate found something he knew I would like and changed the channel. Had he not been there with me on that day and I was in the house alone, I'm confident that I would have completely lost it. He was truly my rock. Of course, I would get worse over the next few days, particularly after her memorial service…

I hadn't showered or bathed in many days, not since her passing, so Jon drew me a bath on that first night. He had even kept me company whilst I was in the tub, sitting across from me in the wicker chair and telling funny stories, doing his best to keep up my spirits. Afterwords, he had cooked a lovely dinner for me, which I had done my best to choke down. Then we sat out on my deck for a while, talking and sipping cocktails. Jon only had one drink, explaining that he wanted to remain clear headed for me. He had recommended that I limit myself to 2

drinks, but I wound up having closer to 5. Inevitably, I became weepy and lost my shit. My best mate simply sat and listened, holding my hand or cuddling with me when I got especially upset.

At one point that night, my brother Lawrence called and checked on me. He was less than pleased to learn that Jon was over, insisting that he was up to no good and would get me drunk or high then try to rape me in my sleep. He knew of Jon's antics when I had been in hospital recovering from my appendectomy, but I had told him that Jon was sober as a judge this time around and was therefore a completely different person. I also reminded my brother of how supportive my best mate had been when our parents and sister had gotten killed. Lawrence had become very drunk some time that week and had cried on Jon's shoulder, but hadn't remembered anything the next day. Knowing how prideful Lawrence was, Jon and I had elected to keep the incident a secret.

When I was too tired and shitfaced to keep my eyes open, Jon helped me to bed, and he even cuddled with me until I dozed off. I had been experiencing nightmares but with my best mate at my side, I had slept like a baby.

Several days later was my wife's memorial service and I had gone by myself, since it was intended for just her relatives. Jon did chores around my house while I did this. Afterwards, her family and I had lunch at a local restaurant and reminisced about her. When it was all over, I hugged and kissed all of them goodbye, promising through tears to stay in touch and get together again soon. The event had been draining for everyone, especially my wife's parents, who had been in complete and utter shock at what had happened to their daughter. As for me? I managed to remain calm and collected until I arrived back home, at

which time I staggered through the front door and made a beeline for the bedroom, where I curled up into a ball on the bed and cried hysterically. Jon joined me within seconds, holding me.

"Let it out mate," he whispered as he spooned me. "It's all over. You made it. I'm proud of you." He let me cry some more before continuing to talk. "I have a proposal for you," he began. "I think you need a vacation, and I wanted to offer for you to stay with me at my place for a week. I will pay for everything and we can relax on the beach, maybe take a day trip, perhaps to a national park or even Disney, if you would be up for it? I think a change of scenery would be healthy for you right now. You could get out of the house, spend time with me and Lisa, as well as Nick and Chris? Dale, too? They would all love to see you. What do you say, mate? Would you be interested?"

I sniffled and wiped my eyes. "Yes," I mumbled. "I need to get away."

"Brilliant. I will book the plane tickets today. You deserve to be happy and enjoy yourself. It's what she would have wanted for you."

We lay there in silence on my bed for a while, and I would be lying if I said I felt so loved and so safe being held like that. I eventually dozed off, at which time Jon went to the pharmacy to pick up my anxiety meds and antidepressants, and booked first class tickets for the following week to Los Angeles. Little did I know how much my mental state would worsen over the next 7 days...

The funny thing with grief is that it's non-linear; some days you think you are healing and that everything will be ok, and other days you feel like life is hopeless. Sadly, the "hopeless" days prevailed for me, and perhaps 2 days before I was scheduled to leave for California with Jon, I decided I wanted to join my wife. I wanted to end my time on earth.

It was an overcast day with plenty of wind. I lay in bed until late morning, waiting for Jon and Daryl to leave for the grocery store so I could execute my plan. The tide was high, and the water suitably choppy. It was the perfect day to go for a swim, if death by drowning was one's goal.

Through tears, I walked around my beach front home, looking at each photograph on the wall. They all featured my wife and brought me back to the pleasant times we shared. I eventually settled on a picture of her and me on our wedding day, smiling from ear to ear at the camera. I brought my face closer to the picture.

"I'll see you soon, butterfly," I choked as fresh tears streamed down my face. With those words, I opened up the sliding door to my house and stepped out into the overcast day.

In a daze, I hobbled onto the sandy beach then walked to the water. When I waded out up to my waist, I sensed a presence behind me and turned around. Surely enough, Jon and Daryl had returned from shopping and were headed towards me.

"Ken?" Jon called out as he walked towards the water, Daryl following behind.

I wanted to say something, such as "sorry" or "goodbye," but I couldn't speak. So I simply smiled sadly and turned away, taking some final deep breaths before diving into the choppy water.

I let myself sink to the bottom, letting go of most of my breath and wanting so badly to let death take over. Why couldn't I get myself to inhale or swallow water? I was ready to be reunited with my butterfly but what happened next was testament to the fact that it wasn't yet my time.

Jon swam up to me and wrapped his arms around me, then carried me to the surface. We were both choking. Waves were everywhere and the tide was high, making swimming all the more difficult. But Jon managed to do just that, and while carrying me, no less. We reached the shore within moments, a hysterical Daryl coming to greet us as we collapsed onto the sand. Jon never let go of me and held me even more tightly as I sobbed into his shoulder, my body wet and cold yet warmed by my best mate's love and his strong embrace. My sobs were the product of disappointment at my failed suicide attempt as well as relief that I was in good hands.

"Don't ever do that again," Jon said in a choked up voice. "Your life is valuable, mate. I know you miss your best girl. We all do. But you WILL heal from this. I promise. I love you. I will always protect you." His green eyes were kind and paternal, and there were tears in them. Jon, for all his dickish ways, truly loved and cared about me. It was this love, along

with the love of Daryl, Lawrence, and a select few others, that would help me heal.

Daryl was bawling his eyes out, having nearly lost both of us. Jon invited him to join us in the embrace, reminding his little brother with a wink that there was no way that he would let either of us drown. Daryl simply nodded and cried as he hugged us both.

After a few more tearful moments, Jon suggested we go inside for some tea. He helped me and Daryl off the ground and half carried me to the house while Daryl followed closely behind us, wiping his eyes.

Jon and Daryl changed into dry clothes and helped me do the same. I felt like a bit of an infant, a grown man getting help with a simple task, but I was so shaken up that I allowed them to help me any way they could. Once we were all dressed, it was time for tea. Daryl went to make a fresh pot while Jon lovingly took me over to the couch and wrapped a cozy blanket around me, a sweet smile on his face.

"May I sit next to you?" He asked.

I nodded, welcoming his nurturing presence. He held me tightly, running his hand through my hair. "I'm glad you're alive."

His words, whispered in my ear, resonated with my soul. Tears of gratitude filled my eyes. I cleared my throat.

"I'm so sorry I did that," I said in a shaky voice. "It was rather stupid of me. I just…I just felt so alone. The pain has been too much." I broke down once more, crying into Jon's shoulder.

"Oh, Ken," he whispered. "You are so loved. And you're not alone. I'm going to help you. You will let me do that, yes?"

I nodded, sniffling. "Yes."

"But you have to promise me you won't hurt yourself like that again." He held my face in his hands, gazing at me intensely.

I looked Jon straight in the eyes, which had tears in them that managed not to fall. His lip trembled. He appeared much like a dam threatening to break, keeping it together by sheer force of will. At that point in my life, I had rarely seen my best mate become emotional, so it was a big deal when it did happen. Right away, I was able to see the incredible amount of pain and heartbreak I caused him by trying to take my own life, and I knew he would be devastated if he lost me. I nodded. "I promise, Jon."

He smiled warmly. "That's my boy."

We held each other once more. Just then, a tearful Daryl walked up to us, setting down cups of tea. He sat down on the couch, joining in on the embrace.

"I couldn't handle losing you," Daryl said to me through sobs as he hugged me. "You're my best mate and business partner. And you're my brother's best mate, too. Oh, bloody hell..."

Jon and I wound up consoling Daryl, who was once again completely shaken up. After a few moments of tearful silence, I decided it was a good time to start sharing funny stories of the three of us, like the time Jon hid his pet boa constrictor Samantha in a basket full of laundry to scare his father, who had a fear of snakes. He had told Daryl and me before doing it, and the three of us were able to watch in horrified delight from upstairs as Jon Sr. let out a high pitched scream that contrasted with his usual deep voice, before calling out to Jon.

"'Jonathan?!'" I imitated Jon and Daryl's uptight father, changing my facial expression to mimic his, while putting my hands on my hips. "'Please come get this godawful, scaly creature out of the laundry basket!'"

Jon and Daryl howled with laughter at my imitation, as did I. It was the first time I let go a real laugh since my wife had passed, and it felt bloody good. Suddenly, Jon's wheezing laughter turned into a coughing fit. He sounded more than a bit congested.

"I have some kind of a stupid cold," Jon explained. "Gave me a reason to take a break from smoking, anyway."

"I noticed you haven't lit up once since you've been here," I said. "You did mention when we talked on on the phone that you and Lisa had a virus of some kind."

Jon nodded. "It happens."

Time would reveal that Jon was actually nursing a mild case of the flu along with bronchitis, and due to stress and lack of sleep brought on by taking care of me, it would develop into walking pneumonia. It would take weeks for him to recover. In the meantime, however, he simply had a cough.

We three blokes had some tea and ate some dinner, electing to order takeout just for fun. I still wasn't quite ready to leave the house yet, and hadn't done so, aside from attending my wife's memorial service. As for Jon? He would develop a rather awful case of insomnia, later revealing that he was afraid I was going to attempt suicide again if he were to risk sleeping.

His decision to remain awake backfired after a day or so when, after an especially draining 24 hours, he fell asleep on the couch with a cigarette in his hand. He had decided to treat himself to a cancer stick after not smoking for over a week, but the tiredness overcame him, and he had burned himself awake when the lit end made contact with his bare leg. He wound up with a rather severe burn and also wound up with a minor

scar, as well as a bald patch on that particular spot on his thigh. Luckily, my best mate has rather light body hair and a bit of a tan, so it's hard to see unless he points it out. Still, I feel rather awful that, because of a depression of mine that has since abated, he has a scar that will never go away.

By the time we were leaving for California, Jon had gone without sleep for 48 hours. The 5 minutes of dozing while smoking didn't count, since awakening to the sensation of being burned outweighed whatever rest he had gotten. There were dark circles under his eyes and his cough had worsened, but he still remained positive and talked about all the fun things we would do whilst in Malibu.

"We're going to have a blast," Jon assured me while we were in our plane seats, en route to California. "We're gonna-"

He began coughing, trying his best to do so into the crook of his arm. The hacking continued for several minutes, after which time he smiled and assured me he was "fine," and just had "a bit of a cold."

"You don't sound so good," I said. "Perhaps you need to see a doctor when you get home? I've been worried about you."

Jon shooed me. "I will be alright, mate. You just focus on healing yourself. This ain't the first rodeo my poor lungs have had to deal with, and I reckon it won't be the last." He winked.

I chuckled at Jon's legendary optimism. Incidentally, we did wind up having a great time. There were some sad and tense moments, especially when Lisa had shown up at the airport to pick us up and began crying as she held us. She was grieving as well, having lost a dear friend. As for her cough? It was worse than Jon's, perhaps due to her refusal to stop smoking while sick. When my best mate had gently scolded her, she had seemed insulted, becoming even more so when Jon insisted on being the one to drive home. When I had later asked him why he didn't want Lisa driving us, he had confessed that he was able to make out the smell and taste of alcohol on her breath when he had kissed her and hadn't known the extent of her impairment; nor did he care to find out, hence his decision to take the wheel.

The palm trees, dry air, and rolling hills were a welcome departure from the typical New England landscape, and I did my best to leave behind all the grief and sadness that had become the norm over the previous few weeks. I breathed in the warm air and took in the sights as we rode in Lisa's convertible, hoping to god that this trip would somehow reset my brain and allow me to start anew, or at least function.

When we arrived at Jon and Lisa's palatial home in postcard-perfect Malibu, I was wiped out. Some of the staff was there, including Dale, who was also a friend of Jon and Lisa's. He did everything from bartending to cooking to cleaning, and also worked as a model when not working for Jon. He helped with the luggage and got me situated in the guest room. I took a much needed nap, savoring the feel of the lush bedspread.

Once I had awakened, Jon and Lisa invited me to join them at the pool, and we enjoyed some drinks and conversation. Lisa offered me some weed and I couldn't resist. After a few hits off her pipe, I was beginning

to feel rather normal, or at least less depressed. Nick showed up after a while, delighted to see me but also very sad for my loss. Like Lisa and Jon, Nick had been friends with my wife too.

"I'm so sorry, buddy," Nick said as he hugged me tightly. "She will be missed."

"Thank you," I said sincerely as I smiled and backed away, taking another hit off Lisa's pipe and offering some to Nick, who took a generous hit before giving Jon a hug, then Lisa.

I was able to see Jon tense up when Nick and Lisa embraced. In fact, he rapidly stood up from his seat and aggressively kissed her for several minutes straight. It was clear she had to fight for air and struggle to break free from Jon. My best mate had been jealous of Nick and Lisa's friendship from day one, always having to make it known who Lisa belonged to.

The tension dissipated as the weed and booze consumption increased. My best mate remained impressively sober, still in "caretaker mode." I so admired how much he cared about my well-being, refusing to get shitfaced even when in the comfort of his own home.

At Lisa's urging, we moved the party inside, where she drunkenly led us to the master bedroom. She began kissing and undressing Jon. Nick also began to disrobe and I followed suit, but I was still unable to become aroused. Grief had a way of ruining my libido but until my plumbing worked properly again, I didn't mind watching. Before long, the three of

them were swapping spit and fondling each other. Lisa urged me to join the love fest, but I respectfully declined, preferring to be a voyeur instead.

My best mate checked in with me often, making sure that I was alright. I was more than alright, and rather welcomed the distraction that the kinky visuals provided. Things started out with Lisa going down on Jon as Nick tossed Lisa's salad. Jon occasionally reached over for my hand and squeezed it, smiling at me as he did so.

After a while, Jon dominated Lisa, flipping her over and holding her down with his strong arms. He then ordered Nick to eat his arsehole while he pounded the hell out of Lisa. He pulled out after perhaps ten minutes, climaxing all over her large breasts. Then he licked and sucked the cum off of her and kissed her deeply, feeding her the load.

"I'm riding your cock next," Jon spat at Nick as he turned around. "Get on your back."

Nick nodded and switched places with Lisa, who got up to get herself a drink and have a smoke. Nick spat on his erect cock, and Jon lowered himself onto it until every inch of Nick's member was burrowed inside of his arsehole. Jon's hands traveled to Nick's throat as he rode him, and he began to squeeze.

"Since you have been flirting with my little lioness all bloody night, you must pay the price, Tricky Nicky." My best mate's voice was a low growl.

Nick began to choke and gag as his face turned purple, and he grabbed at Jon's hands. But the grip only intensified. It became very clear that Jon had no intention of letting up and was tempted to really hurt Nick. I scurried over to Jon and did my best to pull him off Nick. Lisa, seeing what was going on and witnessing my struggle as well as Nick's, helped me. After a great deal of physical effort and verbal coaxing, Jon backed away from Nick, who, true to his easy going nature, insisted what happened was ok and "the name of the game."

The rest of the California trip went rather smoothly, aside from Jon once again having to compete with Nick by nearly smothering Lisa while kissing her in a restaurant parking lot. Also, his cough continued to worsen, as did his fiancée's, and by the end of my trip, they were both coughing almost nonstop.

In many ways, that trip was healing for me and helped me move forward with my life, to where I could actually function well enough to return to work. Most of the trip centered around relaxing activities like swimming in his Olympic size pool, scenic drives along the pacific coast highway in Jon's convertible, luxurious days at the spa, and sunbathing on the beach. On my second to last day there, Jon, after taking copious amounts of cough medicine, insisted we visit a theme park and I'd had so much fun. Lisa, having developed a fever, respectfully declined my best mate's offer to join us. Jon had completely spoiled me, paying for all the food and other various expenses, and even insisted on spending the night in a fancy hotel that was a short distance to the park. It had been so indulgent and over the top, but it was what I needed to feel loved and to focus on something other than my pain and grief.

On my last day at Jon's, he surprised me with a check for $50,000, explaining that I needed it to cover funeral expenses and loss of income that resulted from the situation. His cough was really bad by this point, with almost nonstop hacking. At my insistence, he agreed to see a doctor the next day and was going to bring Lisa with him, since she was in even worse shape and hadn't stopped smoking. I tried handing the check back to him, insisting it was too much and reminding him of all he had done for me already.

"Nonsense," he said with an eye roll as he handed it back. "Take the money, mate. You need it and you deserve it." He coughed into the crook of his arm.

I sighed, taking back the check. "Alright, if you insist. But I still want to pay you back one day."

Jon shook his head. "It's a gift. Remember what Butterfly said many years ago? To accept kindness when it's given to you? She was right. There's no strings attached here. No need to pay me back or get me anything as a gift. This is to help you, mate. I love you."

My eyes teared up. "I love you too, mate."

We embraced. I was able to hear the deep congestion and wheezing in his lungs as I held him. Once I packed my things and called a taxi, I said tearful goodbyes to Jon, Lisa, and Nick then rode in the cab to the airport and flew back home, my outlook somewhat improved.

I returned to work after a few more days of relaxing at home, then, little by little, began to get my libido back. Although I missed my wife, she appeared in my dreams often and most of the dreams were sexual in nature. I found myself waking up with an erection after these dreams, and, not before long, began to masturbate again, and to pictures of girls I knew. My favorite? Tracy, who had yet to turn 18. It would only be a matter of time before she became the first girl I fucked after my wife's passing, ending a dry spell and continuing my journey into the twisted world of edgeplay.

Back in the present day…

My entire body ached as I lay in the tub, the red water becoming lukewarm. Why couldn't I just go back in time to that moment before my wife had died? Why was I stuck in this godawful limbo? Why was I still alive? I thought of these things as I drifted into a dead sleep, my head barely clearing the surface of the water.

An indeterminate amount of time later…

"Come on, wake up, mate!"

I could hear his voice but was unable to move, speak, or open my eyes. Somehow I was able to sense that I was no longer in the bathtub. I so wanted to tell him I was alright but I wasn't breathing, at least not yet, and, as such, communicating wasn't possible.

He pushed on my chest and breathed into my mouth, trying to force life into me where none existed. Then I heard her voice.

"Hey, caterpillar."

That had been one of my wife's nicknames for me.

"It's not time for you to get your wings yet," she whispered. "Only I can be a butterfly. I'm always with you. Live your life. We will meet up again one day. Stay alive for Anna, and for Jon, and for Daryl. For me. For yourself."

Just then, I felt a rush of air enter my lungs and I gasped for breath, coughing on occasion. My eyes cracked open and I was able to see that I was on the floor of my bathroom. Jon and Anna were there, and they both began to hold me, crying as they expressed their gratitude that I was alright.

"What happened?" I asked dazedly. "I got so drunk and fell a couple times, breaking glass and falling on it. Then I had dozed off in the tub. I was so upset, Anna. I thought you had abandoned me."

"Not at all," Anna began soothingly. "I had gone to the store to pick up something for you, but when I came back, you wouldn't answer the door or your phone. I had a feeling something was very wrong, so I

called Jon and he broke down the door so we could get inside. Then we saw all the blood on the floor and knew you were badly hurt. Jon also had to break down the bathroom door, which had been locked. When we got to you, your head was below the surface of the water. Lord knows how long you were down there for, but you're alive." She began to cry.

I sat up, running my uninjured hand through her long red hair. "I'm glad I'm alive," I admitted with a shaky voice. "Because I have a chance to tell you something I've been wanting to tell you for a while."

"What's that?" She said with eager eyes.

I looked over at Jon, who nodded with encouragement.

"I love you, Anna."

The tears fell like rain as we held each other, and it was as if a dam had broken. Unable to contain himself, Jon let out a cheer, beyond relieved I had come clean about my love for her after keeping it to myself for so long.

At Anna's and Jon's insistence, I went to the emergency room and got checked out. I wound up needing stitches for my hand and antibiotic cream for my bum but I was in passable shape otherwise. Afterwards, the three of us went out to dinner, talking about anything and everything. It felt so great to finally be able to express my feelings

towards Anna, and to know that she reciprocated them. As for my best mate? He had saved my life once more, and I was so grateful for him.

Several hours later...

"Bloody hell," I gasped as I held the heavy golden contraption. "Is this a BAFTA award?"

Jon nodded as he sat in my living room, lighting a cigarette. Anna had fallen asleep in my bedroom, so it was just us 2 boys.

"I won best supporting actor two years ago. For that movie I did in England. I never told you or anyone else because I had decided the experience had ruined my relationship with Lisa and made my issues with drugs and body image that much worse. The hell I had to go through still traumatizes me, sitting for hours in the makeup chair every day and being forced to wear a fat suit, getting co-star Noelle pregnant and watching her suffer a miscarriage, and having many a tearful video chat with Lisa, where I did my best to reassure her I wasn't abandoning her and that things would be different when I got home. When I learned of my nomination, I made up my mind that I wasn't attending the ceremony. As luck would have it, I fucking won, and wound up doing my acceptance speech over video. In it, I mentioned Candy's late father, THE David Klein, for helping me master an American accent. But I told nobody, not even my mum, that I had won. Nor did I let anyone watch the award show, OR movie. Until now."

Jon took out a DVD and held it up. It was a reboot of a popular werewolf movie, set in London, much as the original had been. He played the lead character's best friend. His face, among other stars in the movie, graced the cover. His makeup, glasses, and fat suit rendered him almost unrecognizable, but the intensity of his gaze gave away his identity.

"I can't wait to watch it!" I exclaimed.

Jon nodded with a smile. "I think it would be cleansing to do so. A new beginning, of sorts. This movie and the award no longer have to be sources of shame, nor do they have to represent unpleasant memories for me. They can represent hope and accomplishment. We don't have to let the troubles of our past determine our future."

I smiled, holding up my shot glass of whiskey. "Cheers to that!"

Jon held up his own shot glass of scotch and toasted. "Le Chaim!"

We both knocked back a shot and settled down to watch Jon's movie and then watched his short but touching speech, where he thanked not only his acting coach but also his mum for encouraging him to pursue his dream, his father for helping him develop a good work ethic and a thick skin, his younger brother for demonstrating the importance of remaining positive in times of adversity, Lisa for standing by his side, Candy for teaching him to enjoy simple pleasures while her acting coach father wasn't forcing him to practice pronouncing his R's, and me, for being the best mate any man could hope for. I had cried when he mentioned me, giving him a big hug. As for the movie? I had loved every

minute of it, even though there were sad parts, such as when his character transformed into a werewolf and got shot and killed by a police officer.

I thought of what Jon had said about not letting past traumas determine one's future, and used that bit of wisdom as a motivator to talk with Anna about my wife. When we lay in bed that night and I was spooning her, she and I had talked about our respective former spouses and the times we had shared. Anyone who knew me was well aware of the fact I almost never referred to my wife by her real name, simply calling her Butterfly. So when Anna had asked me what her real name was, it felt almost foreign to me, because it had been so long since I had spoken it aloud.

"Her name was Melody."

Anna smiled. "What a beautiful name."

I sighed as I held her. "Yes, indeed. Melody Veronica Lopez. She was my butterfly."

"She's still with you," Anna whispered.

There was a peaceful stillness in the air around us, and I could sense Melody's presence, almost as if she were smiling down on me, happy that I had found someone to love.

"I know."

Then we drifted to sleep.

The next morning when I sat outside on my deck, I saw a beautiful monarch butterfly come flitting up to me. She circled around my head for a few moments then perched atop my lap, sitting unusually still as if she were watching me. Melody had paid me a visit!

"Great to see you again," I said to the butterfly, who appeared to wave at me before flying away.

"Who were you talking to?"

I jumped at Anna's voice, smiling and laughing. She sat down next to me, holding my hand. "Just an old friend paying me a visit," I said with a wink.

She smiled as the wind blew her long red hair. "I love you, Ken."

My eyes filled with tears of gratitude. "I love you, Anna."

Chapter 10 (Epilogue) - Whips, Chains, Wedding Bells, and Baby Carriages

"Do you, Andre Johnson, take Todd Turner to be your lawfully wedded husband? To have and to hold, in sickness and in health, until death do you part?"

Andre sighed with a smile on his handsome face as he stood in a tuxedo, immediately knowing the answer to the question. It was a swanky black tie affair at the Mark hotel in Manhattan, with about 50 people in attendance.

"I do."

The justice of the peace asked the same question of Todd, who had been crying tears of joy since his father walked him down the aisle several minutes prior. Todd's father was an old fashioned southern baptist who had once disowned his only son for his homosexuality, but now accepted his lifestyle after learning that Andre had helped Todd quit his cocaine habit, thus saving his life.

"I do." Todd's voice was soft and quivery, and he began to cry harder, as did many in the audience.

"By the power invested in me by the state of New York, I now pronounce you man and man. You may kiss."

The crowd cheered ecstatically as Andre and Todd locked lips and held each other. It was so wonderful to see Jon's old friends from New York City finally tie the knot after so many years together. Their wedding was the first in a long line of weddings that would take place over the next couple of years.

Next on the list were Daryl and Tracy, who had a lovely ceremony on the beach in cape cod, with a reception at a dance hall that was also on the water. Daryl had bawled his eyes out when he saw Tracy walk down the aisle, which made almost everyone else cry. I had been the best man, and Jon and Nick were groomsmen. Amy was Tracy's maid of honor, with Anna and Candy as bridesmaids. I was beyond happy for Daryl, and was confident things would work out great for him and Tracy. It turned out I was right, and they wound up having a baby girl within the first year. Oh the irony of my Baby Girl having a baby girl!

Then came Amy and Eugene, who had a ceremony and reception on a farm that had a beautiful barn, which was tastefully decorated for the occasion. They had both cried when reciting their vows, and it was touching to witness. Neither bride nor groom elected to have bridesmaids or groomsmen, wanting to keep the event simple. Since Amy's father was no longer living, her mother had walked her down the aisle. Watching Eugene and Amy dance their first dance had been absolutely adorable, and they had both blushed a ton while they weren't stepping on each others feet. After a few drinks, however, they were both way more outgoing and had a blast singing karaoke, which the DJ had offered at no extra charge.

Not long after, Jon and Candy got married, deciding on a destination wedding to Bermuda. They had arrived by cruise ship, and Jon had paid for the wedding party to join them on the cruise. It wound up being yours truly as the best man, followed by Daryl, Nick, Mario, and Chris as groomsmen. Jon's friend Jesse flew in with his boyfriend Steve and was beyond happy to be there, using the opportunity to take a much needed vacation. Noelle arrived from NY with her new German born boyfriend, Hans, who looked quite a bit like Jon and, unlike her ex, treated her like gold. On Candy's side, it was Anna, Lisa, Tracy, Amy, and her cousin Irene, who was the maid of honor. Her friends Ellie and Adrian attended, with their teenage children in tow. Adrian, after years of being single, met a mysterious man at the wedding, who happened to be one of the vendors that enjoyed mingling with the guests. He had a thing for Candy's friend in particular, and they wound up exchanging numbers by night's end. Only one thing Adrian forgot to ask of the gentleman: his name. Candy would tease Adrian about forgetting this minor detail for a long time. Incidentally, Adrian would eventually marry this mystery man, whose name turned out to be Ferdinand.

Candy's former landlady, Gladys, was the closest thing Candy had to a parent figure and had walked her down the aisle. As her plus-one, Gladys brought her son Roger, who lived in California and knew Jon. In fact, Roger had been homeless for a time and Jon had helped him out, offering him a job as a live-in chef and housekeeper at his home in Malibu until Jon had moved, at which time Roger took a job at Lisa and Nick's cafe. Roger was now doing well enough to afford his own apartment in LA.

True to his word, Jon had asked Candy to be his "queen" while performing in the band with Mario. The venue was a restaurant and bar

located at a beachfront amusement park in WestChester County, New York. Most of us were in attendance at that concert, and had been overjoyed at the opportunity to witness such an epic proposal and performance. My best mate had called Candy onto the stage, serenading her before getting down on one knee and popping the big question, with a gigantic diamond ring surrounded by rubies. She had tearfully accepted, and they had kissed passionately before doing a lovely duet together. After the song, they stepped down into the crowd where they hugged, shaken hands, and taken selfies with us and many others, then disappeared hand-in-hand into the park, making a beeline for the Ferris wheel, where they had kissed for the first time decades ago.

The event took place at a lavish beach front resort that overlooked the beautiful pink sand and blue water. The ceremony and part of the reception was black tie, before switching into a more casual beach theme. I mean, how could Mr. Jon Moore NOT wear a fancy tuxedo for at least part of the evening? Candy's dress was a stunning white satin number in a halter top style, with a mermaid style skirt. They had both looked like movie stars. The colors were navy, white, and gold. Jon and Candy had danced beautifully to a live band, twirling around to an ensemble that included everything from a ukulele player to violinists. At some point, Jon Sr. had sung to Jon and made a touching speech that made my best mate cry. It was so lovely to see father and son get along and enjoy a close relationship after so many years of friction. Jeannie was the photographer, and captured all this beauty on her camera.

The sexiest and most depraved part of my best mate's wedding, however, was the way the bride's red lipstick stayed fresh throughout the evening. Whenever Jon kissed Candy in private,, he bit her lip hard enough to draw blood, and, by mixing it with just a touch of gloss, she was able to use the blood as lipstick. The guests, aside from myself, had

no idea, and Candy got compliments all night long on her lovely lips. It was at that moment I decided to do the same thing with Anna on our wedding day.

By the time I had proposed to Anna, Candy was pregnant with twins and my best mate was absolutely over the moon with excitement. It seemed everything was on an upturn for everyone I was close to and it felt amazing. Of course, the night of the proposal I had been a nervous wreck but managed to calm down after one of Jon's fatherly pep talks.

I had waited for a lovely sunny day and suggested that Anna and I take a drive to a lovely state park in Connecticut that had a waterfall. Once there, I walked us to a beautiful vantage point, where the waterfall was visible in all its splendor. It had looked like a painting come to life. Then I turned to her, got on one knee and opened the jewelry box with the gorgeous ring inside.

"Yes!" She had exclaimed through tears. And I was the happiest bloke on earth.

We got married on the beach in late June, deciding on Newport, Rhode Island as our locale. The day has been like a fairy tale. Daryl was my best man, followed by brother Lawrence, Jon, Nick, and Mario as groomsmen. Anna looked like a vision in her white, off the shoulder lace dress, and her maid of honor was Candy, followed by Tracy, Amy, Lisa, and Brittany as bridesmaids. I loved how my darling redhead had made friends with my little dollies, former neighbor, and best mate's ex in the years she and I were together.

While my parents were both gone, Anna's were still alive and she had the pleasure of having her father walk her down the aisle. As for our first dance? Jon had given us tango lessons, and we had done quite an amazing job. Daryl, despite his shyness, gave a rousing speech, which I suspect was partly due to the vodka tonics he had consumed but he managed to bring me, Anna, and most of the wedding party and guests to tears. By night's end, we all were good and sloshed but still coherent enough to recall everything, and after spending the night at a fancy hotel in Newport, went on a mini moon to our favorite casino in Connecticut before taking a cruise to the Bahamas.

Fast forward perhaps a year later, and several of us in our circle became parents. Candy gave birth to the twins, one boy and one girl, and they had arrived into this world via home water birth. The boy's name was James Connery, named after Jon's late twin brother. The girl's name was Irene Susan, named after Candy's mother and cousin who shared the same first name, and her late grandmother's first name for the middle name. The boy looked like a miniature version of Candy with his blue eyes, and the girl looked like her father with the green eyes and dimpled smile. Needless to say, they were both blonde.

Anna and I had a baby boy, who I wound up naming Gordon Charles, after my late father. We called him "Gordy" or "G" for short. He looked like a combination of Anna and me, with my dark hair and Anna's green eyes. It was surreal being a dad, and, much like my best mates Daryl and Jon, I had bawled my eyes out the first time I'd held my baby. Anna had chosen a birthing center to have her baby, and she'd had the most amazing experience. I was looking forward to a beautiful future with the three of us.

As for Anna's and my relationship arrangement? She had grown to love the concept of an open marriage, having seen how healthy a relationship my polyamorous friends had. In fact, she was the one who encouraged me to explore the idea of having a second lover, one who I would spend time with when I wasn't spending time with her. Someone who, if I desired, would be as much of a partner to me as my own wife. The notion thrilled me, and I knew immediately who I had in mind.

It was an unpredictable choice for me because, despite identifying more and more as bisexual, I still preferred women over men. Yet, at the same time, the decision made sense because we had been so close to each other our entire lives. We understood each other and had been through so much together. Aside from that? The sex was fucking amazing.

Candy gave her blessing, more than a wee bit on board with her husband having a boyfriend, especially if that boyfriend was me. Her only condition? That she was occasionally allowed to watch us fuck. Both being exhibitionists, Jon and I happily agreed! We even encouraged her to join in most times, which she almost always would.

Others in our circle jumped aboard the polyamory wagon, and even Daryl was ok doing occasional threesomes with Tracy as long as it was another girl. Similarly, Eugene and Amy branched out on occasion, but only with Tracy, who did so strictly with Daryl's permission. It was beautiful, having the freedom to love without limits.

One winter day, I was in the midst of an epic orgy with Candy, Jon, Anna, Nick, Lisa, Noelle, and Hans, when my best mate got a call from

his agent. They wanted Jon to audition for a lead role in a movie being shot in New York City and Boston, with some scenes in Miami, Florida as well. His agent had also met Candy, having come across some of her comedy acts when she had decided to do some stand-up routines at open mic nights. He had thought she had the perfect look and personality for a supporting role and wanted HER to audition as well. Her formal acting experience had been limited to stage work but she decided she had nothing to lose.

"We best call Amy, our lovely nanny," Jon said as he hung up with his agent, who he had put on speakerphone so Candy was able to talk to him. "Looks like we are flying out to California."

Needless to say, Jon and Candy both landed the roles. The next few months were a whirlwind of activity for my best mate and his wife, with plenty of travel and long hours. With a bit of help, they were able to juggle professional time with family time, seeing to it that the twins could come along during filming.

It was challenging for Jon, who had to gain 30 pounds of muscle for his role, and make sure his British accent was "British" enough. He admitted to me that, he wasn't able to look at his body in the mirror while making the movie and hated listening to his voice, almost preferring to speak in an American accent.

"How ironic that I went from a slim Brit playing an American man in a fat suit while starring in a British film, to playing a hulking Brit starring in an American film?" Jon commented with a smirk. "Back then, I didn't sound 'American' enough and had to bust my arse to perfect my

American accent, and now I don't sound 'British' enough. Way to be culturally ambiguous." He shook his head in amusement.

"You were right when you made that joke," I began. "The one when you said that by the time you get a lead role as a British man, you will have mastered an American accent."

We both laughed. Unsurprisingly, Jon nailed the accent, doing his best to work on a more pure sounding London dialect instead of his natural London/Cockney one that got him mistaken for Australian on a regular basis. His father helped coach him, as did Candy. The movie wound up being a hit, earning several nominations and awards.

The success wasn't without consequences, however. In fact, Jon relapsed with his eating disorder once again and began to use cocaine to lose the weight he had gained. Up until that point, he had been off the coke for four years and was a devoted husband and father, completely spoiling his family whenever he could and being very affectionate. His behavior reverted back to the way it had been years ago when he was with Lisa, being either cocky and insensitive or emotionally distant.

Things came to a head when Jon had come home one night at 3am incoherently drunk, staggering into the living room with a baggie of coke and dumping the contents of it onto a table that was merely feet away from where the twins had fallen asleep. He didn't even have a chance to cut himself a line before Candy went ballistic, demanding he go to rehab and making it very clear she loved him but hadn't signed up for this. She moved out of their home that same morning, taking the

twins and staying in Gladys' newly renovated, still-vacant duplex and refusing to return home until Jon got his act together. Although the place was furnished, Candy still wanted some of her own stuff and the twins' belongings, so Anna and I had helped her move them into the duplex. Gladys, who was retired, loved helping Amy with the babies while Candy worked her part time job at the gym and volunteered at the hospital. Thanks to Jon's generosity as well as her own financial success from the acting gigs, Candy didn't have to work but still enjoyed staying busy. Plus, with the drama happening at home, it kept her mind occupied for the 3 1/2 months she lived there.

My best mate-turned boyfriend had been horrified at the idea of losing his beloved wife and babies and would do anything to keep them. After waking up on the couch to an empty home with blood caked under his nose, a pile of cocaine on his end table, and a note from his wife telling him she was leaving with the kids and not coming back until he got clean, he called me up sobbing, explaining that he had fucked up royally. After getting into detail about the extent of his cocaine use, he took my advice and started his journey into sobriety that same day. He completed a medically supervised detox then checked himself into rehab. Candy had shown me a video she had taken with her cellphone the night of the cocaine incident, and it was heartbreaking. Jon could barely speak and had crawled his way to the couch after falling to his knees in the living room. On top of that, it seemed that he didn't know where he was. Candy had been tempted to call the paramedics but she had seen him in that condition several years prior, and knew he would be ok once he slept it off.

After 90 days in a top notch facility, he was clean and sober, and at a healthier weight. Ironically, his former high school rival-turned fellow rehab patient Scott Foley was a counselor at the rehab, and had lost over 200 pounds. He had helped Jon get back onto his feet, insisting on

staying in touch after his discharge. As a strange coincidence, Scott worked part time as a personal trainer and expressed interest in working at Jon's gym, since it was a closer commute to his house. Impressed with Scott's weight loss story and familiarity with eating disorders, Jon agreed to hire him. Scott would eventually work his way up to gym manager, becoming good friends with Jon as well as Daryl and me.

Jon returned home to a full house, his wife and twins greeting him tearfully with open arms along with his family and friends. Balloons, decorations, and random gifts adorned his home. He gave a lovely and tearful speech, where he thanked everyone in attendance and mentioned me in particular for encouraging him to get help right away.. He then made sure to apologize to Candy, both publicly and privately, for putting her through such pain, and expressed gratitude for refusing to give up on him. She had embraced him after the speech, crying tears of joy and assuring him she took her vows seriously, that she was proud to be his "queen" and his "little angel," and would be there for him no matter what. Minutes after the speech and tearful hugs, Jon's agent made a surprise visit, deciding to announce in person that Jon and Candy received nominations for Best Actor and Best Supporting Actress. So, what had started out as a "welcome home" party had turned into an "academy award nomination" one. Best of all, however? Jon never relapsed on drugs again.

About two years after Gordy was born, Anna and I had a second baby. Much like her mum, she was a lovely red haired girl. We named her Bridget, after my late sister. I so loved being a father and embraced my role fully. I wound up putting an addition onto my house, making it more suitable for a family of four and also giving me a private space to do my writing.

That's right: with all the twisted shit that has happened in my life and the fact that I was becoming increasingly bored with most pornography, I began dabbling in erotic literature. My fourth book is due to come out any week now, and little do the readers know that my stories are works of nonfiction. Well, mostly., I have had to change some of the names to protect the guilty, along with some other little details which only I will know.

So hard to believe. Three books in just under four years, and a fourth one on the way. It's incredible what you can accomplish when an insatiable sex drive coincides with an uncanny knack for detail.

Thank you for reading, and stay horny my friends. A prequel is in the works!

Made in the USA
Middletown, DE
05 April 2023

27754375R00351